Praise for A Storm in the Stars

"An elegant sojourn in the early 19th century inspired by the travels and travails of the Romantic poets Shelley and Lord Byron. The world of this novel especially brings Mary Shelley's own brilliance to satisfying life." – Alix Christie, author of *Gutenberg's Apprentice*

"Don Zancanella breathes fresh life into the radical enchantment of Mary Wollstonecraft Shelley and Percy Shelley—one of the great love stories of all time." – Samantha Silva, author of *Love and Fury: A Novel of Mary Wollstonecraft*

"A panoramic sweep through the lives and viewpoints of the Shelley circle, this compassionate novel is beautifully told." – Alix Hawley, author of *All True Not a Lie In It*

"What a beguiling group of characters—Mary and Percy Bysshe Shelley, Wollstonecraft, Godwin, Lord Byron, Keats. Misfits and creative spirits, they fought convention and sought to live authentic, genuine lives of meaning. This is an ambitious novel that succeeds magnificently in taking us into the minds and hearts of these fascinating, complicated, and brave individualists of the past, all of whom can inspire us in the present." – Elizabeth J. Church, author of *The Atomic Weight of Love*

Also by Don Zancanella

Concord
Western Electric

A Storm in the Stars

A Novel by

Don Zancanella

Delphinium Books

A STORM IN THE STARS

Printed in the United States of America

For information, address DELPHINIUM BOOKS, INC.,
16350 Ventura Boulevard, Suite D
PO Box 803
Encino, CA 91436

Library of Congress Cataloguing-in-Publication Data is available on
request.
First Paperback Edition: August, 2023
ISBN 978-1-953002-28-0
23 24 25 26 27 LBC 5 4 3 2 1
Jacket and interior design by Colin Dockrill

"Sister, I hear the thunder of new wings."
—Percy Bysshe Shelley, Prometheus Unbound

Prologue
London 1797

In August of 1797, a comet appears over London, splitting the night sky. To William and Mary Godwin, awaiting the birth of a child, it seems an auspicious sign. But when the babe emerges from its mother's womb, the placenta fails to follow. A surgeon is called. Upon his arrival, everyone, even the midwife, is sent from the bedchamber. William listens at the door but can hear nothing. At last the surgeon steps into the hall, his hands covered in blood.

"How fares my dear wife?" William asks.

"Quite well. I was successful in my efforts."

But the doctor is mistaken. Two days later signs of infection appear. William places the infant in the care of a nurse and then sits beside his wife's bed. When she's awake, he reads to her from *The Faerie Queene*. After a while she whispers, "Some lines from Canto Nine, if you please." He nods and skips ahead.

Her fever rises and he holds a cold compress against her brow. Yet even as she fails, he refuses to pray. Among his most deeply held beliefs is that God does not exist.

The surgeon returns but this time has nothing hopeful to say. In fact, he seems eager to be out the door.

Mary sleeps for a few hours only to awaken soaked in sweat. With the help of a neighbor woman, William bathes her. He feeds her what she'll accept, a little porridge, a little broth, but forgets to feed himself. She shakes so violently, he fears the bed will collapse. "Husband, save me," she says. Then, late one night she begins finding it difficult to breathe, and before help can be summoned, she dies. She was called Mary, so the child shall be called Mary as well.

Part One

1802–1814

Mary

Mary and her sister, Fanny, are to accompany their father on a walk. Mary has recently begun dressing herself, but her older sister still helps with the buckles on her shoes. "Not too tight," says Mary, to which Fanny replies, "But tight enough so they won't fall off." As it's the height of summer, they won't need shawls or hats.

Their destination is St. Pancras Church, a place they've visited many times before. The churchyard is lovely and green and canopied with trees. It is also where their mother is buried.

Their father, who people call Godwin or William or sometimes only Sir, looks no different from other fathers she's seen. His hair is brown, his clothes are rumpled, and his expression can be genial or stern. "We shall take the path through the meadow," he says, "if it is not wet with dew." She knows he's telling them this because last time their stockings got soaked. The other route goes past a brick works. If they choose that one, their father insists they hold tight to his coattails, herself on one side and Fanny on the other, so they won't be run over by a cart.

In addition to taking them on walks, their father reads them fairy tales and has recently begun teaching them arithmetic, geometry, and the histories of Rome and Greece. Their school room is his library, in which hangs a portrait of their mother. She looks down upon them with eyes that, depending on the light, can seem kind or fierce. Their father sometimes apologizes for the times he was unable to give them a mother's care, such as when Mary had earaches or when Fanny had the pox, which left her face with scars.

As it happens, the sun has burned the dew off the meadow, so they leave the busy streets behind. The path is barely visible, winding through tall grass. When they reach the small stream that crosses the meadow on its way to the Thames, their father carries them to the other side. After that it isn't long before they can see the church, its pale gray walls and stout bell tower reminding Mary of a crouching badger rather than, as some churches do, a bird about to take flight.

Mary is dimly aware that a visit to her mother's grave should be accompanied by sadness and regret. Yet when they come here, her father takes pains to make the outing a pleasure. In his pockets he has apples or perhaps a slice of cake, and he allows them to play hide and seek among the trees. He seldom admonishes them for laughing too loudly or wildly galloping about.

However, there does come a time when he calls them over to stand before their mother's headstone. Mary looks forward to this moment because this is where she first learned to spell her own name. *Mary Wollstonecraft Godwin*, it says in large, deeply cut letters, followed by some other words and numbers, which she can read after a fashion but not yet comprehend. Each time she comes, she traces *Mary* with her finger and sometimes the other words as well. Today the bushes nearby are covered in fragrant purple flowers. Mary feels sorry for Fanny because her name is not carved into the stone.

Often, they have the churchyard to themselves, with only the sexton working nearby. But today, as the morning has passed, a crowd has begun to gather. At first, they can't understand why, but then their father directs their attention skyward. Mary looks up and the first thing she sees is a large crimson orb gliding through the air, higher than the highest trees. An eagle with outspread wings is painted on its side.

"Papa, what is it?" Fanny gasps. Mary looks at her father, eager to hear his reply.

"I believe it's called a Montgolfier. What luck that we picked this morning to visit. Quite marvelous, wouldn't you agree?"

As the orb floats nearer, they see suspended beneath it a wicker basket, and in the basket, three men waving madly at the throng below.

"Oh yes, yes it is," Fanny replies.

Then, as if to demonstrate their mastery of the air, one of the men climbs over the side, opens a large, parasol-like apparatus, pushes away from the basket, and descends smoothly to the ground—albeit with alarming speed. For a moment everyone is silent, uncertain if he's survived. Suddenly, he leaps to his feet, doffs his hat, and the crowd sends up a cheer. A dog runs in circles and barks.

Through it all Mary remains silent, too awestruck to speak.

That night, as always, they kneel and pray. In the past, their father has explained this practice by saying, "Although we are not believers, certain customs are worth keeping because they lend order to our lives." Nonetheless, Mary finds it strange, this brief conversation before bed with someone she can't see and who, if he truly is listening, never bothers to reply. When their prayers are concluded, their father extinguishes the taper and departs.

Now, in the darkness, she thinks about the orb. How beautiful it was, how unexpected and how strange. She'd like to discuss it with Fanny, but Fanny is asleep. This always happens. As soon as Fanny lays down her head, her breathing becomes steady and serene, while Mary's mind remains animated by the day's events.

During their walk home, she made her father spell the word he used and was pleased to learn it begins with an *M*. It's a long word, a peculiar word, with several parts. She can picture all the letters but can she remember how it sounds? She puts her lips together and thinks hard. "Montgolfier," she says.

Shelley

In a large country house in Sussex, in a room on the second floor, a boy and his four sisters sit gazing at the fire. The boy is telling them a story about the Great Tortoise of Warnham Pond and the fairies who attend it—and the snake with which it does battle, and the many ancestors of the tortoise, all the way back to the time before the house existed, before England existed, when trees and animals reigned.

As usual, the boy's sisters are thrilled. He glances at Margaret, the youngest, and sees her small hands are clenched in fists and her eyes are filled with tears.

"Bysshe, you're scaring them," Elizabeth says. She's only a year younger than Shelley and addresses him as an equal.

But he continues, as if in a trance.

"And then the most ancient of them all opened his mouth and spoke: 'Spirit of Nature! Soul of the mighty spheres!'"

"Bysshe, I said you're frightening Margaret," Elizabeth says again. "Let's do something else."

He stops, shakes his head, and looks about. "Sorry," he says. "You're all right, aren't you, Peg? Would you prefer to play Summoner? You be the spirits and I'll call you up."

This may be their favorite game of all. In it, the girls are dead, and he brings them back to life. It works especially well when they have their nightgowns on as they do tonight. That makes them seem like actual ghosts, white, diaphanous, visible but without substance, especially when the only illumination in the room is from the writhing flames of the fire.

The girls lie on the floor like the petals of a flower. He stands at the center in silence. At first they giggle, but he waits them out. Then begins the incantation. Some of the words are Latin and some are made up. Starting with Hellen, the second youngest, he raises each from the grave. Polly has a dreamy half smile on her face while Margaret appears determined not to cry.

Touching each one's forehead, he draws them up, backs as stiff as planks, as if he's pulling an invisible cord. Once they are all on their feet, he looks at his sisters, their hair down, their gowns seeming to billow out despite the absence of a breeze, and even Elizabeth, the oldest and most sensible one, appears exhilarated and ready for more. Which he will now provide.

"Earth's pride and meanness could not vanquish thee," he proclaims, spreading his arms wide. "So go now, sleepless spirits, and carry hope in thy smiles." Then, without warning, he spins away and casts a handful of powder into the fire. The flames erupt, turning from yellow-orange to green to an intense blue-violet. They crackle and throw off sparks and flares, the highest of them reaching over the mantel before collapsing back into the hearth. The girls scream, but all of them together aren't as loud as his own laughter, which, if he isn't careful, will bring their father up the stairs.

When at last calm has been restored, Elizabeth says, "What was that you threw in the fire?"

"I can't say. A magical . . ." But he has now returned to earth. "Copper chloride, obtained from Mr. Dobbs," he explains, naming the parson who tutors him on Monday and Wednesday afternoons.

Shelley loves his sisters dearly, loves to entertain them, whether by raising them from the dead or taking them on expeditions out across the fields. And if not that, then by reading aloud through the languorous afternoons of summer, using his voice to make the rest of the world disappear. Sometimes he even writes stories himself. In his opinion they're as good as the ones in books.

Then one evening his father calls him to his library and informs him that the time has come for him to go off to school. He knew this was coming; over the past few months, intimations have been made. Still, it is a shock.

"Next year?" he says hopefully.

"Next week. You'll want to be there at the start of the term. Your mother will help you pack."

He hears a noise at the door and turns to see his mother listening, waiting. So all of this was planned.

"You'll meet boys your own age," she says brightly. Then she takes his hand and leads him up the stairs.

For some reason he can't bring himself to fight back. He has quite a temper, especially if cornered, but it's as if this is foreordained. He's capable of reading books filled with words even his father can't pronounce, so why does he need school?

Later, he goes out to the garden. Already he's feeling nostalgia for this place, these people, this time. Elizabeth is watching him through the window. She motions him over—what does she want? Then suddenly he understands. Leaning across a shrub, he positions his cheek so she can kiss it through the glass.

On Friday, he and his father depart. As he waves to his sisters from the window of the carriage, he begins to understand the full significance of this event. There will be no more summoning, no more fairy stories, no more treks into the woods. There will be no more explosions of purple fire.

Jane

Seldom has five-year-old Jane seen her mother so animated. What good fortune it is to find themselves living next door to the great William Godwin, author of something called *Enquiry Concerning*

Political Justice. Jane hasn't yet learned to read and doesn't understand what it means to be an author, but her mother can't stop talking about the wonderful man and his book.

Their previous residences offered little excitement. Sometimes they had only one room for the three of them, she and her older brother, Charles, sharing the same bed or sleeping on a pallet of quilts and blankets on the floor. More often than not, the roof leaked and rats got into the meal. Occasionally, her mother brought home men, men who called themselves uncle or who didn't need to be called anything because they paid Jane no mind. On their way out the door, they might offer her a farthing and breathe on her with hot, fish-smelling breath. Then one day their mother told them things would be getting better because she'd managed to obtain a little money, although where it came from, she didn't say. That was when they moved next door to William Godwin—who, they are told, is a Man of Note.

Before long, their mother is talking to him over the garden fence. To Jane, he doesn't look like much. Middle-aged, dressed in drab clothes, with a large nose and wispy hair—like a country vicar without a church. Yet he puts her mother in a dither. Even at age five she can see it. Not only does her mother spend hours getting dressed, but her voice changes. Where once it was tired and indifferent or sometimes shrill, she now all but sings her words, at least when Mr. Godwin is near. This causes Jane to admire him. Anyone who can make her mother less irritable deserves her regard.

She's still getting used to their new situation when she catches sight of a little girl next door. There she is now, looking down from the window, her head covered in red-gold hair. Jane nudges her brother and points, unsure whether to be excited or afraid. You can't always tell about other children—some will happily be your playmate while others will pelt you with stones. For a time her fear overrides her curiosity and she refuses to go outdoors. She doesn't want the curly-haired girl watching her. But she would like to know her name. With luck it will be Flora, which is what Jane wishes she'd been called.

It isn't long before she has an opportunity to find out. On a bright spring morning, her mother says, "I have a surprise for you. Today we are going with Mr. Godwin and his two children to Lambeth to watch a play."

Jane glances at her brother, hoping he'll join her in an act of resistance, but Charles claps his hands and asks what the play is about.

"It's called *Puss in Boots*," their mother says. "About a cat in service to the king." Then she shoos them upstairs to get dressed.

Jane has to admit that a cat in service to the king sounds intriguing. As she searches for her white gloves, the pair she keeps for special occasions, she worries that the girl next door will make fun of her shoes or hair.

When they finally go outside, she is surprised to discover not one girl but two. The second one is older, nearer Charles's age, with rough cheeks and straight brown hair. She is called Fanny, and the small one, Mary.

By the time they have attended the play, gotten a hot gingerbread, and watched a trained bird fly in circles above its master's head, she has decided that Mary is neither hateful nor unkind, but shy, clinging to her father's hand as they walk toward home. In the play the cat thrashed an ogre who had the power to change shape.

From that day forward, regular traffic between the two houses commences. Their mother runs next door on every possible pretext and Mr. Godwin visits their house almost as much. Charles wishes one of the Godwin children were a boy, but Jane enjoys playing with both girls, Fanny as much as Mary, and the two of them together most of all. Mary and Fanny can already read, which she finds remarkable and a source of envy. However, it's not surprising given that their house is filled with books. Conversely, she knows how to work with a needle, which, owing to their lack of a mother, Fanny and Mary do not.

Shelley

The school his father has selected for him is called Syon House, and from the first day, he finds it a perfect hell. It all begins when he doesn't know how to play marbles. Apparently, every boy in England learns to play marbles by the age of six, and yet here he is at ten without the first idea of what to do. It's his father's fault. Surely he knows how to play marbles and surely he knows how important the game is at school. Keeping it from his son had to have been intentional.

"My god, that's not how you do it!" shouts Tom Philpot, his voice so full of disbelief that Ian Blake squeals with laughter, causing the other boys to follow suit. No one offers to teach Shelley how to play, and even when he copies the others, going down on one knee and using his thumb to shoot, they mock him or correct him or throw conkers at him until he runs off to hide. Upon finding him, they call him a Molly boy and someone says, "Molly Shelley, Shelley Molly," and from then on, that's his name.

He doesn't mind the actual schooling, the lessons and the work. His teacher, Dr. Adam Walker, knows more than old Dobbs by far. Dr. Walker tells them about electricity and gravity and the constellations and says there might well be living creatures on Venus. Not animals like foxes and hedgehogs but men with gossamer wings, an idea Bysshe embraces. It's almost as if he knows such men exist without being told. One morning, in assembly, Dr. Walker shows them his orrery. The sun is brass, the planets are celluloid, and their orbits are dictated by lengths of copper wire. Dr. Walker asks if anyone would like to turn the crank and Shelley's hand shoots up. As he walks toward the front of the hall, he's a bit nervous, but he follows Dr. Walker's instructions and discovers that putting the universe in motion is a very agreeable act.

On Saturday afternoons they are allowed a few hours to do as they please. For most of the boys this means sport, but Shelley walks straight into Brentford, where a small bookshop carries cheap Minerva editions, the ones with blue covers that can be had for sixpence each. He's partial to ghost stories as well as tales of war and death. He selects one, leafs through it, puts it back, selects another, leafs through it, puts it back, can't decide, can't decide, but the shopkeeper is peering at him over the tops of his spectacles, and more important, if he's late getting back, he'll not be allowed to go again. In a panic he makes his selection and then gallops out of town, along the lane under the elms and through the gates of the school. Maybe tonight the cook will let him read in the kitchen after curfew as she did last week.

Even better than the bookshop are his periodic trips home. The instant he steps from the coach, Lizzie and Hellen and Polly and

Margaret all dash toward him and leap into his arms with such force, they fall to the ground in a tangled heap. Then they run upstairs or out to the garden, and he begins telling them everything he's learned. There's never enough time, but he feels a responsibility to educate them to the best of his ability. They are always mesmerized by him.

"Lizzie, you will not believe what I've brought with me," he says. "It's called a Leyden jar."

"What's it for?" she asks.

"For electricity. As you shall see."

In no time they are back to their old ways, the girls serving as acolytes to Bysshe's sorcerer. He unpacks the jar as the girls look on. Once it's assembled, he sets about furiously rubbing a glass rod with a bit of rabbit fur, then passes the rod along a wire projecting from the top of the jar.

"Now," he says, "who's first?"

"First for what?" Hellen asks.

"First to experience electricity."

Elizabeth looks at him suspiciously: "Experience it how?"

"Give me your finger." He holds out his hand toward her, knowing she won't be able to resist.

"This had better not hurt," she says.

That afternoon, his father takes him out to shoot snipe. This part of being home he doesn't much like but nor does he resist. As they stroll across the fields, he is instructed about the dredging of ponds, the trimming of hedges, and an annoying farmer who can't manage to keep his livestock on his own land. Apparently he's not showing the proper signs of attention, because at a certain point his father stops and gives him a reproachful look:

"You ought to take an interest. Are you expecting the help to do it all?"

He shrugs. "I heard every word. The ponds need to be dredged."

"Don't be impertinent."

"I can't see why you care about someone else's cows. What harm do they do?"

His father shakes his head, mutters something to himself, and continues on.

Still, it's a good day's shooting. For reasons Bysshe can't fathom, he's been a fine marksman since a tender age. He takes three snipe in three shots.

"Look at this!" his father says to his mother and sisters as he opens his bag to show them their take. Yet through it all, in the back of Bysshe's mind, is the thought that when he comes into his inheritance, he'll make sure his mother and sisters are well provided for and then sell the damned place off.

Mary

Before a year has passed, her father and Mrs. Clairmont are married, and the two families become one. "How fortunate that they moved in next door," her father tells Mary and Fanny. "On occasion fate treats one well."

Mary wants to believe having a new mother will be as satisfying as her father says it will be, but Mrs. Clairmont is rather stern. Without delay Mary and Fanny are introduced to the concept of chores and to the importance of tidiness throughout the house. Her new siblings, Jane and Charles, are pleasant enough, but sometimes she wishes she and Fanny and their father could take walks and read books, just the three of them, as they did before.

Then, while Mary is still getting used to how things have changed, Mrs. Clairmont announces that she is to have a child. Furthermore, they will be moving to a new house in a different part of town. It's all happening so quickly, Mary hardly knows what to think.

"Why must we move?" she asks her new sister, Jane.

"To open a bookshop. Mother says your father will write books and she will sell them. She says we have no income and need to get one."

"Your mother told you this?"

"Of course not," Jane replies. "I listened behind the door."

And so, during the summer Mary turns seven, a new baby, William, joins them, and they decamp to a house near Smithfield, at 41 Skinner Street, north of Black Friar's bridge. The house is five stories tall, so they can have the shop on the ground floor, her father's large personal library on the next one, and the family quarters above. The first time Mary sees their new lodgings, she looks up and notices the face of a man carved in the stonework above the door. He's an ugly fellow, with a mouth that seems caught halfway between a laugh and a snarl. The instant she sees him, she freezes in her tracks, unable to go inside.

Taking note of her alarm, her father says, "That, my child, is Aesop. Remember the yellow book we read, the one with a bird on the frontispiece? Those were his stories. An appropriate guardian for a bookshop, wouldn't you agree?"

She nods but casts her eyes downward to avoid meeting the figure's gaze.

Unfortunately, their new neighborhood is not as pleasant a place for walks as the one they left behind. To the right is something called Fleet Market, where carcasses of pigs and chickens and rabbits are on display and where the gutters run with something so thick and black, Mary can scarcely believe it when her father tells her it's blood. To the left is Bridewell Prison, where it's not uncommon to see a forlorn-looking mother with a flock of underfed children being escorted inside.

"Look at those poor wretches," says their father when they are out walking one day. "See how they are treated like lawbreakers when they have broken no law? What does sending the poor to such a place accomplish?"

But their new mother (whom Mary still thinks of as Mrs. Clairmont or her stepmother, never as simply *Mother*) says, "Of course we don't know what caused them to become poor. It may be that they spent their money on immoral pursuits."

"What sort of pursuits?" Mary asks.

"Watch your tongue," Mrs. Clairmont replies.

Her stepmother seems to be having difficulty becoming fond of her. Indeed, certain aspects of Mary's very nature set Mrs. Clairmont on edge. Chief among them is what she terms *willfulness*, as when Mary does her chores her own way rather than according to whatever inflexible system some adult has devised. Mary's father once explained to her that he found her both diffident and outspoken. "This is an unusual combination," he said. "You spend much of your time in hiding, and yet when you emerge, you speak your mind."

Despite the unappealing surroundings, their new residence is easily accessible from all parts of London, so they have many more visitors than before. Not surprisingly, given her father's fame, the visitors are Men (and occasionally Women) of Note: the inventor and philosopher Humphrey Davy, the painter Mr. Constable, the actor Mr. Kemble, Charles and Mary Lamb, and even William Wordsworth, should he happen to be in town. They talk and drink and eat and laugh and talk more, about all manner of things, most of which Mary is only beginning to understand. One day it's poetry, another, the nature of stars, and a third, the fact that there is no rational way to prove the existence of God. Fortunately, her father, over the objections of her stepmother, allows the children to dine with the guests.

One afternoon, Mr. Lamb and his sister come for tea. He is small of stature, kind to children, stammers when he speaks, and always smells of gin. She has a red face and probing eyes. Before they've been there an hour, Sam Coleridge shows up as well. Whenever he visits, he winks at Mary and says, "Hartley sends his love." This refers to a time when she and Hartley Coleridge were very small and Hartley declared his intention to take Mary as his wife. Now that she is a bit older, the mere mention of his name causes her to blush.

The men go to her father's study while Miss Lamb remains with Mrs. Clairmont and attempts to converse. It's an awkward affair. They have such different interests, and Miss Lamb, as everyone knows, is a strange one. So strange that, instead of going off to read a book, Mary stays to observe.

"I am considering the purchase of a Persian carpet," Mrs. Clairmont says.

"A Persian carpet. I should like to visit Persia," replies Miss Lamb.

"This room is cold and I expect a Persian carpet would make it more tolerable."

"It is said that Zahhak had vipers growing out of his shoulders," declares Miss Lamb. "If their heads were cut off, they promptly grew new ones."

Mrs. Clairmont looks to Mary for help. However, Mary

would rather hear about Zahhak than the carpet. "Didn't they bite Zahhak?" she asks. "Since they grew out of his shoulders?"

Miss Lamb shrugs. "One would think."

With Miss Lamb, such exchanges are not the exception but the rule.

After tea is served, Mary expects Mr. Coleridge and the Lambs to go home, but no, they return to her father's study to continue their discussion. This time Miss Lamb goes with the men. Mary picks up her book but has a hard time concentrating because her stepmother keeps walking in and out of the room. She hears her grumble about the cost of keeping two fires burning, and about the possibility that she'll have to feed the visitors again. When they reappear, well into the evening, the possibility becomes a fact.

During supper, most of the talk is about Napoleon. The discussion is somewhat difficult for Mary to follow. As far as she can tell, they all had high hopes for him, but those hopes have been dashed.

"He has not been a man of his word," says Charles Lamb.

"We expected too much," says her father. "I'm beginning to think human nature is a larger obstacle to change than any system of politics or body of law."

But Coleridge isn't interested in France. "Let them do as they please," he says. "What does it matter to us?"

Her father looks a little sad. She wishes he didn't spend all his time thinking about the great problems of the world. There are so many things he doesn't like. He doesn't like greed, he doesn't like property, he doesn't like religion, he doesn't even like marriage, although now that he has got himself a wife again, he's stopped making comments about that.

When supper is over, Mary and the other children are sent up to their room. They protest, but Mrs. Clairmont stands firm:

"Mr. Coleridge is going to read his new poem, and it's not for young ears."

The instant she's gone, Mary and her stepsister Jane begin to plot.

"I want to hear it," Jane says.

"Me as well. What about you, Fanny?"

Fanny shakes her head. She never breaks a rule. And Charles

has already opened a book. He'll not sneak back down because he's older and considers such behavior immature.

Jane, however, revels in rule breaking, so she leads the way. Down they go, toward the light and the sound of voices, taking care to step softly, cringing whenever a stair creaks, trying not to laugh. One flight above the parlor they begin to hear Coleridge's voice. He's still introducing the poem; Mary can tell by his tone. Once they reach the hallway, they'll slip into the room and hide behind the sofa.

As they squeeze into place, back-to-back, knees up, the reading of the poem begins. Mary shuts her eyes and tries to make sense of the lines, grasping bits and pieces as they come: "*The Wedding-Guest sat on a stone . . . the sun came up upon the left, out of the sea came he!*" Mr. Coleridge reads very expressively. His voice rises and then falls so low it becomes almost a growl: "*The bride hath paced into the hall, Red as a rose is she . . .*" A bride. Mary glances over her shoulder and catches Jane's eye. Her stepmother said it wasn't for young ears. She hopes she was telling the truth.

Before many more lines pass, Mary is entranced. The story is thrilling and the pictures the words create in her mind's eye would cause her to gasp if she wasn't worried about being found out:

> *About, about, in reel and rout*
> *The death-fires danced at night;*
> *The water, like a witch's oils,*
> *Burnt green, and blue and white.*
>
> *And some in dreams assurèd were*
> *Of the Spirit that plagued us so;*
> *Nine fathom deep he had followed us*
> *From the land of mist and snow.*

When she looks again at Jane, she sees that her eyes are glistening, filled with tears.

"Are you all right?" Mary whispers.

"I'm frightened."

"Don't be. It's only a poem." But even as she speaks, she knows it's more than that. When combined in such a manner, words take on meanings they don't have when they stand alone. They become an incantation. They leap and shimmer. They become a waking dream.

She turns and embraces Jane, drawing her close. They stay like that until the poem ends. Then, as the adults are applauding, they tiptoe back upstairs.

Shelley

He spends three years at Syon House and his feelings about the place never change. Except for Dr. Adam Walker, there is no one there he cares about nor anyone who cares about him. Peace comes only when he can sneak off into the woods to read. As a result of his time in school, he has come to hate all three of his names. They made fun of Shelley so he tried Bysshe. They made fun of Bysshe so he tried Percy. And when they made fun of Percy, he lost his temper and flew into a rage. He'd been holding it inside for such a long time that when he leaped upon the boy who'd been teasing him and began pummeling his face, the other boys stepped back in astonishment. After it was over, he thought *Now I'm surely done for*, but to his surprise, they started leaving him alone—not so much because they considered him dangerous but because they considered him mad. "Mad Shelley," they called him—another to add to the list.

After Syon House, he moves on to Eton, which is no better. The harassment is more systematic, and he's not the only one suffering, but it's equally difficult to bear. It's as if the stronger boys are not only allowed to torment the weaker ones but are actually expected to do so. However, this time he knows how to respond. Before the first month has passed, he stabs another boy with a three-tined fork, pinning the tender skin between his thumb and forefinger to a table in the dining hall. The boy howls. Thereafter, when he walks down the corridor, everyone veers to one side. Which he finds agreeable— better to be feared than attacked.

He has tried appealing to his father for relief. Couldn't he be educated at home? Or perhaps there's a different sort of school, one that would better match his temperament and interests. Although if he tries to imagine such a place, all that comes to mind is absolute freedom and a library full of books.

When he feels so starved for companionship, he can't last another day, he goes to visit his sister Elizabeth. She's in school now as well, not far away. Sometimes they only talk through the fence, but other times they sneak off. As always, she is a willing accomplice, whether in borrowing a farmer's horse to ride or building small structures out of sticks and setting them ablaze.

On one such occasion he arrives to find Elizabeth waiting with a friend, whom she introduces as Harriet Westbrook. At first he's annoyed—is this going to interfere with the outing they'd planned? But her friend is a pretty girl with heaps of curly hair, and it might be fun to have another person with them.

After they've been introduced, he says, "I was thinking today we might go to Windsor. I've heard tell of a ghost there, just off the London road."

Elizabeth frowns. "What sort of ghost," she asks, as if certain ghosts might interest her while others most definitely would not. Yet Harriet Westbrook is instantly drawn in. "A ghost! What a brilliant plan!" she exclaims.

"It's an historical ghost. A black coach with two black horses belonging to the physician who came to treat Charles II when he was on his deathbed. Every night it returns."

Before he can continue, Harriet jumps in and takes up the plot: "He, the physician that is, hopes that this time he'll be able to save the king." Clearly she approves. Not simply some wandering spirit, but a ghost with a purpose who wants to right a wrong.

"Precisely," Shelley says, flattered by her attentiveness. He's now glad Elizabeth thought to invite her. Her imagination seems to complement his.

Yet Elizabeth remains unconvinced. "Bysshe, we have to be back before dark. I'm assuming this ghost appears at night."

"We can slip in behind the cottages," Harriet tells her. "The other girls will provide an alibi. We've done it enough times for them."

Elizabeth and Harriet go back inside to get warmer wraps, and then, their faces made pink by the cold air and the prospect of adventure, they depart. As they walk along the lane, they fall into a discussion of spirits and fairies and other denizens of the unseen world.

"What I find most terrifying," says Harriet, "is the Devil. He's all-powerful, and once under his spell you have no recourse."

"Are we speaking here of the Christian Devil?" Shelley asks. "Or of a more English Devil, the kind one might meet on the road between Maidenhead and High Wycombe?"

"I didn't know there was a difference," she replies, sounding genuinely surprised.

"Of course there is. The first one lives in Hell and the second here in England. Devils from Hell run naked and the others dress in clothes."

From Harriet he hears a delighted giggle and from Elizabeth a harrumph.

Upon reaching Windsor, they turn down Park Street. It's already getting dark. The sky is purple, here and there lamps are being lit, and a cat skulks into an alley to begin its nightly hunt. Soon, Shelley stops in front of an old, poorly maintained alehouse and motions across the road to a vacant piece of land covered in weeds and stunted trees.

"There," he says. "The coach is supposed to come straight out of that field, turn down the road, and vanish into the night. The horses are enormous and the driver's eyes are said to glow."

Elizabeth sighs. "So we do nothing but stand here and wait?"

"My dear sister. You are unusually disagreeable tonight. We do not stand *here*. We stand over *there*," he says, and leads them across the road. "Apparently, a livery once occupied this location. Perhaps we'll find the ruins."

"How do you know such things?" Harriet asks.

"I read about it in a volume I found in the library. A sort of guidebook to the nether world. You have no idea the number of ghosts in this part of England. At least one in every town." While it's true this ghost is mentioned in the book, the size of the horses is his own embellishment, as are the coachman's eyes.

They cross the road and enter the field, wading through burdock and sedge. He's enjoying the attention being paid to him by Harriet. He'll have to tell Elizabeth to bring her along again. Beyond the weeds are some small trees and then larger ones, but before they get that far, he stops and directs them to sit on a fallen log.

"Resist the urge to speak," he says.

"I can speak if I choose to," Elizabeth replies.

He's about to say something cutting in response when they hear a noise behind them, a rustling in the trees. Harriet grabs his arm and squeezes it with surprising strength. They glance back but see only shadows. "This is quite stimulating," Harriet says, but Elizabeth isn't so pleased. "Bysshe, I'm frightened. I hope you're not playing some kind of trick."

"Hush," he says. "I promise to keep you safe."

Now they are silent for an extended period, ten minutes at least. He loves to perch on the boundary between the seen and the unseen. By nature he's a skeptic, but he wishes he were a believer. That is, he would be delighted to encounter a spirit, yet if he did, he would feel called upon to determine its origin by purely rational means.

At last Elizabeth speaks: "What time is it?"

Shelley shakes his head. "Haven't a watch. Nearly midnight, I expect."

"We really must get back."

"A little longer," he says, and then, feeling the need to make the evening worthwhile, "Look over there, among the trees."

"I don't see anything," says Elizabeth.

He doesn't either. Maybe they ought to give up and return. Then out of the darkness comes Harriet's voice—a whisper, partly frightened, partly exhilarated: "I think . . . I think perhaps I do."

"Yes!" he says. "The trees, they do move. The branches bend. The horses! Cover your faces, how horrible they look!"

And for a few seconds, he's not sure whether he's making it up or simply reporting what he sees. Harriet shrieks, Elizabeth cries out, and the shadows and moonlight become what the moment requires.

A week later he receives a letter from Elizabeth. In it, she tells him how she has secretly been feeding a stray cat behind the rectory, how she sprained her wrist while playing hoops, and how she's been reading a novel by Maria Edgeworth and will send it to him when she's done. In closing, she writes, "My friend Harriet may be in love with you. I feared you would have that effect on her. She said she found you delightfully wicked. I pity the poor thing." Shelley gives the matter little thought. He can scarcely remember her face. Of more importance is the fact that he has just finished making a steam engine out of a tobacco tin and a piece of lead pipe and can't wait to start it up. He takes it to a hidden spot at the edge of the grounds. It rumbles. It shakes. It explodes.

Mary

The day after Mary turns eleven, she visits her father in his study and says, "I wish to read one of the books my mother wrote."

He looks up, his expression changing quickly from puzzlement to recognition. "Of course you do. Has someone told you not to?"

"No, but . . ." He's teasing her. Mocking the jut of her chin. "Where are they?"

"Here, behind me. She was best known for this one, which she wrote during the days of the French Revolution. There was a time when if you had *A Vindication of the Rights of Woman* on your bookshelf, you need say nothing further. Everyone knew where you stood."

That sounds intriguing enough but also rather intimidating. Instead, she reaches for *Thoughts on the Education of Daughters*. She can see her father watching her out of the corner of his eye.

"I'm not sure that's the best place to start," he says. "Seeing as you have no daughters yet."

Nonetheless, she opens it, only to find herself staring at a page on which the word "breastfeeding" occurs several times. Swallowing a gasp, she slaps it shut.

"Try this one," her father says.

Mary reads the title: *Mary: A Fiction*. She throws her father a look of disbelief. If anything, this is more unnerving than the previous one. Perhaps this is a bad idea.

"She liked the name "Mary." It was her own name and it's the name of the girl in the book. And then I gave it to you."

Now she understands. For a brief, disquieting moment, she thought the book was about *her*. But that would be impossible because her mother wrote it before she was born.

"What sort of book is it?"

"It's the story of a young woman. How she grows and who

23

she loves. I'm afraid it doesn't end happily, but that's no reason to avoid it. I fancy it captures some truths."

Mary looks at him. Sometimes he pretends to like things he dislikes and vice versa, as a means of influencing her. Does he want her to read it or not? She retreats from the study, the book tucked under her arm.

She thinks about her mother often. Although she never met her, she misses her. How is that possible? Not getting on well with her stepmother doesn't help matters. Her stepmother likes Jane better than Mary, which, given that Jane is her real daughter, is to be expected. But she also seems to prefer girls of Jane's *type* better than Mary. Jane is musical and sweet and cries when she's afraid or when she's touched by some moment of melancholy, whereas Mary herself is not at all musical and seldom cries, at least not in front of adults. Based on what her father has told her, she imagines her mother as a sort of goddess, like Athena in the Greek myths. In her mind, she was loving without being sweet and had a countenance that demanded respect. That Mary Wollstonecraft was in France during the Revolution makes her seem fearless, although Mary doesn't know if she was truly in danger. Maybe she was in a room somewhere, writing another book.

Of course there are untold numbers of children who have never known their mothers—she's met a few herself. And she now has a stepmother, for whom she ought to be thankful, whether or not they get along. But she wishes she could visit her mother's grave more often, as they used to when they lived farther out. It wasn't only the headstone with her name on it; it was the peacefulness of the place, the flowering shrubs, the tolling of the church bells, and the long, soft grass that the sexton seldom cut. There's no such spot anywhere close to their current residence, although if she can't live in the country, she's happy to be living in a house overflowing with books.

In addition to operating the shop, her father and stepmother have decided to begin publishing books for children. This means the house is twice as busy as before. Where once there were customers during the day and visits from her father's friends in the evening, there are now writers and illustrators calling from morning till night. Wherever she looks, there are manuscripts and stacks of new books just arrived from the bindery and heaps of engravings which may or may not end up in a book. This on top of all the books from other publishers and all the books that belong to her father and all the books and papers that seem to have found their way in simply because this house invites them, welcomes them in from the cold.

But right now there is only one book that matters, *Mary: A Fiction*. She intends to start today, even though it will mean setting aside Scott's *The Lady of the Lake*. All the way to the top of the house she goes, to the seldom-used attic, where on occasion she and the other children put on plays. There she sits, back against the wall, a small window at the peak of the roof admitting light, and begins to read.

The story commences with uncommon dispatch. A woman is born into wealth. At a dance she falls in love with an officer, but her father insists she marry someone else. All this in the first chapter. She reads a bit further and before long begins to understand that the husband is a cad. He visits his "pretty tenants," while leaving his wife at home. Nonetheless, she soon gives birth to two children, a daughter called Mary, and a son named John. The woman has little interest in rearing a daughter, but as the Mary in the book grows up, she educates herself by reading and by absorbing the lessons Nature so readily provides.

And so the afternoon passes. For long periods her mind is filled with nothing but the characters and the events in the book. Occasionally she pauses to marvel at the fact that she is reading about people made from her mother's own words. There are even passages she feels she herself might have penned: *She entered with such spirit into whatever she read, and the emotions thereby raised were so strong, that it soon became part of her mind.*

Yes, exactly so.

At last she stops but only because it's gotten too dark to see the page. Her father was right to say the story is not a cheerful one; still, it's quite absorbing. When the Mary in the book is of an appropriate age, she's forced to become the wife of a man she dislikes. Yet even more than the plot, it's the various ideas expressed that Mary finds fascinating. For example, one character holds that animals have souls. At first she is taken aback. How is that possible? Then she reconsiders. Why shouldn't they? If there are such things as souls, animals certainly have as much right to them as people. How clever her mother was.

That night before bed she hands the book to Fanny.

"I got this from Father," she says. "Have you read it?"

Fanny looks at the spine. She doesn't bother opening it. Instead, she shakes her head and gives it back.

"You have no interest in it?" Mary asks.

"Not really. Is it good?"

"Is it good? It's by our *mother*. How can you resist? You actually *knew* her. You have memories of her, do you not?"

"I've read a few pages of a different one. But she's no longer with us and"—she points at *Mary: A Fiction*— "that's merely something she wrote. It's made of ink and paper. Whatever its merits, it cannot kiss me. It cannot take me in its embrace."

Mary looks at her, furrowing her brow. They seldom speak of their mother, at least not directly. Fanny is so mild, so lacking in passion and curiosity. Which is why everyone likes her. She never starts a quarrel and takes orders without complaint. Fanny's father was the man Mary Wollstonecraft was in love with before she met William Godwin. For all Mary's interest in her mother, she tries not to think too much about the fact that she had children by more than one man. Yet that may explain why she and Fanny are so different. Sometimes she likes Fanny even better than she likes herself, while other times, she'd like to slap her. How can Fanny not wish to read the books her mother wrote?

"Do you remember what she looked like?" Mary asks.

"Not well. I confuse what I remember with the picture in Father's study."

"You should feel lucky to have your memories. *Because I have none at all.*"

Fanny, who until this moment has been seated at her desk, turns to face her sister. Seeing Mary's distress, she stands and takes her in her arms. "I am a thoughtless creature," she says. "Our mother's books are precious. I take back what I said."

Mary finishes *Mary: A Fiction* late that night. The Mary in the book begins traveling so as to avoid her husband. Then she meets a man named Henry and falls in love. As the book draws to a close, there are hints that before she can achieve true contentment, she may die. There are other hints that she will live out her life in loveless dolor. Which it shall be is left for the reader to decide.

She puts herself to bed, her heart discomfited by how the story turned out. The Mary in the book was intelligent and resourceful, but that wasn't enough to save her. She ought not to have allowed herself to be pushed into an unhappy marriage. She should have refused to be mistreated, even if it meant renouncing love in all its forms.

In the morning, she decides to write a story of her own. It's more difficult than she expected. She wants it to be a story about love, yet she knows so little about the subject, she can scarcely fill a page. Abandoning that, she tries writing about how Athena helps Hercules slay the Nemean lion. That doesn't go much better. How does one invent speech? How does one cause characters to move about on the page? How does one create a world into which the reader can enter? If her mother were here, she would ask her these questions and many more.

Jeff Hogg

Thomas Jefferson Hogg arrives at Oxford in the autumn of 1810. He has a squarish body, legs like small oaks, and a nose like the beak of a hawk. He knows no one who is attending university nor does he or any member of his family know anyone who has *ever* attended university. He can see the buildings from a long way off, gray spires and towers piercing the water-blue sky. Last week he turned eighteen.

He intends to be a solicitor but quickly discovers that for all the institution's pretentions to learning, there is little actual teaching and hence little in the way of studies required of him here— certainly nothing that would prepare him for the law. Once a week he must submit a few lines of Latin translation, and once a fortnight he must meet with his tutor. And that is all. Before long, he's dreadfully homesick and wishes he'd never left Durham. Thus he begins to mope. He starts drinking more than he should. He sleeps to excess, at least twelve hours out of twenty-four. He wonders if he has come to the wrong place. Perhaps this is some sort of institution for the promotion of indolence. Could it be the real Oxford is farther down the road?

Then one afternoon he passes a door that has never been open before. Until now he has seen only his own room and the one beside it. They are identical, sparsely furnished stone cells with a few books and carelessly dropped pieces of clothing scattered about. However, this room, with its door standing ajar, causes him to stop and gape. Yes, there are books, boots, papers, and clothes. But there are also glass flasks and copper pots, spyglasses and dueling pistols, an instrument he knows to be a solar microscope because he once saw a drawing of one, numerous stains upon the table and rug, loose pieces of money, a bottle of Japanese ink, a knife large enough to gut a stag, and beside the knife, a mirror and cup, implying that the knife has been used in place of a razor, to shave some fellow's beard. While he is standing there, a tall, slight boy with longish hair and exceptionally blue eyes emerges from the jumble. It seems he was sleeping on a rug in front of the hearth.

"What ho!" he cries. "I have a visitor! Enter if you dare."

"Just looking at your . . . your kit."

The boy surveys his room. "I told them it wasn't large enough. They didn't seem to care."

"The knife. You use that . . . ?" He makes a shaving motion across his jaw.

"I couldn't find my razor, so I had no choice. I remember using it to cut a loaf . . . maybe you could help me look for it. A fresh set of eyes."

Hogg is intrigued. It's as if he's stumbled upon a cave filled with treasure. With someone living in it. They fail to locate the razor, but after they give up looking, they have a glass of wine and begin to talk, and then a second glass and continue to talk, and a third glass followed by more talk: about Oxford and where they each came from and the art of shaving and the art of fishing and philosophy and politics and literature and girls.

"How do you feel about journalists being expelled from the House of Commons?" the boy asks.

"I didn't know it was happening, but I suppose it's a bad idea . . ."

"Indeed it is. A transparent effort by those in power to conceal their scurrilous acts."

Hogg is so relieved to have someone to converse with, he nearly weeps. Thus begins his friendship with Percy Bysshe Shelley. He stays until five a.m.

Shelley is unlike anyone he's ever met. He is at once ambitious and careless, serious and unrestrained. He is studious, although only in regard to the things he cares to be studious about. He is opposed to strong drink but sometimes makes exceptions. He has no interest in wealth as an objective and hates all forms of injustice—a fact Hogg finds especially remarkable upon learning Shelley is the son of a baronet. And while he gives the impression of being a laggard—it's there in his very posture, the boneless way he leans against the frame of a door—Hogg has never seen anyone work so hard. Where Hogg has long ago concluded that the best use of his unconscripted hours is sleep, Shelley fills his with books.

He reads so much. Rousseau, Gibbon, Paine, Voltaire, Godwin, and Adam Smith, Milton, Tacitus, German writers Hogg has never heard of, and stacks of blue bound adventure novels he thought fellows their age were supposed to have outgrown. It is not uncommon for Shelley to read until he falls asleep, and then, a few hours later, wake up and start reading again, from wherever he left off. Although sometimes, instead of reading, he'll awaken and begin to talk:

"I do not understand why more isn't being done to explore the continent of Africa. A country such as ours, with its vast resources, ought to be able to send out dozens of men, hundreds even, in boats, on horseback, in hot air balloons. The entire place could be mapped in a matter of weeks."

Hogg is just back from supper. He tried to roust Shelley before he left so he wouldn't miss a meal, but Shelley waved him off. Yet now he leaps to his feet and begins to pace.

"Of course, whatever was found would be plundered. Do you think those who live there now are happier in their destitute but natural state, or would they prefer to be under England's tyrannical heel?"

"You only assume they're destitute," Hogg replies. By now he is used to entering Shelley's stream of thought laterally, without worrying about the stream's direction or source. He prides himself that doing so requires a nimble wit and considers it good training for the law.

"If you're saying it's a matter of perspective, I'll grant you that if given a choice between a mattress of feathers and a mattress of straw, some'll choose straw. There's a passage from Hume that speaks to this rather directly. I'm certain it's here somewhere." He pauses and grabs for a book. And so they continue into the night, Hogg thankful that he went to supper because Shelley can go for long periods without food, his body like some mechanical contrivance that runs on books and talk.

On rare occasions, Hogg can get him to talk about his family. This Hogg very much enjoys.

"Sometime soon I shall introduce you to my sisters, and you will fall immediately in love," Shelley says. "You have never met more beautiful and accomplished creatures. My mother will treat you like a son and my father will compare the two of us and be confirmed in his belief that when it comes to an heir, he was cheated."

There's no chance a man of his father's station would hold such an opinion, but Hogg plays along. "If I did fall in love with one of your sisters, what would you—"

"It would probably be Elizabeth. I would tell her to expect to be poor but happy. And when you have children, I will come live with you and serve as their tutor and take them off to romp in the woods whilst you earn bread for us all."

At times the pictures Shelley paints with his words are so delightful, Hogg laughs out loud.

Jane

While Mary reads and Fanny helps around the house, Jane has begun taking lessons in French and music—the purpose being, in the words of her mother, "to improve upon your natural gifts." Mary and Fanny were not asked if they wanted lessons. It's somewhat confusing—they are all part of a family, but Jane and Charles are still their mother's children, while Mary and Fanny belong to Mr. Godwin. Only little William, born out of the union of Mr. Godwin and her mother (an act she sometimes tries to picture, then banishes from her mind in revulsion) will grow up feeling truly at home.

She wishes her relationship with Mary were more congenial. Some days they are as close as blood sisters while other days they seem like strangers who have only recently met. Mary is certainly the more bookish one. She is now reading Rousseau and Locke and says things like, "Belief cannot be compelled by violence." In reply, Jane says, "*Je ne connais pas.*"

Still, she prefers Mary to Fanny. While Mary can be accused of being headstrong, Fanny is too often inward and morose. Mary is always interested in adventures, in going places without their parents' permission, even to the coarser precincts where girls of good families ought not to be seen. Whereas Fanny prefers staying home to help care for baby William while their mother tends the shop. Jane's not sure if she is prettier than Mary or if Mary is the prettier one. Jane has to admit she is jealous of Mary's fair skin.

On one of her outings with Mary, Jane meets a boy. They have gone out to buy string, the kind used to tie up bundles of books. "Go directly there and back. Do not dawdle," her mother says. They nod, but while so doing, Mary catches her eye and winks.

They stop at a sweet shop for peppermints and rock, and at a dress shop for a glimpse of the latest styles. And instead of going across the bridge, they take the long way round, past the Church of St. Sepulchre, simply because they can. At last they go to complete their errand, only to find the clerk at the shop waiting on a boy their age—also, coincidentally, purchasing a ball of string. He glances over his shoulder as they enter and then turns away. When the clerk goes off to fetch his order, Jane gathers her courage and speaks:

"What do you suppose he's going to do with it, Mary?" she says at full voice. She's astonished at her own boldness. It's almost rude. Apparently, Mary agrees because her eyebrows go up and her hand covers her mouth.

Again the boy turns, but more slowly this time. "Pardon?" he says. He has sand-colored hair, and his lips are full and pink.

"The string," Jane says. "What's it for?"

"For tying things, I suppose. I wasn't told."

This causes Jane to laugh and the boy to laugh in turn. Mary smiles, but by now Jane has no interest in her; she's focused entirely on the boy. They chat back and forth, their remarks seeming to Jane to be full of wit, until at last the clerk reappears and the boy prepares to depart.

"Would it be terribly forward of me to ask your name?" he says.

She raises an eyebrow. The hairs on the back of her neck stand up. "It would be, and it's Jane."

As they make their way home, she feels positively elated—partly because she has never before had an unsupervised exchange with a boy and partly because it came so naturally to her. She could have talked with him all morning long. She had only to open her mouth and cunning remarks emerged. Best of all, she showed Mary up. Mary may read more books, she may be more well-spoken about the arts, about history, and the news of the world, but isn't the most important thing the ability to attract young men?

When they get home, Jane finds Fanny. "You'll not believe what happened," she says, and then proceeds to tell her about the boy. She says nothing about Mary except that she was present. Fanny can infer the rest.

"Will you see him again?" Fanny asks, her eyes unusually bright.

"I'm not sure how I would. He knows my name but I don't know his. Maybe he'll seek me out."

Fanny claps her hands together. "You could seek *him* out. You could go back to the shop and ask the clerk to look up his account."

That hadn't occurred to her. What an outrageous suggestion!

"Do you think they'd tell me? No, I couldn't. Even if they gave me his name, I'd need some pretense for paying him a visit. And if Mother found out, she'd have my head. It's too dangerous by far." And so she continues for several minutes more, speculating, imagining, agonizing, her mind filled with pictures of his pink lips and sandy hair. She doubts she'll act on Fanny's suggestion, but she's thrilled that such a possibility—tracking down a boy like a hunter tracking a deer—even exists.

When she looks at Fanny again, the light in her eyes has begun to fade. She is becoming sad Fanny once more.

"I wish . . ." Fanny says but then stops.

"Yes? What do you wish?"

She lowers her eyes. "I wish I was you."

Jane looks at her, a bit stunned. "Not Mary? I should think—" But she doesn't pursue the matter because it feels somehow cruel to do so. For what Fanny is probably saying, perhaps without even being fully aware, is she wishes she were someone other than Fanny Godwin.

Before her mother and Mr. Godwin married, Jane was the only girl child and therefore had no one to compare herself to. But she can see that such comparisons, although tempting, lead nowhere good.

Jeff Hogg

While walking in the countryside near Oxford, Shelley tells Hogg he thinks they ought to write something together, something subversive and rebellious, something that will take their ideas (*Yours, mostly*, thinks Hogg) and thrust them into the world.

"What sort of ideas?" Hogg asks. They are on a winding country path, with a row of elm trees on one side and a brook along the other. As much as he enjoys their talks, he sometimes wishes Shelley were a young lady. A buxom one, in a blue frock.

"The sort that people know in their hearts to be true but are afraid to express for fear of censure."

Hogg realizes at once what he's referring to. "You want us to write something about atheism?"

It is among their favorite topics of discussion, although before Hogg met Shelley, he thought merely uttering the word would get one thrown in prison or struck down by the hand of God. A hand, if Shelley is correct, that does not exist.

"Not simply *about* atheism, but an endorsement of it. We shall have it published and thereby embolden those who value rational thought."

"Published?" Hogg says, kicking a stone along the path. "Only if your goal is to get us tossed out."

Shelley shakes his head. "We'll publish it anonymously. I

know a man who will do it cheaply and won't say a word. He'll help us cover our tracks."

Hogg considers the idea. It would cast them as revolutionaries, and what could be more appealing than that? He has sometimes wished he could take part in a great rebellion. Then again, if one ends up with one's head on a pike, the appeal would be rather less. But Shelley often makes suggestions and doesn't follow through. He decides to hope for that.

The next time Hogg sees him, he has a sheaf of papers under his arm, a completed first draft.

"Take it and read," Shelley says.

"Will it diminish my faith in God if I do?"

"It will lay waste to it. It will wipe it clean away."

"Just what I've been looking for," Hogg replies. He's startled to hear himself saying such a thing. In Shelley's company he's gone from being an indifferent believer to a proselyte for the other side.

Their requisite repartee concluded, Hogg sits and thumbs the pages. "Your handwriting . . ." he says.

"I know. It's damnably hard to decipher. Would you like me to read it to you?" Shelley attempts to take the manuscript back, but Hogg moves it out of reach.

"You needn't bother. I'll do the best I can."

The title Shelley has given it is "The Necessity of Atheism," and the tone of the text is cool and logical, almost mathematical in its reasoning. His argument is that mankind benefits from Truth, that Truth can only be arrived at through Reason, and that religion distorts Reason in ways that prevent the discovery of Truth. It's not a long document—when printed up, it will be a mere pocket-sized pamphlet—but it makes the case quite well.

"So what do you think?" Shelley asks as Hogg turns the final page.

"It's masterful. And as I said before, it will get us thrown out."

"They won't know who wrote it. Your job is to prepare a clean copy, add a few flourishes of the legal variety"—he often says Hogg talks and writes like a solicitor already—"and then we'll take it to Slatter and Mundy to have it printed up."

"And our names will be nowhere upon it?"

"They will not. Furthermore, Slatter has agreed to display it in the window of their bookshop and sell it for six pence a copy. The ancient ecclesiastics who oversee this place will be appalled. The title alone will cause them to soil themselves."

Until now Hogg hasn't fully realized that the chief purpose of this publication is to rile the heads of Oxford. But it makes sense. The heads of Oxford are in a position to determine the very nature of truth and compass of belief. Why not challenge them? Hogg finds himself alternately caught up in his friend's boundless enthusiasms and worried about where those enthusiasms will lead. It's like being on a runaway horse—once you're on its back, all the worry in the world won't keep it from going where it must.

Hogg edits the manuscript, adding the requested legalisms. Then Shelley takes it to his friend who will carry it on to Worthing, there to be printed and bound. And so, before ten days have passed, it appears full-formed in the window of Slatter and Mundy's shop. The instant Shelley sees it, he dashes inside, picks up a copy, and begins exclaiming about how fine it looks. The other customers turn and stare.

"How many have you sold?" Shelley asks.

The old fellow behind the counter looks bewildered. He obviously doesn't know who they are. "None yet. We only put 'em out this morning. Do you wish to purchase a copy?"

For a moment Hogg fears Shelley is going confess to being the author. But instead he says, "I'll take ten," and throws him a glance—a glance he'd call conspiratorial if it didn't betray such delight.

As they leave the shop and turn up the street, Shelley begins handing out copies, one to each of the first ten people they pass, without regard to whether or not they look sympathetic to the athe-ist cause. The last one goes to a boy who couldn't be older than eight. "Take it home to your mum," Shelley says. "Tell her it's what they *don't* teach you in school."

That afternoon they discuss what they should write next. If this is as successful as they expect it to be, what other cause might they take up? Hogg suggests capital punishment and Shelley agrees— although there is also the slave trade or the enclosure acts. While they're talking, a messenger arrives at Shelley's room calling on him to meet with the Masters and Fellows of the College first thing the following day. They look at one another as the messenger departs. Hogg can see Shelley's mind turning. No doubt he's trying to imagine a benign reason for such a summoning. They both know none exists.

"Well, that was bloody fast," Shelley says at last. "How do you suppose . . . ?"

"Slatter and Mundy, of course. They turned you in. Most likely before they even put them in their store. I wasn't named because you're the one they dealt with." Such a disaster. He feels himself begin to perspire.

"Impossible. I'm their best customer. I've purchased more books from that shop than any other student at this college. Why would they betray us? What cowards! What toadies! I'll not spend another shilling there."

"We must form a defense," Hogg says. "What shall be our strategy?" Yet while he's saying this, he's also trying to picture himself telling his father what happened. It's a scene too terrifying to entertain.

"I'll deny it. Our name is nowhere on the book. If anyone says otherwise, I'll call them liars."

The next morning, Hogg watches as Shelley goes off to his doom. But when he's been gone for only a few minutes, he decides he must be brave. Never once did his friend say he, too, must accept some of the blame. What a good man Shelley is. He splashes cold water across his face, pulls on his boots, and runs out the door.

He has to make several inquiries to find out where the Masters and Fellows are meeting. When he finally locates the room, he barrels past the porter and bursts inside. There he finds seven white-headed old men seated at a high table at the front of a large assembly hall, with Shelley standing before them, looking distressingly thin. He makes a note to himself that, whatever the outcome, he must convince him to eat.

Now that he's here, Hogg is not sure what to do. There's a sea of empty chairs before him—should he sit at the back or go up and join his friend? It appears he's too late. The terms of Shelley's expulsion are being stated—an expulsion, they are now saying, which shall be irrevocable and begin this very day.

Before they can conclude, Hogg makes his way up the center

aisle and begins to speak. He's trembling, but to remain silent at such a moment is not an option. He wouldn't be able to face Shelley. He wouldn't be able to face himself.

"Mr. Shelley did not write the document in question nor did he contribute to its composition, publication, or distribution. Therefore his punishment is unjust."

"Who then is responsible?" The speaker is seated at the far left. He looks like the rest of them except for an unsightly goiter. This is what it must have been like to be examined in the Star Chamber. He's afraid he's going to pass out.

"I . . . I don't know. And since there is no name on the pamphlet, you cannot know either." He feels as if he's making good points, but Shelley is shaking his head. "A case, it seems, of *nemo dat quod non habet*," he adds, unsure if this is a situation in which that principle can be invoked. He is conscious of how they must appear— Shelley slender and well favored, with a face that might almost be called beautiful; himself sturdy but unrefined, like a common laborer just in from the fields.

"You're Mr. Hogg, are you not?" Now it's the one who was speaking when he entered. His eyes are sunken and yellow; they fix upon him with great ferociousness nonetheless.

"I am."

"And you, too, deny any involvement?"

"I do."

"Then you, sir, are expelled as well. Like Mr. Shelley, you had an opportunity to take responsibility for your actions. And like Mr. Shelley, you chose not to. Return to your rooms and prepare to depart."

As they walk back across the green lawns, Hogg feels a tightening in his chest. He grabs Shelley by the arm and bends over to catch his breath. How quickly one's fortunes can turn. How stupid they were to think no one would find out.

"Are you all right?" Shelley asks.

He straightens up and nods. "I shall remember this moment all my life. The day my future turned to ash."

"You, Hogg, are an uncommon brave soul," Shelley says. "You came to save me."

"You set out to save me first."

They are silent for several steps, lost in painful contemplation. Then Shelley speaks again. "What are you going to tell your father?"

Hogg shakes his head. "I haven't the faintest idea."

Mary

The older Mary is, the more difficulty she has getting along with her stepmother. The answer to every question is *No.*

"No, you may not roll your sleeves."

"No, you may not have a puss cat."

"No, you may not leave the shop unattended. It's empty now, but who can tell when a customer might arrive?"

Admonition after admonition, and if she argues back, it only makes things worse. Although Mary has now been told she *must* call her stepmother *Mother* to her face, the word catches in her throat. Jane and Fanny and Charles have no such difficulty. They speak of their current parents as if their family were never other than it is today.

Unfortunately, her stepmother's opinion of her seems to be infecting her father. He, too, is beginning to view her as stubborn, self-centered, insufficiently feminine, and nettlesome. "My," he says, "it seems I need only touch you and I come away with a small but painful thorn."

"I was happier when we lived near St. Pancras," Mary tells him. "But it's obvious my happiness is of little concern to you."

"Don't be foolish. We moved here for the sake of business. To sell books, one must be located near those who buy books, not in some remote locale."

"And are you selling many books?"

His eyes narrow and he looks at her over the tops of his glasses. She knows it was the wrong thing to say, but there's some truth to it. She has often heard her father and stepmother discussing money, especially how desperately they need it and how hard it is to get.

After a pause—she can tell he's considering the best way to

respond—he simply says, "That's none of your concern."

It's true that there are benefits to living on Skinner Street. Even with limited funds there is much to see and do. Aware that she has developed an interest in Mr. Coleridge's poetry, her father invites her to go with him to hear a lecture on Shakespeare that Coleridge will be giving at Corporation Hall. Jane asks to come along, and they dress for the occasion.

"Wear your brown silk," Jane says. "The one with the Vandyke points."

Mary nods. She has only one other dress for going out, so there's not much to choose from. When she's done laying it on the bed, Jane looks at her expectantly. It's her turn now. "The cream with the yellow flowers," Mary says. "It looks very pretty on you."

They take a hired cab, an indulgence, and as they enter the crowded room, Mary feels suddenly bashful but also honored to be attending. However, Jane is of a different opinion. "This does not look promising," she says. "I thought it would be more festive. I thought there might be food."

Some have taken their seats while others mill about, greeting friends and chatting in small groups. The men smoke and the women cling to their husbands' sleeves. Her father stops to talk with Mr. Lamb and also points out an extravagant-looking fellow and tells them it's Lord Byron.

"Is he noteworthy?" Mary asks.

"He is an excellent young poet," her father says.

As soon as her father is out of earshot, Jane pulls her close. "Lord Byron?" she gasps. "Don't you know? He's a *scandalous* young poet. He's in love with his own half sister. Or so I've heard it said."

Mary turns to look at him. He is standing alone, on the far side of the room. His hair is brown and curly and his forehead high and unblemished, perhaps as a sort of wall to protect the genius that lies within. In profile his face reminds her of statues she's seen, those that have perfectly formed noses and insouciant lips.

"Heard it said by whom?" Mary asks.

"The girl at the cheesemonger, for one. Unlike you, I talk to people. I have a natural curiosity about the world."

"You like to gossip is what you mean." She says it dismissively, but in truth she wants to know more. In love with his half sister? How could such a thing be? "Have you read his poetry?" Jane asks.

"Not yet, but after seeing him tonight, I most certainly will."

Mary enjoys the lecture, but it goes on too long. She especially likes what Mr. Coleridge says about *The Tempest*: "It is a species of drama which owes no allegiance to time or space." As the daily progress of human life cannot escape time and space, how heartening to know there is a work of art that does.

"I thought he was rather unfocused," her father says afterward. "His ideas are always sound, yet tonight his presentation lacked order and style."

"I can't wait to tell Fanny we saw Lord Byron," says Jane. "I tried to make her come with us, but she thought it would be dull. Little did she know . . ."

Fanny does agree to accompany them on their next outing, to attend a wedding. In fact, this time the entire family goes. The bride, who is extremely elegant, wears a light blue muslin dress, a silk shawl embossed with flowers, and a cap trimmed with lace. Afterward, they all enjoy discussing the dress, the ceremony, and the party that followed—at least until Mary and her stepmother clash.

"He seemed quite nice," Fanny says, referring to the groom.

"I shall be very particular about whom I marry," Jane says.

Mary shakes her head. "I shall marry someone who will take me away from here." But when she turns, she is chagrined to discover her remark has been overheard.

"What a high opinion you have of yourself," her stepmother says. "Are you distressed that you have a bed to sleep in? Are you weary of being fed?"

"I only meant—"

"I know what you meant. You condescend far too often. And your father gives you too much leave to speak your mind."

For the next few seconds she fights an inner battle to restrain herself from replying; in the end she succeeds. What a mistake her father made in marrying this woman, and such an unfairness that her true mother died.

The following day, her father calls her into his library and asks if she'd like go away to live with an acquaintance of his in Scotland.

Mary is dumbstruck. "You wish me to go away?"

"Only if you choose to. Although I have not met Mr. Baxter in person, I have corresponded with him on several matters. It is clear to me he is an upright and congenial man. He has lost his wife but has three daughters. If you don't find the situation agreeable, you can come home."

She shakes her head, still not fully comprehending, on the verge of tears. "But why?"

"I have always held that it is useful for young people to go out and see the world. Some men have the wherewithal to send their children on extravagant tours. I do not. And to be candid, Mary, you seem unhappy. You and your mother quarrel overmuch."

Now the tears do come. She feels as if she's being banished. Then again, maybe he's right. Going all the way to Scotland by herself would be frightening, but . . .

Before she can complete the thought, her father speaks again. "Perhaps it would make things easier if we were to agree on a particular span of time. What say you to five months? Don't tell me you've never thought of running off. I have seen it in your eyes."

She goes up to her room but comes back later in the day to request more information. Where in Scotland do these Baxters reside, what else does he know about the daughters, and how soon would she leave?

"Dundee," he replies, fetching a map. "One daughter is named Isabel. Like you, she is fifteen. She has a younger sister and also an older one who is married and no longer lives at home. Regarding your departure, whenever you desire."

Well, she thinks, *it would be an adventure.* And she could be rid of her stepmother for five whole months. She would miss her father and resents the fact that he doesn't seem worried about missing *her.* But perhaps her absence will cause him to realize her true value. As for the others, she suspects she'll miss them in pieces—that is, on certain occasions or for certain aspects of themselves—although perhaps not much at all. She asks Jane what she thinks about her father's plan, but she is busy reading Lord Byron's most recent book. "I had no idea he'd be so amusing," she says, and then, "Go if you like. It makes no difference to me."

That evening she seeks out her father yet again. As usual, he is in his library, bent over some manuscript, his nose only inches from the page. She feels bad that he now has to read children's stories with an eye to sales, in place of the politics and philosophy he loves. What if the real reason he's sending her away is to save money? That hadn't occurred to her until now. But she's made her decision. When he looks up, she speaks:

"I've decided to go. I shall do so with enthusiasm."

"I'm very pleased. I hope I didn't make you feel unwanted."

"I was caught by surprise. You shouldn't tell a person she's going to Scotland without a preamble of some kind."

"You are entirely correct. There should have been a preamble."

"How will I get there?"

"It's something of a journey. Five days by sea."

And so it happens. Only a week later, her father takes her to the docks, where she boards a ship called the *Osnaburgh*. She's been at sea once before and got terribly sick, but she's convinced herself that this will be an enjoyable voyage, that she will meet interesting people and get her sea legs quickly. Yet the instant she sets foot on deck, stark terror overcomes her. Everyone on board looks irritable, and the water is gray and choppy, causing the still-moored ship to lurch and tilt. Even more disturbing, it has suddenly occurred to her (why it didn't occur to her before, she can't explain) that when she arrives in Scotland, she will be required to meet many new people. Why would someone as shy as herself choose to be placed in such a position? She looks back at her father and he waves. If she sought out the captain and begged to be put off, would he allow it?

Before she can act on her misgivings, the anchor is drawn up, the sails fill, and she feels the ship surge forward beneath her feet. They are underway.

Shelley

Now what? Hogg kept saying if they were discovered, they'd be thrown out. He considered it possible but assumed the likeliest punishment would be a simple reprimand. He feels sorry for Hogg. Poor fellow. He says he's going north.

"What will you do with yourself?" Shelley asks.

"I'm uncertain. But until I decide, I intend to lie low in York."

They were in Shelley's room, from which he was being evicted. Making a sweeping motion, he said, "You always admired my microscope. Please take it. And any books you'd like."

Shortly after Hogg's departure, Shelley left Oxford as well and is now in London, living in one shabby room. His father knows about his expulsion and is furious. He says he should not come home nor should he expect his allowance to be forthcoming. So how is he supposed to survive? They exchange letters, some conciliatory, some outraged, some hurt, but Shelley refuses to apologize, refuses to ask for mercy. His father writes a lengthy letter explaining why religion is necessary and right. Immediately, Shelley responds:

> *My dear Father,*
>
> *Your very excellent exposition on the subject of religion pleased me a great deal. I have seldom seen Orthodoxy so clearly defined. You have proven to my satisfaction that those who are incapable of independent thought should follow the faith of their fathers and thereby be constrained from taking regrettable actions. But for rational beings such as myself . . .*

In his next letter, his father says he's not sure he cares to correspond with an atheist. In *his* next letter, Shelley says, "You made me what I am. Why not take credit for your work?" Then comes one Shelley refuses to answer. "Perhaps you are mad," his father writes. "Perhaps I should commit you to the sort of institution that houses the criminally insane."

He and his father have had disagreements before, but he's always told himself they are the kind any son has with his father, disagreements the old must necessarily have with the young. Yet now he's beginning to see things otherwise. He doesn't believe for an instant his father will have him locked up, but it's becoming clear that the two of them are so different in temperament and outlook—and especially in values—that they will grow further and further apart as time goes on. He and Hogg ought to be praised for what they did, not accused of madness. By Jove, they ought to have been given a prize.

Three years from now a substantial portion of the estate will be his, no matter what his father thinks. But three years is an awfully long time to wait. It occurs to him that his situation is not unlike that of Antigone. She, too, did something society disapproved of and was harshly punished; she, too, followed the dictates of her conscience and refused to allow others to tell her what was right. Not that he has any intention of hanging himself. This is England, not ancient Greece.

Over the next few weeks he sleepwalks almost every night. It must be the stress. He disrobes, puts himself to bed, and wakes up fully clothed. He disrobes, puts himself to bed, and wakes up at his desk, pen in hand. One night he even wakes up shivering on the street, a pair of ragged boys gazing down at him, pleased to have found someone worse off than themselves. The next morning, he goes to a doctor and obtains some laudanum. When he gets home, he takes a dose, falls into a deep sleep, and doesn't awake until the following afternoon. He feels rested but strangely weak, as though his blood has congealed, molasses-like, and clogged his narrow veins.

To assuage his loneliness, he writes Hogg long letters—letters in which he analyzes the nature of loneliness. How one's thoughts begin to feed on themselves like a cannibal feasting on his own flesh. He has great ambitions to do something remarkable in the world, but now he's been exiled from Oxford and exiled from his ancestral home. He writes a letter to his sisters in which he tells them their father is not to be trusted, but a servant intercepts it and sends it back. There was a time when he pictured himself coming home from Oxford to his adoring parents and siblings and turning Field Place into a center of natural philosophy and the arts, where he would make great discoveries and write remarkable books. But Oxford and possibly even Field Place are lost to him now.

He goes for long walks and one afternoon finds himself passing a coffeehouse in Grosvenor Square. A girl is standing in the doorway, and she looks so familiar, he stops.

"Pardon me, but I believe we've met," he says. It's his sister's friend Harriet, the one they went ghost-hunting with. As soon as he speaks, her eyes go wide and she shouts, "Percy!"

It's such a relief to see someone he knows. She insists he come inside and sit. She introduces him to her sister Liza, who is tall and severe looking, whereas Harriet is not so tall and has a merry, impish face. Harriet explains that their father owns this coffeehouse. Yes, the very one in which they are now sitting! She asks him about his studies at Oxford—is the work tremendously hard?—then quickly adds, "Of course it's not hard for you."

He surveys the premises. It's an ordinary-looking establishment, with dark furnishings, brass fixtures, and windows stained black by smoke. In reply to her question, he says, "I am at Oxford no longer. I found it . . . uninspiring. I'm now thinking of doing some traveling, perhaps to France." He has never been to France, nor has he given much thought to going there. Yet now that he's spoken the word, it sounds like an excellent idea—although he'd need some money first.

For a time he is left alone as the sisters go off to fetch him something to drink. Only two other customers are present, over by the window, their heads wreathed in smoke. The bulk of their trade must come later in the day.

"My sister attends the Clapham School," Liza says when they return. "The Clapham School is considered quite fine, but Harriet often complains about it. Far too much in my view." Harriet is the same age as his sister Elizabeth, sixteen, while Liza appears almost twice that, which may explain her disapproving tone.

"I would leave the Clapham School as you left Oxford, but my father won't allow it," Harriet tells him, throwing her sister a disputatious glance. He suspects this is an ongoing quarrel. Yet if anyone can understand her problem, it's Shelley: a school she dislikes and a father who thinks he knows best.

"Don't talk nonsense," Liza says.

Instead of responding, Harriet turns away from her sister and attends to Shelley. "And after you return from your travels? What do you expect to do then?"

"I should like to study medicine. Although at present I cannot because I am poor as a rat." A trip to France and the study of medicine! When under pressure, the mind's ability to invent steps forth.

"How unfortunate," Harriet says. "Is there no one to whom you can apply for help?"

"I'm sure Mr. Shelley can manage his affairs," Liza says. "It's rude to suggest he cannot."

"Not rude at all," he says to Harriet. "Thank you for your concern." And then, after a moment of uncomfortable silence, "I am enjoying my coffee a great deal."

The longer they talk, the more it appears Harriet may be as oppressed by her sister as by her father. And the longer they talk, the more appealing she becomes.

As he prepares to take his leave, he says, "May I see you again?"

"We are not often here," Liza replies, with a finality that gives him little hope. But Harriet says, "However, you may visit us at our house. We have coffee there as well."

He walks up the street, feeling positively buoyant. When he awoke today, he was dreadfully lonely, and now he has been invited to call on a pretty girl. Liza may disapprove, but she's obviously a scold.

He goes to see them the very next day and is delighted to find Harriet home alone. She invites him into the parlor; the house is not very grand, but it's well kept and capacious enough. She is wearing a green dress that matches her eyes. They exchange observations about the weather, and he is pleased when instead of coffee she offers him tea. Also some biscuits, which, given that he's been restricting the amount he eats to save money, come as a welcome supplement. As they sip from their cups, Harriet asks about Field Place. She once visited Elizabeth there and thought it a paradise.

"I expect it's an excellent place to hunt," she says.

"I no longer hunt. I've recently renounced the consumption of flesh."

Her eyes open wide. "For what purpose?"

"For the purpose of health and to reduce the amount of barbarism visited upon sentient beings. I've stopped drinking wine as well."

He can see he's made an impression. Perhaps too much of one—she hurriedly changes the subject to something that won't invite so alarming a response.

"Will you return to Oxford? When you're back from France?"

"Oxford? After France?" he says, momentarily at a loss

about what he told her the day before. "Certainly not. Their ideas are narrow and the living quarters too small. By the by, where's your sister?" he asks, fearful she's lurking about.

"She goes every day at this time to give painting lessons to an old lady—a family friend."

He thereby resolves that any future visits will occur at exactly this hour.

A few days hence he returns. Harriet wears a cotton dress and he can't take his eyes off her, in part because the cotton is thin. This time she asks him why he left Oxford. She's says she's heard some gossip but wants to hear his account. When he tells her about the pamphlet, her eyes go wide again. If anything is more shocking than vegetarianism, it is atheism. He fears he's scaring her off.

"I've heard of such people, but I've never met one," she says.

"'Such people,' as you call them, are not monsters. As I hope you can see."

"Then to whom do you pray?" she asks.

"That's just it, I don't."

He wonders if she'll want to see him after today. His beliefs may have been more than she can bear.

But she invites him back again and again. She asks to read the pamphlet and anything else he thinks would help her understand his views. He's touched by her eagerness and sincerity. The world is so filled with cynicism that finding someone who doesn't expect the worst is an absolute delight.

Jane

As soon as Mary is absent, Jane begins to miss her. Before she departed, half a year didn't sound like much. Now she can't believe she'll be away for so long.

Of course there's always Fanny, who is agreeable and exceedingly kind. Yet she has no sense of adventure. When Jane suggests they obtain a set of cards and teach themselves to play Faro, Fanny contends that gambling can lead to ruin. When Jane suggests they convince their parents to take the family to Vauxhall Gardens, Fanny says, "Who will mind the shop?"

Her parents are no more amusing. Of late, they have been consumed by worries about money. They make little effort to hide the matter from their children—indeed, they talk about it over breakfast nearly every day. "There is simply no telling what sort of books will sell," her mother complains. "An idea that seems promising at its conception ends up as a stack of unsold volumes blocking the stairs." Their latest hopes are pinned on a book of stories from Shakespeare being written by the Lambs. Mr. Lamb is doing the tragedies and his sister the comedies. However, Mary Lamb can be unpredictable, so they're worried about her part.

Jane has some compassion for her mother. Her mother thought she was marrying the great William Godwin, author of *Enquiry Concerning Political Justice,* a book everyone of consequence has read. But now what does she have? A fading philosopher and an unsuccessful bookseller. Regarding the money problems, Jane has yet to feel herself inconvenienced or deprived, but she remembers what it was like when her mother had no husband and she and Charles had no provider. There were nights when they had nothing for supper. On one occasion they were turned out on the street for lack of rent. Therefore, she feels a chill when she overhears Godwin speak of debtors' prison "if business does not improve."

One activity Jane does find entertaining in Mary's absence is helping her father with the mail. Before Mary left, one of her chores was to read aloud the letters he received while he penned replies. This task has now fallen to her. She didn't realize how wide his celebrity is. Several letters from admirers arrive every week. The two of them sit in his library, she in an uncomfortable straight-backed chair and he at his great brown desk.

The letters take a variety of forms. Some ask him questions about his philosophy, others simply sing his praises—"From this day forward I shall endeavor to live according to your book." and some are from young writers asking him to read what they've written with an eye to helping them get in print. Particularly amusing are the ones from women curious to know if he's married. Finally, there are those seeking money. They can be either predatory or sad. When she reads one of those, she thinks, *If only they knew.* After a while, she realizes many of letters come from a small group of individuals who write again and again.

Occasionally, a letter speaks in a voice that causes both herself and Godwin to lean forward in their chairs. *Perhaps you will be surprised to hear from an unknown reader*, one such missive begins. Well, not so surprised, thinks Jane. Indeed, it happens all the time. But in the next few lines, the writer tells about himself in a manner she finds unusually affecting: *My life has been short but eventful. I have seen much of human prejudice, suffered much from persecution. Yet the ill treatment I have received has proven my principles to be worthy and not in any regard corrupt. I am young, but I am also steadfast in the cause of justice and truth.*

"Forthright and fluidly expressed," Godwin says when she pauses for a breath. "You'd think such attributes would be commonplace; unfortunately, they are not."

She continues, and the next part makes them laugh: *The name of Godwin has always excited in me feelings of reverence and admiration. However, I had enrolled your name on the list of the honorable departed. I had felt regret that your being had passed from this earth of ours.* So the poor fellow assumed the great William Godwin was dead.

The writer closes by asking Godwin to meet him at some future date. His name is Percy B. Shelley—a stranger, as he says.

She watches as Mr. Godwin composes his reply. "I'll invite him to visit the shop during hours," he tells her. "Maybe he'll purchase a few books while he's here."

Before her mother married Mr. Godwin, before they moved into this house and started this business, Jane had no idea there were people in this world so besotted with books. She thinks of those who come to visit and stay well into the night. Not only do they discuss books, they *talk like books*, paragraphs, pages, entire chapters issuing from their mouths. Likewise it appears there are young men who will write a letter filled with passionate thoughts to a man such as her father whom the young man has never met except in the pages of a book. She finds it all rather odd. She has nothing against books—she likes poetry and novels especially—but they are diversions, not the core of life.

To Jane's surprise, a second letter from Mr. Shelley arrives in less than a week. She didn't expect him to be the kind who would write more than once. This one has the same admirable directness of tone as the first one but includes more specific facts:

> *I am the son of a man of fortune in Sussex. The habits of thinking of my Father and myself never coincided. Passive obedience was inculcated and enforced in my childhood: I was required to love because it was* my duty *to love—which obviated the intention. I was haunted with a passion for the wildest and most extravagant romances: ancient books of Legend and Magic were perused with an enthusiasm and wonder almost amounting to belief . . .*

Godwin holds up his hand to indicate he wants her to stop: "*The son of a man of fortune,*" he whispers, mostly to himself.

The next page describes in detail the writer's expulsion from Oxford for printing a pamphlet in defense of Atheism. Perhaps this is the real reason for his letters. Jane's knowledge of Mr. Godwin's beliefs is not extensive, but she is aware that he has been attacked in the press for his refusal to believe in God, in religion, even in the institution of marriage. But her father seems far less interested in this part than in the one that follows:

> *I am heir by entail to an estate of 6000£ per annum. Yet my principles have induced me to regard the law of primogeniture as an evil.*

When she's done, he says, "A young man whose principles may prevent him from accepting money he is being offered. What then will become of the money?" He pauses. "I think my previous reply to Mr. Shelley was too cool. I shall invite him to come for tea."

Shelley

He continues to call on Harriet Westbrook whenever he can, sometimes at the coffeehouse, sometimes at home. Unfortunately, Liza is often present, or if not she, then Mr. Westbrook—one or the other hovering nearby. Westbrook is a man of business and acts as that label implies. He smiles at his customers, growls at his employees, and treats his daughters as assets that he will sell to the highest bidder when the time comes. Therefore, he seems puzzled by Shelley. Shouldn't a young man of his background be doing something of consequence instead of visiting in the middle of the day? He often asks him when he's planning on leaving the country, a note of hope in his voice.

"Simply getting my affairs in order," he replies. Or "waiting 'til the weather improves."

Despite being chaperoned, there usually comes a time when he and Harriet are alone and able to talk. Among her favorite topics is the one she brought up the first time they met: how much she dislikes the Clapham School. Shelley encourages this line of thought. It may be the job of fathers and schoolmasters to tell those who are imprisoned that they should practice forbearance, but he considers it *his* job to sympathize, perhaps even to help her escape.

She says, "I'd rather perish than go back. They treat us so harshly and punish us for the smallest errors. The lessons are more tedious than you can imagine. The food is always cold and they never give us enough."

"Have you told your father how much you dislike it?"

"Many times. He says I'm too young to know my own mind. Perhaps he's right, but I *do* know when I'm being abused. I lost my hair ribbon, and when I told the matron I knew who took it, she slapped my face." The memory brings tears to her eyes. She tries to blink them away before she continues, "And when I protested, they withheld my supper. I have only one friend there and she may not come back next term."

He'd like to go to her father and insist she be allowed to quit. Better yet, he'd like to take her in his arms and console her . . . she being so pretty and all. Instead, he says, "Have you any paper?"

She looks up, wipes her eyes. "What sort?"

"Ordinary writing paper. Several pieces."

She leaves the room and returns with a sheaf of perhaps twenty sheets in hand. He takes one and folds it, folds it again, turns it over, folds it yet again, and with a few more deft moves, produces a handsome paper boat.

"Very clever," she says. "For what purpose?"

"To take your mind off your troubles."

She raises an eyebrow. "You'll have to do better than that."

"You do one."

"I wasn't watching closely enough. You'll have to show me again."

"Maybe you dislike the Clapham School because you are an inattentive student," he says, pretending exasperation. "Now do as I do, stepwise. Make your creases sharp."

When they finally stop, there are twelve paper boats spread across the table, all identical except for two crooked ones she made when starting out.

"An armada," Harriet says.

"And now we must set them afloat."

He throws on his coat, helps her with her cape, stuffs his pockets with boats, and pushes her out the door, managing to avoid being seen or heard by Liza. The Serpentine in Hyde Park is only a few minutes away. Once there, he checks the wind, picks a good spot, and they launch their creations one by one, giving each a gentle shove, letting the light breeze that's blowing from the southeast carry them away. What Harriet doesn't know is the making of paper boats has been one of Shelley's favorite pastimes since he was a small boy. One he never tires of and has never outgrown.

"So have you forgotten them?"

"What?"

"Your worries."

"My dear Percy, I have no idea what you're talking about," she says and smiles without reservation as her beribboned tresses are mussed by the breeze. She calls him Percy and he permits it. The name sounds pleasant coming from her lips.

The next time he visits, he steals a kiss; the time after that, she takes him to a hidden pantry in the coffee shop, where they embrace and kiss again and again. He pulls her to him and she surprises him with her ardor. She nips his throat and ear and he puts a hand where no maiden has allowed him to put a hand before.

So they continue, day after day, sometimes in a concealed corner of the garden, sometimes in the parlor at the Westbrook house, where, Shelley having become such a common presence, they are occasionally left unwatched. When he's not with her, he's begun writing a long poem, one which will take up British politics, the false history of Christianity, and the grandeur of the planets in motion. He thinks about Harriet as he writes and about the poem as they kiss. Harriet's pull upon his body is as powerful as any force in nature, as the moon upon the tides.

At last they end up in a small bedroom at the top of the house, one kept for visiting children and the occasional spinster aunt. He blocks the door with a chair, but they are both so nervous, they remove only the clothing necessary for the act, which is performed quickly, with few expressions of passion and not one spoken word. When it's over, Harriet tries to act as if everything is as it was before, but he notices she's crying.

"My sweet, what's wrong?" he asks.

She shakes her head. "Nothing. Tears come with strong emotion, do they not?" She wipes her eyes and forces a smile. "Would you like to stay for supper? I can ask the cook."

He takes her hands in his and says, "We have nothing to be ashamed of. One day men and women will be able to do as they please without fear of condemnation. But I say, why wait?"

Mary

From the front of the Baxter house, she can see the Firth of Tay and, from the back, a line of green hills, beyond which stand the craggy ridges of the Highlands, where perhaps dragons sleep. Whaling ships dock in the Firth, bringing with them wind-blasted men and casks of foul-smelling oil. Other vessels arrive from India, laden with spices and jute. Mr. Baxter owns a factory that makes cloth for sails. While her own father seems almost to beg the public to buy his books, Mr. Baxter says the demand for canvas is such that he can barely keep up.

Thus far, her father's description of the Baxter family has been borne out. Mr. Baxter is kind and tolerant, governing the household with a gentle hand, and she likes her new "sisters," Isabel and Christy, very much. Upon her arrival, all of them were so welcoming that her fears about being in the company of strangers quickly disappeared.

It's been only a few years since the Baxter girls lost their mother, so Mary has that in common with them from the start. Isabel is her age exactly and seems pleased to have her as a houseguest, especially since Christy is often helping her father at his place of business. The eldest of the three sisters is married and no longer lives at home.

Before coming here, she wasn't fully aware of her father's— and mother's—wide celebrity. Everywhere she goes, she is introduced as William Godwin's daughter or as Godwin and Wollstonecraft's child. Indeed, Isabel considers Mary Wollstonecraft to have been one of the great women of history.

"It must be daunting to have such a mother," she says. "It's as if you have royal blood."

"All I know of her is what my father tells me—and what I find in books."

"But she lived in France at such a momentous time! Was she acquainted with Madame Roland? Did she ever meet Robespierre?"

"Madame Roland?" Mary says, embarrassed by her ignorance. She thinks she's heard the name before but can't recall where. When she confesses as much, Isabel says, "Oh, you must read her memoir. I have my own copy. She was an extremely brave member of the Girondists. Right before she was to be guillotined, she said, 'O Liberty, what crimes are committed in thy name.'"

It turns out Isabel is fascinated by all aspects of the French Revolution. She goes to her room and returns with Madame Roland's memoir and several other volumes she says Mary must read.

Mary is pleased not only with the Baxter family but with Dundee as well. It's a charming town, with winding streets and more churches and sweet shops than she can count, with unobstructed vistas in all directions, some toward the hills and some toward the slate-gray sea. She and Isabel go on long walks, during which they discuss literature, history, and whatever else their curiosities call forth. It is on one such ramble that she discovers Isabel has a second passion, a darker one. She takes her to a field, in the center of which is a barren mound. There, beneath a sky heavy with clouds, she explains that they are standing on the spot where witches once were burned.

"They tied the accused to an iron wheel and then set a fire beneath it. The wheel was turned until her head was in the flames and her feet pointed toward the sky. It was believed placing the witch in such a position would speed her journey to Hell." As Isabel speaks, the wind increases and her shawl whips about.

"I don't believe in Hell," Mary says.

"Not at all?"

Mary shakes her head definitively. "Neither Heaven nor Hell."

"Where then will your spirit go after you die?"

Mary shrugs. "I suppose I shall find out when the time comes."

"What an interesting person you are," Isabel exclaims. "I myself am torn. I worry that if I don't believe in Hell, my chances of ending up there increase. Do you see what I mean?"

Yet as far as Mary is concerned, it's Isabel who's the interesting one. They share a room, and as they lie in bed after the lamp has been extinguished, Isabel explains that she has seen more than one ghost and promises to take Mary to where the fairies live. She even knows a good deal about a monstrous demon wolf reputed to live in the south of France.

Sometimes they go to visit Isabel's married sister, Margaret, and her husband, David Booth, in the village of Newburgh, on the other side of the Tay. Booth is even more of a reformer than Mary's own father—in fact, for him the term *radical* seems almost too mild. It turns out that Isabel's knowledge of the French Revolution comes as much from Booth as from the books she reads. "We ought to have done the same thing here," he says. "But now I fear the moment has passed." He is also a great student of the natural world and takes them on walks along the water, where he explains the workings of the tides and knows the name of every bird. Although he is forty years of age and Margaret is twenty-five, he is the more vigorous of the pair, as Margaret is often ill.

One day, while Mary and Isabel are on their way home after a day spent with the Booths, Mary says, "I don't think I would like being the wife of a man almost as old as my own father. David is certainly admirable, but admiration is not enough."

Isabel is of a different mind: "Oh, he is far more than admirable. He is kind and witty and so very intelligent. Imagine having him at your disposal every night."

"Isabel! At your *disposal?*" Mary replies, shocked at the image her words call to mind. And then Isabel bursts into laughter as she realizes what she's said.

When summer comes, the Baxters take her traveling. They go north into the wild-most parts of Scotland, to Pitlochry, to Inverness, and then all the way to the end of the earth, otherwise known as John o' Groats. She starts out expecting it to be an arduous journey, but there's such a party of them—Mr. Baxter, Isabel, Christy, their married sister Margaret and husband David Booth, three hired coachmen, and Mary herself—that it's quite enjoyable. They find strange but accommodating little inns miles from any town, and when there is no inn, they set up camp amid the gorse and broom. The people they meet along the way are delightful. Almost without exception they seem pleased to have visitors, amazed that anyone would bother to venture so far into the wilderness merely to see the sights. In London she never heard a single good word uttered about the Highlands or its denizens. "If you go there, expect to be murdered," is what she was always told.

Even if the people weren't so accommodating, the landscape alone would make the trip worthwhile. The great ridges and steep-sided valleys, the rushing waters and endless skies are like nothing she's ever seen. One afternoon they watch a thunderstorm take shape at the far end of a glen. The clouds are like purple-gray mountains, and as the rain sweeps across the land, shafts of rose and yellow sunlight shine down as if through windows of stained glass. "The glory of God is all around us," Mr. Baxter exclaims. "Commit this vista to memory so you may recall it in times of despair."

During the long days in their coach, they read to one another. She and Isabel take turns with *Pamela,* passing the copy back and forth, but when it's Christy's turn, she reaches into her satchel and produces George Lyttelton's *Communication with the Other Side.* Mary hasn't spent much time with Christy, but it turns out her fascination with the occult matches Isabel's. While their coach rumbles along, she reads them passages in which Baron Lyttelton explains how, by way of certain "spiritual imbrications," he managed to make contact with Peter the Great, Pericles, even Queen Christina of Sweden, years after they were dead. It's perfect traveling literature—

as Christy reads, the miles pass effortlessly by.

Then one night the three girls are sharing a room in an inn north of Inverness when Christy suggests they imitate Baron Lyttelton and attempt to contact the spirit world. After all, it doesn't get dark until almost midnight and they're having difficulty falling sleep. They laugh and declare, each in her own way, that the idea of speaking to the dead is ridiculous, and then, a moment later, commit to try. But whom should they contact?

"Henry the VIII," says Christy.

"What would you ask him?" says Isabel.

"If he has any regrets. What about you, Mary, to whom would you like to speak?"

She bites her lip and thinks. The answer has to be clever. Something that will make them laugh. But she can't come up with anything so she deflects the question from herself. "I know who Isabel wants to hear from: Madame Roland. Or Marie Antoinette herself."

"I've a better idea," Isabel says, "Mary Wollstonecraft. We must try to reach her!"

Mary gasps. The game is no longer a game. She shakes her head and says, "No. I shan't permit it."

"Mary," Christy begins, but before she can continue, Mary stands and steps toward the door. She won't have them pretending to summon her mother and putting words, probably ridiculous ones, in her mouth.

"I think we're all tired," Isabel says.

But Mary won't be soothed. She takes her shawl off the back of a chair and says, "I think I'll go for a walk."

Outside, she stands for a moment and looks up at the sky. It is neither day nor night, but an in-between time, the long, silver twilight of the far north. Setting off up the road, she crosses over a low rise and veers into the heather, following a stone wall. She feels cast out and alone—not because of anything Isabel and Christy said, not because her father sent her here, but because she has no actual memories of her mother. Yet whenever Mary Wollstonecraft is mentioned, she is reminded that her mother really did exist in the world, she really did talk and laugh and write and eat and sleep and Mary feels her presence. Perhaps spirits are to be feared, but she would feel no fear if at this moment her dear mother came walking toward her out of the shadows, out of the purple tangles of brush, out of the invisible world Baron Lyttelton seems certain exists.

Upon their return to Dundee, Mary finds a stack of letters waiting, some from her father, and some from Fanny and Jane. She opens them, orders them by date, and then waits until later that night when the house is quiet to sit down and read. She appreciates it when they write and likes to linger over each letter, even if all they contain are accounts of ordinary life. However, this batch is different. In every one there are remarks about a new friend her father has made through the mail. An aspiring poet and philosopher named Shelley, he seems to have impressed the entire family. Jane says their father is "taken with him," Fanny calls him "Father's new admirer," and her father speaks of his "subtle and well-formed mind."

While such remarks pique Mary's curiosity, they also cause her to worry. She has noticed, as her father has gotten older, that he tends to seek out admiration rather than allowing it to arrive unsolicited. He is not a vain man, but it pains her to see that the respect offered him by his family is not enough. On a few occasions in the past, unscrupulous fellows, thinking William Godwin must be rich because he is well known, have attempted to inveigle themselves into his house and attain favors. She hopes this Mr. Shelley is not one of those.

Shelley

It all happens so quickly. Harriet has been out of school between terms, and when it comes time to go back, she refuses. She looks at him with tears in her eyes and says, "Please help me. He'll try to force me and I lack the strength to resist."

He is at once thrilled and taken aback. What will her father do? Westbrook is a man of business. The decisions he makes are based on facts and the facts are all on his side. The only way to help her is to take her away.

"If you leave, he may not allow you back," Shelley says, thinking of how his own father has been treating him.

"I know. But I won't mind because I'll be with you."

He has shared with her his thoughts on marriage—that it

ought to be abolished because its primary purpose is to repress. So does she really mean for them to live as lovers and have her reputation ruined? He poses the question to her directly, without embarrassment, and gets this reply:

"I thought you might . . . reconsider. You love me, do you not?"

"I do. But I have my principles."

"Then what am I to do?"

"Is the Clapham School really so intolerable? I shall visit often . . ." He feels like a traitor for saying this. He has encouraged her rebellion and now he's having second thoughts.

"I will end my life."

"Don't be foolish. You'll do no such thing."

He leaves her without a decision having been made. He understands her position but won't compromise his own. The next day he writes a letter to Harriet's father pleading her case. The response comes by return post: *In this matter your opinion is of no value. Do not write again.*

Now they can meet only in secret. Her father's suspicions have been aroused. Shelley sends her a message asking her to come to the Serpentine. She is there before him, standing utterly still, a winsome statue gazing out across the pond.

"You look very beautiful," he says, approaching from behind.

"Oh! Percy, you startled me."

From the pockets of his overcoat he retrieves a handful of boats. He kneels and begins to push them away from shore.

"Again?" Harriet says. "Have you noticed they all sink to the bottom before making it to the other side?"

The last one launched, he stands and says, "If we were to marry," but before he can complete the thought, she interrupts.

"I told him about us. He said he will never give his consent."

This infuriates Shelley. His hands go into fists and his chin juts forward. "Then we'll go to Scotland. There, the law allows a contract of matrimony to be signed without the father's consent. Let him try to stop us." He takes her hands, looks intently at her small, questioning face, and kisses her. Then they walk arm in arm through the cold afternoon until it begins to get dark.

After they part, he has much to consider: money, which he'll try to borrow from Hogg, who is still in York; transportation, which will require money; and a well-thought-out plan of escape, for it's obvious her father is becoming more watchful by the day. First, however, he must tend to his principles. If a girl of sixteen goes off to live in sin with a man of nineteen, her whole future will be lost. So marry they must. But why have principles if they can be so easily set aside? Perhaps he'll put the question to William Godwin, with whom he's been corresponding lately. According to Godwin's writings, marriage corrupts society. Yet among the facts that have emerged from their correspondence is that Godwin is himself married. Apparently, even great philosophers allow their principles to bend.

He meets her two Sundays hence, on Chapel Street, shortly before noon. They won't leave for Scotland until tonight, so they'll need to spend the day in hiding. At an alehouse they choose a shadowy table in the corner. Harriet is wearing a purple dress with a black velvet collar. As lovely as she looks, he can't have them attracting attention and directs her to conceal the dress with her cape. They feel excited and wild and dissolute. Where else in London are there two such reckless souls? Whenever anyone comes through the door, they prepare themselves to see her father's face. Although neither of them are drinkers of ale, they do so now, to mark the occasion. They toast their future and their love. He's gotten five pounds from Hogg and has to keep reminding himself that it must last them all the way to Scotland. He assures her there is more money forthcoming, but that assumes he can make peace with his father. A large assumption, that.

As night begins to fall, they walk briskly to the Green Dragon Inn on Gracechurch Street, where they board the night mail. When they hear the crack of the driver's whip and feel the coach lurch into motion, she clutches his arm. The other passengers offer opening pleasantries—after all, they will be going some distance together—but for the most part he and Harriet keep to themselves. They pass large, dark buildings that stand like gray hulks against a fading sky. They pass small, dark houses that huddle near the road. And then suddenly they have left London behind; where before there was a city, there are the looming silhouettes of trees, the black tracery of fence lines, and undulating fields made indigo by the light of the moon.

For three days they continue northward. Meals are taken at coaching inns, where the quality of the food ranges from poor to indigestible. Passengers get off and new ones replace them. By the middle of the second day, none of those who started with them in London remain. Eventually, it's just the two of them, so they sleep, Harriet nestled warmly against him. When the driver stops to change horses at York, they consider getting off and going to find Hogg, but Harriet says, "My father might be following us. We can't allow him to catch up." So they leave a note for Hogg with the innkeeper and continue on. At the next stop, a Scotsman joins them. He peruses a newspaper for a time and then sets it aside.

"A border marriage, is it?" he asks.

Shelley feels himself blushing. Is it so obvious? Harriet demonstrates her claim on him by taking his hand.

"It is indeed," he replies.

"I've seen 'em younger than you," says the Scotsman. "No reason to be ashamed."

It's a relief to share their secret, even with a stranger they'll never see again. They ask him where one goes to obtain a license and, once they have the license, where they might be wed. As it happens, he's a barrister and tells them everything they need to know.

The next morning they reach Edinburgh, and before the day is out, they are married. All they had to do was sign a document in front of witnesses. Three cheers for the liberality of the Scots. Then, properly and indissolubly wed, they secure lodgings. They eat a frugal supper of sausages on toast and go to their room. As soon as the door is secured, he all but pounces on her. It's nothing like their first time. They remove every piece of clothing and caress one another's skin. The bed creaks and her face is flushed. They do what they wish, as husband and wife, not just once but again and again.

"Goodness me," Harriet says. "Our fathers would murder us if they knew."

"Speak not of such matters. We choose our own path now."

"Oh, my dear Percy. You rescued me," she says, and smiles. Such a sweet, trusting smile. He wants to be hers entirely, but there is a part of him that remains outside the moment, observing, questioning. A part of him that remains dubious, not of her or of the two of them together, but of himself.

"I'm nearly out of money," he says, becoming uncomfortable with the intensity of her gaze.

"Worry about that tomorrow. I'm confident you'll find more."

To Shelley's surprise, she's right. The next morning the innkeeper brings them a message. A young man is waiting outside on the street. Shelley opens the window and sees Jeff Hogg looking up.

"Am I seeing a married man?" Hogg asks.

"You are. Am I seeing a monied man?"

"Monied enough. Come down and let me take a look at you both. For that privilege, I'll pay you well."

And so they spend the day together, walking the length and breadth of Edinburgh, dining on Hogg's money, and feeling almost giddy with freedom. Late in the afternoon, they climb to the top of the hill known as Arthur's Seat. There, he and Hogg engage in a long discussion about Time. Shelley holds that it is a product of one's perception, while Hogg holds that it is a physical fact.

"Take for example," Shelley says, "how the same number of hours can seem long while one is engaged in difficult labors and short while reading a book."

Hogg replies: "But time is also measured with mechanicals, by which I mean clocks, or by the simple movement of a shadow as the sun crosses the sky."

"True, but suppose man were immortal. What meaning would time have then?"

How easily they fall into their old pattern. Yet as they talk, Shelley keeps an eye on Harriet and wonders what she's thinking. Is she impressed by their erudition or merely bored? Perhaps she'd have married the first man who offered to free her from bondage. Perhaps she thinks she's married a pretentious ass.

On Saturday, only one week since they left London, they move to new lodgings. There are two bedrooms, one for Shelley and Harriet and one for Hogg, who can't bring himself to go back to York.

"I wasn't aware how much I missed your company," Hogg says. "And Harriet is delightful. We shall form a little commune and write inflammatory prose."

The next morning they hear bells and follow them to their source. In the churchyard, among the headstones, they find a wooden bench and sit, himself on the left, Hogg on the right, and Harriet in between. Through open windows they can hear the preacher's voice.

"What are we doing here?" Hogg asks, after some minutes have elapsed.

"Listening to a Scots preacher make a fool of himself. My God, what rubbish. Not a word he says is true."

"You claim to be a supporter of the lower classes. Is it not the lower classes who occupy the pews inside?"

"When you support someone, you don't pander to them. When they're wrong, you tell them they're wrong."

They go back and forth until at last Harriet interrupts: "You'll laugh at what I'm about to say." She waits until both pairs of eyes are on her. "I always thought I would marry a clergyman. But look at me now."

Mary

Not long after their journey north, tragedy strikes. Isabel's older sister, Margaret, always frail, takes ill and dies. It happens with stunning rapidity—on Friday evening she develops a fever, on Saturday her husband goes for a doctor, and by Sunday morning she is gone. Every member of the family is brokenhearted. Mary, who has begun to view herself as one of them, mourns alongside Isabel and Christy, sharing their pain.

Their church community gathers around. The Baxters are members of a small sect known as Glassites, which, as far as Mary can tell, values communal decision-making and communal action and doesn't rely on an ordained minister to lead the flock. Groups of four or five come to the house with pots of stew and remain to pray into the night. That David Booth is an apostate is a fact they seem willing, given the circumstances, to overlook.

In the days and weeks that follow, Isabel prefers to be alone. Without their walks to fill the hours, Mary reads, often books she previously thought beyond her. Milton is a particular discovery—the majesty of his words takes her breath away. She also begins reading her mother's book, *A Vindication of the Rights of Woman*. She doesn't seek it out; rather she finds it tucked away on the shelves of the Baxter family library and thinks, "Since it's here, why not?" Somehow this time she's not intimidated. Indeed, if this is the book that made her mother famous, she ought to know what's inside.

Not surprisingly, given the title, it's very different from *Mary: A Fiction*. In this book her mother argues that women should be educated so they can be true companions for their husbands and so they can no longer be treated like slaves. Yet she also points out that tyrants may prefer them to remain ignorant because ignorance and blind obedience go hand in hand.

She is usually a fast reader—people watching her sometimes remark on how quickly the pages turn. However, this is different. She reads a few lines and stops, reads a few more and stops again. It is almost too much to take in. Her mother writes that truth is hidden from women and *they are made to assume an artificial character before their faculties have acquired any strength*. Mary wonders to what extent this has happened to her already, and vows to become better educated. She wants no truths to be hidden from her; she wants to acquire strength.

Unexpectedly, on a rainy afternoon in March, Isabel comes to her and says that David Booth has asked her to be his wife. Mary is stunned. How long has it been since Margaret's death? A month? Six weeks? Taking note of the look in Mary's eyes, Isabel says, "We intend to wait a seemly amount of time before announcing our intentions. But our decision has been made."

"I was unaware he was courting you," Mary replies.

"I can't say he did—not in the sense you mean—but we already know each other so well . . ."

Of course they do. Since Margaret was frequently ill, Booth spent as much time with Isabel these past years as he did with his wife. And Mary knows how Isabel feels about him. Nonetheless, they had best wait a good long time before marrying, or people will talk.

"I'm pleased for you," she says. "He will make a fine husband, I'm sure."

Isabel lifts her chin in a way that bespeaks unswerving pride. "I was in no way coerced. But look around this place. Perhaps I scare the young men off. In any event, few have come calling. I could do worse than David, don't you agree?"

Mary does agree, but she can't imagine getting married to *anyone*, let alone a man his age. On the other hand, reading *A Vindication* has caused her to question her feelings about the nature of love and marriage. Her mother argues that passion is short-lived and friendship between husbands and wives is the ideal. Maybe Isabel has studied Mary Wollstonecraft's book.

Unfortunately, Isabel and David are unable to resist telling others of their plan, and when they do, the members of the Baxters' church speak out against their union. They consider it sinful for a man who was married to one sister to marry another from the same family. Mary can do nothing but observe and console Isabel as best she can. Mary's father brought her up to question all things and to follow only those rules and injunctions that stand the test of logic. Like most religious traditions and practices, this one does not.

"Couldn't you . . . couldn't you leave the church?" Mary asks. She's been reluctant to suggest it, afraid to overstep, but on this particular morning Isabel looks thoroughly bereft.

"David has said the same thing. But I wouldn't be leaving the church only. I would be leaving my father and my sister. What we want may not be possible. I think we must give up."

Then, to her surprise, Mr. Baxter, devout as he is, says he will support his daughter and Mr. Booth in their decision, no matter the cost. Mary finds Baxter's defense of his daughter very moving.

"In this matter I'll not be dictated to by man or God," he thunders before the entire congregation, even though the elders of the church have promised to excommunicate the entire family if the marriage occurs.

After that there are no further impediments. David Booth gives Isabel a ring with a small diamond in it, and one evening, when all the members of the family are invited to gather at Booth's house for a meal, Mary and Isabel sneak off to the second floor, where they write their initials on a windowpane with the ring. It feels to Mary as if Isabel does it as a final act of girlhood and perhaps also as a sign that being married won't cause their friendship to change.

Yet their friendship must change because Mary is soon to return to London. She has spent several months more in Scotland than was first intended. No longer does she feel that she was sent into exile; in fact, quite the opposite. Her time here has been filled with pleasure and inspiration. If the intention was to free her from her stepmother, it worked, for in all her time away, she has given her stepmother little thought. Still, she looks forward to seeing the other members of her family again and her dread of the sea voyage back to London is nothing like the dread she felt prior to the voyage out.

In advance of her departure, she spends several evenings writing down all that happened to her in Scotland. All she saw and all she experienced and all she learned. Once she begins to write, it comes rushing out, descriptions of Dundee and of the Baxter family, their travels, their social gatherings, the religion they practiced, the foods they ate, Isabel's face and the sound of her voice, the ships in port and at full sail, the look of the Firth in sunshine and in showers, and the stories she's been told, the amusing, the historical, and the strange.

Jeff Hogg

Although Edinburgh is pleasant enough, Hogg persuades Shelley and his new bride to go south to York. They've run through his money and they'll find cheaper lodgings there. Harriet is a sweet girl, quite pretty, and she seems eager to be a good wife. She always calls Shelley "Percy," which Hogg finds comical. Doesn't she know he detests it? As for Shelley, he takes considerable pride in having saved her from school and family. He says, "Her life is now her own." However, Hogg thinks what she really wants is to be cared for. Will Shelley do that, too?

She enjoys reading to them and does it well, her voice contemplative or charged with excitement depending on the text. He could listen to her for hours, although Shelley has a tendency to nod off. Then he's up half the night, pacing the floor, wanting to talk about politics. His father has cut off his allowance, but he thinks he can convince him to reinstate it. And when that happens, his intention is to use the funds to further political and social causes of various sorts.

"What could be worse than the current aristocratic system?"

Shelley exclaims. "There are in England ten million souls, yet only half a million living in a state of ease. The rest earn their livelihood with never-ending toil."

Hogg approves of the sentiment but knows Shelley's righteous indignation can overwhelm his judgment. As admirable as his passion is, there's always a worry: Where will it lead?

They find a place in York to share, two rooms for the three of them, rather shabby, in a house owned by a pair of sisters. One is tall and gaunt and the other rosy-cheeked and rotund. After some negotiation with Shelley, the sisters withdraw into the hallway and whisper back and forth. Then they return and the deal is done. Apparently the money they'll get from renting the place is more important to them than the possibility of something scandalous occurring under their roof. As for Hogg, if scandalous activities ensue, he'll happily take part. Shelley is always talking about how love ought not to be constrained by society's conventions, marriage chief among them. Well then, why not put the theory to the test?

When Shelley isn't present, he teases Harriet about it. "I propose a radical experiment. You kiss me and tell me how I measure up."

She blushes. "There's nothing radical about that at all. Men have been trying to trick women into kissing them down through the ages."

The next day he tries again. This time Shelley is in the room. "Suppose something were to happen to Bysshe. Would you allow me to take his place?"

Shelley looks up from his book. "You have my endorsement."

"Have I no say in the matter?" Harriet asks.

"That's why I'm asking," Hogg says. "To give you a chance to have your say."

Harriet sniffs. "Nothing is going to happen to Percy. We shall all of us live to be very old. He and I will continue to be in love and you will go off and find a bride of your own. She will have boney elbows and knees and crossed eyes. But you will be devoted to her nonetheless."

When it appears the weather will be mild for a time, Shelley leaves to go visit his father. His father has decided that only by being in the same room with him will he be able to settle their differences.

"Settle their differences" is what he says, but what he means is "pry a little money out of his grip." He hasn't an especially high opinion of his father. Deep down in his heart he may have as much love for him as any other son would, but it's well buried. And once buried, some things are never dug up.

"Good fortune and a speedy return," Hogg tells him, but his mind is already on Harriet. He can't help himself. If he thought Shelley would be angry with him, he wouldn't try, but that's the thing. If Harriet says yes, Shelley might actually think better of them both. He likes all things unconventional and what could be more unconventional than engaging in free love?

"Just once," Hogg says to her. They've had a good supper. They've had some wine. They are seated together on a well-worn divan and the fire is crackling in the grate. She doesn't seem too annoyed. Could it be she's coming around?

"You're incorrigible," she replies.

"I'm being serious. He won't care. Come closer. Allow yourself to be wooed." Then, seeing no movement on her part, he puts his arm across the back of the divan. Not quite touching her, yet near enough.

"Perhaps he wouldn't care," she says, her demeanor suddenly fierce. "But I would." Then she pushes him away—although small, she is strong—and locks herself in the other room.

He stands at the door and calls out to her: "I apologize. I promise not to touch you. Am I such a beast?"

"Please go away," she says. "I'm overtired and need to sleep."

Hogg goes walking through the dark streets of York and thinks back on his relationship with Shelley. When he came to Oxford and felt thoroughly out of place, Shelley took him in. He certainly didn't have to. Most fellows with his advantages would have glanced at him and sent him away. And when he could have asked Hogg to shoulder some of the blame for their blasphemous essay, he chose not to. The reason he's willing to give money to Shelley is that when Shelley has money, he shares it freely with him. For those reasons and many others, Hogg would never do anything to hurt Shelley, but he's so mercurial, it can be difficult to know what he wants.

The next day and the day after, he and Harriet hardly speak. She reads or sews and goes to bed early while he finds reasons to stay away. At a tavern he drinks too much and gets into an argument about politics, the kind of argument he and Shelley get into all the time, but the dolt in the tavern wants to settle the matter with fists instead of words. Hogg gets the better of it—he flattens the man with one blow—and goes home feeling rather smug. To his dismay, Harriet is unimpressed. "Percy doesn't partake of strong drink," she says.

At last Shelley returns. He is pleased with the outcome of his trip home. His father has promised to continue to send him money, although how much and how often is unclear. For now at least, his pockets are full. Immediately, he reimburses Hogg for the money they've spent since his arrival. Then suddenly he says it's time to go elsewhere. Maybe Ireland. Maybe Wales. Maybe to Nottingham to join the workers' revolt. He's working on a poem, one that will present his arguments in a form the censors won't find so easy to suppress. It will be a philosophical poem, setting out the path to a revolution in society. Lately, Shelley has been in a state of almost constant outrage about the textile factories. Every day the mill owners replace more men with machines. And if the men retaliate, the government hangs them by the neck. He intends his poem to strike a blow for the workers. Hogg studies him. This is the Shelley he loves. If there's a chance his feelings about Harriet will cause a rift between himself and his friend, he'll desist.

He awakes the next morning to find himself alone in the flat. They have left a note. They thank him for all his help but have decided to go west. They'll write when they are settled. Yes, Shelley is definitely mercurial. Hogg dresses and goes downstairs, where he finds the sisters waiting for him. They want their money. He shakes his head and laughs. Exactly like Shelley to give him money one day and leave him with a bill the next.

Shelley

He and Harriet move on to Keswick, where he hopes to meet William Wordsworth, but the poet is not at home. He goes to visit Robert Southey, whose poetry he admires less than Wordsworth's, and stands outside his house for three days in the rain before he has the courage to knock at the door. When they finally meet, Shelley is unimpressed, and it soon becomes apparent Southey feels the same about him. Southey tells him he oughtn't to call himself an atheist. Surely he must believe in some species of God:

"You needn't choose Christianity. Do some exploring in the texts of the great religions. Pick whichever you like." Having offered the young fellow his wisdom, Southey sits back and draws reflectively on his pipe.

In response, Shelley says, "Sir, I am well acquainted with texts of the great religions. But I believe in no God, Christian or otherwise." Southey tries again and yet again to convince him that religious faith is a necessity but to no avail. In scarcely more than an hour, Shelley is back outside in the rain.

Then one bright morning, he receives a most delightful letter. His father and Harriet's father have gotten together and decided to provide them with 200 pounds a year. This is beyond the small allowance his father offered when he last visited Field Place. They will not be wealthy, but they can stop being poor. Yet no sooner has this good news arrived than something less good follows. There is a knock at the door of their tiny cottage, and when he opens it, he finds himself nose to nose with Harriet's sister, Liza. "I have come to live with you," she says.

He knows he should be welcoming, but having her move in with them is a wretched idea. "For what reason?" he asks. Harriet stands behind him. She pinches his flank. Is she signaling him to hold his ground or be more polite and invite her in?

"My sister is too young to be gadding about England with a married man. Her mother concurs."

"But she is a *married woman*," he replies. "Married to *me*."

"Indeed," Liza says and forces herself inside.

"You might have written ahead," Harriet tells her as she takes her shawl.

"What difference would that have made? Where shall I put my bags?"

So now they have money, but they also have Liza. If he could get rid of her, he'd happily go back to being poor.

That evening, after Harriet has gone to bed, he finds himself sitting by the fire with Liza. Tall, long-faced Liza with a mouth full of yellow teeth. "I came here out of concern for Harriet," she says. "Our father is willing to take you into his business. What exactly are your ambitions? You say you are a writer. Then what is it you're writing?" She looks around at the sparse furnishings and bare walls. "Is this how you intend to live?"

What he's writing is a poem he calls *Queen Mab*. Also an essay, "An Address to the Irish People," which he hopes to deliver in person. In it, he urges them to rise up against England, but first to educate themselves and prepare for a long struggle: *Temperance, sobriety, charity, and independence will give you virtue; and reading, talking, thinking and searching will give you wisdom; when you have those things you may defy the tyrant.* So no, he doesn't intend to live like this, at least not in Keswick. He wants them to go to Dublin and assist in the struggle for Irish independence. With the money from their fathers, they can leave sooner than he'd originally planned.

He's recently resumed his correspondence with William Godwin and now asks him for a letter of introduction to be used among the Irish rebels. Godwin seems to know everyone with revolutionary tendencies the world over. He keeps company with radicals in London and, rumor has it, met his late wife, Mary Wollstonecraft, at a dinner given by none other than Tom Paine.

The following evening, Shelley tells Liza that, as they are moving to Ireland, she ought to go back home. "I admire your regard for Harriet's welfare, but I am fully capable of caring for her. I have the means and I have the will." The three of them are seated around a tiny table, eating black bread and potted cheese.

"I shall not leave my sister," she says. "Especially now that you have revealed your plan to visit Ireland. Ireland is a foul place, as anyone who reads the newspaper knows."

"I do not intend to *visit* Ireland. I intend to settle there. Tell her, Harriet. This is what you chose."

Harriet gnaws at her thumbnail and looks at him with her large, childlike eyes. "I cannot banish my sister. I promise, she will be helpful and won't interfere."

In the end, they arrive at an agreement: Liza can remain with them if she doesn't meddle. Admittedly, he appreciates how she occupies Harriet. He hadn't been prepared for the amount of attention a wife requires. Since they've been married, he's come to realize how much time he needs with his own thoughts. Uninterrupted hours. Uninterrupted days.

They now begin making preparations for Ireland. There is little packing to do. All they own is what they brought with them when they eloped. Besides his clothes, he has but one small trunk containing a brace of pistols, a sextant, a microscope, some books, and a supply of laudanum, which he uses on occasion as an aid to sleep.

When there are reports in the press about Ireland, they read them around the table at night. Some tell of English agitators being thrown in jail.

"If I'm imprisoned, you must visit me every day," he says bravely.

"If *I'm* imprisoned, you must write a poem about me," Harriet teases. "A long one, with line after line about the beauty of my hair."

At last the day of their departure arrives. They travel to the port town of Whitehaven and buy passage on a packet that will leave at midnight. The agent tells them to expect rough weather—wind, rain, and high seas.

The color leaves Liza's face. She says, "Perhaps we should wait a day."

He refuses to be detained. As he leads them toward the wharf, he says, "The Irish people have waited long enough."

Less than an hour out of Whitehaven, they meet the predicted storm. The little boat is battered and pushed far off course. Liza glares at him and Harriet spews over the side. He overhears one of the sailors say they'll end up in Greenland if the winds don't change. At last, thirty hours after they began, they dock in the far north of Ireland. They take a coach to Dublin at first light and arrive exhausted late in the day. That night after Liza is asleep and he and Harriet are lying in one another's arms, she tells him she's with child.

"I wanted to wait until we got here before I gave you the news," she says. "I was afraid you'd change your mind and not let me go."

"I would never do such a thing," he says, but in truth he's a bit dismayed. He wants them to be quick on their feet, able to travel and live on very little, and a child won't help. But what's done is done. Putting his reservations aside, he says:

"I shall be a different father than my own has been to me."

Over the next few days they settle in Dublin. They find rooms in a commercial district and, from the windows one floor up, observe the passing scene. Oxcarts, handcarts, and horse-drawn drays compete for the right of way as children and dogs dash around, under, and between. It seems twice as crowded as London and three times as poor. Across the road, a house that looks fit for one family appears to be accommodating four, and not one child has shoes. To Harriet he says, "The rich grind the poor into abjectness and then complain that they are abject—they goad them to famine and hang them if they steal a loaf."

Once they are unpacked, he goes in search of a printer to reproduce his tract. Three thousand copies should be enough. This time he doesn't intend to put it up for sale; he intends to give it away. That was the problem with what he and Hogg did in Oxford. They depended on the bookseller for distribution. Better to put one's words directly into readers' hands. In the end the cost forces him to settle on fifteen hundred.

Five days later the printer's boy delivers the finished copies. Shelley sits down to examine their work. The product is a little disappointing. The ink isn't of the highest quality and the document is longer than he expected, more pamphlet than broadside, but it's too late to revise. He riffles the pages, pausing to reread his favorite passages. *Arise*, he thinks, *arise and renounce your servitude. Love and justice will conquer all.*

The next morning distribution begins. Harriet accompanies him and together they deliver copies to the homes of prominent politicians. They leave copies in public houses and coffeehouses and in the vestibules of churches. On a busy street corner he reads some lines at full voice. Unfortunately no one stops to listen, and when he holds out a copy, his hand is pushed away. Women with their market baskets cast wary glances in his direction. Men in brown ulsters break stride only long enough to glare.

Then, to his surprise, Harriet says, "Give me those," and instead of waiting for the next woman to reach out for one, she simply drops a copy in her basket. The woman doesn't object. Next, Harriet dashes into the street and begins tossing copies into coaches. A girl wearing a blue cape is crossing and Harriet tucks one inside her hood. Soon she's laughing, glancing back at him, making a game of it, and he finds himself laughing as well. He thinks about their child and admonishes himself for having been less than fully enthusiastic upon hearing the news. She is such a pretty, lively thing. She's trying very hard, but she's so young that he's beginning to wonder if taking her from her home and parents was a mistake.

When they're done, they walk back across Dublin exhilarated, inhaling the chill air.

"Now what?" she asks him.

"We wait. We wait for the spark to become flame."

Jane

Mary has returned. She was away longer than expected and now has roses in her cheeks from the Scottish climate and two tartan dresses, one red and one blue, which she contrives to wear as often as possible. Too often, in the opinion of Jane. She knows envy is not an attractive trait, but sometimes it cannot be forsworn. Mary now tells Scottish ghost stories and even affects a Scottish lilt. Then again, she did bring gifts for everyone. Woolen scarves all around.

When Mary was sent away, Jane understood it to be because she had been quarreling with their mother. It was a punishment and Mary deserved it. But somehow she seems to have turned it to her advantage. It appears she loved Scotland and was sorry to leave it. She made friends with the Baxter sisters, especially Isabel, and did all sorts of enjoyable things—rode horses, went sailing, traveled to the far north. While everyone here on Skinner Street led their usual dull lives.

Still, she did miss having Mary to talk with. Shortly after Mary left, her brother, Charles, went away to school, and as Fanny is always helping in the shop or going off to care for the children of some other family, she began feeling rather lonely. Now she and Mary have some catching up to do.

"I'm sure ghosts are delightful," Jane says. "But you have yet to answer the most important question. Did you meet any interesting young men?"

"One or two. But none I wanted to bring home."

She frowns. "You must not have tried very hard."

They are in their bedroom, on the fourth floor. From their window they can see across the rooftops of London to Ludgate Hill and the dome of St. Paul's. Many late afternoons have passed with their eyes upon it. As the sky goes dark, the dome catches the setting sun and begins to glow.

"Speaking of young men, tell me about Mr. Shelley," Mary says. "How did Father come to know him? You all seem quite entranced."

"He writes witty and impassioned letters. He comes from a family of quality. Like most of those who seek out Father, he considers himself a radical. Such is the extent of my knowledge. We haven't met him yet."

"He's never visited?"

"Not yet. And now I believe he has left London. Perhaps he's gone back to Sussex. He may have become suspicious of Father's motives—his last letter suggested as much."

Mary looks at her, puzzled. "His motives?"

"When Mr. Shelley implied he might become Father's benefactor, Father was too eager to accept."

Mary sighs. "On the matter of money, his logic deserts him. He wants it and holds it in contempt at the same time."

"I have no such difficulty," says Jane. "If someone offers me money, they shall suffer no contempt."

Jane wonders if her relationship with Mary will be different now that they are older and have had some time apart. Will they truly be sisters, together because they wish to be and not because they must?

Mary seems more mature than when she left and Jane wonders if she does, too. Partly as a means of declaring her adulthood, she has been thinking about changing her name. She knows a girl about her age named Ann who has begun calling herself Daisy. She did it on a whim, without asking her parents' permission. She simply got out of bed one day and insisted her name was Daisy—and kept on insisting until everyone complied. If Jane were to change hers, she would choose Clara. Clara Clairmont, which she considers mellifluous, not to mention easy to remember. Memorable is one thing she would certainly like to be.

"What have you read lately?" Mary asks, changing the subject. "The Baxters had plenty of books, but as you know, they are Glassites. They disapprove of novels. As well as strong drink and games of chance."

"Oh, then you haven't seen Maria Edgeworth's latest. It's called the *The Absentee*." She proceeds to describe it in detail. The reading of novels is one enthusiasm she and Mary share.

"I did read my mother's book, *A Vindication of the Rights of Woman*," Mary says.

Jane nods in acknowledgment, but rather than asking her to elaborate, she continues her own list: "Also Lord Byron's new poem, *The Corsair*. It's full of pirates. Some say the Corsair is Lord Byron himself."

"I have heard of it but have yet to lay my hands on a copy," Mary replies.

Jane (now beginning tentatively to think of herself as Clara) dislikes such discussions. Most of the time she can't compete with Mary on literary and intellectual grounds. And given that they are part of such a literary and intellectual family, the difference between them has been a source of distress. However, she is a much better musician than Mary and that serves as compensation. In truth, Mary is no musician at all.

Jane/Clara leaves Mary in their room and goes down the stairs past her stepfather's study and into the shop. Her mother is arranging books. That's how she spends most of her time. Stacking books. Placing books on shelves. Moving books from one table to another. But now she hears her daughter's footsteps and stops to look up.

"You must be pleased to have Mary home again," she says to Jane.

"I suppose so. She's full of stories about Scotland. It sounds like a wretched place. I'm so glad I wasn't made to go there. I do wish

she wouldn't wear those dresses all the time. She's only showing off."
She concludes with a disdainful toss of her head.

Still, Mary hasn't read *The Corsair*. That's what she gets for
going off to Scotland for the better part of a year. Nor does she have
a beau to show for it. Now, if *she'd* been let out from under this roof,
free and far from home, she'd have done something dramatic, something that would have gotten everyone's attention. At the very least
she'd have gone away Jane and come back Clara.

Later that evening they hear the sounds of celebrating in the
streets. A boy runs by shouting that Bonaparte has been deposed. The
whole family goes outside. Flags appear and church bells ring. But
though it is a victory for England, it is a loss for their father. He hates
monarchies, especially the French Bourbons, and had begun to hope
they were a thing of the past. He tells Jane, Mary, and Fanny that they
should now expect the royalty to reassert itself, not only in France, but
across the Continent and in England. "And Louis the Eighteenth will
take his seat on the throne as if awakening from a bad dream." After a
brief pause, he puts a more optimistic face on it, as is his wont: "However,
such is the movement of reform. Two steps forward, one back."

As Jane/Clara and her sisters get ready for bed, she asks them
if they ever tire of their names. She can tell they find her question
puzzling, but she's not ready to reveal what she's planning, not yet.

"I'm only curious," she explains. "Think about it. You have no
say in what you are called and have to live with it until you die."

"Well," says Fanny. "My name, properly *Frances*, is from the
French and means *free*. Although that is not what I am, it is a condition I hope to achieve."

They look to Mary. She says, "I have no quarrel with *Mary*.
Yet as my mother once wrote, you shouldn't be trapped in a cage not
of your own making. Although she was speaking of womanhood at
the time, I don't know why the same logic wouldn't apply to a name."

They do not know she is now Clara but she looks at them
through Clara's eyes. Clara shall be more affectionate and generous
than Jane. Clara shall be more reliable and hardworking than Jane.
Already she is satisfied with the change.

Shelley

His words fail to set Dublin ablaze. Maybe it was too long a document, too many words. He's passionate about politics, but could it be he has no aptitude for it? He arranges to meet with well-known radicals John Curran and Hamilton Rowan, but nothing comes of it. They listen politely and send him on his way. He arranges to give a speech in a hall on Fishamble Street, but nothing comes of it. The attendance is modest, and when he's done, the applause is modest as well. It's quite frustrating. He genuinely wants to do good in the world but is having trouble figuring out how.

"They look upon me as an opportunist," he tells Harriet, "a freebooting Englishman who is simply looking for a cause."

Harriet replies with consoling words, but he can tell she's no more convinced he has something to contribute to the Irish people than was the audience at Fishamble Street. Still, it's nice that she pretends.

Exhausted by his lack of success, he puts himself to bed and falls into a deep sleep. At times he hears Harriet and Liza talking, but it's as if they are speaking one of the lost languages of Ur. When he finally wakes up, all he can think of is food, so Harriet cooks him up an immense plate of fried potatoes, which he consumes like a wolf.

"Are you feeling better?" she asks.

"Much. I'm also reconsidering our presence here."

Her eyes brighten and there's a twitch at the corner of her mouth. Try as she might, she can't conceal the fact that this pleases her. She says, "You've done all you can for now. Perhaps we can come back another time."

That evening he confirms it: They are returning to England. "My prayers have been answered," Liza says. Their sojourn in Ireland has lasted fewer than five months.

So where to next? Given that he left certain debts behind in London, he'd feel a little nervous showing his face there. Perhaps Devon would be better. It's both beautiful and remote. Based on something Shelley has read in Smollett, they decide on Lynmouth, where the East Lyn and West Lyn converge and flow into the sea.

"If it's as you say, I shall be satisfied," Harriet says. "I want our child to be born away from the city, away from the noise and filth."

In contrast to their previous crossing, the Irish Sea this time is placid as a lake. Their boat docks at Chepstow and they proceed westward down the Somerset and Devon coasts, the landscape becoming more lush and appealing with each passing mile. He's not sure what to expect of Lynmouth but it turns out to be as inviting as he'd hoped. Every window box is filled with flowers, the wooded slope leading back and away from the village is a deep blue-green, and there is a single small house available to let. Clearly they were meant to leave Ireland—otherwise, they wouldn't have found this.

They quickly settle in. Lynmouth is much quieter than Dublin. Shelley reads and writes while Harriet and Liza keep house. They visit the shops and talk with the townsfolk, who seem pleased to have a young mother-to-be and her husband moving in—although they must wonder how the husband provides support. Liza cooks; she's not especially good at it, but he's never been fussy about meals. Thus, whole weeks begin to pass as quickly as days. Harriet plants a small garden and he praises her for it. He should praise her more often—she positively glows.

She says, "I like to picture us here with our children years from now. Very snug and happy we shall be."

"How many children are you imagining? It's not a large house."

"However many come. However many we are blessed with. I hope this first one takes after you."

Each time she mentions their child, he is momentarily taken aback. He's not sure he's ready to be a father. One evening he's having a bad headache and takes a dose of laudanum for the pain. While under the drug's influence, he has a terrifying vision: Harriet goes into labor and produces a lizard—with a tail and yellow eyes.

He doesn't believe in premonitions, especially those brought on by laudanum. And yet it is only when, on the third day of summer, the midwife emerges from behind the closed door and takes him to see his new daughter—who has pink skin instead of scales—that he feels relief. He kisses Harriet and does his best in the days that follow to stay out of the way. For once he is pleased to have Liza present. She takes over and runs the house even more forcefully than before.

He and Harriet confer on the name, a process which delights them both. After much deliberation they settle on Liza Ianthe, Liza because how could they not, given her presence, and Ianthe because it's the name of a character in the poem he is working on, the one called *Queen Mab*. At once a fairy tale, a philosophical argument, and a recipe for revolution, it is the most ambitious thing he has ever attempted. The fairy Queen Mab takes Ianthe's spirit on a journey and shows her the universe. Shows her the violence of the past and the miseries of the present but also how humanity might yet prevail. At the end of the poem he intends to place a series of explanatory essays—about atheism, about love, about the injustice of murder by the state, and about astronomical phenomena such as the reflection and refraction of light. His head is filled with ideas, and since all of them won't fit inside the poem, he'll approach it as a carpenter and build an extra room.

"I think my message about revolution is more fitting for poetry than prose," he tells Harriet. "My letter to the Irish lacked heart."

"It's difficult for the poor to hear any message except that of food and shelter," Harriet replies.

"Very true. But those in power won't give them food and shelter because they fear how they'd spend their time if their stomachs were full. Therefore, I offer poetry, which engenders compassion. It may succeed where cold logic has failed." More and more he hates the established order. In Ireland he saw immense poverty and that has changed him. It seems that unless the rain is beating down on their own heads, most men will do nothing to keep others from getting wet.

Harriet starts to say something else, but Ianthe begins to cry and she is drawn away. She takes the child from her cradle and goes outside. How completely one tiny being can fill a house. Now he understands his own father's tendency to turn the children over to a nurse.

Through one of the house's deep-set windows he looks out upon the purling waters of the Lyn. Before they moved in, the place had been vacant for years, so the rent is next to nothing—a good thing because they're nearly penniless again. He'd hoped the amount they're getting from their two fathers would be enough but it seems the more money he gets, the more he spends. Already, from the local bookshop, he has ordered Sir Humphry Davy's *Elements of Chemical Philosophy*, *Xenophon on Government*, *Thaddeus of Warsaw*, and *A Vindication of the Rights of Woman* by Mary Wollstonecraft, the late wife of his recent valued correspondent, William Godwin. Also a pint of ink.

When *Queen Mab* is complete, he gets it printed. This time he's more conservative—five hundred should be enough. But how to distribute them? Lynmouth is a tiny place, and even if every last resident bothered to read it, no revolution would ensue. He decides to mail copies to members of Parliament, to prominent journalists, to those in positions of influence. They'll find his ideas shocking, but the first step toward change is to have one's complacency upset. Harriet and Liza help prepare them for mailing and he feels a great sense of satisfaction when they are finally out of his hands. Then, for the few that are left, he has an idea. Something he did as a boy. He goes back to the shop where he ordered the books and buys some large sheets of brown paper, the kind used to wrap meat. When he gets home, he places the paper on the table and tells Harriet and Liza he needs their help.

As he begins folding the first sheet, Harriet claps her hands and laughs. "He's making boats," she tells her sister. "It's ingenious, you'll see."

"Ah, but you're wrong," he says, his hands moving swiftly as he speaks. "I'm making airships. To be launched into the sky." Attached to each one will be a copy of his poem. Who knows where they will end up? Throughout human history, one man with . . . but even as he is explaining to himself why this is a good idea, he knows it's a ridiculous idea. Ridiculous but also oddly compelling and undeniably fun. Truth be told, he doesn't care if they drift all the way to India or fall into the sea.

Part of his genius is his enthusiasm. Indeed, it's such a force that even a peevish person like Liza can be carried along. At first she stands back holding Ianthe and says, "I refuse to believe it." Yet she keeps returning to the table where he's working, watching him cut the paper and crease it and attach lengths of string.

When the first one is complete, he takes a nub of candle and suspends it in such a way that the paper won't catch fire. "The Chinese call them sky lanterns," he says, and checks to make sure the women are suitably impressed.

They work all through the afternoon, seated at the table next to the window, the sun streaming in. Harriet and Eliza take turns, one helping fold and glue while the other tends the child. A little before nightfall twenty-three airships are ready to take flight.

A narrow field beside the river is the place he selects. There, they begin lighting the candle beneath each paper lantern, making sure the poem is well attached before launching them into the sky. A passing farmer leading a donkey stops and watches, shakes his head, goes a little farther, stops again, and finally continues on. The brown paper shines like hammered copper, so beautiful that Harriet and Liza can't help but exclaim. To add to the drama, he recites a few lines from *Queen Mab*:

> *Heaven's ebon vault,*
> *Studded with stars unutterably bright,*
> *Through which the moon's unclouded grandeur rolls,*
> *Seems like a canopy which had spread*
> *To curtain her sleeping world.*

When they're done, when every lantern has floated so far into the black sky, it can no longer be seen, they return to the village. Harriet and her sister walk ahead of him, Ianthe in Harriet's arms. It has been a fine day and they seem quite happy, but Shelley feels inexplicably alone. What is his purpose? How in this world can he be of use? At times he is overcome by passion and it pours into whatever stands immediately before him, whether Harriet or the people of Ireland or his poetry. But after such spells he always begins to feel empty again—as he does now. He thought a loving and beloved companion might change him. Can he and Harriet really spend their lives together? She tries to share his interests, but there are so many of them and they move so quickly, she has difficulty keeping up. It's not her fault, but neither is it his.

The following day he tells Harriet he must go to London. "I

intend to meet with some publishers, including a man named Godwin," he says. But he keeps from her the fact that he is thinking about offering Mr. Godwin some money. Since they hardly have enough for themselves, she'd surely be distressed by his eagerness to give it away.

Part Two

1814–1816

Mary

Now that she's home, she works in the bookshop most every day. She does so partly out of boredom—compared to Scotland, the house on Skinner Street offers few diversions—and partly as an attempt to improve her standing with her stepmother.

She doesn't mind helping customers, a task Mrs. Godwin finds demeaning when those visiting the shop are beneath her station and embarrassing when they are above. If the shop is empty, Mary goes to a chair she's placed behind a bank of shelves and reads. She is continuing her study of Milton. To her surprise, she finds herself admiring Satan. He has such vitality. And the angelic war over heaven is breathtaking: *Lead forth to battle these my sons invincible. Lead forth my armed Saints by thousands and millions ranged for fight.* She stands and dances about the shop, overcome by the glory of the Blind Poet's words. When a passerby stops and peers in through the window, she scurries out of sight.

One thing working in the shop has revealed to her is how few books they actually sell. Although she's been aware of her father's financial difficulties, he's never shared the details. Now she can see it plain. If things don't improve, debtors' prison may not be an idle fear. That is why he's so interested in the assistance his new correspondent, Mr. Shelley, might provide. Unfortunately, his letters have begun to say less about his wealth than about his efforts to cause the Irish to revolt.

"Do you think it's really possible?" Mary asks. "Can a lone Englishman go to Dublin and start a rebellion?"

Her father shakes his head. "He's clearly a passionate young man, but he's far too naïve. Besides, it appears he's given up on Ireland. He's now somewhere in Devon. He seems to be having difficulty finding his place."

Mary muses, twisting a lock of hair. "He looks up to you, does he not? Can't you tell him to devote himself to a more sensible cause?" But the phrase she's used is the wrong one; she knows it the instant the words leave her mouth.

"Oh, Mary, *a sensible cause*? I fear the only sensible causes are those that don't need our help." His gaze shifts from her face to the painting above the fireplace. "Your mother," he begins and proceeds to tell her how in the midst of the revolution in France, she was never fainthearted, never afraid to act on her beliefs. Even though Mary has heard it before, she's filled with pride tinged with shame. How admirable her mother was. How much she has to live up to.

No doubt her father is correct: Mr. Shelley should not be looked down upon for attempting the impossible. Still, it would be nice if he followed through with his offer of support. Unlike her father, Mary has a practical streak and considers bread as important as liberty. In fact, calls for liberty often begin with calls for bread.

The more fraught the atmosphere in the house, the more she misses Isabel, the other members of the Baxter family, and the seaside near Dundee. She'd like to talk to Isabel about what married life is like. If she were still there, she has little doubt her friend would take time away from keeping house so they could roam the hills together. Sometimes she even misses the feeling of tranquility that would come over her when she'd attend Sunday services at the Baxters' church and was forced to sit quietly with her own thoughts.

Since returning from Scotland, she often feels she doesn't fit in. Fanny seems happy with her lot, caring for the children of some wealthy merchant, or sewing and writing letters when she's at home. Jane believes her life will begin when a young man comes along and takes her as his bride. Mary is content with neither point of view. Perhaps Scotland ruined her. Some say travel takes you out of yourself; if so, she has yet to find her way back in.

Still, she does enjoy the liveliness of London and the many opportunities it presents. She and Jane go to see an exhibition of the paintings of Joshua Reynolds, portraits so vivid she can almost imagine the subjects' thoughts. Soon after that, her father takes her to Mr. Turner's studio, where she is so stunned by his painting of the building of Carthage, she becomes short of breath. She also attends lectures, one given by a man who believes there's a tropical city beyond the top of Norway, another which includes a demonstration of how electricity can make a dead frog jump, and a third by some fellow who claims the soul can be caught in a bottle and preserved after death. One night, instead of going to bed, she stays up and joins in a conversation her father is having with some friends. Napoleon has recently been exiled to Elba and everyone has strong opinions about it. When she decides to be brave and express hers, the men listen attentively even though she is a girl. As she makes her way upstairs after they've all gone home, she thinks how interesting the world is and how much she wants to know about its many and diverse parts.

At last Mr. Shelley troubles himself to pay them a visit. When he arrives, Jane, who has lately begun calling herself Clara, peers down from their bedroom window as he makes his way up the walk. "Oh my. He looks splendid," she says.

Mary stands behind her, then nudges her aside to get a better view. "Are you sure you don't mean consumptive? He's quite pale. He must be in poor health." She's exaggerating but feels the need to say something contrary because everyone is so excited to meet him. Not that they are excited without reason: If he offers their father a loan, their lives will be improved. Maybe it will even come as a gift, a pot of money that won't have to be repaid.

"Take care what you say," Jane says. "Father wants us to be on our best behavior. I expect it's you he's worried about most."

They listen to the voices below, waiting to be called. Mr. Shelley's is light and clear and conveys excitement. He sounds as pleased to be meeting their father as their father is to meet him. Jane checks her hair in the glass and Mary slips on her shoes. A few minutes later they are invited down to be introduced.

"These are my daughters," their father says proudly as they descend the stairs. "Jane is very musical and Mary recently returned from an extended visit to Scotland." As he's explaining that he has three other children, baby William in the nursery, Charles away at school, and Fanny tending the shop, their mother interrupts:

"It should also be mentioned that Jane speaks excellent French. Mr. Shelley, please plan to stay for tea."

Mary notices that his clothes are of good quality but worn in a disheveled manner. She suspects it's an affectation meant to show he places little value on appearance. His waistcoat is improperly buttoned and he chooses not to wear a cravat. However, he does look clean.

"With pleasure," he says to their mother, and then to Jane, "We have had our differences with the French but of their language I cannot speak ill."

After a few more pleasantries, their father escorts him to his library. The instant they're out of sight, Jane says, "He's younger than I expected. He said something about his wife in one of his letters. I wish she had come as well."

Mary disagrees. "He's here to conduct business. It's not a social call."

Later, when they have assembled for tea, their father asks Mr. Shelley questions about his family, while he asks their father questions about *Political Justice* and what he's writing now. The girls listen attentively, but Mary interjects a remark about her father's book. As always, her native shyness diminishes if she's talking about politics or literature or art.

"Mary," their mother says. "How can you speak of that which you have not read?"

Before she can reply, her father says, "Oh, but Mary *has* read *Political Justice*. More than once, I suspect."

"I could hardly avoid it," she says with a shrug. "For as long as I can remember, there have been copies lying about. One trips over them on the staircase. We used them to build castles for our dolls."

In response, Mr. Shelley bursts into laughter—laughter so high-pitched and wild, no one seems to know whether to join in or look away. "Of course you read it," he says. "How could you not? You built castles for your dolls!"

Mary can't decide what she thinks of him. He's unlike anyone she's met before, in appearance as well as speech. He has the characteristics of a gentleman but also an appealing strangeness, as if he is lit from within.

After the dishes have been cleared, Jane sings, beautifully as always. Feeling the need to compete with her, Mary mentions that she has recently begun translating Virgil's *Aeneid* as a means of filling her idle hours. To her surprise, Mr. Shelley seems more interested in her scholarly endeavors than in Jane's nightingale voice.

"Will you allow me to see it?" he asks. "I admire Virgil a great deal and consider translation an invaluable art."

Mary feels herself begin to blush. If she'd known he'd want to read it, she wouldn't have mentioned it. Now she has no choice. "Perhaps when I'm done. But I must warn you, my Latin is poor— although not as bad as my Greek."

"I charge you with false modesty," he replies. "Your sister plays her music in public, does she not? Don't be afraid to claim your gifts."

She's beginning to wish this conversation would end. Who is he to charge her with anything? To change the subject, she says, "You wrote to my father about your work in Ireland. Tell me, were you successful?"

He grimaces and lowers his eyes. Part of her intention was to prick his confidence but perhaps not so effectively. Now he looks distressed. Jane throws her a reproving look as her father interrupts:

"We shall have to hear about Ireland at some future date. There are a few more items Mr. Shelley and I must discuss before he departs."

When Shelley is finally gone, they all gather around their father to find out if he was successful in securing the loan. He says, "Jane, he found you delightful. Mary, your intelligence shone like the morning sun. And my dear, your hospitality was beyond reproach. As for the loan, Mr. Shelley says he must first discuss the matter with his banker. But how we can be found unworthy, I cannot perceive."

Later, as Mary and Jane are getting ready for bed, Jane says, "He likes you more than me. Although the question you asked about Ireland was impolite."

"He has a wife. I assume he likes her more than either of us."

"I've heard rumors . . ."

"How have you heard rumors? We only just met him."

"I have friends in society. Unlike you, I do more than read books."

Jeff Hogg

After eight months of training in a conveyancer's office in York, he has come to London to look for a job. Since he and Shelley parted, they've carried on an irregular correspondence, but it hasn't been enough—he can't wait to be in his company again. Hogg has other friends, but none of them is so compelling to be around. An evening's conversation with Shelley is worth a week spent in the company of some other man.

If Shelley's letters are any measure, he's having difficulty staying put. He's gone from Keswick to Ireland to Devon, and now seems to be near London, Windsor to be precise. Unfortunately, his feelings about his new wife seem equally unstable. Certain remarks in his most recent letter suggest he may soon leave her behind. How long were they together? A year? Fifteen months at most. Hogg is saddened but not surprised. In the beginning Shelley idealized her. He thought that after he saved her, she would become his muse. But she is simply a gentle, unassuming girl. Now, if he thought Harriet would have *him*, he'd gather her up and take her back to York. Unfortunately, he suspects that in her view, his association with Shelley has disqualified him. If he is destined to have a wife, it will have to be someone else.

In an effort to locate Shelley's exact whereabouts, he contacts Tom Peacock, a mutual friend. Like Shelley, Peacock aspires to be a writer, but he shares none of Shelley's recklessness or intensity of thought. Rather, he's soft-spoken, lives with his mother, works days as a clerk, and pens satirical sketches at night.

"Where has he gotten to now?" Hogg asks him at a tavern, over a glass of ale.

"He asked me to find a place for them in Windsor, which I did, but his wife arrived without him. She says he's taken rooms in London, off Cavendish Square." Peacock always seems to know where everyone is and how they're spending their time. And if a friend needs help, he's the first one to lend a hand. But right now Hogg doesn't care where they're living. He cares that they're living apart.

"Then is it over between them?

"She didn't say and I didn't think it my place to ask. In any event, I have more important news to relate. Shelley is now a father. The two of them have a child."

Hogg is stunned. He can't picture it. Shelley never mentioned the fact in his letters. It takes him a moment to find words:

"And still he left her?"

"So it appears. You know how he is. He'll go away for a few days, upbraid himself for bad behavior, then come rushing back."

Yet Hogg can see he doesn't believe it. They both know that once Shelley begins moving in a particular direction, he almost never turns back.

Following Peacock's lead, Hogg sets out the following day and locates Shelley in a dingy room near Cavendish Square. "So glad you've come," he says upon opening the door, and then before Hogg can even say hello, he picks up an enormous book and begins to read aloud—it sounds like Spinoza, but he's not sure. Hogg waits patiently until he's done, at which point Shelley looks up and says, "Damned interesting, don't you think?" Then they laugh and embrace as in the Oxford days. The man may have failed as a husband, but he has lost none of his exuberance or ability to welcome a friend.

"Tell me everything," Hogg says. "From the day you left me in York holding your outstanding bills until now."

"After which you shall reciprocate."

"If you wish. Although I must warn you, offices are dreary places and I have yet to appear before the bar."

The events Shelley relates are as entertaining as he hoped they'd be. His meeting with the pompous and uninspiring Robert Southey. His attempt to foment rebellion in Ireland (accompanied by amusingly self-deprecating details). Harriet's insufferable sister. And the birth of his daughter, Ianthe, which Hogg still finds hard to believe.

"You, a father?"

"Indeed. But not a good one, I'm afraid. I'll see that she gets an education and try my best to make sure she's never destitute, but that may be all I have to offer." He pauses and his expression becomes forlorn. "I miss my dear child every day."

"Whatever happened? I thought you and Harriet had made a fine beginning. Is there no hope of reconciliation?"

"Very little." Tears fill his eyes and he looks skyward. Never before has Hogg seen him look so despondent. "It was all a mistake. She asked me to take her away, to save her from her father, and I couldn't refuse. We should have waited. I ought to have told her it was a bad idea."

"You're certain it was she who suggested it?" It may be too late for blame, but he doesn't feel Shelley should let himself off so easily. Harriet didn't force him to do anything. No one forces him to do anything.

"It seemed so to me . . . in the heat of the moment . . . She's a fine girl. She'll recover quite well, rest assured." For a few seconds he seems to be contemplating the truth of his previous statement. Then suddenly his face brightens: "I have news. I've met the most ravishing young woman. William Godwin's daughter. Mary Wollstonecraft's daughter."

"Of course you have."

"Do not mock me, sir."

"I can't resist. I certainly see why you'd be interested. Such a pedigree."

"She lives up to it, I promise you."

Hogg looks away. There are times when Shelley's behavior is difficult to understand. Even if he and Harriet don't belong together, must he be so eager to replace her? "I assume she knows you're married. Might I ask her age?"

Shelley is on his feet now, pacing. His hands flutter about and the speed of his words increases. "She does indeed. I have no secrets. I think she's sixteen. Or seventeen. I'm not really sure."

"So you're in love again."

"I'm afraid so."

He envies Shelley but pities the girls he falls in love with. It seems unlikely that there exists anywhere a female who will be able to keep pace with him. Poor Harriet. She didn't stand a chance.

"Some men make arrangements, you know," says Hogg, trying a different approach. "They have a wife and children but also pursue other . . . interests, as opportunities arise."

But Shelley shakes his head. "I expect my love to be all-consuming," he says. "When it ends, it ends. I refuse to split myself in half."

Seeing no way forward on that issue, Hogg asks him how he's living. He's never known Shelley to have enough money. It's more carelessness than profligacy, and he's generous to a fault. If, as it appears, he's supporting a wife and daughter in Windsor and himself in London, he can't be doing well.

"I've taken out a post-obit loan," he says with an embarrassed smile. "A rather large one. That way I can care for Harriet and Ianthe and myself and still give a little to William Godwin, who, truth be told, is in a bad way."

"Oh, you haven't," Hogg says, referring to the loan. In his view, post-obit loans are among the worst forms of usury. One is given money with the promise that it will be repaid in full when one's inheritance comes in. The terms are never less than appalling.

"I most certainly have. My father thinks he can keep what's rightfully mine to himself simply by staying alive. So I've borrowed against it."

"You realize this has no effect on him, don't you? It means only that you'll get far less when the time comes."

"I refuse to wait. The time is now."

And so they talk on into the night. Shelley rails about the mistreatment of the poor. He expostulates on the evils of royal privilege. He makes a case for vegetarianism. Finally, they get to the subject he cares about most. He asks Hogg if he's had a chance to read the poems and essays he's been sending him. "Most assuredly," Hogg says, but it's not entirely true. The man is so prolific, it's hard to keep up. At twenty he's written more than those twice his age. He writes as others breathe.

Then, as the sky is turning from black to violet, as the stars begin to fade, it's Hogg's turn to describe what he's been doing for the past few months. But his warning turns out to have been on the mark: The stories he tells are dreadfully dull, to no one more than himself.

Shelley

His first meeting with William Godwin was a bit like his first meeting with Southey—a man of great accomplishment who turns out to be more interesting when viewed from afar. However, there's one important difference: Godwin's daughter Mary. Good Lord, what a beauty. Not to mention intelligent and well-spoken. He was unaware the man even had daughters, let alone one like her.

His intention had been to thank Godwin for the letter of introduction he provided for his trip to Ireland, while also apologizing for giving the impression he has money to spare. But after he met Mary, all his plans changed. Suddenly, he found himself telling Godwin that although he was presently short on funds, he'd find a way to help.

Now he's begun visiting the Godwin household as often as possible, inventing reasons to do so. On one occasion he asks Godwin to read his missive to the Irish people even though it is now a dead letter, its usefulness passed. On another he browses in the shop and purchases an armload of books. There is even a time when he steps in to care for Mary's half brother, little William, sitting with him for so long that Mrs. Godwin has no choice but to invite him for supper. So as not to make a scene, he eats the meat she serves but feels ill for the rest of the night.

Mary's beauty can't be denied, but it's her inquisitive mind that makes him want to see her again and again. At first she is shy; then gradually her true self begins to be revealed. Among her most appealing qualities are these: She speaks only when she has something sensible to say and never because she's charmed by her own voice; she is deeply curious about history and the arts and natural philosophy; she cares little for gossip; and she is an intrepid reader, approaching fearlessly the most daunting of books. When they first meet, she is reading Gibbon and draws Shelley into a debate about the role played by Christianity in the fall of Rome. Next it's Petronius's *The Satyricon,* which, although he considers himself sophisticated, he may not be able to discuss with a female. Does she really expect him to share his observations about Quartilla's lechery or the attempts made to cure Encolpius of his impotence? It's almost as if she has chosen the book to get the upper hand.

"The chapter in the brothel," she says. "Tell me your thoughts about that."

"I cannot," he says. "I cannot."

Sometimes their conversation takes a personal turn. She tells him about Scotland and her friend Isabel and he tells her about Field Place, his unpleasant experiences in school, and his trip to Ireland, which he laughingly admits was an utter failure.

"I tried to convince them to be tolerant of religions other

than their own," he says. "They didn't take well to that."

As for Harriet, he says nothing about her unless it can't be helped. Instead, he tells Mary about the tender feelings he has for his sisters and his mother, and how often and on what subjects he and his father disagree. She listens carefully and replies:

"Boys quarrel with their fathers. It's as old as the world, is it not?"

"Without a doubt. But we go beyond quarrels. He once threatened to have me locked away."

"For what cause?" Mary asks. They are seated on a simple wooden bench at the back of the shop, the air filled with the smell of books.

"He claimed my failure to believe in God was evidence of madness. He went so far as to have the papers drawn up."

Her brow furrows with interest. "How then did you escape?"

"His own solicitor explained to him that being mad is different from being wrong."

"And what did you say to him—to your father, I mean?"

"That it's society that needs changing and not me." He pauses and smiles. "'Tis a pity *society* can't be locked up."

The next time he visits, he presents her with a copy of *Queen Mab*. He considers it an expression of admiration and a commitment, although toward what end he can't yet say.

"What shall I learn from this?" she asks. She's teasing, but he plays along.

"Something about me and something about how mankind might improve itself by way of compassion and service. Also about the true nature of virtue, which is unlike the false virtues children are often taught."

"It sounds high-minded."

Is she trying to provoke him? Were it someone else, he'd take back the poem and tell her she's lost her chance to read it. But the look in her eyes only increases his desire to know her response.

When he returns the following day, she has already finished it, even the essays at the end.

"You read quickly," he says. "Or you skipped the parts you found dull."

"Neither. I stayed up half the night."

He's quite nervous. If she hates it, everything will change—he'll turn and walk out the door. "Well, what did you think?" he asks.

He can tell she's nervous, too. She turns the pages over in her hands. She walks to the window and looks down at the street. At last she speaks: "*Love withers under constraints; its very essence is liberty; it is compatible neither with obedience, jealousy, or fear; it is there most pure, perfect, and unlimited where its votaries live in confidence, equality, and unreserve.*"

He goes to her and takes her hands. "You committed it to memory," he says. "My exact words."

She lowers her eyes and returns the poem to him. There, on the first page, below the title, she has written something in carefully formed script: *I am thine, exclusively thine.*

He can say nothing. He gathers her in his arms and kisses her face, her lips.

Clara, formerly Jane

On the whole she is pleased with her new name, although reminding the members of her family to use it has already gotten tedious. "Clara," she says firmly when they revert to Jane, "if you please." Her biggest supporter in this is Mr. Shelley, who now visits several times a week.

"One should be called what one wishes to be called," he says. "It's the responsibility of others to comply."

"Suppose she changes her mind repeatedly and comes up with something new every week?" Mary asks.

He turns to Clara. "Is that your intention?"

"Most certainly not."

"There," he tells Mary. "Your argument has been refuted."

"And what about you," Clara asks him. "What do you wish to be called?"

"Shelley is my preference," he replies.

The first few times he came, it was to talk with their father, to work out the terms of a loan. Yet it soon became obvious that seeing Mary was his goal. For a few short days at the beginning,

Clara thought he might be having thoughts about *her*. Then one time she saw his face as Mary entered the room. They do have similar interests—books and more books—about which they can talk for hours. They also like to argue, in a flirtatious way. Perhaps most intriguing (to Clara anyway) is how everyone seems to have forgotten about his wife. It's as if she were dead rather than in Windsor, only a half-day's journey away.

Things being as they are, Clara has now begun to function as Mary's chaperone. If Shelley wants to take her out walking, Mary says, "Please, I won't feel comfortable unless you come along." Their father is such a freethinker, he wouldn't care if Mary and Shelley went unaccompanied to an inn, but their mother would be apoplectic. And Clara doesn't mind helping. That Shelley so clearly prefers Mary seems unfair, but he's a bit earnest and scholarly for her taste. She has difficulty picturing herself as a philosopher-poet's wife. On the other hand, it's possible he'll tire of Mary. Since she returned from Scotland, she's been annoyingly full of herself.

They usually walk to Charterhouse Square, but sometimes Mary insists they go all the way to St. Pancras Church. The trees and flowers there are lovely this time of year. No matter their destination, there always comes a time when the two of them go off alone. While they're away, Clara sits under a tree. She understands the purpose of these walks, and whatever her feelings about Shelley, she's neither a child nor a pest. When they come back, she teases them by saying, "You were gone for over an hour. What significant matters were you discussing, if I may inquire?" Their clothes are often in disarray, even more than is customary for Mr. Shelley. In, one might say, *scandalous disarray*. If you were to ask a family friend which of the girls in the Godwin household is most likely to misbehave, they would probably point to her. But Mary might surprise them one day.

This time when they return, it's even more obvious that they've been tumbling about than on previous occasions. Shelley's shirt is open and Mary's hair is down.

"Really, you should take a moment before you come out from amongst the bushes," she tells them. "It's a matter of self-respect."

"You're entirely correct," Shelley says. "I have bad manners and deserve to be scolded." He then makes a show of refastening his clothing, which prompts Mary to smile. When he's finished, he says:

"Tell me, Clara, have you ever seen hydrogen lit on fire? It's an absolute spectacle. The three of us ought to do it sometime."

"I'm sure Mary knows what you're talking about," she replies. "But I do not. Nor do I wish to. I'm happy to walk out with you but keep your eccentric ideas to yourself."

As they return to Skinner Street, she lets them be together and hangs back. They make a nice pair. But his poor wife—she's forgotten her name—what will become of her? She's heard him say she's ensconced in a nice cottage and that her mother often visits to help care for the child. But that's the sort of thing a man who wants to be done with his wife would say, especially around a new girl.

Occasionally Clara does wonder if she could steal him. She knows she's prettier than Mary, but Mary has a far higher tolerance than she could ever muster for his pretentious talk. And he for hers. She's never seen two people get so excited about books. Although reading is a pleasant enough pastime, there are other things of value in life. Of course, Mary is the daughter of William and Mary Godwin, so one ought not to be surprised. But she herself would prefer a man who is more appreciative of music and the pleasures of society, as well as one for whom actions take precedence over words.

Shelley

He counsels himself to be cautious and then promptly ignores his own advice. Events are unfolding with alarming swiftness, and it was rushing things with Harriet that got him in the fix he's in. Yet he also feels that each step he takes with Mary is a step toward something extraordinary. Even as he kisses her, he is considering what to do next: 2,500 pounds for Godwin, a letter to Harriet in which he describes, as gently as possible, the terms of their permanent separation, and then he and Mary can go off somewhere and begin their new life.

He writes to his friend Tom Peacock and asks him to look in on Harriet from time to time. Peacock is an affable fellow and will do his best to keep her spirits up. Peacock knows Shelley has no intention of moving back in with her and Hogg knows, too, but does *she* know? He fears she may be with child again but tries to put it out of his mind. Whether she is or not, she'll be better off without him. Her parents will care for her, and it's also possible he'll die young. Or if he doesn't, the kind of life he has in mind for himself is no life for a girl like Harriet. He wants to write poetry and involve himself—however he can—in fighting injustice, neither of which will provide her with the snug home he knows she desires. The sooner she forgets about him, the happier she'll be.

But Mary is no mistake. He is unable to resist her. They try to wait but cannot. In the northeast corner of St. Pancras churchyard, in full daylight, he lays his coat upon the grass. Although they are well hidden behind bushes, her sister Jane, now Clara, is reading a book not far away.

"I think I am ready," Mary says, "but you must tell me what to do."

"No instructions shall be necessary," he replies. Her own mother's grave is off to his left; as he lowers himself upon her, he can see it from the corner of his eye.

When it's over, she says, "It was as I hoped. Now I am truly yours," and, "I didn't know I had such madness in me."

"Some might call it mad," he replies. "Some might even call it wicked. In truth it is neither."

"I feel rather strange. I wish we could walk all night and not go home."

"We must be considerate of your sister, as she is considerate of us."

"Not so much considerate as curious. If she knew of something more interesting to do, she'd abandon us in a trice."

"More interesting than us?" he says, giving her a kiss on the cheek. "Does such a thing exist?"

Now all he can think about is Mary. These feelings are nothing like the ones he had for Harriet. Where he and Harriet were united in circumstance, he and Mary are united in philosophy and literature and politics and desire, united in body and mind. Mary is also different from Harriet in that she is a dedicated writer, often spending her mornings with her notebook and pen. She has hinted to him that she has high aspirations in that direction; and why wouldn't she, given her intelligence and how much she seems to have read?

However, unlike him, Mary is private about her work. If he asks to see it, she says, "It's not worth your time. I write only to gather my thoughts." Still, he needn't read what she's written for them to have a common understanding about the value of time spent with words. How he wishes he'd met Mary first.

He thinks Clara may fancy him as well, so he needs to be careful. She's a dear girl, a pretty girl, but much more ordinary than Mary. She'll have no problem finding a fellow who will take care of her and do as she says. Providing, that is, she can break free from Mrs. Godwin, who seems to have proprietary feelings toward Clara that she doesn't have for Mary. Shelley finds the woman frightening. She shares none of her husband's interest in throwing off the bonds of convention. Then again, Godwin may not be as unconventional as his writings suggest. This final thought gives Shelley pause—he hopes the same will never be said about him.

He requests a meeting with Godwin and tells him to expect a draft from his bank. It won't be as much as he's been asking for, but as he's sitting across from Godwin, he can't bring himself to say so. He'll find out soon enough.

The following day he goes to Mary and says, "The time has come to tell your father about our intentions. After which we can do as we please."

"Suppose he objects?"

"How can he? He has written at length about the importance of liberty and how relationships between men and women should be unconstrained by religion or law. More to the point, I'm loaning him what he asked for—or as much I can afford, considering my other responsibilities."

However, Godwin does object. And the money seems to have made no difference. It's as if he sees no connection between the two matters. He cares only that his daughter is too young, that Shelley is already married, and that the 2,500 pounds he's been given is only half of what he needs to fully retire his debts.

This infuriates Shelley. After letting his anger build for several days, he walks from his rented rooms to Skinner Street through the pouring rain, comes roaring into the shop, and goes in search of Mary. Mrs. Godwin screams and says, "God save us," as she follows him up the stairs. He finds Mary in her room, only partially dressed, struggling to pull on a robe.

"They shall not separate us," he says. "No one shall keep us apart. They have no right." As he speaks, he takes a pistol from one pocket and a vial of laudanum from the other. "My God, my God, what are you doing?" Mrs. Godwin cries and lunges for the gun. Clara, entering the room behind her mother, takes one looks and shrieks.

"Drink this and fall forever asleep," he says, thrusting the laudanum at Mary. "Then I shall murder myself and we'll meet in the next life." He's bluffing, of course. The pistol is not charged and the dose of laudanum in the vial is too small to do Mary any harm. Mrs. Godwin reaches for the vial, but he's too quick for her. As he dodges away and waves the pistol in the air, he knocks a pot of ink off Mary's writing desk and onto the floor. The black liquid pours forth in a shape he takes to be emblematic of love denied or a soul in pain. He almost stops to comment upon it, yet before he can do so, Mary begins to sob. He should have told her of his plan. "Bysshe, please no," she says and throws herself on the bed. He can hear footsteps on the stairs, heavy ones that must belong to Godwin. He hasn't thought this far ahead. Suppose Godwin himself is armed?

"Mary, the decision is yours," Shelley says, his voice low but firm. "I will do as you say."

Mary sits up and their eyes meet. At first she seems confused; then a look of recognition falls across her face. She says, "Leave peacefully and I will pledge myself to you. Nothing my father can do will change that."

Clara is holding her mother from behind in an attempt to restrain her. "You witless little—" Mrs. Godwin begins, but Shelley holds up a hand to silence her. "And so I pledge myself to you as well," he says, and goes back the way he came, dodging past a stunned Godwin as he bounds down the stairs.

Outside, he stops and looks back at the shop. The stone face of Aesop over the doorway seems suddenly malevolent and he feels as if he's just emerged from a dream. He went there intending to frighten them into letting him have his way, but halfway through, he began to realize it was an imprudent, ill-conceived plan. Thank

God Mary had the presence of mind to guess what he was doing and play along.

Instead of returning home, he goes to the inn where Hogg is staying and hammers on the door with his fist.

"My word!" says Hogg as he lets him in. "What's wrong? What have you gone and done?"

"Nothing to be proud of." He pauses and frowns. "I'm afraid I can't stay here any longer. Godwin intends to stand between myself and Mary, but he has no idea of the strength of my will."

Hogg studies him for a moment and then speaks: "So you want to save a girl from her family once again."

"A remarkable girl. She's unlike any other."

"Perhaps so, but must you act so hastily?"

Instead of answering the question, he says, "Help Peacock look after Harriet, will you? And my children."

"Your *children*?"

"Harriet's expecting again."

Mary

The moment Shelley is gone, her parents attack. They tell her she's foolish, they tell her she's impulsive, they tell her the time she spent in Scotland changed her for the worse.

"You are destroying your reputation," her father says.

"You are destroying *our* reputation," her stepmother says.

Mary commences again to sob. Clara sits by her and strokes her head. Fanny, who arrived after Shelley left, stands in the doorway looking horrified. The bottle of laudanum on the nightstand projects an air of disdain. Use me or use me not, it seems to whisper, your life is of no consequence either way.

"I'll not allow you to see him again," her father shouts.

Mary glances up. She can't remember the last time he raised his voice at her. "Then I suppose you'll be returning the money?"

He looks stricken. It's as if he's only now realizing how his financial relationship with Shelley has become entangled with his daughter's relationship with the same man.

"The money is not—" he begins, but Clara interrupts.

"Oh, Father, you can't be serious. How can you expect Mr. Shelley to be your patron while judging him unworthy of Mary? It's so hypocritical of you."

No sooner are the words out of her mouth than her mother slaps her face. Becoming sisters with Jane—Clara—has not always been easy, but suddenly Mary feels an overwhelming fondness for her. She could have been silent but chose to speak up on Mary's behalf. Clara bolts from the room; their parents shake their heads and follow after her, leaving Mary and Fanny behind, the air hot with anger and pain.

"What will you do?" Fanny asks. Poor Fanny. Ever the bystander. She seldom participates in any conflict but always seems to be there to observe, her eyes filled with dismay.

"I don't know. I refuse to be kept from Shelley."

"You wouldn't . . ." she says tentatively, nodding in the direction of the laudanum.

"Fanny, no, you needn't worry." She smiles tenderly at her sister's concern. "As I don't believe in heaven, dying would be no solution. It would keep me from him forever."

That evening, when she's finally alone, Mary ponders what to do next. Shelley wants to be with her, there's no question about that, but where can they go? He intends to care for his wife and daughter in as compassionate a manner as money will allow. That may sound unkind, but how many men would do as much? His wife has to know by now there is no future for them together. Mary tries to refrain from thinking bad thoughts about her, but it's not easy. One day at St. Pancras, Shelley told her that Harriet is disappointed in how her life with him has turned out:

"I'm not what she expected. She assumed we'd return to Field Place and take up residence there. The wife of a man of property and the lady of a fine house is what she hoped to be."

"Of course she did," Mary replied. "As would most girls. But I promise you I have no such expectations. Indeed, if you try to force such a life upon me, I will rebel." Then she thought but didn't say, *I am Mary Wollstonecraft's daughter, after all.*

Her hair is a mess so she begins to comb it. Rain has been falling all day, and although it's midsummer, she wishes there were a fire in the grate. Her door opens and Clara comes in, already dressed for bed. She sits down beside her and says, "I've been thinking. We should go away."

"Who? The two of us?"

"No, the *three* of us."

Mary is startled, but she understands what's in Clara's mind: Since Mary and Shelley will not allow themselves to be kept apart, they'll likely run off. Therefore, why not take advantage of the opportunity and go along? It would be an adventure and Clara chafes at life in the house on Skinner Street as much Mary does.

"We hadn't planned to leave, but after today we may have no choice. If we do—and if you come with us—what should our destination be?"

Without hesitation, she says, "France. The war is over so travel there is again possible. And my French is quite good. Then perhaps Switzerland. I've heard the people there are tidy and well mannered."

"You've given this some thought . . ."

Clara responds with an impatient wave of her hand: "Write Shelley a letter. You can claim my idea as your own. I'll carry it to him tomorrow."

She's surprised by Clara's assertiveness. Ordinarily, Mary would have told her she was capable of making her own plans, but tonight she's willing to place herself in someone else's care. France sounds as interesting as anything she herself has considered. And Shelley has said more than once that England is becoming more intolerable by the day.

She writes the letter and in the morning hands it over to Clara, leaving it to her to figure out how to get out of the house without being questioned. Then she goes downstairs to apologize to her father and stepmother about last night's row, if only to prevent them from getting suspicious. She knows she's a poor liar and struggles to keep from meeting her father's eyes.

She expects it will be a day or two before Shelley replies. To occupy herself in the meantime, she writes more letters, including one to Isabel in Dundee. Of all the people she knows, Isabel is the one most likely to understand what she is about to do.

As it happens, she doesn't have to wait two days or even one to hear back from her beloved. That very afternoon, Clara bursts through the door and begins a breathless report of how Shelley read the letter on the spot, said theirs was an excellent idea, and that he would, with the help of his friend Hogg, set about engaging a chaise-and-four to pick them up at sunrise two days hence.

"Have you considered the gravity of what we're about to do?" Clara asks.

"Things won't be the same afterward. I understand that," Mary says. But she is unwilling to entertain second thoughts. "How will we know where to find the coach?"

"I'm to go out tomorrow to meet Mr. Hogg at a certain tavern. He will provide further instructions. All this sneaking about is making me feel scandalous—which I confess I rather like."

Left with little to do now but wait, Mary begins to pack. They'll be traveling light, so she decides she can take only two pieces of luggage, one for each hand. The first she fills with clothing, only things she can't do without. The second is for keepsakes and books—in consideration of the possibility that they will never return. Of course she takes her mother's *Mary* and *A Vindication*. Of course she takes her father's *Political Justice*. She recalls a line from *A Vindication*: "Liberty is the mother of virtue." Isn't that an endorsement of the action they are about to take? And shouldn't her father understand as much?

She puts the matter out of her mind. Right now, all she can think about is taking a journey with Shelley. What joy! What extraordinary adventures await!

Clara

It's as romantic as she hoped it would be. Though the real romance is between Mary and Shelley, in some respects she prefers her position. She can partake in the drama without the anxiety of constantly wondering (as Mary must be) am I beautiful? am I desirable? and especially, am I taking care to avoid repeating the mistakes made by the wife he's leaving behind? However, Mary may be immune to such thoughts—she's uncommonly sure of herself and the place she and Shelley meet seems to be some rarified plane of the intellect that has little to do with the usual ways in which the sexes interact.

The night before they leave, neither she nor Mary sleep. At three hours past midnight they are packed and ready, even though the chaise won't be there until five. They wear black dresses so they can move along the dark streets unseen. At half four they creep down the stairs. In the past they might have had to suppress giggles, but not today—this is too serious. Outside it's cool and damp, the fog having drifted from the Thames all the way to their doorstep. A solitary walker passes by on the opposite side of the street. A window slams shut. Overhead, the moon is a yellow smudge.

They left a letter for their parents—Mary wrote it, signing both their names. Clara didn't think they should say where they were going, but Mary insisted. "My intent is not to punish," she said. "And it will be easier for them if they know our destination." Clara isn't so sure. Their father probably expects them to go to Scotland or Wales. Far away yet not too far. France may be enough to break his heart.

The chaise is exactly where Hogg promised it would be. As soon as Mary sees Shelley standing beside it, she drops her cases, dashes to him, and plunges into his arms. He has on a simple cambric shirt, as if to demonstrate that fine clothes are a thing of the past now that only his love for Mary matters. Hogg ambles over to Clara and tells her he would like to come along but can't leave his job. She's relieved. Although he's exceedingly amiable, it would be stressful to spend long days of travel with a man she scarcely knows.

The driver stows their cases and they climb inside. Hogg steps away from the horses. "Good-bye," he says. "As soon as you are established, I'll come to visit." A few seconds later the rumble of their wheels breaks the morning silence and their journey begins.

At first they chatter about how excited they are and what they might have left behind. "We'll be out of the city in no time. There's not another carriage on the road." "I haven't been out of bed this early in years." "Did you remember your hairbrush? I think I forgot mine." A little later Clara closes her eyes as Mary and Shelley whisper in one another's ears. And still later, no longer in London, they escape the fog and watch as the dew-soaked fields become a bright, shining green with the rising of the sun. Hogg told her it would take them a full day to reach Dover. She wishes they could simply fly there like birds—she can't wait to be aboard a boat bound for France.

Occasionally Shelley allows that he's afraid they'll be pursued. When the driver stops to water the horses, he goes out and urges him not to tarry, tells him he'll pay extra if they make good time. Clara reminds herself that he's done this before. He's never shared all the details, but she knows he ran off with Harriet Westbrook against the wishes of his parents as well as hers. One difference this time is that he is so estranged from his own father, no pursuit by him is expected. It's only the Godwins who might try to stop them.

Fortunately, they reach Dover at dusk without incident. Instead of waiting for the packet of the following day, they find a pair of fishermen who are willing to take them across at once, promising a voyage of two hours. Clara hears them debating whether to go toward Boulogne or Calais, and even as they shove off, it's unclear which they've selected. By then Mary isn't feeling well. Perhaps it's the motion of the boat, but this is not the first time this week she's had a sick stomach. Suddenly, it occurs to her that Mary might be carrying Shelley's child. She always knew what they were doing behind the willows at St. Pancras. And there were other times when he and Mary went off together, ostensibly to deliver some books or visit a friend of Shelley's and didn't return for hours.

On the water, Shelley becomes expansive: "Our prospects are as boundless as the sea," he shouts, standing square in the center of the boat, "and my love as deep; the more I give to thee, the more I have, for love is infinite—it encompasses all and cannot be measured or weighed." The sailors cast wary glances and tell him to sit down and shut his bloody yap. If he goes overboard, they'll not fish him out. Mary appears to be feeling worse by the minute. Shelley settles in beside her and she clings to him, presses her face against him, and he strokes her hair. Clara dozes, her head resting on a folded shawl. Soon a squall arises and the boat tips up and dives forward, tips up and dives forward, wave after wave breaking hard across the prow until they are all thoroughly drenched. Clara isn't ready to turn back, but she does wonder if they shouldn't have looked for a larger vessel. Finally, the sea calms and a stiff breeze pushes them straight toward Calais. When at last they glide onto the strand, Mary looks up and offers her an exhausted smile. The sky is red at the horizon and Shelley, seeming to speak partly to Mary and partly to some unknown listener in the clouds, says, "Look, the sun rises over France."

In Calais, they take rooms in the charming Hotel Dessein. It has a lovely garden, but the chief attraction for Shelley seems to be that Laurence Sterne once stayed there. He even asks that they be placed in the same rooms Sterne occupied. Clara's French is better than Mary's and even Shelley's, so she takes charge of the arrangements. This makes her feel useful as well as more intelligent than they for once.

Next they nap, sleeping in their clothes like the exhausted travelers they are. When they awake, much refreshed, they take an early-evening stroll through town. As they walk, she and Mary gossip about the French women's clothing, especially their outlandish hats, while Shelley remains a few paces behind. The plan is to rest here for a few days and then go on to Paris. After that, Switzerland or maybe Italy—Clara would go willingly to either one.

That evening after supper, a girl knocks on their door and tells them a fat woman is downstairs waiting to see them. They are so curious, they all go to see who it might be. As soon as Clara reaches the foyer and looks through the doorway to the lounge, she knows her mistake. She should have translated "fat" as "large," because her mother, though not at all fat, is as tall and broad-shouldered as a man. Their eyes meet and she sees in her mother's face equal parts fury and relief.

"There you are," she says, striding toward them.

"You needn't have come," Shelley says. "They are under my care."

But Clara has never seen her mother look so strong. "Step aside immediately, or you shall regret it," Mrs. Godwin says. Then, taking her daughter by the hand, she leads her away from Mary and Shelley and toward her own ground-floor room. It's all happening so quickly, Clara can scarcely breathe. Who'd have thought the Channel wouldn't be enough of a moat to protect her. Once inside the room, she is ordered to sit. Her mother secures the door and says, "We shall spend the night here and go home in the morning. You are a foolish girl and have been deceived by Mr. Shelley. I know not what promises he made but they will not be kept."

"What about Mary?"

"Before I departed, I offered to collect her as well. However, Mr. Godwin said she must return on her own. She is his daughter, so I will follow his wishes."

"Yet you think I can be compelled?"

She shakes her head in a way Clara is familiar with, a way that means the question you have asked is not worthy of a response. Instead, she says, "I need to know what you and Mr. Shelley have done."

"What we have done?"

She explains that there are those who write about free love as an ideal, as something that might come to pass when society reaches perfection. And then there are those who think they can use it for their own base purposes in the present day. After pausing for a moment, she adds, "Shelley is of the latter persuasion, I fear."

Clara blushes. Her mother has never spoken to her of such things before. She's aware of her stepfather's opinions as set down in his books, but if her mother means what she thinks she means, she is horrified. She may have run off, but she is not depraved.

"Mr. Shelley and I have done nothing except converse. And we shall do nothing. How could you even ask?"

They are silent for a time. Her mother begins to unpack her bag and Clara watches. Presently, she asks if she can go upstairs and get her things. "You may not," her mother says, and sends a chambermaid to fetch them instead.

Clara sits beside the window and watches night descend on the garden outside. Her mother tries to start a conversation about matters other than going home, but Clara refuses to respond. Eventually, she puts on her nightclothes, gets in the bed they will share, turns her face toward the wall, and pretends to sleep. She has decided she will not be crossing back to England in the morning. Yesterday was the most thrilling day of her life. She experienced elation and terror and even felt *courageous*, a quality she'd never expected to claim for herself. And really, has she done anything so wrong? It's Mary who is cohabiting with a married man—probably doing so with vigor this instant in their room overhead. Clara wants only to be herself. Different from Mary, who thinks her ideas and values are so exalted that they can be understood only by a few other perfected souls. Also different from overcautious Fanny, who refuses to take the smallest risk, even if the reward for doing so is great. No, just *herself*, who has come along on this trip not for anything immoral but for the sake of a little amusement, a little adventure, of the kind that can't be found in the house on Skinner Street.

Shelley

"Bloody hell, how did you do it?" he asks. The three of them are standing in front of the hotel as a carriage with Mrs. Godwin inside rattles away. He's genuinely impressed. When Mrs. Godwin arrived, he was sure Clara was lost to them. He finds the woman terrifying— if it had been he whom she'd wanted to haul back to England, he'd have surrendered on the spot.

"I swore I'd run away at the first opportunity," Clara tells them. "I pointed out that they couldn't keep me locked up forever."

"And that was enough?" Shelley replies, still finding it hard to believe Mrs. Godwin is returning to London empty-handed.

"I also said I'd do my best to wreak havoc upon her life."

Mary laughs out loud. To Shelley she says, "I expect she's giving us a rather genteel version of what was said. My sister is seldom angry, but when she is, it's a sight to behold. Wreak havoc indeed. Consider yourself warned."

They decide not to stay in Calais but to continue on to Paris that very day, taking the *malle poste* for a fare of eighteen francs. It would have been more convenient to go by coach but that would have cost twice as much and already he's worried about money. However, he's confident that when they reach the city, he can go to a bank and work something out.

In Paris they find a hotel that's less expensive than the one in Calais. Since they've been in France, he and Mary have barely slept. Instead, they engage in amorous congress, talk for hours, and then engage again.

"The Scots call this *hogmagundy*," he says, pausing to catch his breath.

"You're making that up."

"I am not. Burns uses it."

"Then let us hogmagundy again," she says.

Shortly before dawn they drift off and sleep until the fierce morning sun comes streaming in to wake them. Since leaving London, he and Mary have been talking about love in all its forms. They are both opposed to a legal union and to any mention of love everlasting, but that only seems to make their present love more intense. He looks across the bed and, as her eyes come open, says, "We are acting on the prescriptions your father laid out in his book. Ironic, don't you think?"

"And so we shall raise our child accordingly," she says.

He squints at her, unsure of what she means. "You are with child?"

"I think I am. I shall be surprised if I am not. I began to suspect it before we departed."

"What excellent news!" he says and takes her in his arms.

"I would be frightened if not for you by my side."

They hold one another for a long time, saying no words. It's natural for her to feel nervous about the child, but in truth she's the most fearless girl he's ever met. Clara can be defiant, as demonstrated by her encounter with her mother, but Mary is more resolute in her passions and beliefs. From a young age, Shelley knew that he would act upon the world rather than allowing the world to act upon him. In Mary Godwin he can see that same quality. It lies a bit below the surface, but when necessary, it comes out.

At last he gets up, dresses, and leaves the hotel. He visits three different banks to inquire about loans, but the fact that they have no idea who he is seems to be an impediment. On the way home he finds a shop where he pawns his grandfather's watch and chain. In exchange he receives eight napoleons. He's always treasured the watch and is not sure he'd have parted with it if Mary wasn't going to have a child.

That afternoon they visit the site of the Bastille, now only a heap of rubble.

"My mother said its destruction hailed the dawn of a new day," Mary says. "She said the passions and prejudices of Europe were instantly set adrift."

"I wish I had a mother like yours," Clara says, and Shelley has to restrain himself from asking if by that she means *dead*. Next, they try to find a man who was a friend of Mary's mother, but when they locate the address, the landlady tells them he has moved to Marseille.

The following day they decide to continue on to Switzerland. Clara is delighted. She has a theory her father was Swiss—a soldier, handsome and of high rank. To Shelley, it's as reasonable a destination as any. He's heard Switzerland is pleasant and of a democratic temperament, and they all agree Paris is too hot.

"I suggest we walk," he says. "We have no appointments to keep and it will allow us to meet the people and see the beauty of the land." He expects them to complain, but surprisingly they seem to consider it an adventure. And it's a good thing. Although he might get them to Switzerland by coach on the money he has, they'd have to forsake food.

They quickly pack up and by early afternoon are en route, heading out of the city in a southerly direction, accompanied by a donkey they purchased at a livery stable to carry their things. The sky is blue and cloudless, the road is often shaded by trees, and it's impossible not to feel hopeful and free. Even the donkey seems to be enjoying himself. None of them brought much in the way of luggage so his load is light.

As afternoon shades into evening they begin to worry they'll have to sleep out, but at a crossroads they find an inn. It's small and dark and the bed all three of them are expected to share is fit for only one. One human, that is, but also a thriving family of lice, pleased to see new bedfellows have arrived.

Shelley tries to fall asleep but can't, so he gets up and goes outside. It's gotten cooler and he walks about the ramshackle garden gazing at the low-hanging moon. His life is moving forward very rapidly—it wasn't so long ago he and Hogg were being expelled from Oxford and he can scarcely count the number of places he's been since. Yet it doesn't seem fast enough. He wants to take Mary's hand in his and run. In his head is a list of the next five or six things he intends to write. In his head is a list of issues he needs to read about and actions he wants to take to improve society for the better. And in his heart is their child. He's so pleased to have found Mary. Harriet had already begun to hold him back. Leaving her now instead of five years from now was the merciful thing to do. The stable is nearby and he goes to check on the donkey. It's sleeping so peacefully, he's envious—sometimes he wishes his mind were not on fire.

The next day they begin to see evidence of the recently concluded war. The conflict between England and France had been going on since Shelley was a child. He remembers asking his father to explain it to him when he couldn't have been more than five. Later, when he'd begun reading newspapers, the dispatches from the front (or rather the many fronts across Europe) formed a daily chronicle not unlike the weather reports from Newcastle-upon-Tyne—that is, always the same and always grim. Then a few months ago, the Allies finally prevailed, a treaty was signed, and Napoleon was banished to Elba—where Shelley pictures him roaming the hills in a blind fury.

All around are burned houses, felled trees, orchards stripped bare, and fields overgrown with weeds where healthy crops should be. They maneuver around shattered wagons and overturned limbers and the occasional skeleton of a mule. He thinks if they are quiet, they might hear the keening of ghosts. In the villages through which they pass, half the houses appear to be unoccupied and the only people they see are a few ragged children who rush out to beg. Clara finds it horrifying, but Mary seems fascinated: "I can understand why the ancients believed in gods of war. It's difficult to picture mortals doing all of this."

Then, as they are beginning to leave the battle-scarred fields behind, Shelley steps in a rut and sprains his ankle. He tries to continue walking, but the pain is too great.

"Leave me here," he says. "I'll persuade a passing farmer to give me a ride."

"Get on the donkey," Mary says firmly. "We can carry our things."

He protests, but Mary is not having it: "Do as I say," she insists.

So they continue, Mary and Clara with a bag in each hand, and him astride the beast, his feet almost touching the ground. Each hour seems to pass more slowly than the one before it, and suddenly Switzerland seems discouragingly far away.

Mary

As dusk arrives, she begins to worry that tonight's lodgings will be even more foul than last night's. They pass one place that appears adequate, but Shelley says it looks too costly. She asks him if he's being thrifty because of possible future expenses or because his purse is empty now. He pretends not to hear.

Little by little, she has come to understand how indifferent he is to money. Although it's one of the qualities she loves about him, she fears it may become one she'll regret. The inn they finally settle on has not only lice but rats—they hear them scuttling in the wall. Worse yet, the proprietor follows them into their room and takes Clara by the hand. It appears he thinks it's his right to have her warm his bed. But Shelley rises to the occasion. Still hobbling from his sprain, he stands toe to toe with the despicable fellow and uses a combination of hand signals and broken French to indicate Clara is not to be molested.

"*Retirez vos mains*, you infernal beast," he says. "*Arrêtez. Arrêtez* this instant!"

Surprisingly, he is successful. It's something about his eyes— he can look terrifying when enraged. The proprietor thus dispatched, Shelley bolts the door and all is well, except that Clara fawns over him to excess. Mary wishes it were she he'd saved.

The night is a long one. They are relieved when the day dawns and they can put the wretched place behind them. On their way through the village, they find a stable and trade the donkey for a considerably larger mule. At least now Shelley's dragging feet won't leave furrows in the dust.

And so they continue mile after mile, day after day, until they've been walking more than a week. The inns don't improve and afternoons are still hot, but they're thankful it hasn't rained. Better to be using their umbrellas for shade than to keep dry.

They pass through Langres and through Champlitte, and in the evenings, in whatever dismal establishment they happen to find themselves, Mary reads to them from *Mary: A Fiction* until they fall asleep. Shelley seems to enjoy it, but Clara finds fault with the actions of the characters—"Who would behave like that?" she exclaims— and soon her moodiness carries over to other parts of the day. It's difficult to blame her. She chose to come along, but no one warned her it would be like this. She probably expected the worst to be a dusty coach ride and at the inns, moldy bread.

Eventually, as they trudge along in the heat and buzzing flies, Mary becomes irritable as well: "If your wife could see us now, what would she think? I wager she'd be glad you left her behind." As soon as the words pass her lips, she wishes she could call them back.

Shelley's reply startles her. "I invited her to come with us. I told her I saw no reason we couldn't all be together, if only for Ianthe's sake. Unfortunately, she declined."

Mary is momentarily speechless. At last she gathers herself and speaks: "You would have us all live together? What an outrageous thought!"

"Your father has written—"

"My father has written many things which no rational person would act upon. I sometimes think you mistake me for a kind of philosophical ideal. I promise you I am nothing of the sort.

Again, she regrets her too-hasty words, for Shelley lives his life in pursuit of philosophical ideals. His eyes begin to fill with tears and he turns to conceal his face.

Later she apologizes and he pretends it was nothing. How strange that she should feel guilty for not wanting Harriet Westbrook to live with them. About her, Mary knows very little, but the image she has in her mind is of a slight, callow thing, one who likes pretty trinkets and is not especially bright. Of course she may be wrong. Harriet could have many admirable traits. Suppose they had met under other circumstances and become friends? She shakes her head to dislodge the thought. Such a friendship never happened and never will.

Perhaps sensing that more quarrels lie ahead, Shelley offers to tell a story. He says, "This was one of my sister Elizabeth's favorites when we were young:

"In ancient Rome, during the reign of Theodosius, there lived seven young men who were accused of practicing Christianity, which had been outlawed by the state. The authorities offered them numerous opportunities to recant, but they refused and were exiled to a cave outside the city walls. Then a spy in the service of the emperor discovered that all seven happened to have fallen asleep at the same time. Seizing the opportunity, the emperor dispatched soldiers to seal the cave's entrance and trap the seven inside.

"They remained asleep for one hundred eighty years. Some say three hundred. Until one day a farmer noticed a peculiar gap in the stonework through which he felt compelled to look. What he saw astonished him—seven young men lying side by side! Naturally, he thought they were dead, but when he managed to enlarge the opening, they began to come awake. And as he spoke with them, it was gradually revealed that they thought Theodosius was still emperor and that they'd been asleep for only one day."

"A parable," says Mary. "I'll wager I can guess what comes next."

"Let him finish," says Clara. "Had they grown tremendous beards?"

"I know nothing of their beards," Shelley continues, "but when they went into town, they soon noticed Christian churches, people praying publicly, and other evidence that where once Christianity had been outlawed, it was now the religion of the state. The seven men spent the remainder of their lives glorifying God."

They are silent for a time, the only sounds their footsteps on the road and a flock of linnets chittering in the trees.

At last Clara speaks: "That's all? They awoke and saw the truth? Are you not an atheist?"

"I have an alternate interpretation," Mary says. "The story is about how a way of thinking which is scorned today may come to be accepted tomorrow. Christianity may turn to atheism and despotism to democracy. War may become peace. However, unlike the men in the story, we are doomed to live in the world as it is. Until philosophy and medicine can bring us back from the dead, the future is but a dream."

"I like it," Shelley says, but Clara is unconvinced. "Alternate indeed," she says.

For days they've been seeing the Alps in the distance, and now at last the road begins to climb. Shelley says they should purchase seats on the next thing with wheels that passes by, without regard to the cost. But before they can do so, a storm moves in. Lightning bolts strike the peaks, the wind drives the rain into their faces, and in no time they are soaked through. Soon the mud is ankle-deep and Clara slips and falls. When she gets up, she's sobbing, not because she's hurt but because she's entirely covered in gray muck. They take refuge under a tree and look out across the blue-gray fields.

From where Mary now stands, she can see not only the mud and rain and barren landscape but also the singular path she has taken to get there. First there was her mother, whom she never knew, a storied mother, a mother of the revolution, a mother whose books both speak to her and mystify her; and her father, always bent over his own books, always worried about money, finding some contentment (or perhaps mere convenience) with Mrs. Clairmont. Then Scotland and Isabel and the ghosts of Scotland, but all of it suddenly made small by her first sight of Shelley, their first words, their first kisses, their intimacies (at which point the word hogmagundy pops into her head and she almost begins to laugh), and some months from now, their child.

So on this wet afternoon in eastern France, a few miles from the Swiss border, the mountains towering above them, she remains exhilarated, despite how cold and tired she feels. She doesn't care if they reach their destination or if they have enough money. She simply wants to cling to these days, these days she knows won't last forever, these days of Shelley and wonder.

Clara

At last the rain stops. It always does. They put on dry clothes. In the next hamlet they do as Shelley suggests and hire a carriage. Such a pleasure it is to be riding instead of trudging through the mud. Clara falls asleep and awakes to find they are deep in the forest. She falls asleep again, and this time when she comes awake, it's entirely dark, so dark she can close and open her eyes and see no change. "Mary," she says, and then, "Shelley," but neither answers. She knows they're still sitting across from her only because she can hear them breathe. Thus she is alone with her thoughts for miles and miles. She remembers a time before her mother remarried, when they took a trip to see a man in Hull. Under the seat of the coach her mother made a nest of blankets and there she remained for the entire journey, curled up like a cat. When they reached Hull, the man wasn't there, but they found a room anyway and stayed for several months. She falls asleep a third time—is it hours that have passed or days?—and when she opens her eyes, the mountains are behind them and all around are sunlit meadows where sheep and cattle graze.

"Switzerland," Mary says, upon seeing she's awake.

Clara blinks her eyes at the bright outdoors. "I'm suddenly starving," she says. "When will it be possible to eat?"

They choose as their destination Brunnen, beside beautiful Lake Lucerne. Their first impression of Switzerland is so positive that they immediately set about finding a house—and when they do, Shelley signs a six-month lease. Mary says, "We can visit Zurich," and Shelley, "I shall enjoy looking out on the lake as I write." Clara wants to join in but isn't sure what to add. Then it comes to her: "I'll plant a garden." She knows little about plants or gardening, but how hard can it be to learn? In her mind she begins to construct a picture of her life here. It will be so different from Skinner Street, because it will be only the three of them and because of the presence, everywhere she looks, of flowers and trees.

Then, only four days later, as if waking from a dream, they come to the realization that it can't last. They have no money and no plan for getting any. Shelley says, "I suppose I could send a message to Hogg, but whatever he'd send wouldn't get us through the week." He's equally honest about his writing. "I have yet to sell anything for a significant amount and may not ever do so. The truth is, I'd as soon give it away."

"We came so far," Mary says, as if to credit them with an accomplishment, however lacking in substance it may turn out to have been. They are seated in the grass, eating what's left of yesterday's frugal lunch: a little bread and cheese.

They look at one another, dumbstruck by their poor planning. The first one to begin laughing is Clara. She repeats what Mary said, "But we came *so far*." Then Mary begins to laugh, and finally Shelley, all of them laughing until they're breathless, laughing until tears run down their cheeks, and they fall back and look at the sky.

Once they recover, they agree to do the only thing they can:

turn around and set out for home. Clara wonders what Shelley was thinking. As the man of their party, wasn't it his responsibility to take the long view? At the very least, he ought to have told them how empty his purse was.

"I shan't walk back to Paris," she says. "I don't know how I'll get there, but it won't be on my feet."

"We'll go north and then travel by boat," Shelley replies. "I promise, it will be much easier. If we have to walk, I'll carry you on my back."

She studies his face. She studies Mary's face. Mary's eyes dart at Shelley. These days they are always conspiring, which makes her feel left out.

That night they stroll beside the lake and lament the memories they'll never have. Then the next morning they depart, just like that, without even informing the poor fellow from whom they rented the house.

About their mode of transport, Shelley keeps his word. He has barely enough money to buy them places on a coach, which takes them to the Rhine. There, they board a barge to Rotterdam. It is while they are on the river that Mary confirms Clara's earlier suspicion. She is indeed with child.

"Is that the true reason we're going back?" she asks.

"We're going back because we have no money. And if we haven't enough for the three of us, there'd be still less for four."

One afternoon on the barge Shelley gets into an argument with a man about slavery. The man, a Dane, says it's a necessity while Shelley says it's an abomination. The Dane asks Shelley what he does to make his living and Shelley tells him it's an impertinent question. The Dane presses him and Shelley sputters for a moment before declaring himself to be a poet. At that, the Dane scoffs and walks away.

In Rotterdam they leave the barge and board a ship which will carry them across the Channel. The captain realizes only after they are under way that they're too poor to pay for their passage. Fortunately, he doesn't throw them overboard. But once they dock at Gravesend, he insists on remaining with them until he gets what he's owed.

"This really is uncalled for," Shelley says as they walk up the street away from the docks. "I'm good for it, I vow." The captain is holding a fistful of Shelley's shirtsleeve and won't release him. "Not 'til I'm paid," he mutters.

They hire a cab and Shelley, after a moment's thought, directs the driver to take them to the coffeehouse owned by his wife's father. When they arrive, he jumps out and disappears inside.

Clara looks at Mary in astonishment. "What on earth is he doing?" she asks.

"Borrowing some money I suppose."

"From Westbrook? Is he mad?"

Mary shrugs. "At times I think he is."

The captain of the ship is sitting right beside them but acts as if he doesn't hear a word they've said. He's not interested in where the money comes from, only that their account is settled.

Minutes pass. "Maybe we should go inside?" Clara says, but Mary shakes her head.

At last Shelley emerges and smiles broadly, not a hint of anxiety on his face. It's as though getting a loan from the father of one's estranged wife is the most natural thing in the world.

To the captain, he says, "As you can see, I'm a man who pays his debts."

"I can see a great number of things about you, none of which I like," the captain replies. And then, having no reason to remain with them any longer, he exits the cab and goes up the street on foot.

Shelley laughs, but to Clara it sounds forced. He directs the cab to continue on to Skinner Street, where they arrive unannounced at midday.

Clara is prepared for a great bloody row, but their parents receive them with such meekness and gratitude, all she can feel for them is pity. More than anything else, they seem bewildered—greatly relieved to see their daughters safe at home, but also disturbed to see they are still with Shelley, the scoundrel who stole them away. Godwin embraces Mary and gives Clara a peck on the cheek. Shelley extends his hand, but Godwin keeps his at his side. It's a complicated moment, made more so by the fact that the Godwin household has been living off Shelley's money for the past month. Only Fanny displays emotions that seem unmixed. As soon as she sees them, she begins to sob.

"I feared I'd never lay eyes on you again," she says.

In truth, Clara is embarrassed about the entire journey and suspects Mary is, too. They departed with such bravado, and now, here they are creeping back, making it obvious that they hadn't been able to thrive on their own. But not Shelley. He seems entirely unfazed. Clara wonders what he and Mary will do next. It's one thing to hide off in some corner of the Continent and live a life debauched and dissolute, but quite another to do so in London, where punishments for nonconformity can be harsh.

Later, when she has a moment with Mary alone, she puts it to her directly: "So what are your intentions? Will you live here? Or are you and Shelley setting up house?" Mary replies with something indistinct—she's not sure, Shelley has an idea, they have a place in mind—but Clara soon stops listening because the real subject of the question is herself. Must she go back to living at Skinner Street and return to the life she led before? Going to the occasional party? Meeting tedious young men? Providing grudging assistance in the shop? Yet what choice does she have? At least Mary has options, scandalous though they are.

But then, to Clara's surprise, Shelley finds a house for himself and Mary on Church Terrace in Pancras and invites her to come along. Although the place is small and in poor repair—not nearly so nice as the one they had for four days in Switzerland—she'll have a room to herself, at least until Mary's baby comes. It happens not a moment too soon because they've received notice that their father wishes to have no further contact with any of them.

Shelley shrugs. "I cannot blame him. When another man steals your daughters, you have a proper complaint."

They have barely a stick of furniture, so Shelley disappears for a few hours, and later in the afternoon, a squadron of deliverymen arrive. They bring beds and chairs and writing desks and a handsome oval table, around which they can take their meals, and a sisal rug. This is the first time either she or Mary has lived in a place of her own, and they both revel in the simplest acts of proprietorship. Should this chair go here or by the window? Isn't it remarkable how a vase of yellow flowers improves a room? Shelley stands watching, a look of satisfaction on his face.

Clara thinks she's beginning to figure Shelley out. Back when they first set off for France, she wondered if he was so bold, so self-confident, so contemptuous of conventional morality that he aspired to take them both into his bed. But now she thinks he simply likes having a sort of made-up family, a clan, consisting of as many people as there are places to sleep in the house. She wouldn't be surprised if he invited Jeff Hogg to come and live with them—although Hogg is so large, he'd require a purpose-made bed.

She does wonder what Mary's opinion is. Perhaps she and Shelley would prefer to be alone. As a sort of test, she says, "You're certain I'm not a bother . . ." Mary laughs. "No more than usual, I daresay." Clara also suspects Shelley will have difficulty paying for the place. He receives money from his family but always spends more than he gets. Her suspicion is confirmed when, shortly after they've moved in, a bailiff comes knocking at the door.

"I need to speak to Mr. Shelley," the bailiff says. Mary stands in the doorway as Clara listens from an adjoining room.

"What is it you need to see him about?" Mary asks.

"That's between the law and Mr. Shelley. Although I am at liberty to say it has to do with his debts."

"His debts?"

"His prodigious debts. We've been waiting for him to return."

As soon as the bailiff is gone, Mary turns to Clara. She can't tell if the expression on Mary's face is one of anger or fear. Probably both. "I'm going out to find him," she says. "He went to buy figs. He insists they are only in season for a short time and he didn't want us to miss out. But figs or not, he ought to sleep somewhere else tonight."

"Did you know about this?" Clara asks. "About his debts, I mean."

"Not the particulars, but it's easy enough to deduce."

Over the next several days Shelley stays with friends, never spending more than a single night in any one place. Tom Peacock serves as go-between, carrying messages and making sure Mary knows where she can meet her beloved: St. Paul's one day, The Cross-Keys Tavern the next, and then back at the house on Church Terrace on Saturday night because at one minute past midnight the Sunday prohibition against making arrests begins. Every time she returns, Clara insists on a report. She finds it rather exciting and wants to know all the details. The letter in which Shelley instructs Mary to meet him at St. Paul's makes her heart race:

You may find me at St. Paul's at one. My dearest and best love, your affection is my only & sufficient consolation. I have no personal interest in any human being but you, & you I love with my whole nature.

If only someone would send a letter like that to *her*. Yet as romantic as it all is, Shelley's absence is making Clara nervous about their accommodations. She still fears they will have to move back under their parents' roof.

"He can't continue like this," she tells Mary. "To whom does he owe the money? I thought he got an allowance from his father every month."

"He does, but he gives some to his wife, some to my father, some to other friends in need. Then, with nothing left, he makes purchases on account. At present he owes money to a haberdasher, a shoemaker, the man who sold him the chairs we're sitting on, and the landlords of the last two places he lived before we left for France."

Not long thereafter they relocate to rooms on Blackfriars Road. Clara isn't sure if this is because his debts have been paid or if it's a part of some subterfuge to keep his creditors at bay. Whatever the reason, he stops hiding and the bailiffs stop showing up.

Jeff Hogg

Shelley has lost all interest in Harriet, but Hogg still has a place for her in his heart. He can certainly understand Shelley's point of view. Would it be to anyone's benefit if they were to stay together—he bored with her, she coming to hate him, his children growing up in a house filled with simmering disgust? That describes half the households in England and the country is worse for it. Yet it's also true that Harriet is blameless. As far as he knows, she never mistreated her husband, never lost faith in him as a man. In an effort to live up to his duties, Shelley did try to visit her, but when he arrived at the Westbrook house, her father barred the door. After that, Hogg attempted to look in on her, but he had no better luck:

"I'm a friend," he said, peering over Westbrook's shoulder to see if Harriet was hovering inside.

"You are an associate of Mr. Shelley and therefore no friend of my daughter. He has stabbed her in the heart."

"You are mistaken. I am here because I hold your daughter in the highest—" Yet before he could complete the sentence, the door was slammed in his face.

Then, on a blustery day at the end of November, he hears from Tom Peacock that Harriet has given birth to a son.

"What does Shelley intend to do?" Hogg asks.

"Give her some money, I suppose."

"That's all?"

"She's a lovely girl, but he's done with her. And what's the point of him going to have a look at the child? He'd feel terrible and so would Harriet. It would give her false hope."

After Peacock is gone, he decides that if Shelley won't go to see her, he will try again. Maybe Westbrook won't be home. However, the servant who answers the door redirects him to Windsor, to the house Shelley found for them before he ran off. Thus he doesn't have to contend with her father—Harriet answers the door herself.

"Jefferson, how good of you to come," she says, looking genuinely pleased. She's as pretty as ever although, not surprisingly, looks tired. She invites him inside, little Ianthe clinging to her skirts.

"I have a girl coming in to help," she adds, perhaps noting the concern in his eyes. "I'm not usually alone. Would you like to see Charles?" *Charles*. This is the first time he's heard the child's name. He is in a cradle across the room and they go and stand over it.

"Sleeping soundly," Hogg whispers. He has had little experience with infants and isn't sure what else to say.

"He looks like Bysshe, don't you think?" she whispers. The child stirs and they step back. "Can I make a pot of tea?"

"I won't put you out," he says. She begins to insist. but he shakes his head.

"Tell me about Bysshe. Is he well?"

He tries to think of something that won't be upsetting. "He's sworn off sugar as a means of protesting slavery in the West Indies. But now he can't stop talking about how much he likes cake."

She laughs, but it all seems exceedingly bleak. Here she is, alone in Windsor, without family or friends. As if she's read his mind, she says, "When I heard your knock, I thought it was Tom Peacock. He stops by from time to time."

"Do you have enough . . . of what you need?" he asks awkwardly.

"My father is generous," she replies, but her eyes dart about the room as if she's embarrassed by the furnishings—or by their absence. On the rough table are two pieces of pewter, a flickering rushlight, and nothing more.

"Bysshe is sending you money, too, is he not?" It's what he's been told, but something makes him want to confirm it.

"Oh, yes. That goes without saying. After all, he's my husband."

He finds the remark heartbreaking. Father of your children perhaps but husband in what respect? "I could help out if you need me to. If not for money, then . . ." He shrugs, unsure of how he could be of use. He wishes he'd said yes to the tea. He'd like a reason to stay. More than that, he'd like to hold her, comfort her. He fears that if he doesn't express his feelings now, he never will. But he hasn't the nerve.

"You're sweet. As I said, I have my father. And Tom Peacock. Bysshe must have told him to look in on me. So no need to trouble yourself."

On his way back to London he works up a head of anger toward Shelley. He never should have taken advantage of the poor girl. She can try with all her might to be cheerful, but she is still a deserted wife. Then again, maybe Shelley is right—maybe they should all move into a house together and then none of them would ever be lonely. Would that be any less moral or any less logical than the way things are configured now?

He goes directly to Shelley's current place of residence on Blackfriars Road. At least he thinks that's where he's currently living—they keep moving about. To his surprise, it's the correct address and all three of them are present. However, before he can say a word, they rush at him with news: Mary is with child.

"If it's a boy, perhaps we'll name it after you," Shelley says.

Hogg appreciates the gesture and tries to join in the celebration but finds it difficult. He's still thinking of Harriet—the contrast between the feeling of abandonment he experienced in her presence and the joy in this room. Shelley knows him well enough to sense something is wrong.

"Poor Hogg," he says, clapping him on the back. "I won't steal your name if you don't want me to. Besides, it will probably be a girl."

"You may have my name and use it now or in the future," he says. "As children seem to come easily to you, you'll want to be stocking up."

Shelley

He chooses not to respond to Hogg's remark. Yes, Mary is pregnant, and yes, upon their return, he found a letter waiting for him with the news Harriet had given birth to their second child. So what is he to do? He tried to pay Harriet a visit but was turned away. He sends her money and not a small amount. He can tell Hogg wants better for Harriet. So does he, but again, what is he to do? Changing the subject, he tells Hogg how he managed to dodge the bailiffs. His friend is duly entertained and leaves in a much better temperament than the one in which he arrived.

In the midst of these events, Shelley has begun a new poem. It's to be about a wanderer, a poet who sets out to explore the world. But what the wanderer is searching for is neither treasure nor undiscovered lands nor even love. No, he is searching for that which is not of this world, what the Greeks named the *theurgy*, the presence of beneficent magic in nature and its influence on human affairs. At certain points in his life Shelley has been overtaken by the feeling that he will not live much longer; this poem will be his attempt to explore what lies beyond life, not something as simpleminded as heaven or as desolate as the grave, but that which only poetry can engender—an awakening of the body and the spirit in a transcendent place.

He's aware he can be remote when he's immersed in a poem, but Mary seems to understand. Indeed, it's often *he* who has to intrude on *her*, interrupting her reading and writing to demand her full attention when he can tell part of her mind is elsewhere. "May I borrow you for a moment?" he says, and reads a few lines aloud:

"The Poet wandering on, through Arabie, and Persia, and the wild Carmanian waste, and o'er the aerial mountains which pour down Indus and Oxus from their icy caves . . ."

She looks up from her book: "I'm sorry. I wasn't listening. Indus and Oxus? Please begin again." This he loves about her. Harriet would have feigned appreciation, but he'd have known it was all an act; whereas, when Mary finally attends to him, her focus is so unwavering, it is as if he has become some wild animal's prey. He quotes from Ovid and she corrects his quotation. He uses the words *joy* and *exultation* in the same line and she asks him if one wouldn't do. A little while later, with no warning whatsoever, she tells him their child will be born with wings.

His eyes go wide. He recalls the laudanum-induced dream in which Harriet gave birth to a lizard-child. Although wings are less hideous than scales, he'd prefer the baby have neither. Even in jest, there are things that ought not to be said.

"Don't make such predictions—suppose it comes true?"

"I should think you'd be pleased. You wouldn't want to father an angel? In your poems you often—"

"An angel in this world would be monstrous. It would be hunted down and killed."

"Perhaps not. Have you so little faith in people's ability to perceive that which is exceptional?"

"Oh, they perceive it. They perceive it and punish it for being different."

"Then we shall move to some island where no one can bother us. Me and my Bysshe and our child with wings."

Later that same day the always amiable Peacock makes an unexpected visit, so Shelley takes a break from his writing, tells Mary and Clara to get dressed for a walk, and the four of them go out to the ponds on the other side of Primrose Hill. Naturally, they launch a few boats, which he happens to have in his pocket. He can't help himself. If he doesn't set something afloat or on fire approximately every fortnight, he begins to feel he's losing his powers.

As Mary and Clara make a circuit of the pond, he asks

Peacock how Harriet and the children are doing. When Hogg visited, Shelley wasn't prepared to hear it, but he's ready now.

"As well as one would expect. The baby came early, but he's healthy enough."

"I really ought to make a visit."

Peacock stops and looks at him. "To be honest, I'm not certain she'd appreciate it. I think she's divided about you. Wishes you'd come back to her one day and wishes you'd drown the next."

"But the boy, Charles, he's doing well?"

"I just told you he was." He pauses, shakes his head. "What you really want is for me to tell you *she's* doing well and that I'm unable to do."

They walk on in silence. Of all the emotions, guilt is the most unpleasant—especially when what's wrong can't be fixed. He's relieved to see the women come around the lake so they can proceed toward home.

His financial problems he has solved with yet another post-obit loan—although *solved* may be too positive a word. If he continues his current practices, his father's considerable estate will, upon his death, go directly to the lenders, every farthing, like water soaking into parched ground. But what is he to do? Stop giving money to Harriet? The few things he buys for himself and Mary are not the problem. It's all the people he feels he must support. He will soon be a father three times over. It's true that the amount he spends is sometimes more than he has, but it doesn't seem fair that he should be persecuted for that.

As the days pass, he realizes he's being more attentive to Mary than he was to Harriet while waiting for their first child. He can blame part of the difference on Harriet's sister, who was always in the way. Clara is sometimes in the way, but she is more tractable. Although Mary and Clara are the same age, he thinks of Mary as a woman and Clara as a girl. As long as Clara is entertained, even at a modest level, she remains satisfied. In the evenings he tells them stories, the kind he used to tell his sisters. Clara listens to every word while Mary, exhausted from the changes in her body, falls asleep.

Then, quite unexpectedly, news arrives from Field Place that his grandfather has died. He was old but not, as far as Shelley knew, in poor health. His father's father, he was the bearer of family stories, and although Shelley never felt particularly close to him, he is surprised by how affected he is by his passing. It is from his grandfather that he learned about the Romans in Britain and about the ancient tortoise of Warnham Pond. He wishes he'd gone to visit him during the past few months, but given the rift between himself and his father, doing so would have been unwise.

At least now there should be more money. Not the whole of Field Place and the family estate, not yet, but an amount his grandfather held in reserve. He's not going to feel ashamed for wanting it either. It will make life much easier, and if he refused it, it would stay with his father. He can see no sense in that. He informs Mary and tells her he must return home immediately to protect his claim.

"Would your father really try to take what's rightfully yours?" she asks. "He needn't pay you an allowance and yet he does . . ."

He hates everything about this. There are so many other things in the world more important to think about and discuss. He says, "Here's a fact I've never told you. He pays me an allowance only because Harriet's father insists on it. Once they both realize I'm not going back to her, he'll stop."

Mary looks slightly stunned. "So if you buy me some trinket, it's her I ought to thank? How disgusting." She makes to leave the room but stops short and turns. "Go if you must," she says, "but please, when you get there, don't make matters worse."

Early the following morning he departs. He goes on horseback and works on his new poem in his head as he rides. He has decided to call it *Alastor*, at the suggestion of Peacock, after a character from Roman myth who is the poet's spiritual guide.

When he arrives at the house, they're expecting him. How can he tell? A servant, a fellow he's familiar with, is stationed at the door to prevent him from coming inside.

"But I live here," he says.

The servant lowers his eyes. "I'm sorry, but I have my instructions, sir."

Thus denied entry, he sits down on the doorstep, takes a book from his pocket, and begins to read. Someone will have to come out eventually. His family always calls him stubborn and they will know he can outwait them. Before he's read ten pages, he hears the door and looks up. It's Elizabeth, wearing not the look of joy he expects, but something akin to sisterly disgust.

"Lizzie, it's so good to see you," he exclaims, getting to his feet.

"You ought to have warned me you were coming. I could have smoothed the way." She narrows her eyes. "Who is Mary Godwin anyway?"

"She is . . ." He shakes his head, not because he has no words, but because he has too many words. Instead of describing her, he says, "You and Mary are a great deal alike. You will become best friends." Stepping back so as to see her fully, he adds, "Where did you get that lovely dress?"

"When I heard you'd run away to France, I was so angry with you. I told myself when I saw you again, I'd slap your face."

He turns a cheek toward her. "Which I deserve. Draw back and let fly, hard as you like."

"Come," she says, and they walk into the garden, through the gate, and into the woods where as children they spent so much time. He asks about Hellen and Margaret and Polly and she relates what she knows about their activities at school. He promises to arrange a proper visit when this is over—or better yet, she should come to London and visit him there. Their new place in Blackfriars has extra rooms so she can stay as long as she likes.

"Who knows, maybe you'll fall in love with Hogg or Peacock," he says.

She lifts an eyebrow. "Are all your friends animals or do you have human ones as well?"

He finds it difficult to be back here, where he had such happy days. He enjoys seeing Elizabeth, but the house seems almost angry, its heavy bricks like gritted teeth, the door a kind of scowl. If it belonged to him, he'd raze it and let primeval nature take over. He'd live in a hut and watch the bindweed and brambles have their way.

Perhaps experiencing similar feelings of discomfort, Elizabeth says, "I should go back. They're probably watching from the window as we speak. I shall ask Father if he has anything to communicate to you. Wait by the door."

Once again he protests—how humiliating that he should be kept waiting outside Field Place. It's as if he were a peddler with muddy boots. But Elizabeth ignores him and disappears inside.

As he expects, they keep him waiting again, simply because they can. He paces in the garden. He sits and reads. Some movement at the window catches his eye, but it's only the curtain being blown by the wind. He pictures them discussing him at length: "I know what is customary, but what does he *deserve*?" "In my view, nothing. Nothing at all."

At last the door opens again. It's the same servant, the one who blocked his way. This time he has something for him—a folded document, which he lays in Shelley's palm. He shakes it open, scans the page, and then shoves it firmly into his pocket. He is to receive 1,000 pounds a year, with one-fifth going to Harriet. Is it fair? Is it what he *deserves*? He doesn't care. It's so much more than he's getting now, he's delighted. He can stop worrying about Harriet and Ianthe and the baby, give some to Godwin, and still have some left over for the children yet to come. He once thought inherited wealth was an evil of primary magnitude. He chooses not to think about that now.

The business at Field Place disposed of, he can't wait to return to his poem. On his way back to London, he urges the horse onward, puts the inheritance out of his mind, and becomes the wanderer, feeling the sun, the wind, the breaking of the waves against the hull:

> *The day was fair and sunny: sea and sky*
> *Drank its inspiring radiance, and the wind*
> *Swept strongly from the shore, blackening the waves.*
> *Following his eager soul, the wanderer*
> *Leaped in the boat, he spread his cloak aloft*
> *On the bare mast, and took his lonely seat,*
> *And felt the boat speed o'er the tranquil sea*
> *Like a torn cloud before the hurricane.*

He looks up and the clouds overhead are exactly so, shredded, moving with great rapidity, and for a brief instant he feels as if the words in his mind and the world around him are one.

133

When he gets home—and after today, it's clear to him that his home is not Field Place, but wherever Mary is—he tells her about the annuity.

"Good. She is provided for," Mary replies. "You can be done with her and feel no guilt."

"I hold no grudges against Harriet, my father, or anyone else," he says. "What I feel most is relief." Then he goes off to write.

For weeks thereafter, he works on his poem. He writes from the hour he awakes until the hour he all but drops from exhaustion. He forgets to take meals. "Mary, have I eaten?" he asks. "I think perhaps I did, but I cannot recall."

Then, just as he is about to throw himself at the concluding lines, the one event that can disrupt his work arrives: Mary's lying-in. Her labor begins shortly after midnight on a Saturday. He runs for the midwife while Clara stays behind. Although he knows exactly where to go, he somehow takes a wrong turn and spends a few minutes of panicked confusion trying to regain his bearings. Thus, when he finally returns, the midwife in tow, the birth has already begun. Mary has reminded him on several occasions how her own mother died when she was born, so for a moment he takes the worried look on Clara's face to be a sign of the catastrophe he fears. But the midwife assures them all is well, and so it is. Mary gives birth to a boy as the stars outside recede into a brightening sky.

Even though her father still refuses to speak to them, they name the child William Godwin Shelley. Clara calls him, in gentle mockery, "the offspring of freedom and love," while Hogg says he looks a great deal like his father and such a tragedy that is. Fanny comes to visit and Shelley feels sorry for her because she's so divided. She stayed home when Mary and Clara left and is now viewed by their parents as the loyal one. But she fawns over baby William like the most devoted aunt imaginable. "We shall call you 'Willmouse,'" she says, and thereafter it's the name they all use.

"Do you think Father will ever want to see me again?" Mary asks.

"Of course he will," Fanny says. "Already I've seen signs that he's prepared to relent. And a grandson will provide an incentive."

They have some money, they have a child. They have friends

and family to gather round the hearth. His new poem is nearly done. Still, he is uneasy. He wants all these things, but also something more.

Clara

"Jane" was a child's name, too innocent for her by far. And yet she's beginning to think "Clara" is dowdy, an appropriate name for someone like Fanny, who stays home all day and does needlework, but a poor one for herself, who now finds needlework a bore. She would prefer a name like Mary. Mary's name came from her well-known mother—a mother who even before Mary was born gave the name to a character in a book.

Setting aside the problem of names, she ponders Mary's romance with Shelley. In the beginning, she found watching them thrilling because she'd never seen love up close before. A bit later she found it absorbing, in the way a naturalist finds it absorbing to watch hedgehogs mate. But since the baby's arrival, Mary seems overly pleased with herself, as if being fertile were a talent instead of a fact of animal life; and Shelley has adopted a sort of *paterfamilias* air, which is at odds with who he really is. It's rather much.

She doesn't mind Shelley when they're alone, after Mary has gone to put Willmouse to bed. Then they sit side by side, and even without Mary present, he tells her stories. The ones about animals are Clara's favorites. As she did not grow up in the country, everything he says about badgers and stoats comes to her as news. Sometimes he looks at her in a way that makes her think he's about to offer her a kiss. It would be hard not to accept. It's not merely his beauty. It's the passion he brings to the things he cares most about—Mary, poetry, justice, liberty . . . What, she wonders, would it be like if he were to turn such intensity toward her?

One night she says, "I would be quite lonely here without you."

"Are you afraid I'll leave?"

"No. But imagine if you had never written to Father. If you had never come to us. How different our lives would be."

He studies her as if trying to ascertain her thoughts. He says, "Is there a reason you're telling me this? I should not wish to misunderstand."

At the very brink, she forces herself to retreat. "I have no hidden motive. I value your friendship. You have made Mary happy and I'm thankful for that." Had she gone forward, imagine the chaos that would ensue. Besides, Mary and Shelley seem well matched. If he made love to her, he would consider it to be in addition to Mary, not instead of.

However, the moment is not without effect. It causes her to decide she wants an adventure, one that doesn't involve Shelley or Mary, one that is hers alone. And she knows exactly where to begin. As every member of London society is aware, Lord Byron is presently in town. She's never met the man, but his celebrity means she knows a good deal about him—from what he eats for breakfast, to his travels in the Ottoman Empire, to his use of Macassar oil on his hair (which makes him smell of cloves, or so the newspapers say). In truth, it would be difficult to *avoid* knowing such facts, so widespread is his fame. More to the point, she knows that his wife, Ada, Lady Byron, the mother of his daughter, has left him, but not before accusing him of having an unlawful relationship with his half sister as well as unnatural relationships with certain men, allegations Clara refuses to believe.

But how to meet him? She could try to solicit an invitation to some social event where he's expected to be present, but that might prove difficult. They move in different circles—Byron among those of wealth and status; herself (by way of Shelley) among intellectuals of the middle class and artistic poor. She could enlist her stepfather's help—surely he knows someone who knows Byron—but since she's returned from France, they're not on speaking terms. In the end, she decides to write to the poet directly. She's heard he receives dozens of letters each week, many from eligible young women, so she'll need to be persuasive, neither too coy nor offensively bold:

> *An utter stranger takes the liberty of addressing you. Please pardon the intrusion and listen with a friendly ear. It is not charity I demand, for of that I have no need.*
>
> *I tremble with fear at the fate of this letter. I cannot blame you if you receive it as an imposition. But mine is a delicate case. My feet are on the edge of a precipice. Yet do I leap*

forward at the peril of my life.

> *If a woman, whose reputation is unstained, should throw herself upon your mercy—if with a beating heart she should confess the love she has borne you for many months, if she were to offer you her fond affection and devotion—could you accept her and receive that affection in some secret place?*

When she writes the last word, her hand is shaking and she can feel the blood rushing to her face. Is she really going to commit such an audacious act? She's heard there are women who make a habit of attempting to insinuate themselves into the lives of the wealthy and powerful. Perhaps this is how they begin. Among the many things she knows about him is that he lives at 13 Piccadilly Terrace. She posts the letter and waits.

He fails to respond. Of course. Why should he bother himself with such pathetic pleadings? It's not as if he needs another lover. Now she's embarrassed to have sent it and pictures him reading the first two lines, then throwing it on the fire. Or even worse, having a derisive laugh.

Then again, perhaps he read it and thought, "If she's really so intent on meeting me, she will write again." So she does, but this time she's more direct.

> *Lord Byron is requested to state whether seven o'clock tomorrow will be convenient for him to receive a lady who wishes to communicate with him on business of peculiar importance.*

There is no actual *business* to be discussed, but implying money is somehow involved might open doors. Such is the way with men, or so she has been told. Trying to get him to reply is beginning to feel like a game. What will it take?

> *She desires to be admitted alone & with the utmost privacy. If the hour the lady has mentioned is convenient, she will come; if not, perhaps his Lordship will suggest an alternate appointment. The Evening is preferred.*

Once again he fails to reply. In her third letter she says she's considering a career on the stage and asks if he has any theatrical friends who might advise her in this pursuit. He's on the governing board of Drury Lane Theatre, so perhaps such a request will be deemed more appropriate than the ones she's made before.

When she's about to give up hope, a letter arrives bearing such an elaborate seal, it can only be from Lord Byron. She gasps and clutches it to her breast. What if he rejects her? Worse, what if he mocks her? She opens it and her eyes scan the page. *Eight o'clock*, it says. *Thursday*, it says. Followed by his address, which she already knows by heart.

The following day, the annoying, irksome day between now and when she will see him, she can scarcely think. She tries to learn a new piece of music, but her attention wanders; she tries to nap but can't fall asleep. Mostly she gazes out the window at the sky. The same is true for Thursday, at least until midafternoon when she begins to dress. She has already made up a story about attending a lecture with a friend, so when the time comes, neither Mary nor Shelley knows her true reason for going out.

Upon arriving at Lord Byron's house—his very grand house—she looks up and down the street to make sure she's not being watched. According to what she's read, collectors of gossip who write for the penny press surveil the great poet at all hours and she wants to protect her good name. But when she knocks, the doorman says Lord Byron is out and won't be back until late.

The next day, in a most agitated state of mind, she writes again, telling him that she is William Godwin's stepdaughter and the stepsister of Mary Godwin, whose mother was Mary Wollstonecraft. This time his reply comes immediately. Within the hour. He wants to meet her and Mary both. The fact that it took Mary to get his attention is infuriating, but one does what one must.

"Mary," she says, "I need you to go out with me this evening after supper."

"For what purpose? You've been secretive lately. I'll have to arrange for someone to watch Willmouse. How long will we be gone?"

"Perhaps a couple of hours. I've been invited to meet Lord

Byron. He doesn't live far away." She can feel herself begin to color, merely from the act of saying his name.

Mary turns toward her, her eyes wide with astonishment. "He wishes to meet *you*?"

"Indeed he does. I've been corresponding with him," she says, trying to sound nonchalant. "He's offered to advise me about how to begin a career on the stage."

"I didn't know you were interested in such a career."

There's a vase on the table before her and she spends a moment centering it. Mary's correct, she has no actual interest in acting, but for now she feels she must maintain the ruse: "I might be. I'm considering it. But that's not the point." She then continues, describing in detail her letters and her prior visit to his house.

"You're aware of his reputation?"

She lifts her chin, annoyed by Mary's tone. "I wish to form my own opinion. What can be the harm in that?"

In the end, Mary agrees to accompany her—less, Clara thinks, from sisterly duty than from pure curiosity. How many people receive invitations to Lord Byron's house? They already know he's remarkably handsome. It's not an opportunity to be passed up. Mary arranges for the baby to be looked after and then they spend a great deal of time getting ready. Clara even allows Mary to help with her hair. When they're done, she thinks they both look fetching—and this time, at Piccadilly Terrace, the doorman admits them at once.

For some minutes they are left to wait in a dimly lit foyer. Then a manservant appears and guides them down a long hall and into a parlor which is being heated to excess by a blazing fire. Clara has seen Byron twice before, once when they went to hear Coleridge speak, and once from a distance, walking in Kensington Park. But she is unprepared to encounter him as he is now, resting languidly on a horsehair settee. He's even handsomer than she remembers, with a broad forehead, lustrous brown hair, and a wide but shapely mouth. And his glance, well, it's positively unnerving—she comes to a sudden stop and takes Mary's hand for support. A large black dog on a patterned rug opens its eyes to take note of their arrival before going back to sleep.

"Miss Clairmont and Miss Godwin," he says, rising to meet

them. "How... how good of you to come." He speaks softly and with some hesitance, which surprises Clara—she expected a more imposing manner, and for that to be reflected in his speech. He certainly didn't dress to receive them. It appears all he has on is a dressing gown and some sort of loose breeches. And on his feet, slippers that look as if they came from the Far East.

He invites them to sit and asks for refreshments to be brought. "Coffee," he says, "from Sumatra, by way of Amsterdam. It arrived on Friday." He looks at them expectantly and strokes his chin.

"I believe the island of Sumatra was visited by Marco Polo," Mary says. Although her remark is clearly an attempt to help by filling the silence, Clara wants to pinch her for showing off.

"I am an admirer of your father," Lord Byron says. "I consider *Political Justice* to be among the great works of our age. However, I was unaware he had daughters. Certainly not such pretty ones." After a brief pause, he adds, "You may tell him of my regard for his book, but I advise you to keep the rest to yourselves."

Clara feels herself blushing and struggles to find something to say. "We will definitely tell him," she says. "He'll be flattered, I'm sure."

The coffee arrives, and although they exclaim over its flavor, to Clara it tastes no different from any other coffee she's had. Yet she's heard that barely a handful of beans from the Far East can cost more than a London tradesman earns in a month. How wealthy he must be!

Because of the letter she wrote, Clara feels she must ask him about the theatre and begins to do so now. She explains that she has always enjoyed going to plays and has been told she has a lovely voice. But before she can get any further, he dismisses the idea with a wave of his hand: "I can tell it's not your calling. To be successful onstage, a woman must be both beautiful and desperate. Only one won't do." Clara blanches. How is she to respond to that? Fortunately, Mary steps in and says that it doesn't matter what Lord Byron says, Clara's mother would never have it. In response he laughs and the conversation moves on.

He asks them what they do to pass the time, and to Clara's ears, their answers make them sound like imbeciles. Next he asks them about their travels; this goes somewhat better. They describe their trip to Switzerland and he seems genuinely impressed that they undertook their journey at such a tender age.

"As you might expect, the further we got from Paris, the worse the roads became," Clara says. "But the mountains are a wonder. They far exceeded my expectations and I hope to see them again."

"Now that the war is over, we can travel freely," he says, as much to himself as to them. "One forgets how oppressive England is until one experiences life elsewhere. People here talk of liberty, but seldom act on their beliefs."

Clara feels the evening slipping away. Her goal from the first letter she wrote has been to seduce him, to make him fall in love with her, and thereby transform her life. Into what, she doesn't know, but surely it would be extraordinary. It's common knowledge, now confirmed by her own eyes, that he's an extraordinary man. And then it comes to her: She must offer to sing for him. It's the one thing that sets her apart.

Her suggestion seems to please him. And Mary looks happy as well. Maybe she, too, thought the conversation was losing its spark. He takes them to another room, where there is a pianoforte that looks virtually untouched.

"Have you any requests?" she asks.

"Something beautiful and sad," he says. "A song to heal a wounded heart."

Clara wants to ask if he's referring to himself, but she's not brave enough to do so. However, Mary is: "The heart that needs repairing . . . by any chance is it yours?"

He smiles and shakes his head. "No, and it never could be, as mine is made of rock."

She accompanies herself as she sings a song from the *Yorkshire Garland*, which has been quite popular, this season as well as last. When she's done, he compliments her and she feels for the first time as if he's attending to her person and not to some general idea about witless girls he had before they met.

"I am partial to the songs of Greece and Anatolia," he says. "Perhaps you could learn one for me."

"I would happily do so," she says, "but I'm not sure where . . ." And then from the corner of her eye she sees someone standing in the corridor, visible only in silhouette. She gasps and Lord Byron follows her gaze.

"Dr. Polidori," he says. "You ought to announce yourself before you enter a room. This, ladies, is my new physician. He comes to me from Edinburgh, where he learned his trade."

"I apologize for interrupting," the doctor says. "It appears I took a wrong turn." He's tall and Clara thinks he might be handsome, but he remains in the shadows, difficult to see.

"I don't believe you," Byron says. "You were drawn here by the music. No wrong turns were involved. Tell Miss Clairmont what you thought."

"An artful performance," he says. "You play and sing very well."

Clara keeps expecting him to join them, but he continues to hover outside. After an uncomfortable moment, he says, "I shall now return to my room."

When the doctor is gone, Lord Byron says, "An awkward fellow, don't you think? Or perhaps only a bashful one. Hiring him may have been a mistake. I am not unhealthy, but when traveling out of the country having one's own physician is a precaution worth the expense."

"Do you intend to leave the country?" Mary asks.

"As I said before, I may go to Paris. The truth is, I am always intending to leave whatever country I'm in. It's only a matter of when."

Not long thereafter, Clara and Mary prepare to depart. "I've enjoyed our correspondence," Clara says. "I hope you will allow it to continue."

He laughs. "Do I have any choice in the matter?" And for at least the third time since they arrived, Clara can't tell if she's being pursued or mocked. She wants to run out the door as much as she wants to fly into his arms. She looks to Mary for guidance, but Mary's expression is one of concern—no doubt she considers any continuation of this liaison a mistake.

As he walks them to the door, she notices his limp. She knew about it before they came: in fact, she read in some terrible, gossipy newspaper article that he exaggerates it to invite sympathy. But in her eyes he moves with remarkable grace.

Mary

Shelley has exciting news. He's found a publisher for *Alastor*. They have a celebration, the three of them—four counting Willmouse. Shelley has high hopes for his poem and has already begun contacting various publications to ask if they'd consider doing a review. "*Queen Mab* was too much polemic and not enough art," he says. "People didn't know what to make of it. *Alastor* is where my life in poetry begins."

Mary wishes she could say something about Lord Byron. It seems odd to speak of poetry without telling him they've met. But she promised Clara she wouldn't. She still finds it amazing that Clara talked herself into his house. She understands why she finds him intriguing. Yet there is no doubt in her mind that he is also dangerous. As demonstrated by tigers, intriguing and dangerous often go hand in hand.

Later that night, in bed, she breaks her promise —it's too rich a piece of gossip to keep to herself.

"My God!" Shelley says. "Lord Byron? Clara? *She's* pursuing *him*? And you went with her? Well, what happened? What was he like?"

She describes it all as best she can, but he keeps interrupting. "You simply walked up to the door and presented yourselves? I wish you'd told me. I'd have come along to watch."

When she's done, she implores him not to say anything to Clara, but also asks if he has any advice. "What should I tell her? How should she . . . *deal* with him?" she asks.

"Tell her she has my admiration. However, I predict she'll never hear from him again."

Yet before a week passes, Clara comes to her and says, "He has written me, just as I hoped. He wants us to meet."

Mary contemplates her voice, her demeanor. She can't tell if she's boasting or seeking approval. "Would you like me to come with you again?"

"Certainly not. He has invited me to join him at an inn."

"An inn?" Mary is incredulous.

"The location of which I am pledged not to disclose."

Mary begins trying to talk her out of it, but quickly realizes she has no standing—it was Clara, after all, who accompanied her when she and Shelley took their romantic walks at St. Pancras churchyard and when they ran away to France. To tell her she's not old enough to offer herself to a poet would be the height of hypocrisy. She could argue that Shelley's motives were pure while Byron is a known rake, but Clara has already been made deaf by love.

The night Clara goes away, it's snowing, and Mary, still uneasy about the liaison, tries again to convince her it's a mistake.

"This is an action you cannot reverse."

Clara, already on her way out, stops at the bottom of the stairs: "Mary, I am not a child."

"Wait for better weather. Suppose the carriage can't get through . . ."

Yet she can see from Clara's expression that she'd walk there if necessary. Before Mary can say another word, Clara has put up the hood of her cloak and gone out the door.

Sometime later, Mary sits down with Willmouse and begins to nurse. As she gazes into the fire, Shelley speaks.

"Tell me your worries," he says.

"The obvious one. That she will be hurt."

"I expect that's inevitable. We are, after all, talking about love."

"The more prominent a man is, the more damage he can do."

Shelley looks up. "I'm not sure that's true. Do you consider me prominent?"

She can't tell if he's teasing or being ingenuous, so she refuses to answer. After a period of silence, she changes the subject. "I've begun writing a story about my time in Scotland. It features a sailor home from a voyage and the changes that occurred while he was away."

"I expect things will have gone downhill."

"I daresay. The girl he left behind has lost interest in him. While he was absent, she had time to meditate on his flaws. They are greater in number than she realized and most of them can't be repaired."

Clara doesn't return until the following day, and when she does, she goes directly to her room. Some hours later she emerges and takes Mary aside.

"It was wonderful," she tells her. "I tried to imagine . . . I had no idea . . . I was afraid I'd be heard by other lodgers, so loudly did I cry out." She throws herself across the bed in a posture of abandon, her arms cast out to either side.

"How forthright you are," Mary says. "Did he make any promises?"

"Not with words."

"Don't be coarse. You understand my meaning."

"He said I'm remarkable and lovely."

"I'm sure he did. Other than that, what did you talk about?"

She looks puzzled, but then says, "I took one of Shelley's poems with me. We spent some time discussing that."

"You're a clever girl," she replies, partly as sarcasm and partly as genuine praise.

Clara sits up, propping herself on her elbows. "He's soon to leave the country. Maybe I'll go with him."

"Do you expect to be invited?"

"I don't know why I wouldn't be. Not after last night."

Mary finds this frustrating. Everything she'd like to chide Clara for doing, she herself has done.

As an afterthought, Clara says, "His physician asked about you."

"His physician? I thought you met at an inn."

"We did. This morning we returned to his house."

Mary shakes her head. An inn, his house—it appears Clara is capering about London of her own accord, and with abandon. "Well, what did he say?"

"'Where is your companion? Has she taken ill?' So I said, 'Of course not, and it's impertinent of you to ask.' Then Lord Byron chastised him. I don't know why he needs a doctor in the house. I dislike how he hovers about." Then suddenly Clara's eyes brighten. She's forgotten an important part. "Before I left, he showed me the animals he keeps. Were you aware he has such a menagerie? Not only a dog, but a falcon, a small monkey, and an Abyssinian goat!"

Later, after Clara goes to bed, Mary and Shelley talk.

He says, "I can hardly believe it. I was sure he'd turn her away."

"She can be very persistent. And you should know, she took

one of your poems for him to read."

A look of surprise falls across his face. "Did she now? What was his—but I suppose I should ask her myself." He pauses for a moment, as if to order his thoughts. "He's considered quite dissolute, you know. Scandal follows him wherever he goes. Then again, I don't trust the newspapers. There may have been extenuating circumstances. Furthermore, anyone who writes as he does has my respect. Dear Clara, bedded by the author of *Childe Harold's Pilgrimage*. Fancy that."

During the succeeding fortnight, Clara goes off to visit Byron several more times. Perhaps sensing that Mary doesn't approve, she begins sharing her thoughts with Shelley, pulling him outside into the garden and whispering in his ear. Seeing the two of them together so frequently makes Mary slightly jealous, but Willmouse takes up much of her time, and Shelley does love gossip, especially of the literary kind. She has encouraged him to talk sense to Clara, to tell her to guard her feelings and protect her reputation. But it occurs to her that he, too, is smitten by Lord Byron, if only from afar. And for good reason—if Byron were to say a few kind words about Shelley's poetry, editors would be clamoring for his work.

Although Mary finds Byron intriguing, lately it's her father she's been thinking about the most. He hasn't exactly disowned her, but nor has he reached out. When she writes to him, he either replies with the briefest of notes or doesn't reply at all. In one letter she suggested they meet. He wrote back that he was eager to do so but uncommonly busy at present and would contact her when he had time. As bland as his words were, they made her cry. Yet when Fanny comes for a visit, she assures her all is well: "He really is very busy. Give me a little time and I will hatch a plan. Together we will mend up our precious family and become as we were in days gone by."

Yet before any such plan can be put in motion, Clara comes with news: "Lord Byron has left the country—for Switzerland," she exclaims.

Mary is at her desk. "I'm so sorry," she says, turning to meet her gaze.

Clara removes her bonnet and throws it aside. "Don't be. I intend to follow."

Mary hardly knows what to say. How can she possibly do it?

What evidence exists that he wants her to follow?

"You should discuss it with Bysshe. I've already told him about—"

"There's nothing to discuss. My decision has been made. I need only work out the best method of travel."

Mary can tell she's serious. But also frightened. Clara wants desperately to follow Lord Byron, but how can she do it, alone, so young and without means? And then it comes to her. All three of them should go. Why not? What is there to keep them here? It will take no effort at all to convince Shelley. He is always ready to set off for *somewhere else*.

"You cannot make such a long journey by yourself," Mary says.

"I have no choice."

"Our last trip to France was rather unpleasant," Mary says. "If we undertake this one, it may be no better . . ."

Clara's eyes open wide as she begins to understand. "Our last trip to France was delightful. We stayed in many picturesque inns."

"You will have to help with Willmouse. Traveling with a child is no small task."

"It would be my pleasure," Clara says, and then exclaims, "Oh, Mary!" Mary can tell she expected to be told following Byron was impossible. There is little more satisfying than having someone champion your deepest desire.

As Mary predicts, Shelley agrees without a second thought. Indeed, he takes up the idea at once and begins to make it his own: "Let us exit this corrupt society. Let us flee senseless laws and conventions and raise our child in freedom. Let us do as we wish instead of as we are told. Let us above all be brave."

Mary laughs and kisses him. For his delightful exuberance. For his absurd exuberance. She cares not whether their destination is Geneva or Rome or some city she's never heard of. She cares not what obstacles they may face.

"We shall have to hire a coach," she tells him, a touch of firmness in her voice.

"Of course. Were you expecting us to walk?"

In the days that follow, the three of them make preparations, most of them centered on Willmouse's needs—extra clothes, extra blankets, extra everything, and she's already begun to worry about the rats and lice. At times she can't help wishing it were only herself, Shelley, and the baby, going off to live in a cottage by the sea. One with a large window, by which to read and write. And yet she's also caught up in Clara's excitement. She knows exactly how she feels.

"I sent him a letter explaining I'd be as happy to be his friend as to be his lover. I do hope it reaches him," Clara says. Her tone is one of pride, but Mary almost laughs. She hopes the life Clara ends up with is the one she desires.

As they're packing, Clara takes her aside and says she has something important to tell her: "Clara" is no longer adequate. She feels it makes her sound drab. From this time forward she prefers to be called Claire. *Claire Clairmont*. Mistress of Lord Byron. Perhaps one day soon, his wife.

Part Three
Summer 1816

Dr. Polidori

Such a grand coach it is! Byron's manservant, Fletcher, says it was modeled after Napoleon's. Whenever they come upon a village, he is astonished to see crowds have assembled in anticipation of their arrival and line the streets to watch them pass. Some of them wave and cheer, but more often they simply stare. He wonders how much the ordinary Frenchman knows about Lord Byron. Enough, apparently, to lay down his tools and gape.

As they left London only a few weeks after he was hired, he worried about being trapped in a coach with his new employer. Could he sustain a conversation with such a wit? But to his relief, the coach is so large, it has two compartments, one for Lord Byron and one for himself and Fletcher, with a partition in between. Although he was hired as Byron's physician, Polidori's services have yet to be required. Surely the man will say something if he begins to feel ill.

The manner in which they departed was so peculiar, he couldn't help but marvel. At nine o'clock in the evening on a Thursday, Fletcher, a slight, wiry fellow with an expressionless face, informed him that two days hence they'd be embarking on an extended journey and he should prepare accordingly. He tried to imagine where— Cyprus? St. Petersburg? The mysterious lands beyond the Black Sea?—but almost as an afterthought, Fletcher said, "Switzerland." It was something of a letdown. Byron had spoken to him about his travels to Greece with such fondness that Switzerland seemed tame. Nonetheless, he packed his belongings and was waiting by the door the morning they were to leave, a full hour before the specified time.

As he stood and watched, trunk after trunk was loaded onto the coach, with additional items, including the animals he keeps, into a freight wagon to follow. The traveling party was to consist of only the three of them plus the coachmen, but a bystander might well have thought they were packing for fifteen. At last Fletcher directed him to get inside, but before he did so, he overheard the following exchange between Fletcher and Lord Byron:

FLETCHER: Sir, it's not too late. I could still arrange for an agent to sell the contents of the house and forward the proceeds when the transaction is complete.

LORD BYRON: That's not necessary. Leave everything as it is. Don't bother locking up.

FLETCHER: The scavengers will descend like locusts. There will be no order to it.

LORD BYRON: Let them strip it clean.

As the driver cracked his whip and the horses surged into motion, Polidori looked back and saw a clutch of ragged men already approaching the door.

Fletcher, anticipating the question, said, "Everywhere he goes, he sets up house fresh. When we depart for somewhere new, he takes only what's necessary and leaves the rest behind."

He wondered briefly what constitutes the necessary and what constitutes the rest—and how wealthy one must be to have so much of both.

"How do they know when to come," Polidori asked. "The scavengers, I mean?"

Fletcher looked at him meaningfully. "Oh, they have their spies."

Polidori made a mental note of the morning's events so as not to forget anything of importance. Two days prior, having been informed that they were leaving England, he had approached the publisher John Murray with an idea: He would keep a journal about the excursion, with the intention of writing a portrait of Lord Byron, as well as a description of postwar France. He said he planned to do it in secret, without permission, for the simple reason that permission wouldn't be granted. Murray's response? "Bring it to me when you're done and I'll give it a look. But make it entirely about Byron. I don't give a damn about France."

Now, as they move slowly across the French countryside, he sometimes tries coaxing Fletcher to tell him more about Byron, the sorts of things only a valet would know. But Fletcher does as a man in his position ought: keeps his lips sealed. Yet when Fletcher turns the tables and asks Polidori about himself, he obliges. He's not vain but nor does he dislike the sound of his own voice.

"My father came to England from Italy," he says, and begins to narrate his life story—his London childhood, his education at a school in remotest Yorkshire. Before he can get to his medical studies in Edinburgh, Fletcher yawns extravagantly and nods off.

Thus the days pass. They read, they sleep, they speak to one another but seldom about anything of import, and they look out at the green forests and tawny fields. Polidori has set himself the task of reading all of Lord Byron's published work—or at least all the volumes they've brought along. He begins with *English Bards and Scotch Reviewers*, proceeds to *Childe Harold*, and continues on through *The Corsair*. He has no difficulty understanding Byron's popularity. His poems, especially the more recent ones, combine adventure, love, and the exotic in roughly equal parts.

In the evening they stop at whatever inn presents itself. Fletcher claims Lord Byron prefers convenience to luxury. Last night he disappeared after supper, and when Polidori asked Fletcher what became of him, he said, "You saw the chambermaid, the one with the red lips? My bet is he went upstairs and fell upon her like a thunderbolt." So perhaps it is convenience of a certain type he seeks.

Eventually they bear north toward Belgium, aiming to get to Switzerland by way of Bruges and Antwerp. It seems Byron despises the Bourbons, and since they have been placed back on the throne by Napoleon's exile, he wishes to spend as little time as possible in France. It's certainly not the quickest route to Switzerland, but it means they will soon lay eyes on Waterloo, where the Duke of Wellington, with the help of the Prussians, put an end to the emperor's reign.

Well before they reach the famous battlefield, they begin to see signs of war. Caissons sit abandoned; tree trunks, their limbs sheared off by cannon shot, stand like blackened spars; and nearly every house along the road that hasn't been flattened or burned has been converted into a shop to sell relics collected from the field of strife. At one such establishment Byron purchases a cutlass, a brass helmet with a purple plume, and a bloodstained book. Polidori buys a blue officer's scarf. Fletcher, after taking a moment to peruse their purchases, shakes his head.

"Nothing for you?" Polidori asks.

"I prefer not to traffic in what the dead have left behind."

Their next stop is the site of conflict itself. The newspaper accounts called it a charnel house, but the grass has already grown back and here and there a cow stands placidly, as if this were an ordinary pastoral scene. Soon, the men separate, each choosing his own path. Polidori glances over at Byron and decides this is the first time he has seen him whole, his shining brown hair, his expressive mouth, his broad chest, his crooked foot. He looks both invincible and somehow childlike, a pampered rich boy who has the makings of a warrior king.

A bit later Byron approaches from behind and speaks:

"Such carnage. Such a blood feast. My cousin Frederick died here . . . somewhere. I thought perhaps if we visited, I would understand. I thought there might be a monument, a column commemorating the lives lost." He looks out across the battlefield for a moment before continuing. "Maybe it's for the best. As the land was before, so let it be again." Then, as if in confirmation of this, he orders Fletcher to turn his goat out to graze.

Claire, formerly Clara

They left London after Byron but appear to have arrived before him. No one in Geneva has seen him or his party and it's impossible that the Lord Byron she knows would arrive and fail to be seen.

Their journey across France was less arduous than the previous one, owing to the fact that wheels move faster than feet. And Shelley has more money this time so the places they stayed were less grim. It helps that they're older and more experienced—two weeks ago she turned eighteen.

They've taken rooms on the third floor of the Hotel Angleterre, on the shore of the lake and an easy walk to town. Although the English call it Lake Geneva, the Swiss, she has learned, use the French name, Lac Leman. Since the others are asleep, still exhausted from their trip, Claire decides to go for a walk along Lac Leman—she prefers the French.

Downstairs, before she leaves the hotel, she inquires about

Lord Byron. The proprietor, a gruff man with an ornate black mustache, looks up from his account book and shakes his head. His expression is one of annoyance—this isn't the first time she's asked.

"I know nothing of him," he growls. "There are other hotels. Why not check with them?"

"But I was told—"

"I know nothing of him," he repeats and turns back to his work.

Once outside she pauses to consider her choices—left toward the countryside or right toward Geneva—and decides to go into town. The people she passes smile and nod at her, and she tries to picture what it would be like to live here, not for weeks but years: a glorious blue lake to look upon instead of the foul-smelling Thames. She thinks she might make a habit of this, a postprandial stroll to inhale the healthful air. Then suddenly she begins feeling light-headed. Just before they left England, she came to the realization she's pregnant but kept the news to herself. She might have told her mother, but such a hurricane that would have provoked! Now, however, she's finding the secret more and more difficult to keep. So, for a confidante, Mary will have to do. A child. It's not what she intended, but she's not surprised. How will Lord Byron react? If there were a place to sit down, she would, but there's no stoop or bench in sight. Instead, she stands in a doorway and leans against the wall. After a few minutes she recovers but decides to cut her walk short.

Back at the hotel, the sleepers have come awake. Shelley is preparing to go in search of a boat to rent and Mary is dressing.

"Has he arrived?" Mary asks.

"Not yet," she says, and then with false confidence, "but I'm sure he'll get here soon."

"He may have stopped in Paris," Shelley suggests.

She frowns. "I certainly hope not. Why did you even say that? I won't be able to think about anything else for the rest of the day."

She turns to the window and gazes out over the lake. Shelley has often spoken of boating on the lake at Field Place, but this is the first time they've lived in a location where he can take up the practice again. "What sort of craft do you prefer?" Clara asks.

"A modest one. But large enough to have a mast."

"This is quite different from the last time we came . . ."

Shelley shakes his head. "The last time we shouldn't have been so quick to give up."

"We were very wet and very tired," Mary says. "Besides, we were out of money."

"Whereas now we have enough."

While his tone is one of complete confidence, over his shoulder Claire and Mary exchange a dubious glance. In truth, she's never sure what Shelley's financial situation is. Every remark he makes casts it in a different light.

When Shelley is gone to find his boat, Claire takes Willmouse in her arms and begins to talk to Mary as she carries him about the room.

"I shan't be having breakfast," she says. "I'm not feeling well."

"Travel can cause dyspepsia. At least it does so in me."

"It's not that. I think I may . . . for a few weeks now . . ." She looks at Mary and then at the floor.

"You and Byron," Mary says.

"I believe so. In fact I'm certain. I've been wanting to tell you since we left England."

Mary sits down and sighs. "Well. This adds significance to his arrival."

Suddenly, the true weight of the situation descends upon her. She shifts Willmouse from one arm to the other and grimaces before she speaks. "Oh, Mary, you must help me. I don't expect he'll approve. Nor am I prepared to care for a child alone. I'm frightened. What shall I do?"

When her condition first became apparent, she placed the facts of it in a locked room in her mind. Then they started their trip and there were many other things to think about. Dear Mary. Sometimes they find themselves at odds, but she needs her now as never before.

"Of course you'll tell Lord Byron the minute he arrives. And there's no reason Shelley shouldn't know. Other than that, there's little you can do but wait. It's not so bad. I shall guide you through."

As Mary continues speaking, Willmouse begins to squirm. "Down!" he says, but when Claire sets him on the rug, he reaches up for her again.

"Suppose I tell him and he takes no pleasure in it?" she says.

"When I went with you to see him, I was surprised to find him less arrogant than I had been led to expect—by the newspapers, I mean. Don't judge him prematurely. There's no telling how he'll react."

"My mother will be outraged. She'll place all the blame on me."

Mary takes Willmouse from her and immediately he calms. Together, they all stand at the window and look out at the sunlit lake.

"You and I have chosen to do what we must," Mary says. "I'm sure some will declare we have thrown ourselves away, but this morning I feel as happy as a new-fledged bird. I hardly care what twig I fly to."

Claire loves Mary's optimism and would like to share in it, but Mary is an uncommon creature. Perhaps it comes with being so intelligent. Or perhaps it's merely a pose. She hopes when Byron arrives, she will feel a similar happiness. If only he would arrive.

Shelley

He finds himself an excellent little boat, a dozen feet long with a center mast and sail. He thinks it's called a pram, or perhaps a wherry, but wishes it were a Yorkshire Billy-boy, merely so he could use the name.

Tying it at a dilapidated dock near the hotel, he runs inside and up the stairs to fetch some passengers—Mary, Claire, Willmouse, or all three of them, it doesn't matter as long as he has someone to take for a sail. In the end only Mary comes, leaving Willmouse with Claire.

"By what right do you call yourself a sailor?" Mary teases as she climbs aboard. The hull rocks and the sail snaps in the breeze.

"Prepare to be astonished," he says and shoves the boat away from the shore.

"Prepare to be drowned, more like."

He spends the next few minutes arranging things, glancing now and then at Mary in the prow, giving her a wink. The truth is he has no experience sailing on bodies of water as large as this, but he loves the idea of it, of being able to skim ahead of the wind not for minutes but for hours or even days. As they get farther from shore, the breeze increases and the sails fill. The boat tilts with the wind and Mary gasps, afraid it's about to heel over. He shakes his head and laughs.

"I was building boats and putting them on the water before I entered school. When people asked me what I wished to be when I grew up, I said a sailor or a salamander—the first for the joy of it and the second because they are amphibious and have beautiful stripes."

He needs to adjust the sail, but first he pauses to look at her. There she is in a yellow dress, her hair surrounding her face like a shining copper wreath, and he thinks she's more beautiful at this moment than she's ever been. More beautiful than any woman he's ever known.

Soon they are a good distance from the hotel. The mountains become more visible, peak beyond peak beyond peak, their tops white, their flanks jagged, the spaces between them lost in shadow. Something about the sun and the water and the grandeur of a sail stretched tight by the wind makes him feel fully free, no longer encumbered by his father, by Godwin, by London, by Harriet, poor dear that she is, by Hogg, poor dear that *he* is, and even by himself. Free of all the hindrances and impediments and obstructions that prevent his thoughts from finding their true form.

"Would you like me to recite something?" he shouts.

"I would prefer you didn't. I'm enjoying the silence. The sound of the water."

"Do you think he's really coming?"

"Who? Byron? I know nothing of him or his plans."

"Haven't you any conjecture to offer? Maybe he heard she was going to be here and changed his mind."

"Don't be unpleasant."

"It's just—there are so many stories about him."

"She'll be devastated if he doesn't come."

Far up the lake they can see clouds, dark and swirling, a rainstorm in the making. Yet overhead the sun still shines. He finds speculating about Byron and Claire fascinating. One party he knows quite well and one he knows only by way of gossip. From his perspective, it is as if they are awaiting the arrival of a character from a novel, one with whom an ordinary flesh-and-blood girl is deeply in love.

"I want us to settle down and work," Mary says, spoiling his reverie. "Now that we have a comfortable place to stay."

He dips his hand over the side and tosses some water at her. "You are a taskmaster. But first I want to savor our freedom. The weeks before we left were unbearable."

"My poor father was a bit deranged, I'll grant you. I'm sorry he treated you poorly."

"You needn't apologize for him. I remain a great admirer of William Godwin. I take some responsibility for his vexation. I promised him more money than I could provide."

The wind changes and he adjusts the trim. The lake is lovely, Geneva is picturesque, the mountains are magnificent, and it appears the storm clouds are dispersing. But he is so ferociously in love with Mary, any place, any weather, will do.

"We oughtn't to leave Willmouse with Claire for so long," she says. "I don't like to take advantage."

"We'll hire a governess. A competent Swiss girl who will look after our child and generally run our lives." Then, one hand on each gunwale, he pushes himself to his feet. As he does so, he says, "I now intend to kiss you and not only that. I will do my best to avoid turning us over as I proceed."

Thus, despite Mary's concerns about Claire, they don't reach land until dark.

Mary

Two days later, Willmouse wakes her up at dawn. Maybe he's roused by a strange sound, maybe by the unfamiliar coloring of the sky outside. So as not to disturb the others, she decides to take him for a walk.

She kisses sleeping Shelley on the forehead and they tiptoe down the stairs and out into the gray morning. When they reach the edge of the lake, she puts his toes in the water. He squeals and claps his hands and she can't help but laugh. Back at the hotel a light comes on in the kitchen, but the other windows remain dark. Then she realizes something is wrong. Shelley's boat isn't where he left it. Someone must have taken it during the night. What a dastardly thing to do. Before she can go back inside and report the theft, something far out on the water catches her eye.

"Look," she says to Willmouse and points to the distant sail, a white triangle reflecting the first rays of the morning sun. "I'd say it was your father, but we left him in bed."

Is it coming toward her or sailing away? She puts up a hand to shade her eyes. Definitely toward. The boat has two occupants, one dressed in black and the other in maroon. Then suddenly it occurs to her who it is: Lord Byron and a companion, perhaps his physician, sailing directly at them, only a few minutes from shore.

"Oh my!" she says and rushes back to the hotel, clutching Willmouse to her breast and taking care not to stumble and fall.

She climbs the stairs and bursts into the room to wake Shelley and then next door to roust Claire. "He's here, get up, Lord Byron has arrived!" she cries, and hurries back down to the lake. Breathing hard, she stands with Willmouse in her arms and watches the vessel approach. She's surprised by how excited she is. What should she say? Perhaps, *Welcome to Geneva.* Perhaps, *I hope you enjoyed the use of our boat.* Or perhaps, most accurately, *My sister Claire will be so relieved.*

Seconds later she hears the door of the hotel slam behind her and glances back to see Shelley and Claire running down the slope toward the water, both of them laughing like children, Claire's face aglow with happiness. Shelley looks as though he put on whatever clothing was at hand, while Claire has managed to make herself look pretty with only seconds to accomplish the task. "I knew he'd come!" she exclaims.

Byron appears smaller than Mary remembers, still broad-shouldered, but not as tall. Yet his clothes fulfill her expectations: a maroon brocade coat entirely unfit for boating and a shirt with an extravagant lace collar and silk cravat. The physician—what was his name?—looks uneasy, his eyes darting about as if searching for a means of escape.

"You are very bad," Claire says as the boat's prow meets the gravel bank. "I feared you had decided not to come."

"How could I possibly do that, knowing you'd be here?"

Knowing you'd be here? Is he improvising in the moment, or was he somehow informed in advance? Or did he simply assume that a girl as infatuated as Claire would find a way to come?

"It's awfully early for a sail," Mary says.

"Not early at all," Byron replies, stepping onto land. "We arrived after midnight and, upon seeing this thing moored in such a convenient spot, put it to use. We've been on the lake all night admiring the stars." He makes no effort to secure the boat, but leaves that to the doctor, who completes the task with Shelley's help.

Introductions follow. She is reminded of Dr. Polidori's name and finds it amusing when Byron's eyes betray a moment of puzzlement as Clara calls herself Claire. Shaking Shelley's hand, Byron says he knows his work. At first Mary wonders how that could possibly be, but then she recalls Claire's use of one of Shelley's poems as an aid to conversation the night she fell into his bed. She leans toward Claire, who is positively aglow, and whispers into her ear, "He's here at last." Claire nods, her eyes glistening with tears of joy.

As they walk to the hotel, Lord Byron asks Shelley about the accommodations. Shelley tells him they are acceptable but that the proprietor has complained they're too loud. "I blame young Willmouse," he says, but Mary corrects him:

"It's not Willmouse; it's you. Your laugh and the way you run up and down the stairs in the middle of the night."

"I shall give him more to complain about," Byron says. "I keep late hours as well."

Claire hangs back and Mary motions to her to say something, anything, but she has been struck mute.

As they prepare to part, Byron turns to Shelley and says, "I want you to join me at supper."

He looks to Mary. "Have we any plans?"

"None whatsoever," she says.

When Byron and Polidori are gone, Claire seizes her hand and holds it tight: "He looks very well, don't you think?"

"I suppose he does. And if he takes ill, he has that peculiar fellow to attend to him."

"You ought not to denigrate the doctor," Claire says. "Should Willmouse get the croup, you'll be pleased he's nearby."

"Let us have breakfast," Shelley says. "We can gossip about them while we eat."

And so they do. Now that Shelley has laid eyes on Byron and made his acquaintance, his interest seems to have increased fivefold. He says, "Do you think he will stay long?" and, "I like him already," and "He is an amusing conversationalist, or so I've heard."

Claire sighs. "There's no end to what he can do."

"I hope you don't gush in his presence," Mary says. "It can make you sound needful. Or worse, insincere."

They don't see Lord Byron and the doctor for the rest of the day. Mary bathes Willmouse and Shelley writes letters, but Claire can't sit still. She paces, perches for a moment on the edge of a chair, paces again, goes outside to walk along the lake and is back only minutes later, looking for something to do.

"Get a book," Mary says. "Maybe you can read."

"What should I wear?"

"For supper? I didn't hear him invite you. But perhaps I misunderstood."

Claire looks at her as if she's daft. "Of course he wants me at supper. What a ridiculous thought."

Sometime later Lord Byron's valet comes down and informs Shelley that supper will be served in his lordship's room. He makes no mention of Claire.

Mary watches her face. For a moment she looks stunned. Then her eyes brighten and she shrugs. "Let the poets go off together. I'll have him to myself tomorrow. I'm feeling tired and shall proceed to bed."

Mary wants to protect Claire. No doubt the best way would have been to keep her from meeting Byron in the beginning or at least keep her out of his bed. Now, however, she's torn between wanting Claire to be successful in her romantic quest and hoping it will be brief and not result in too much pain. Yet that's too optimistic— there's nothing brief about a child.

In the book Mary's mother wrote, women are advised that passion is fleeting while friendship lasts. Between herself and Shelley both exist, but she fears Lord Byron has little interest in allowing a woman to be his friend.

Dr. Polidori

Lord Byron is closemouthed about his personal affairs. Miss Clairmont was a frequent visitor during the last days in London, but it was never mentioned that she'd be waiting for him here. On the jetty this morning she looked as though she wished she could leap into his embrace. As for Miss Godwin, she seems to have become Mrs. Shelley, but that, too, went unexplained.

After a nap, Fletcher tells him to dress for supper. When he's ready, he knocks on Lord Byron's door and is invited in. Polidori continues to be uncertain about his role. If he were merely an employee, he would take his meals on his own, as Fletcher does. If he were a friend or colleague, he would take his meals with Lord Byron but not be ordered about.

In any event, he is looking forward to supper with Mr. Shelley. Byron tells him Shelley is a proponent of a vegetable diet. And of free love.

"What are you suggesting?" Polidori asks, before Shelley arrives.

"That he eats no meat."

"Not that. The other."

"He considers matrimony obsolete. Men and women should cohabit as they see fit."

"How do you know this?" he asks.

"It's in something he wrote."

"Are you saying he and Mrs. Shelley and Miss Clairmont . . . but they are sisters, are they not?"

"I don't believe they are. If you wish to be scandalized, make sure your facts are correct."

He can't tell if Byron is being serious or not. Two women, whether at the same time or on alternating nights, is as fascinating as it is shocking. He has enough difficulty convincing one woman to take him to her bed. Perhaps his lordship is having him on. It wouldn't be the first time Byron amused himself by proffering erroneous facts.

The meal is brought to the dining room of Byron's large suite. There, the three of them sit at a small table, as at a café, eating pigeon and a salad of dandelion greens. Shelley asks Byron about his journey and Byron replies in unexpected detail. Polidori watches Shelley closely, and indeed, he eats only the greens. When Byron notices him looking, he breaks off his description of their travels and asks Shelley to explain.

"Dr. Polidori is interested in your eating habits. In why you shun flesh."

Shelley looks up from his plate. "All animals are sentient beings and each is an individual unto itself. I would no more eat this bird than you would eat your dog."

"Are you certain you are not simply doing it as a provocation?" Byron says. "Look at me. I have great respect for animals." With his knife he gestures toward the monkey in a cage in a corner of the room. "And yet I eat them without qualms."

"Provocation?" Shelley replies, pointing to his plate. "This bird is the provocation. It ought to be in flight."

In response, Byron stabs his fork into Shelley's pigeon and takes it for himself. Polidori fears he'll be offended; he has every right to be. Instead, Shelley erupts into high-pitched laughter. Byron laughs, too, although his is deep and as resonant as a bell. Not to be left out, Polidori begins to laugh but feels uncomfortable doing so.

He manages to get through the remainder of supper without saying a word. Later, however, over port—which Shelley declines—they begin discussing literature and Lord Byron forces him to join in.

"Polidori is a dramatist," he says. "Tell Mr. Shelley about your work."

He wasn't expecting this. In truth, he's surprised Byron even knows about his writing. When he interviewed for the position, he mentioned that he was composing a play, but only in passing. At the time he didn't even think the remark had been heard.

"I don't know what to say. Should I fetch something to read?"

"Please do," Lord Byron says.

He hurries to his room and selects his most recent piece, a tragedy about a forgotten prince of Portugal. This is really quite exciting—suppose Lord Byron likes it? He has connections to Drury Lane Theatre and might help him get it produced. Yet no sooner has he placed it on the table than things begin to go badly. Byron snatches it up, opens to a random page, and starts to read. Within seconds he has managed to locate one of his least graceful lines:

"*'Halt! Who approaches from the unguent night?'* Unguent? My dear Polidori, what sort of word is that?"

"It means, well, glue-like. I thought—"

Byron turns to Shelley: "How would you respond to a person who hailed you in such a manner?"

"It does seem a bit . . . out of place. However, I hate to comment on an unfinished draft."

But Byron won't leave it alone. "Look here, on the next page," he says and proceeds to point out other flaws. Polidori feels his face get hot, and when he reaches across the table in an effort to reclaim the manuscript, Byron pulls it away—and begins to read again.

In the end it's Shelley who intervenes: "Return the poor fellow his drama. You have successfully dissuaded me from ever allowing you to read any of my writing. Better I should feed it to the fire."

Later that night, back in his room, Polidori opens his journal. When he met with the publisher and proposed to write a book about his time with Lord Byron, he pictured an amusing portrait that might provide a glimpse of the poet at work. But thus far he's found little amusing to relate. He makes a few desultory notes about supper, leaving out the part where his play was ransacked. Then he closes the journal and hides it at the bottom of his bag.

Although it's well past his customary bedtime, he remains wide awake. He decides to continue his reading of Lord Byron's poetry. Currently, he's in the middle of the *The Giaour*, which seems similar to *The Corsair*. He opens the book to where he left off and has read for perhaps half an hour when he comes upon some lines that cause him to gasp:

> *Hers is the loveliness in death,*
> *That parts not quite with parting breath;*
> *But beauty with that fearful bloom,*
> *That hue which haunts it to the tomb,*
> *Expression's last receding ray,*
> *A gilded halo hovering round decay . . .*

Polidori knows precisely what he's talking about. He's seen it with his own eyes. *A gilded halo hovering round decay.* The sublime beauty of the recently entombed.

Claire

In the room directly below Polidori's, Claire lies in bed and listens to the wind. In her mind's eye, she sees the towering peaks surrounding them. She was able to contain her emotions in the presence of the others, but now she begins to weep. They've been apart for weeks and yet he said scarcely a word to her. Nor did he embrace her. Their eyes met for only a moment before he glanced away. He doesn't know she's carrying his child. She came all this way only for him.

She dries her tears. He was probably tired. After all, they'd been out on the lake all night. How original he is. If she's going to be in love with someone like that, she can't expect him to behave as others do. It's she who needs to change, not him. When she's finally alone with him, he'll show his true feelings. He couldn't resist her before and he won't be able to now.

Every day she thinks about her child. Every hour. Now that Mary knows, she wants to tell Shelley as well, perhaps tomorrow. That will be easy enough. But how will she give the news to Byron? He has a child already, a daughter by his estranged wife, Annabella, but he never talks about her. In fact, the only reason she knows about the child is because it's been in the papers. Everything about him is in the papers eventually—perhaps one day she will as well.

Claire falls asleep thinking about being a mother. She will be a better mother than Mary. There's nothing wrong with how Mary treats Willmouse, but she will be more attentive. She suspects that if a choice was ever required, Mary would select Shelley over her son. When Mary and Shelley are together, they notice nothing but one another. What must it be like to be the object of such adoration? Claire isn't sure she could stand being looked at in that way, even by Byron. It would make her feel responsible for his happiness. Caring for a child will be responsibility enough.

In the morning she takes her time getting dressed. Today is important. She wishes Byron hadn't brought Polidori with him.

What if the peculiar doctor gets in the way? Lord Byron enjoys having people around him, which makes intimacy difficult. He once told her that, on the whole, he doesn't like the company of women except in bed. They were in bed when he said it. Although he meant it in jest, there can be truth in jesting. He started to explain himself, but she stopped him with a kiss.

Now there's a knock at her door. It's Mary; she enters and surveys the room. "Why are you taking so long? The morning is half over," she says.

"I'm almost ready. Is he awake? Have you seen him?"

"Not yet. He's still in bed, I expect. But Dr. Polidori has been up for hours. He joined me at breakfast and told me about his studies. If you have any maladies, he will be happy to look into them. He claims to have much book knowledge but little practical experience at his craft."

"I don't believe Byron likes him. I'm not sure why he hired him."

"I think the doctor has the same question. He seems exceedingly ill at ease."

"In any event, he doesn't interest me. As you know, I have only one interest, which I shall examine, physician-like, today."

Mary cocks an eyebrow in her direction. She uses her eyebrows for expressive purposes better than anyone Claire knows.

"Please leave so I may finish getting dressed," Claire says.

Today she wears green. Even the ribbons in her hair. Although it's not always possible, she tries to have matching ribbons for every dress she owns. Outside, the sun is behind clouds and the sky is gray. The water is completely flat, completely still. It looks as if it could be walked upon, like a great expanse of slate.

She'd like to go straight to his room, but considering how she was received yesterday, she's not sure she should. Instead, she goes to Shelley for advice, finding him in the garden behind the hotel, bent over a book. She has to say his name three times before he lifts his eyes from the page.

"May I sit with you?" she asks.

"Of course." He blinks his eyes. He reminds her of a fox emerging from his den.

"Did you enjoy your evening?"

"Quite. He's an exceptional fellow. But you know that better than I."

"Did he speak about me?"

His eyes dart to the right. Shelley is a terrible liar, so she doesn't even give him the chance. "Don't answer," she says. "I'll see him soon enough."

"What do you make of his physician?" Shelley asks.

"Mary and I were just discussing him. Did he behave badly?"

"He didn't appear to enjoy himself. I don't think Byron likes him."

"That's exactly what I said."

Suddenly, she decides this is the time to tell Shelley about the baby. Doing so could serve as a rehearsal for telling Byron. She knows Shelley won't think less of her, so why not?

"I have a secret," she says.

"About Dr. Polidori?"

"No, silly, about myself." There is a bench facing his, so she sits down and smooths her skirts.

"Let me guess."

Perhaps Mary told him already. "I'll give you three tries," she says.

"You had marmalade on your bread this morning."

"I did not. I ate no breakfast at all."

"You dreamed you were walking through a forest when you came upon a small house. Through the window you saw—"

"No more guesses. You have lost the bet. This is my secret: Lord Byron is the father of my child."

He looks up. Their eyes meet, but she can't hold his gaze. "That was going to be my next guess."

"Now you understand why I've been so anxious to see him."

"He has yet to be informed?"

She nods. "I intend to tell him today."

"Maybe Mary should go with you," he says, looking troubled. She knows he's trying to be helpful but finds it annoying that he thinks she can't manage on her own.

"Why would I do that?" she says.

After she leaves Shelley, she walks along the lake. She should have eaten breakfast. At a shop she buys half a loaf of bread and then continues walking, tearing off piece after piece and stuffing them into her mouth. It's as if she hasn't eaten in days. She hopes no one is watching her. If only she had some strawberries as well.

When she finally goes to Byron's room, it's early afternoon. He's slept long enough. He probably had too much wine last night. Yet when he answers the door, he's fully dressed and looks as if he's been up for hours.

She comes at him so quickly and with such passionate intent, he can scarcely keep his balance. She kisses him and pushes him back onto the bed and tears at his shirt. He says, "My God, what are you doing?" and then laughs. She kisses his chest and unfastens his trousers and begins the process of removing her own garments; he recovers his senses enough to help. He nips at her throat and unlaces her stays. Only when she is naked and in his bed does her anxiety begin to wane. Part of her was convinced this would never happen again.

As he is the only man she has ever experienced in this way, she wonders how he is different from others and how the same. He has a birthmark on his shoulder and her eye is drawn to it. He calls her his pet, which she likes, and also his goddess, which sounds insincere. At a certain point he seems to forget exactly who she is but she's not dismayed. She once heard her mother tell a friend that while in the throes of passion, men care about the woman less than the act.

When they're finished, he gets up and begins to dress, while she remains in bed.

"I knew you would follow me here," she says.

He laughs. "*Me* follow *you*? I'm certain it was the other way round."

"You cannot resist me."

"Is that what you think? Tell me, what is it that sets you apart from others of your sex?"

She hadn't expected him to provide such an ideal platform on which to set her news. But now that it's there, she uses it: "My sweet, I am carrying your child."

He is silent for a time. Apparently, there are occasions when even Lord Byron can't be glib. At last he says, "I suspected as much.

However, do not assume I've made any sort of pledge."

She was prepared for such a statement. Still, she didn't expect it to feel so sharp. She takes care to keep her face impassive and, as she readies herself to speak, to keep the emotion out of her voice.

"I shall assume nothing," she says.

Shelley

They boat almost nightly, rowing out in the gloaming and returning after dark. Sometimes it's he and Mary, sometimes Claire as well, and sometimes he and Lord Byron—or LB, as they've taken to calling him. Mary coined it and he doesn't seem to mind. Dr. Polidori prefers not to boat. Instead, he spends his evenings reading or going into Geneva to call on other physicians, which is just as well. If Polidori came along, he would make LB impatient, LB would make a cutting remark, and Polidori would be left sitting there, trapped in the boat with his detractor, a look of anguish on his face.

When it's only Shelley and Byron in the boat, they talk about philosophy and poetry and politics and many other things, but seldom about women and love. In this respect LB is different from Peacock and Hogg. With them, most discussions, no matter where they begin, end up being about which girl they intend to woo, why they find her appealing, and what methods they expect to use once the wooing begins. Whereas, with LB, women are acquired so easily, no planning or analysis is required. Shelley pities Claire. She hoped to lay claim to a lord, but it's clear he won't be claimed, nor even allow himself to be distracted, by a vivacious though still rather ordinary girl of eighteen.

Tonight the wind blows them to the far side of the lake, and as they row back across, pulling with all their strength, Shelley finds himself being accused of having excessively Utopian ideas.

"Man cannot be perfected," LB says. "He can be beautiful and terrible and of many parts, but he shall never be as you wish him to be. Perfection is available only to those who can step out of time. Which mankind cannot."

"What makes you think I consider man perfectible? When have I said such a thing?"

"You have written it."

"In which of my poems? In which lines?"

"You need me to point them out? I shall begin with *Queen Mab* ..."

To have a poet of LB's prowess discuss his work is gratifying. What writer wouldn't want a critic of such intelligence and wit? It helps that LB is a different sort of poet from himself, less overtly philosophical and definitely more amusing. This fact allows them to exchange opinions without becoming competitive. Yesterday, Byron told him to ignore the fact that *Alastor* has gone unreviewed. He said his own success is due largely to luck and the only thing of value is the work itself.

When LB is done proving *Queen Mab* and *Alastor* are full of Utopian sentiments, Shelley shares some ideas from the poem he's currently writing to see how Byron responds.

"Suppose beauty is not in things but exists instead as a spirit that comes and goes?"

"Comes and goes? In what manner? As a sort of ghost?"

"No, as a result of human thought. As an aspect of the mind."

For a time, Byron draws in his oars and does not speak. There is only the sound of water plashing against wood. At last he says, "If beauty is not of this world, then what use is it?"

Earlier in the day, after observing them in conversation, Mary said, "It's as if you've been friends for years. There's no awkwardness between you." To which Shelley replied, "Poetry is our common language. No matter what I say, he seems to understand."

He considered the remark unexceptional, but she looked stricken. "Is not the same true of me?"

"Need you ask?" he replied, and then wished he'd refrained from speaking.

No good can come of comparing men and women, wives and friends. Doing so results in jealousy and he wants none of that. People say he believes in "free love" as if it were all he cares about, but one reason he finds the idea appealing is because if love were free, it would not consume so much time and effort. It would simply exist.

When at last they are close to land, Byron stands in the prow of the boat and sings an Albanian song. Loudly and off-key.

"What's it about?" Shelley asks.

"I haven't the faintest idea. I speak no Albanian. I simply memorized the sounds."

As they secure the boat to the dock and climb out, Shelley questions him about Claire. Perhaps it's not the best time, but there may be no best time for a topic such as this.

"What do you intend to do about her?"

"Don't worry, I'll provide for the child when the time comes."

So he knows. He'd meant to come at the matter obliquely, to feel Byron out. This makes it easier. They can both be direct.

"I'm sure you will. But she has expectations—hopes—which extend beyond the child's welfare. She's—"

"I can see that, and I'm sorry I allowed them to take shape. But when a girl of such youth and beauty insists on having me, I am unable to resist. I'm sure you understand."

It's true, he does understand, but he also pities poor Claire and the child. She'll have her baby and then Byron will pay her off and never see either of them again.

"What's happened has happened," Shelley says, trying a different tack. "It's her future I worry about."

"As I said, I'll take responsibility for the child. But she is responsible for herself."

Back at the hotel, he tries to enter the room quietly so as not to awaken Mary, but her eyes come open at the sound of the closing door. He sits on the bed beside her and says, "I've just come from speaking with LB. He's a bit hard-hearted about Claire."

She lifts her head from the pillow, says, "What did you expect?" and falls instantly back to sleep. He admires her honesty. She keeps him from thinking the world is more malleable than it actually is.

In the morning, Mary reminds him of his promise to find someone to assist with Willmouse, so he asks the hotel cook if he knows a nursemaid they might hire. The cook names a girl who often brings vegetables to sell; he'll send her up when she arrives.

As soon as they meet her, they can tell she'll be ideal. She has a cheerful but earnest demeanor, speaks excellent English, and says when Willmouse is a little older, she'll teach him German and French. After the terms have been agreed upon and the girl, whose name is Elise, has departed, Mary says, "I feel so relieved."

The intensity of her tone brings him up short. "I was unaware you were in distress."

"I'd begun to worry about how I could care for Willmouse and still have time to write. As you know, I have aspirations of my own. At last I shall have some help."

About her aspirations, he knows and doesn't know. She fills pages with her looping script but seldom shows them to him. In her reading, she asks him to be her guide but she reads as much as he does and her insights are always keen. When they were still in London, he happened upon a list of the books she'd read in the past year. Among them were *Gulliver's Travels*, a book of Locke's essays, *Castle Rackrent* by Maria Edgeworth, two volumes of Gibbon, Defoe on the plague, Labaume's history of the Russian war, Fox's history of James II, and Hume's essays. To name fewer than a third.

"Then I, too, am relieved," he says. "If the expectations of marriage are confining, how much more so are those that come with raising a child."

Mary

She has a dream about Fanny and wakes up missing her. She can imagine too vividly and too painfully the moment when Fanny discovered they'd gone off again and left her behind. Not that Fanny would have gone with them if invited. She couldn't have brought herself to hurt Father. That's one concern Mary doesn't have—she's reasonably certain she's causing her parents no more pain by being here than she would if she were back on Skinner Street. Although she has no doubt her father loves her, takes pride in her, wishes her joy, she also has no doubt that in her case, he doesn't mind experiencing those feelings from a distance. They can love one another from afar.

Now that Lord Byron has been at the hotel for nearly a fortnight, he wants a better place to live. After some discussion, she and Shelley decide to follow suit. The hotel is expensive and they need more room. She would prefer a place with a garden while LB no doubt wants something grand—a place that will cause people to stop and say, with a measure of awe in their voices, "That is where the scandalous Lord Byron lives." It seems to her LB is at once disdainful of fame and a cultivator of it. He wants people to be desperate to meet him so that when they do—assuming they have such good fortune—he can send his man Fletcher to run them off.

Yet if they relocate, where will Claire reside? Will she remain with them or will she persuade LB to take her in? Mary has learned not to underestimate her. One thing is certain: If she's successful and ends up as Lady Byron, she'll finally stop changing her name.

When they inform the hotel's owner of their plans, he's pleased to see them go. He doesn't like them coming in at all hours and doesn't like the noise they make. And although he's never said so, he probably questions their morals. She can't blame him—what must the other guests think?

They secure the services of a property agent, a Herr Meinhardt, who takes them to see three houses in one day—a rambling two-family dwelling, half of which is inhabited by an old man whose wife has recently died; a tall, thin house with a crumbling foundation that looks as if it's about to topple over; and a low, dark hovel so far from the lake that Shelley's boating would have to cease. When they're done, Herr Meinhardt tells them there's nothing else to be had.

"Then perhaps the tall one," Shelley says. "I shouldn't think it will collapse anytime soon."

Mary disagrees. "Please keep looking," she says. "There must be something better." And then to Shelley, in a whisper only he can hear, "He thinks because we're English, he can give us what no one else wants."

Byron and Polidori have better luck—as tends to happen if one has unlimited funds. When she and Shelley encounter them on their way back to the hotel, Polidori gestures excitedly in the direction of a large yellow villa across the lake. Even from this distance Mary can tell it's luxurious, exactly the sort of place LB would select.

She thinks Polidori may be attracted to her. He keeps casting glances in her direction and making vaguely hopeful remarks: "What, my dear lady, are your plans for the day?" or, "I intend to go walking beside the lake. Would anyone care to join me?" Sometimes she turns and finds him standing right beside her. It's bad manners to sneak up on a person; one ought to announce one's approach, if only with a cough.

"Maybe we should try the other side of the lake," Mary says as they look across the water toward Byron's villa. "Herr Meinhardt neglected to show us anything there."

To be honest, all they need is a bed, a table on which to write, a place to put their books, and a carpet upon which Willmouse can roll and creep. She has the feeling that as long as the three of them are together—and that shall be forever—they will be moving from place to place. Still, a garden would be nice. With a bench and patch of grass and a pear tree that blossoms in the spring. Willmouse delights in nature and she in turn relishes his delight.

She hopes her request for help with Willmouse hasn't made her look selfish in Shelley's eyes. Surely he understands how much she adores her child. Before Willmouse was born, she wondered, as perhaps all mothers do, if her love for him would arrive all at once or grow over time. Now she would say it's both—her love was whole and complete at his birth, yet it increases by the day.

That same afternoon several men in Byron's employ arrive with a new boat—a two-masted vessel much larger than Shelley's—and begin loading his things. Crates and cases and trunks, one after the other, until there's scarcely room for the men to sit. When they finally embark, the hull is so low in the water, Mary is left to wonder what riches, literary and otherwise, would be lost were it to sink. Near the prow she can see Byron's falcon, tethered to its perch.

Three days later Herr Meinhardt shows up to tell them he's found the perfect place on the other side of the lake.

"Is it near Lord Byron's house?" she asks.

"Most assuredly," he says. "The Villa Diodati"—calling LB's yellow mansion by its proper name—"is but ten minutes away by foot."

Claire, who has come down the stairs to listen, claps her hands. "That's wonderful. How soon can we move?"

Shelley doesn't look as pleased. "At first I thought it would be good to live near Byron," he says. "Now I think I might prefer a little distance between us. The man likes to socialize too much."

"Are you certain it isn't me you'd like to keep at a distance from him?" Claire asks. "Because if it is, you ought not to bother. I plan to visit him daily, even if we live miles away."

175

Shelley looks defeated and for a moment Mary considers intervening. She knows Shelley cares about Claire's welfare and doesn't want them to quarrel. Perhaps she will say something later. It's obvious they are moving to the house Herr Meinhardt has found for them, and equally obvious Claire will do as she pleases.

Since Mary remains silent, Shelley responds to Claire's remark: "Visit him if you must, but know one thing: Lord Byron is an opportunist. A charming, rather brilliant one, but an opportunist nonetheless."

"I see," says Claire. "A well-mannered devil . . . exactly my type."

Dr. Polidori

He now understands a number of things he found puzzling when they first arrived. Although Mr. Shelley and Mrs. Shelley have a child, they are not husband and wife. Mrs. Shelley is, in fact, Miss Mary Godwin, the daughter of two philosophers, revered in some quarters but known to be radicals as well. Miss Clairmont is in love with Lord Byron and (this last item he's not entirely certain about) may be carrying his child. Most of these facts he learned by eavesdropping, a practice at which he excels.

Were he to read about his traveling companions in the press, he would shake his head in disapproval. He is no prig, but there are limits. Yet now that he finds himself in daily contact with them, he can see they are not markedly different from other young people he knows: They do what pleases them to the extent of their opportunity and means; they boast and make extravagant claims and then feel foolish the following day; they consider the future boundless; they have had little contact with death, so they fear it not.

He, on the other hand, has had numerous encounters with death. Encounters that would cause the others to blanch. One evening, prompted by his continued reading of Lord Byron's poetry, his thoughts return to his time as a student in Edinburgh, and to certain events he has vowed never to disclose:

The professor is extracting a gall bladder. Some stand and some are seated but all lean in for a better view. Today the sub-

ject under discussion is the cystic and hepatic bile. Yesterday it was the peritoneum and tomorrow they'll explore the gut. His feet are freezing and so are his ears. Dissections are done only in winter; if the theatre isn't cold, putrefaction sets in.

When the demonstration is over, he repairs to his favorite tavern and buys himself a drink. If he had a little extra money, he'd take one of the girls upstairs. Since he does not, when one approaches, no matter how appealing, he says, "Sorry," and lowers his eyes.

He sits with his drink and stares into the fire. When he's on his second cup, the tavern door opens and another student enters. It's a fellow he knows, with a pockmarked face and straw-colored hair. Approaching Polidori's table, he says, "We've another job. Do you want to help?"

He nods matter-of-factly. "I suppose I do. I've nothing else on tonight." So back out into the wintery weather they go.

A little way up the street they find another student, this one with dark hair, sheltering in the entryway to a shop that's closed for the night. The yellow-haired one is Roderick and the second one is Tom. Together they walk to the churchyard, arriving as the bells toll nine.

The problem for the members of the faculty who teach anatomy is twofold: too many students—over the past few years the medical school has tripled in size—and the feeling held by the general public that although cadavers are necessary for teaching, necropsy is a kind of defilement—one you wouldn't want a friend or family member to undergo. Thus, a few enterprising students have seized the opportunity and now provide corpses at a fair price.

The soil is soft and easy to dig, and with all three of them working, it's not long before the metal tip of a shovel strikes the casket lid. They needn't unearth the entire vault. With an axe they hack an adequate opening (a couple of square feet will do). They tie a rope to the body—this time a young woman—and quickly drag it out. Then they wrap the stinking corpse in canvas and carry it away.

Now, months later, he wonders how he was able to participate in such ghastly acts. He also wonders what the others, especially

Mary and Claire, would say if he told them what he did. They all pretend to be so worldly. But he'd like to see them break the lid of a casket and behold the face inside.

He shakes his head to banish the memory from his mind. Better to spend his time thinking about live women rather than dead ones, even if they do find him awkward and unappealing. How is he supposed to compete with Lord Byron and Mr. Shelley? Not that competing with them should be his concern. Except for one thing: He is falling in love with Mary. Mary, who is not actually the wife of Mr. Shelley but behaves as if she were. Oddly, the word *wife* makes her even more enticing. She is so unconventional. She is so intelligent. She is beautiful as well as decadent. The combination makes him weak with desire.

When they move into Villa Diodati, Lord Byron tells him to take the room farthest from his. He wants their paths to cross only when it can't be helped. He doesn't say it quite that bluntly, but it's clear what he intends. If he seldom sees Byron, he won't have much to record in his journal, but he hardly cares. Byron is so unpleasant that he may abandon the project entirely. Indeed, now that the Shelley party has moved nearby, he'd rather spend time with them. In the evenings, Mr. Shelley meets Byron at the water's edge and they go off alone, while the women stay back at their new house. He is told they are decorating, so he may offer to help. Then, some evening, while hanging a curtain or straightening a crooked shelf, he will confess to Mary his love.

Mary

On their first day in the new house, she decides to write a letter to Fanny and so sits down at a table by a window overlooking the lake. Willmouse is with Elise in a small room down the hall. The expectation is that Elise will sleep there with him, but Mary doesn't know if she'll like that. She is used to having her son's bed nearby. Yet it's a pleasure to have time to herself. She picks up her pen and begins:

> *1 June 1816*
> *Dearest Sister,*
>   *Since my last letter we have left the hotel and taken a*

house. It is a half hour's walk from Geneva, which, as I may have mentioned, is a walled city, the gates of which are locked at ten o'clock each night. We seldom go into town. There is more than enough to occupy us here beside the lake.

Lord Byron has purchased a boat. Although Shelley has one as well, Byron's is much larger, painted green and gold, and has a keel, a feature Shelley covets. He says, "Look, Mary, it has a keel." "Indeed it does," I reply. As I write this they are on the lake, two boys whiling away the hours of a summer's day.

Now I must tell you something unexpected. You are not to share it with our parents or anyone else. Claire is carrying Lord Byron's child. Unfortunately, he seems to have lost interest in Claire, as befits his reputation. He likes to talk about books with Shelley but finds women of value only for the services they provide. Of course I will do my best to help Claire. That is all I can say for now.

Shelley remains his changeable self. Every day he awakens with an idea for a new poem, a new novel, or a new social revolution in his head. We have hired a girl to care for Willmouse so I too have time to write.

Please send me a penny's worth of White Chapel needles and some black sewing silk. I have been unable to find either in Geneva, most likely because I don't know where to look.

Affectionately yours,
M.

The letter complete, she looks out the window, hoping to see Byron's boat. A storm is coming. The clouds are still some distance off, but she can see them tumbling down from the mountainsides to become trapped above the lake. With nowhere to go, they begin coalescing into massive thunderheads that look as solid as rock. Every day the air seems colder. If this is summer in Switzerland, she's unimpressed.

Claire enters the room and joins her at the window. "When did they say they'd be back?"

"They didn't. but I expect it will be late. We shall have to occupy ourselves."

"To whom have you written?"

Mary holds the letter up so she can see the name.

"Did you tell about me? About the child?"

"I felt I should. I hope that's all right."

Claire shrugs. "I'd hate to be Fanny. Stuck at home with only our parents to talk to. I'd go entirely mad."

"Fanny is better than us. She sees the mistakes we make and then resolves not to repeat them."

Claire wags her head in disagreement. "I'm not sure what mistakes you're referring to. Thus far I have no regrets."

During the next hour the storm continues to advance. The sky darkens and the clouds are like mountains, twice higher than the Alps. The wind blows harder and soon the trees are bending and the window glass shudders in its frame. She and Claire watch, transfixed. Suddenly, lightning strikes the lake, the flash so bright and the crash so deafening, they scream. Seconds later torrents of rain begin to fall.

Mary says, "I hope they're not still out there. Surely they had the good sense to get to shore."

To avoid thinking about the storm-tossed boat, they talk about their parents, taking up the difficult problem of how to regain their respect. Mary suggests writing a letter while Claire thinks only time will help. In the end they decide it's their parents who ought to change. Claire says, "They must accept that our lives will not be like theirs."

A little later, having put Willmouse to bed, Elise joins them. Mary asks her if she expects the storm to end soon and she shakes her head. "I myself would not wish to be out tonight," she says.

"But you've seen Lord Byron's boat. It looks quite seaworthy, don't you think?" She would like very much to be reassured by this girl who grew up near the lake. But Elise's expression remains worryingly solemn and she avoids meeting Mary's gaze.

"LB is a wonderful swimmer," Claire says, stepping in to help. "While in Turkey he swam the full width of the Hellespont, as Leander did to visit Hero in the ancient myth."

Mary looks at the window. Rain continues to lash the panes. "As you well know, Shelley is unable to swim."

Shelley

They return in the middle of the night, as wet as seals. He has always considered himself a willing taker of risks, but Byron exceeds him. Even as the lightning was exploding all around, LB stood up in the boat and shook his oar at the sky. He should have been an actor. He never stops performing, even for an audience of one.

The following morning Shelley looks out the window and knows they'll be staying in today. Another storm is upon them, this one so fierce-looking, so black and expansive, that he suspects even Byron will shrink from the challenge. Not to mention that Mary will forbid him from going near the boat on such a day.

"I worried all last night," she says. "The lightning—what if you were to be struck?"

"When I was at school," he begins, and goes on to tell her about his Leyden jar and how he brought it home to Field Place to show his sisters how electricity works.

At several points in his story Mary shakes her head and laughs. He takes pride in his ability to please her. Lately he feels invincible. Maybe it's her doing. Where Harriet seemed to sap his strength, she adds to it, multiplies it, makes him believe he could absorb a bolt of lightning and, more meaningfully, write a poem filled with images of such wonder that readers will think they've left this drab world for a more glorious one beyond.

"Since we'll not be going sailing, let us spend the day with Byron," he says. "Otherwise the poor fellow will be stuck with Polidori for company and you know how he feels about that."

He informs Claire and the new nurse and soon they are ready to depart. In this weather, even the short walk to Villa Diodati feels as if it's filled with peril. The wind howls and the sun is so blotted out, they almost need a lamp to light their way. Polidori meets them at the door and has to hold on to it with both hands to keep it from being ripped off its hinges. Before they have even removed their cloaks, Byron suggests they stay the night.

Without hesitation, they agree. The villa is large and well appointed, and, while he and Mary have only Elise to help, Byron has engaged an entire staff. And on a day like this, what else is there to do but read and talk? Shelley keeps an eye on Claire, curious to see how she behaves in the company of the object of her desire. When they gather in the drawing room, she seems uncertain about where to sit. LB ignores her and sits beside Shelley to show him some maps in a book. Claire perches on a chair across the room and pages distractedly through a portfolio of prints.

As the day proceeds, they eat no proper lunch or supper but graze on cheese and fruit. They play cards and billiards and persuade Claire to sing. All throughout they talk, and as they do so, Shelley finds himself making note of the form their conversations take: First and foremost, he and Byron never stop; they leap from topic to topic, with natural philosophy and politics predominating. They speak of Galvani's ideas about animal electricity, the Corn Laws, the Treaty of Paris, and the debate between Lawrence and Abernethy on the nature of life. Polidori, awkward as always, makes ill-timed attempts to join in. Byron responds to him with condescending silence, but Shelley sometimes takes pity on the poor fellow, including him in conversation in an effort to soften the effect. Mary mostly listens, while Claire, after her performance, goes off with Elise and Willmouse to some other part of the house. "Save me from philosophy," Claire says as she departs.

Then night falls, the candles are lit, and everyone but Shelley drinks wine. He and Byron are now engrossed in a discussion of Georges Cuvier, whose recent treatise they have both read. According to Cuvier, life on earth has been subject to a series of catastrophes, primarily floods. Each one wiped out the forms of life in existence at the time, leaving new forms to take their place.

Shelley says, "Every class of creatures has its own purpose. Reptiles exist for the sake of reptiles, not for the pleasure of mankind."

"I should like to have seen the great shaggy pachyderms of which Cuvier writes," Polidori interjects. "Like an elephant commingled with a bear."

At last Mary joins in. Byron and Polidori seem to have forgotten she's in the room, but Shelley never does, never would: "As Montesquieu points out, climate is the defining fact of human history. If a change in weather can make the furred elephants and winged lizards disappear, then perhaps we shall suffer a similar fate. Look outside. Who's to say it won't happen tomorrow? Who's to say it wouldn't be just?"

This brings them up short. "What a delightful mind you have," LB says.

Sometime later, Byron offers to read Coleridge's most recent poem, which has yet to appear in print. Claire has come back to join them, now that Elise and Willmouse are asleep. Yet once again she seems ill at ease.

As LB takes his place by the fire, they pull their chairs in close. For the last half hour Shelley has felt himself getting sleepy but the first lines bring him awake:

> 'Tis the middle of night by the castle clock,
> And the owls have awakened the crowing cock;
> Tu—whit! Tu—whoo!
> And hark, again! the crowing cock,
> How drowsily it crew.

LB is a stirring reader, the kind who can enliven the dullest of poems with his voice. Give him Coleridge and you have the makings of an exhilarating event. As the poem continues, Shelley finds himself feeling light-headed, even though he's had no wine. Yet instead of interfering with his appreciation of the poem, the lightness seems to open him to it more completely. Mary is sitting across from him and their eyes meet. Like him, she is savoring every word . . .

> Sir Leoline, the Baron rich,
> Hath a toothless mastiff bitch;
> From her kennel beneath the rock
> She maketh answer to the clock . . .

It's a strange tale, about a woman named Christabel who finds a girl in the woods, abandoned there by marauding horsemen. Christabel takes her home, but when they arrive, she discovers the girl is unable to cross the threshold of her own volition and must be carried inside. There is something menacing about the poem, and Shelley feels himself being overcome by dread. Is it Byron's voice or Coleridge's words or the winds battering the house or something else entirely, something he cannot name? He begins to forget where he is, each word an incantation drawing him more deeply into the poem. Neither Mary nor LB nor Claire is present to him now. Neither the fireplace nor even the very walls of the room are present to him now. Before his eyes, the girl begins to undress, and from deep in his agitated state, he hears these lines:

> *Her silken robe, and inner vest,*
> *Dropt to her feet, and full in view,*
> *Behold! her bosom and half her side—*

Suddenly, it's as if she were standing before him, both unspeakable and real. A window flies open and the storm rushes inside, the wind and the driving rain. He is unable to move and the girl is still present, so close he can hear her breathing. Her skin is torn and suppurating, her ivory ribs are half visible, draped in ribbons of blood and flesh, and in the center of each of her breasts is a golden reptile's eye.

Claire

She's drowsing, nearly asleep, when Shelley shouts something unintelligible and dashes from the room. Mary runs after him, but LB remains where he is. "Would that one of my own poems could prompt such a response," he says.

Polidori crosses to the window and slams it shut. Turning back toward the others, he says, "Perhaps I should follow Mr. Shelley. He may need my care."

Claire's not sure what happened. Polidori seems to be awaiting their encouragement to put his skills to use, but she doesn't say anything. And Byron does the opposite: "I wouldn't bother. I'm sure he'll be all right." It's as if he takes delight in crushing Polidori's hopes. Over the past few days her feelings about Byron have begun to change. She knew he was arrogant and self-absorbed but thought she could transform him. Thought she could make him want her as his wife. Now her main concern is what will become of her child.

Before long, Mary returns, looking distressed.

"Is he ill?" Claire asks.

"He is lying down. He had a vision—something unnatural and depraved."

Polidori leaps to his feet, no longer able to contain himself. He says, "I must go to him," and hurries from the room.

"A vision?" Claire says. "Of what?"

"He said it was a woman, all covered in blood. With eyes . . . with eyes in her breasts."

Claire bursts out laughing. She can't help herself. "How ridiculous," she says.

LB takes an iron poker in hand. After stirring the fire, he speaks: "Ridiculous, perhaps. But imagine encountering such a creature. The sheer absurdity of it would make it all the more terrifying, wouldn't you agree?"

They talk for a few minutes longer. Then, feeling suddenly exhausted, Claire goes off to bed. But before she leaves, she asks LB if she can have Coleridge's poem. To be honest, she wasn't paying much attention and would like to read it again to see what caused all the fuss.

Back in her room, she sits beside a candle, the manuscript on her lap. She is no poet, nor does she wish to be. Why write such terrible things? Before she met LB, she heard people call him mad, but Shelley is the mad one. Sometimes she observes him when he's unaware of her presence and notices how his eyes dart about. She's seen him talking to himself in the garden, whole paragraphs, not merely the occasional phrase. When they first met, she attributed such spells to laudanum or strong drink, but she's been with him enough now to know it's not that. Rather, there is deep within him a capacity for imagining with perfect clarity things that don't exist. She understands completely what Mary sees in him. If you plan on spending your life with someone, you want them to be remarkable. Yet Byron is remarkable and she's fast losing interest in him. Shelley at least is generous—there is little he possesses that he wouldn't willingly give away. And while he can be self-centered, she's never seen him be intentionally cruel. Whereas Byron entertains himself by treating others with disdain. Perhaps she doesn't need remarkable.

185

She only hopes their child will be born healthy and live a happy life.

She changes her mind about reading the manuscript and sets it aside. Maybe in the morning. If she begins now, she'll end up having nightmares. The terrified look on Shelley's face as he ran out may give her nightmares as it is.

Suddenly, she hears footsteps in the hall. They approach and stop at her door. The latch turns. She says, "Who is it?" but the latch continues to move. The door swings open to reveal Polidori—tall, gaunt, in his coal-black suit, a funereal figure but for the almost comical look of surprise on his face.

"Oh, my! I didn't—I do apologize. I opened the wrong door," he says.

"You ought to knock." She's glad she hasn't undressed.

"But I thought this was my apartment. I must have gotten mixed up. I believe I'm across the hall."

"An innocent mistake. Have the others gone to bed?"

"Mrs. Shelley has. But his lordship and Mr. Shelley are still talking. I expect they'll be up all night."

What an odd fellow. He continues calling Mary "Mrs. Shelley," despite having been corrected. The moment their eyes meet, his quickly dart away.

"Then Shelley has recovered."

"He has indeed. I treated him with ether. When I first reached him, he seemed bewildered. Eventually, he came to his senses. I do not believe he has suffered lasting harm."

He turns to leave, but she calls him back: "Tell me, what do you think of Lord Byron? Is he . . . is he *kind*? Is he to be trusted? Do you consider him an honorable man?"

A look of suspicion falls across the doctor's face. She can tell he's deciding how much to reveal. He takes a breath and speaks: "He is unlike any man I have met. Is he kind? Should you trust him? Those judgments are not mine to make." Polidori pauses. "But I am certain he is a genius. Also that he is in some manner tormented, although I have yet to determine why."

It's more of an answer than she expected. She decides to repay his honesty with some of her own. "You seem discontented," she says. "And with reason. I see how he treats you. Perhaps it's not my place . . . but surely there are other positions for someone with your skills."

Polidori has been holding the door half open, but now he steps inside and shuts it behind him. Lowering his voice to a whisper, he says, "I happen to be keeping a diary of this journey for the publisher John Murray. He is interested in my observations of Byron, as well as my experiences in Switzerland. He thinks it could make an interesting book."

"Does LB—does his lordship know?" She's certain he doesn't and wouldn't want to be present when he finds out.

"Most definitely not. He'd never allow it."

"You are braver than I thought. Do you intend to write about me as well?" She's now almost flirting, but only because it comes easily to her. She doesn't find Polidori at all attractive. That he is secretly writing about Byron with an eye to publication adds a margin of interest to his character, although not enough to change her view.

"I suppose I could," he says.

"You *suppose*? Is that the best you can do?" She reaches past him and reopens the door. "Good night. I must get ready for bed."

Jeff Hogg

Once again he goes to look in on Harriet, as Shelley asked. She and her two children have left Windsor and are now in a cramped flat in Bracknell.

"Come in out of the rain," she says. "Such a wretched summer we're having. Do sit by the fire." The baby is in her arms and little Ianthe is beside her. As Hogg enters, Ianthe scoots behind a chair. Harriet's days with Shelley now seem far in the past.

It's a drab, plainly furnished place. He's certain she gets money from her father and Shelley, so she must prefer it this way. Sometimes simplicity is a choice. Ianthe peers out at him and offers a shy smile. Young as she is, Hogg can already see traces of Shelley in her fine features and wispy hair.

"I had some difficulty finding you. I didn't know you'd moved."

"My parents and I quarreled, so there isn't as much for rent."

"I thought Shelley was—" he begins, but she quickly interrupts.

"Yes, of course, but without my father's contribution I needed a cheaper place. I can hardly blame my parents. They had such high hopes for me and now look what I've done with my life."

He doesn't know what to say to that, so he changes the subject, asks how the baby fares.

"If crying is a sign of health, as some say, then he shall grow up to be Hercules. There are still some nights I get no sleep at all. But make no mistake, my little ones are my joy."

Clearly, she is a doting mother, yet after he makes an admiring remark about each of the children, she tells him her parents want to remove them from her care. As tears fill her eyes, she says, "What would I do then?"

"Well," he says slowly, "perhaps I could help." He means it to sound as if the idea is only now coming to him, although it's one that's been in his head since the first time they met. "At present I have no attachment but am not averse to forming one. I earn more than I require to meet my own needs." Will she understand his meaning? Her reply shows she does:

"I like you a great deal. Yet I cannot love you as long as you are his friend. Whenever I am with you, I feel almost as if he is in the room."

He looks at her until he can no longer hold her gaze. Then his eyes drop to the floor between his boots. She's right. To be with her, he'd have to renounce Shelley, and that's something he'll never do.

He departs feeling as if he has let her down, although precisely how, he couldn't say. What will become of her? If her parents truly want the children, maybe she should relinquish them. The years ahead look bleak, especially if you picture them passing within the walls of that dreary room.

A few days later, he is at a gentleman's club when he happens to meet a Cornish baronet just back from Geneva. Before Hogg can ask him about Shelley, he begins describing, with great gusto and amusement, how Lord Byron has set up house on the lake and has with him a veritable harem—: "two daughters of William Godwin and some others, five in all—each of whose lute he strums on a given night of the week."

"Pray tell, what does he do on the sixth night?" Hogg asks, annoyed but playing along.

"Why, start over again, I suspect," the baronet says with a leer. "The fellow who owns a hotel across the lake has set up a telescope. He charges a quarter franc to take a look. I heard one woman exclaiming about how many petticoats she saw hanging on the line. Petticoats! In broad daylight, hanging on the line!"

"Was there any mention of a fellow traveling with Lord Byron? Percy Shelley?"

The baronet shakes his head. "Never heard of him," he says and goes off to find himself another drink.

But Hogg knows Shelley is there—he got a letter only last week:

My dear Friend,

We remain at Geneva, or rather nearby. As I explained in my last, we now reside in a cottage not far from Villa Diodati, where Lord Byron lives. We have become good friends and spend many hours together, when possible in a boat.

Is the weather in England as unseasonable as it is here? Rain falls every day, the wind blows from out of the north, and the sun rarely appears. I expect to awake one morning and find the lake covered in ice. Some are calling it Napoleon's revenge. Others consider it the first sign of the apocalypse. Yesterday as I stood on the pier, a rainbow arched from the foot of the mountains to the opposite shore. But it was a lie, for immediately thereafter, another storm blew in.

I know you are wondering when we will return, but I have no answer. Perhaps you could come here and join us. Mary would be delighted and there is room for you in our house.

Please reply with all the English news: the politics, the literature, the gossip, your labors and your travels, and if you are in love, with whom.

Ever most faithfully yours,
P.B.S.

Dr. Polidori

The weather refuses to improve, so Shelley and the women have gone back to their house for more clothes. They intend to return and stay over again tonight. This morning all the talk was of Shelley's fit. Claire says he was having them on, Mary says he must have been overtired and ought to take better care of himself, and Byron says he found it vastly entertaining and hopes it happens again.

Polidori can't understand what Mary sees in Shelley. Based on his medical training, he'd wager the man won't live very long. He's thin through the chest and lacks color in his face. By the age of thirty he will be used up.

When there's a pause in the rain, he goes out to the balcony and looks across the lake. The mountains beyond are shrouded in clouds. Soon Byron comes out as well.

"Look," he says, pointing off in the direction of the Shelley house. "Here they come now."

At that exact moment, the sun breaks through and Mary, Claire, Shelley, and the hired girl carrying the child emerge from the vineyard that separates the two houses and are momentarily drenched—not, for once, in rain, but in transparent yellow light. Polidori's heart lifts. Mary carries a basket, like a maid on a country road. She is a few steps ahead of the rest, her gait quick and alive.

"You should jump down to meet them," Byron says. "That basket looks heavy. Be a gentleman and take it from her."

Is Byron aware of his feelings? He has said nothing about them to anyone. Then again, the man is quite perceptive—maybe his tone of voice has revealed his love. He looks over the balcony rail. It's not too far down, six feet, maybe eight. With no further deliberation, he vaults over the rail and down to the grassy bank. What he has not considered is the effect of the rain on the turf. As he lands, his feet slip and his ankle turns. Down he goes, as if he were clubbed. He's embarrassed to have fallen, embarrassed to be covered in mud, but the pain from his ankle surpasses all. He writhes and moans as everyone gathers around.

Claire arrives first and says, "You poor dear," while Shelley follows with, "What in God's name made you do that?" Mary adds the one practical remark: "We'd best get you inside before the rain starts again."

As for Byron, he doesn't bother descending from the balcony but only watches as Shelley and Claire help the doctor hobble back toward the door.

They place him on a settee as the Swiss girl hands the child to Mary and takes command. She removes his boot and stocking, then goes outside to fetch an apron-full of leaves. After a short time in the kitchen, she reappears with an herbal plaster, which she applies with conspicuous skill. Polidori finds her medical expertise so fascinating, he doesn't notice that everyone else has gone away.

Soon his thoughts return to Mary. If he is patient, there may come a time when she tires of Shelley and he of her. She would benefit from someone with his characteristics—his practical knowledge and moral strength. At some point, Shelley will bend toward another attractor, whether it be a different female or some consuming ideal. When that happens, he will step in.

He is not at all attracted to Claire. Last night he mistakenly went to her room. Upon opening the door, she looked at him as if he were some sort of mad brute and for an instant he considered playing the part. But he had too little interest to follow through. Perhaps it is because Byron has despoiled her. Although Mary is no innocent either, her intelligence excuses her. Or rather it purifies her and raises her up, above the baseness of the flesh.

Mary

Poor Polidori. There can be few things worse than injuring yourself while trying to prove your manliness. And Byron can't be an easy employer to serve. She wonders what prompted him to take the job. Perhaps he hopes to absorb some of LB's ability to beguile the fair sex.

Byron enjoyed last night so much, he wants them to repeat it. This time, instead of a poem, he proposes they take turns reading from a collection of German ghost stories he found in some dismal little Geneva shop. Although the book is called *Fantasmagoriana*, it carries a more descriptive subtitle—*Stories of apparitions, spectres, revenants, phantoms, etc.* Mary wonders about the *etc.* How horrifying to meet such a creature on a deserted road at night.

As usual, their evening repast is conducted without ceremony. They arrive at the table when the mood suits them and consume without praise or complaint whatever Byron's cook has prepared. But as they begin to eat, the rain turns to snow, and struck by the novelty of such an occurrence in midsummer, they drop their forks and run outside.

"I adore it," Claire says, poking her tongue out like a child and attempting to catch a flake.

Shelley spreads his arms and turns his face skyward. "The seasons are inverted," he says. "What could be the cause?"

LB remains on the balcony, a look of indifference on his face. It's obvious he sees himself as separate and, yes, above the rest of them. Above even Shelley, although this may change in time. Mary can't imagine anyone who truly knows her beloved not holding him in the highest regard. There is certainly no indication to her that Byron is the more intelligent or talented of the two. He's simply annoyingly self-assured.

Soon the ground is covered with white. Then suddenly the snow turns to rain again, a pelting downpour that drives them back inside. They laugh and shake like dogs and hurry off to change clothes. In their room, Mary and Shelley find Elise sitting with Willmouse, who is fast asleep.

"He looks so innocent," Mary says.

"He wanted to go out to see the snow," Elise tells them.

"And you wouldn't let him?" Shelley exclaims.

"I think he shall encounter much snow in his life."

Mary is glad they hired her. She keeps even Shelley in his place.

After Elise removes herself, Mary sits down to change her stockings, examining for holes the pair she intends to wear. While she's thus occupied, Shelley places a hand on her shoulder. "If I exhibit signs of madness again tonight," he tells her, "brain me with a candlestick."

"That would make the doctor happy. He'd have a wound to treat."

Shelley pretends to shudder. "On the contrary, you are not to let him near me. Even if there's blood."

"Don't mock him," she replies, laughing in spite of herself. "The man's in pain."

"In several varieties of pain, I think—one of which is his infatuation with you. Therefore, he'll get no sympathy from me."

When they're done changing, they go downstairs to join the others. Once again they all take seats near the fire, a fire which tonight is a great blaze of the kind ordinarily built only in winter's throes. After a few pleasantries, Byron opens the book and begins.

The story he selects tells of one Ferdinand of Meltheim, a young man who must undo a family curse before marrying his true love. The plot twists and bends back on itself, and at each turn there is a ghost whose miserable doom it is to bestow the kiss of death on the sons of the house. In one especially chilling scene, the ghost, gigantic and clad in armor, creeps down a corridor and approaches the bed where two youths lie cradled in sleep. Eternal sorrow sits upon the ghost's face as it bends down and places its lips against each boy's forehead; whereupon they wither like flowers snapped from the stalk.

When Byron first begins reading, Mary's mind is on other things—on Polidori's infatuation, on Shelley's fit, on Willmouse having been deprived of an encounter with summer snow. Then, unexpectedly, she finds herself caught up in the tale. There's nothing especially artful about it. Indeed, it's the sort of thing that's been told around fires since the beginning of time. Coleridge's poem was engaging and even startling, but this tale is more elemental. It seems less written than remembered, less to be understood than felt. Fear is such a powerful emotion. There is no other that can so quickly flood one's senses, so quickly render one unable to move or speak.

When LB reads the final word, there is a brief pause, after which they exhale as one.

"Quite enjoyable," Shelley says. "Better than I expected."

"Do you think there are such things as ghosts?" Claire asks.

"I don't see why not," Shelley replies. "It may be that they are all around us, but only with certain instruments yet to be invented, can they be seen."

LB scoffs. "Capture one and deliver it to me in shackles. Or in a demijohn. Then I shall believe."

"Is it possible to believe in ghosts without believing in an afterlife?" Mary asks. "Suppose they are merely images of men and women that are somehow left behind."

The debate continues for half an hour. Of them all, Shelley is the most conflicted. Mary knows he loves a mystery, especially one that can't be solved; yet he is also a committed skeptic, so what can he do? Put the ghosts in his poems, of course. Inside his poetry, anything can happen; inside his poetry, only his fancy rules. Mary studies his beautiful face. He bites his lip in concentration and the fire lights his eyes. At this moment she is very happy. They left London and crossed the Alps to be here, on this marvelously inclement night. Truly she has no regrets.

"Read us another," she says.

LB hands the book to Shelley and tells him it's his turn.

After a minute or two of paging through it, he chooses a story called "The Death-Bride." His voice is more feminine than LB's and he reads more rapidly, but before he's many paragraphs in, they are all listening intently and no other sound can be heard. Count Lieppa has twin daughters, one of whom dies. When the Duke of Marino happens to see the living one in Paris, he falls immediately in love. But then he realizes it cannot be her: The strawberry-shaped mark on her neck, which the duke finds so appealing, belonged to the one who is dead. "How can this be?" the duke exclaims. "I know what I saw. I kissed her lovely face." Thus he decides to open the dead sister's grave.

Dr. Polidori

He listens with fascination and a certain rueful regret. Ah yes, a tale of grave robbing. If only they knew. Part of him would like to interrupt and tell them about his own experience, but he'd end up being the object of ridicule. They would consider his participation in such an unholy act shameful. Even worse, they'd accuse him of making it up. His ankle throbs. He has it placed on an ottoman and is medicating himself with a double dram of whiskey. Except for his ankle, he's feeling thoroughly numb.

He can still picture the terrible visage of every corpse. There was the man with eyes as black as shriveled plums, the boy with his mouth full of blood that for some reason had yet to clot, the girl whose face was frozen in mid-scream, and the one who wasn't as fresh as they'd expected and made his supper come up. He assisted with a full dozen before he finally stopped. The money was difficult to forsake, but he was afraid of being found out. There were rumors they were able to get such youthful corpses because someone helped them into the grave. Although he never saw evidence of that, he didn't look very hard.

He glances up and realizes he hasn't heard the last several minutes of the story. How the mind wanders! How it follows a path of its own making! He sometimes feels as if there is himself, Polidori, and then separate from that, his mind, answering its own abstracted call.

When Shelley finishes reading, it's well after midnight. For Byron, this is the shank of the evening, when he's getting ready to start work. However, the rest of them are beginning to drowse—they were up half the night yesterday and are feeling the effects tonight.

Before they can disperse to their rooms, Lord Byron has something to say:

"I suggest we each write a ghost story. It will provide a diversion during these interminable rains."

Polidori surveys the room. They all look slightly stunned—in their minds they were already halfway to bed. He expects Shelley to resist. He won't like being told what to write, even as an amusement. Surprisingly, he looks up and nods.

"I shall write one that will terrify you all," he says. "It will be a true story, about a ghost I saw with mine own eyes."

"True stories are better," says Claire. "At least, those are the ones I prefer."

But Mary says, "Suppose one does not believe in ghosts. What then? Can it be a story about foolish people scaring themselves over nothing? What if ghosts are but wisps of fog? What if the dead are but bones and hair in a grave?"

Once again Polidori wishes he could speak. He would tell her that bones and hair are only the half of it. There is the skin pulled tight across the cheeks, the hands in gnarled fists, the exposed yellow teeth of an involuntary grimace. And above all, the sweet smell of decomposing flesh. To one who would say death is no more than a gentle falling asleep, he would say, *Meet me in the churchyard tonight*.

As he's having these thoughts, Mary speaks: "Doctor, what will you write about?"

"I haven't the gift the rest of you have. Perhaps I shall write an account of the weather in Geneva. Some newspaper back in London might find it worth printing: 'English travelers experience a snowstorm in the *mezzo-termine* of July.'" He'll certainly not write about what he did in Edinburgh. It's disturbing enough to have the memories without recording them in ink.

When everyone has retired, he limps down to the lakeside and looks out over the black water. A herd of ragged clouds, like unshorn sheep, is crossing the moonlit sky. Although he suspects the others think him a fool, he considers himself superior to them all. He is more virtuous, he is better educated, and in his breast is a seed of artistry that will one day come to flower. And those flowers will be more magnificent than anything Byron himself has created. When they see what he has done, they will look back on this time and say, "How could we have misjudged him? How could we not have known?"

Claire

Although she claimed tonight's stories weren't particularly frightening, when she gets to her room, she can't get them out of her head. Last night, even after Shelley's fit and Polidori's peculiar visit, she fell asleep at once. But tonight she's unnerved by every shadow and sound. One side of the room is so dark, a person could be standing there and she wouldn't know it. On the other side, the heavy drapes move, seemingly of their own accord. She'd like to be with LB, even though he's made it clear he doesn't want her company. She wouldn't be a bother. She could sleep while he writes.

After lying awake for what seems like hours, she decides she has to see him. She takes a moment to make herself look as he would want her to look, lights a taper, and steps into the hall. What has she to lose?

His quarters are on the far side of the villa, and as she makes her way there, she herself becomes a ghost. Her steps are so light and quick, she all but floats above the ground. She feels translucent and fragile, as if her skin might suddenly shatter and her bones break apart.

When at last she finds his room, she pauses before the door. There's light coming from beneath it, which she expects. She lays a hand on her stomach and thinks about the child growing there. If she didn't have to see LB so often, his disdain would be less painful. It's not easy to put someone out of your mind when you're sleeping in his house.

At the instant she's about to knock, she hears a female voice inside. She steps back, finding it difficult to breathe. She must be mistaken, but no, there it is again, as clear as water and as musical as a bell. Who could it be? The Shelleys' nursemaid? A girl from the kitchen? Not Mary, she's too in love with Shelley. Or so Claire would like to think. Yet given Shelley's beliefs and Mary's tendency to agree with his beliefs (and Byron's lascivious predilections), anything is possible. She shouldn't have left her room. The voice behind the door goes silent and after a few more seconds of indecision, she goes back the way she came. Whoever he's with, she'd prefer not to know.

She waits until she reaches her own room to cry and even then she doesn't cry very hard. The tears are less for her than for their future child. Thinking back, she wouldn't be surprised if Byron was with a woman the night before their first night together, the night after, and many times since. She can pretend to be scandalized by his habits, but she knew of them from the start.

She quickly dresses for bed, trying to make the time she spends unclothed as brief as possible. Has this house ever been warm? Is Switzerland ever warm? When she's finally under the covers, she begins to shiver. To make herself stop, she draws her knees up and crosses her arms tight against her chest. At last she falls into a dreamless sleep and doesn't open her eyes again until noon the following day. She'd have slept even longer but for a crack of thunder so loud, it shook the bed.

As soon as she's fully awake, she's ravenously hungry. Then she remembers the contest. She knows what the others are like. The moment they see her, they'll ask if she's started her story and want to know what it's about. She's not interested in writing a story of any kind, let alone one meant to cause the reader distress. Yet she's competitive enough, especially with Mary, to want some sort of answer to their query when it comes. So instead of going downstairs, she sits and thinks. And comes up with nothing.

As it turns out, she needn't have worried. None of them has gotten far.

"I can think of many chilling images but no story," Shelley says, and Mary, "I haven't the vaguest idea of where to start."

Polidori describes something similar to the tale of Tom of Coventry, in which a boy who tries to look through a keyhole at some lewd act is struck blind. But it sounds as if he's making it up on the spot.

"That's not a ghost story," Shelley says dismissively. "Claire, what about you? Have you had any success?"

Before she can reply, Polidori defends himself. "It shall become a ghost story when one or more of the characters perish. Is that not how ghosts are made?"

As far as she can tell, he brings most of the poor treatment he receives on himself. But she wonders where he got the idea of someone standing before a door and wanting to see what's on the other side. Might he have spotted her in the corridor last night?

While they are talking about their stories, she studies Mary. When the nursemaid Elise passes through the room, she studies her as well. When a girl from the kitchen brings her tea, she looks to see if her lips are swollen or if there are telltale marks upon her throat. But why bother? All that truly matters is that it wasn't her. Was she really foolish enough to think she could have him to herself? He, who can have any woman he wants? Although she is surrounded by people, she feels quite alone. Perhaps she should take a stroll beside the lake, away from their poetry and chatter. Away from Byron most of all.

Shelley

In truth, he has no interest in writing a story about ghosts. He's never read one that's vivid enough to cause him to fall under its spell. They are all artifice, written by people who pretend to believe because they like how believing makes them feel. In that respect, ghost stories are no different from the gospels. At Eton, he drank wine from a skull in an effort to raise a ghost, but none appeared. He once took his sister Elizabeth and future wife Harriet to see a ghost. He planned to pretend to see one, but Harriet caught him off guard by pretending to see one first. He does believe in a spirit world, beyond the one in which we live. But ghosts as ordinarily understood are like those he and Harriet saw: pretense through and through.

When he writes about the realm of the spirits, his purpose is to guide the reader into a state of enchantment—a state where written language provides what the imagination desires. Perhaps that accounts for the vision he had while listening to Coleridge's poem. Poets, like priests at the height of their powers, can turn words into flesh and blood.

To stop his raving, the doctor treated him with ether. He treated himself later with laudanum. As a consequence of one or both, he slept well enough, but for the whole of yesterday, he felt as if his head were filled with cotton wool. This morning, at last, he is awake and alert, able to enjoy the unexpectedly pleasant weather outside. He and LB have been talking about sailing up the lake to visit some of the sights associated with Rousseau. Maybe this is the day to venture out. Among the first things he and Byron discovered about one another when they met was a common interest in Rousseau. They both consider him a philosopher of great importance, perhaps the most significant and the most capable of speaking to the full range of human affairs in the past one hundred years. Mary's view of him is less sanguine. In *A Vindication of the Rights of Woman,* the book for which Mary's mother is best known, Rousseau is castigated for his opinion that women need little education because their inherent charm gives them adequate power over men. When Mary presented Shelley with this passage, he said, "I do not agree that education should be withheld from women. But is Rousseau not correct that whether or not women are educated, they have natural powers over men?"

This infuriated her. "My mother did not wish for women to be educated to give them power over men but so that they may have power over *themselves*. Go with LB and pay homage to the philosopher. I shall happily stay here."

Considering himself defeated, he did not attempt to rebut her charge.

By the time Byron is out of bed, it's too late to start, but the following morning they set sail. Visiting the sites they wish to see will take several days. Mary and Claire stand on the shore and wave goodbye. They, along with Willmouse and Elise, will remain at Byron's villa with Polidori.

They sail eastward across the lake in the direction of the village of Evian. Although Shelley can't swim (and he reminds LB of this fact every time they are on the lake), he is a competent sailor. They set the craft moving at a rapid pace, taking turns at the rudder and enjoying what seems like the only day of summer they've had in weeks.

At midday, they dock at a lakeside village and find a place to eat. Afterward, they sit in the sun to read. He is a few pages into Rousseau's *Nouvelle Héloise*, which he has always intended to read. He's glad he waited until now—when he looks up from the printed page he sees before him the landscape Rousseau describes. The novel begins with a kiss between a schoolmaster and his student. Though Mary is by no means his student, the scene makes him think of her.

Back on the lake after lunch, he and LB fall to reminiscing about childhood.

"I was my mother's angel," Shelley says, "She viewed raising my sisters as a chore to be completed and to this day mixes up their names."

"Mine called me a lame brat. But she was short and stout and could never catch me, so I guess I wasn't lame enough. Aberdeen was a fine place to grow up. I don't know what would have become of me if I'd been raised in London. It's likely I'd have ended up on the street picking pockets and stealing from the shops. And I'd have been good at it, too." LB pauses thoughtfully and adds, "My mother flogged me for chewing my nails, but she encouraged my love of books."

"I sometimes think all my beliefs and sensibilities were formed in those early days," Shelley says. "What I know to be beautiful and what I know to be good have not changed since I left Field

Place to go away to school. The knowledge I acquired through my formal education amounts to nothing but a veneer."

Later, they argue about Rousseau. Unlike Mary, Shelley finds little to criticize in Rousseau's philosophy. However, he is willing to question certain aspects of the man's life. One point of contention is the children Rousseau had with his servant and lover, Thérèse Levasseur. It's well known that they were all sent away to a foundling hospital, a fact Shelley finds appalling:

"He separated them from their mother. That I can't forgive."

"Thérèse came from a low-born family," Byron counters. "Rousseau saved her by taking her into his house. Then he trusted the hospital to educate the children. He knew they'd do it better than Thérèse."

"Couldn't *he* have educated them?" Shelley asks, unconvinced.

"He saved Thérèse from destitution and she repaid him with her affections. But he never married her. If you take a woman into your bed, do you then become responsible for her and all her offspring until the end of time?"

Suddenly, unexpectedly, this feels like an argument about Claire.

"*You* certainly don't. Not according to what I've seen."

LB rarely gets angry, and when he does, it's with a coolness that makes it difficult to detect. But in this instance, Shelley needs no other evidence than his tone of voice.

"That's the first correct thing you've said," Byron hisses. "I most certainly do not."

For the rest of the afternoon, they put their efforts into sailing, each pretending to be alone in the boat. There are plenty of things to see: magnificent clouds above the mountaintops; a kind of bird Shelley has never noticed before, blue-gray with white wings, gliding just above the waves; and off to the east, a disintegrating castle perched atop a cliff.

That night, in his room at an inn, he writes a letter to his banker in London and another to Godwin. Little by little he has begun to realize he wants to return to England. One mistake some young men make is thinking that bridges once burned can't be rebuilt. A few mea culpas and a willingness to pay for one's mistakes in hard currency can work wonders. He has no doubt there is some reasonable number of guineas that will persuade Godwin and the rest to take them back.

Mary

Not surprisingly, Claire is now interested in everything about children and childbirth. "Some say one should continue wearing stays as long as possible but others say not? What did you do?" she asks.

The truth is, she knows exactly what Mary did because she was present all during the period leading up to Willmouse's birth. But she tells her anyway: "I stopped at the sixth month. I found them painful. I wore a waistcoat as a man does and tied my petticoats on top." After that they have a long discussion about when exactly a child should be weaned.

Claire seems almost relieved to have LB gone. When Mary has had the chance to observe Claire and LB together, at supper, or in the evenings by the fire, she has found herself pitying Claire. It's obvious he is done with her, yet she remains compelled to impress him. When they persuade her to sing, she chooses songs about love and gazes at him the entire time. Some nights, against what Mary is sure must be her better judgment, she joins him in his bed. Claire now claims it won't happen again, but that's easy to say when he's off sailing with Shelley and won't be back for days.

Before they left, Mary told Shelley he ought to talk to Byron about the child to whom Claire will soon be giving birth. His child.

"What would you have me say?" he asked.

"See what he intends to do about it. And about Claire."

"I've already tried, with little success. As I told you, if he doesn't want it, I will provide for it. Claire can't go back to her mother. I'll not allow anyone to suffer that."

She wishes Shelley would share more of how he feels about the children he had with Harriet. How much pain does their absence cause? Occasionally, he says he should take them away from her, but she doubts he's serious; he's simply tossing out words to assuage his guilt.

She hates it when Shelley's away—although to her surprise, she has found some solace in Elise's companionship. Mostly they discuss Willmouse, but little by little she has pieced together some facts about the nurse's childhood, including her rural upbringing and tyrannical father, from whom the position they have given her is serving as an escape.

"Did he strike you?" Mary asks.

"Oh, very often. Also, he kept me without food."

"You poor child," she says and reaches out to stroke her hair. "Your father did not strike you?"

"No. And I am ashamed to say there have been times I deserved it. I've not always been considerate of his feelings."

Elise tilts her head as if to appraise Mary's judgment. "I think he is missing you. You perhaps worry too much."

Thereafter, she vows that whatever happens, Elise will not be sent home.

Of course, neither Claire nor Elise nor anyone else can take Shelley's place for long. There are so many things Mary needs to talk to him about—not only Claire, but Polidori's ridiculous advances, the things Willmouse can do today that he couldn't do yesterday, and the story she's begun to write.

To her surprise, she is the only one who has taken up LB's challenge, at least the only one willing to say so. For several mornings she sat at the small table in her room and wrote not a word. But then one night, after Willmouse was in bed, after Claire had gone to her room, she put her own head on the pillow and saw, behind closed eyes, a pale student of unhallowed arts kneeling beside a figure stretched upon a slab—a hideous phantasm, stirring with an uneasy motion. Her eyes flew open and still the image remained. The student turned and stared at her. The figure on the slab began to breathe. But she herself had no breath and therefore was unable to move or scream. When at last the vision disappeared, she went straight to her desk and recorded what she'd observed.

Now that her tale is under way, she spends every morning with pen in hand. Her story opens on a night like the one when Shelley had his fit, but she changes it to November because no one would believe such weather in July. Instead of being about a ghost, it will be about a humanlike creation, assembled and then brought to life with electricity and chemical infusions, devised by a scholar of such prodigious learning, he has no need for God. But first she must describe the scholar's history— his friends, his family, his education, and the source of his terrible desires.

One evening, after a day spent writing, she comes upon Polidori sitting alone by the fire.

"I rather like the house without them," he says. "Will they be returning soon?"

"I hope so. I didn't expect them to be away so long."

They are silent for several minutes and she contemplates returning to her room. Then he speaks again.

"We have been together these several weeks and with each passing day you have risen in my esteem. I think about you constantly. I—"

He's looking at the fire, not at her. She hoped this moment would never come. He's pitiful, embarrassingly so.

"Your beauty is unmatched and your temperament so . . . so congenial."

"Please," she says, unable to hide the sarcasm his remark invites, "you flatter me too much."

He tries to continue, but she holds up her hand. "Let us be friends," she says, "and not mar that friendship with expressions of ill-advised passion."

Two more times he tries to confess his love and two more times she rebuffs him. Thus he takes an alternate approach:

"I would like it very much if you would tell me about the story you are writing."

She'd rather not, but she feels sorry for him. "You recall the tale we read about the opening of the young woman's grave? Imagine someone, perhaps a man of medicine like yourself, who traffics in such practices and then—"

Her tone is light. She wants, if possible, to lift his spirits, having dashed them so thoroughly a few minutes before. But his expression now changes to one of agitation and does so with such rapidity she feels some alarm.

"I once did such a thing," he says. "I have never confessed it to anyone until now."

"You opened a grave?"

"Indeed. And more than one."

She doesn't know what to say. Yet she also wants him to continue. After such an admission, who could turn away?

"Tell me more," she says.

And so he does, in horrifying detail. He remembers a remarkable amount about each body: its wounds and deformities, its facial expression, even the features he found attractive, as if he'd known the person in life.

"What made you continue? Were you somehow coerced?"

"I did it for the money, but I must admit a certain fascination, at least in the beginning. Have you never wished to do something forbidden? Something society would condemn you for if they happened to find out?"

She looks toward the fireplace, the low orange flames. The feeling he refers to is not entirely alien to her, but it's not something she's willing to discuss. "I think it's time for me to retire," she says, and quickly leaves the room. Yet instead of going to bed, she continues to write her story. And soon she finds herself immersed in the matters Polidori discussed: the circulation of the blood, the function of various organs, and the border between death and life.

In the morning she declares it's time they return to their own house. Claire protests—"I'm quite comfortable here," she says—but Mary insists. "It's too drafty for Willmouse. I fear he'll become sick." She wishes Shelley hadn't gone away.

Two days later she looks out the window and sees Byron's boat. She and Claire hurry out to meet them. When they are close enough for her to see Shelley's face, her breath catches with passion and she anticipates the warmth of his embrace.

"I worried about you constantly," she says.

"Did you?" he replies, leaping from the boat.

"Not truly. I was too busy writing. I scarcely thought of you at all."

When they reach their house, he greets Elise and takes Willmouse in his arms, exclaiming about how he's grown. While he's busy with the boy, she whispers to Elise, and before he knows what's happening, Elise and Claire have taken Willmouse and disappeared.

"They're going for a walk," Mary explains. "Elise is a marvel.

In your absence, we've become friends."

The place to themselves, they embrace and kiss and fall into bed. They've not been separated for this long since they first met. It turns out to be a lovely combination—their familiarity with one another, the way he knows her body and she his, and the need that comes from having been apart, if only for a few days. She even likes the urgency that comes from knowing the others won't be gone for long. "Now," he says. "Please now."

A little later, as they lie in serene togetherness, she tells him how Polidori confessed his love for her while he was gone.

"Did he really? What did he say?"

"He called my temperament 'congenial.'"

"Zounds! He didn't! I shall thrash him."

She laughs. "He also told me stories about his time at Edinburgh. Did you know he was once a stealer of corpses?"

"Polidori, a grave robber? I had no idea. But now that I'm aware, I find it rather fitting. Tell me, were you tempted? When he said he loved you, did you think, even for a moment, of giving him a kiss?"

"Did it enter my mind? Certainly. I have little control over my thoughts. But when I considered how insufferable he would become *after* the kiss, I chose to refrain."

Dr. Polidori

He stands at a window and looks across the lake. The lenses of telescopes at the Hotel d'Angleterre flash in the sun. Yesterday a packet of London newspapers arrived by post and in each one there was an account of the debaucheries being perpetrated by their little group. Some say Mary and Claire are sisters sharing Byron's bed, some say there are other women (whores imported from Marseille), and some hint not only at various couplings and triplings and foursomes, but at the practice of certain black arts. To his relief, he is not named. To his disappointment, he is not named.

He now has difficulty meeting Mary's gaze. Or maybe it's that she is averting her eyes from his. With Shelley and Lord Byron back from their trip, he feels thoroughly left out. Furthermore, there is some sort of intrigue going on, which he suspects has to do with Claire's growing girth.

On the fourth of August they celebrate Shelley's birthday. He is twenty-three years old. In Geneva, Mary purchased a telescope for him. Now they can watch the tourists on the other side of the lake watching them. She has also made him a small hot air balloon, which she and Shelley take out on the boat. Apparently, Shelley is passionate about balloons and can't wait to launch it. Yet what he and Claire and Byron see as they observe from shore is Mary attempting to light a candle, a gust of wind, and the balloon bursting into flame. It's dramatic as well as comical, both of them beating on it and trying to get it into the water before it sets fire to the boat. "Perhaps that will cure him of his obsession," says Claire, "but I rather expect not." While she speaks, the last fiery fragment of the balloon is caught by a breeze and drifts into the sky.

Since the weather continues to be fair, they decide to take their evening meal as a picnic by the lake. But Polidori finds it difficult to be with Mary when Shelley is present, so he goes back inside. There, as he wanders about the villa, he picks up a notebook belonging to Byron. It doesn't look to be anything of importance, lying as it is atop some things meant to be discarded. What he finds when he opens it is the beginning of a story in Byron's easily recognizable script. He can't resist the urge to read.

Like much of what Byron has written, it is an account of a journey, in this instance a journey being undertaken by a man of wealth and good family named Augustus Darvell. Although Polidori isn't particularly intrigued by the premise, Byron can't write a dull sentence, no matter the subject or form. As Darvell and an unnamed narrator advance toward Greece, Polidori soon finds himself hanging on every word. The two are on their way to explore some ruins near Epheseus, where Darvell expects to spend his final days, and where, after his death, the narrator has been instructed to throw his ring into a certain bay. At that moment it occurs to Polidori that this is Byron's ghost story—the one he insisted he didn't write.

He is still reading when he hears them all come inside, but he can't take his eyes from the page. Darvell has now breathed his final breath. The narrator removes the ring from his finger, and as he does so, Darvell's body turns to ash. Suddenly, Polidori knows what will happen next. When the narrator throws the ring in the bay, Darvell will come back to life. He's not sure how he knows this, but he does. Perhaps it's because in their late-night conversations a frequent subject of debate has been the boundary between life and death.

Just then, a noise causes him to look up. Someone is climbing the stairs. The uneven, clumping gait means it's Byron, so he should stop what he's doing now. However, he can't, and turns another page. But there's nothing there. The story is unfinished. He closes the notebook as Byron enters the room.

"The wind . . . did it drive you indoors?" Polidori stutters, embarrassed to have been caught reading his lordship's work.

"There is no wind. What's that you're holding?"

He waves the notebook weakly in the air. "I was only. . . I was just . . . I couldn't help myself."

"Couldn't help yourself? I see. You ought to read something better than my wretched attempt. The problem with ghost stories is they lack wit. Or if they have the wit, they lose the horror. I've no patience with the form."

"On the contrary, I think it's excellent."

Byron snorts. "Then it's yours. Do with it as you please."

Claire

For the past several afternoons she has spent her time making fair copies of Lord Byron's most recent lines. It's the third canto of *Childe Harold*, the one his public has been waiting on for years. She knows she's being taken advantage of, but she forgives him because there's nothing calculated in his request. He says, "Claire, if you are not otherwise occupied, might you do some copying for me?" As though he's entitled to her assistance but also as though she's entitled to turn him down. She doesn't want to alienate him—he could take the baby away. Although Shelley has promised to make sure he has no malicious intentions, she can't take any risks. Try to separate a child from its father, even if it's a child he doesn't want, and there's a chance he'll fight. Byron needs to think giving it up is his idea.

She's having difficulty keeping food down. Mary says it's

normal, but Claire doesn't recall Mary being sick half as much. What will become of her? If she returns to London, it will be in disgrace. But where else can she go and what will she do? She envies Mary, who not only has Shelley but possesses a certain ability to resist being shamed by the opinions of others. No doubt that ability was inherited from her mother, who, by all accounts, stubbornly refused to be shamed.

Since Claire has stopped spending nights with Byron, she stays in her room and reads or, as often as not, weeps. Then one day Shelley comes to her and says they want to make an excursion to Chamonix, to see the famous glacier there. "The three of us," he says. "LB doesn't want to go. It will be a relief for you."

He's right—she could feel herself sinking into despair and a diversion will help. She busies herself with packing and is the first one ready the following day. Mary leaves Willmouse with Elise, so it's only the three of them, as in times past. That alone puts a lightness in her step.

They travel by horseback into the mountains, toward the base of Mont Blanc. They consider themselves familiar with the Alps, having crossed those on the French side twice, but these seem larger, colder, more precipitous and forbidding than any they've encountered before. They marvel at their grandeur. They pull their cloaks tight around themselves and crane their necks in an effort to see the summit. For a time they pretend to be explorers, traversing country never seen by human eyes; but when they arrive at the inn where they will spend the night, they discover it's filled to overflowing with English tourists like themselves. Everyone wants to see the Mer de Glace, which, the innkeeper's wife tells them, is advancing at the rate of one foot a year.

As Shelley prepares to sign the register, he beckons them over. Claire and Mary press close, one on either side.

"Look here. What brainless rubbish," he says, and points to the entries made by previous guests. Some praise the inn for its food, some lodge complaints about the insufficient number of quilts on the beds, but in almost every case they exclaim about how the mountains and the glacier represent the glory of God. "Never have I felt so filled with grace," says one. "The handiwork of our Lord is here for all to see," says another. "When first we saw the glacier, my good wife was moved to prayer," says a third.

"I don't think people give it much thought," Claire says. "They jot down whatever comes to mind."

"My point exactly," Shelley says. "This is a perfect representation of what's in the average Englishman's head."

He reads a few more aloud to drive home his point and then takes up the pen and makes an entry of his own: "P.B. Shelley, Democrat, Philanthropist, and Atheist." In the column marked "Destination," he writes a single word: "Hell."

"You are a provocateur," Mary says, as she signs her name below his. Claire signs as well, but when she's done, she's not sure how she feels. Always before, she's been pleased to be a participant in Shelley's escapades. But lately she's not so eager to be included. She agrees with him in principle, the pious nature of English society oppresses more souls than it saves, but she's content to let Shelley and others like him fight that battle. She would be happy to live quietly in a small house in a village with a piano as her only luxury. And on Sundays, walk to a country church.

The next morning they get up at dawn and meet the guide who will take them to the glacier. He has brought mules to ride and promises them they are surefooted and unlikely to bolt.

When at last they arrive at the glacier, Claire can see why many attribute its existence to God. What other force could have created such a river of ice? It is as wide as the Thames, but with irregular waves and troughs, as if a stormy sea were frozen in place. "It's both grand and monstrous," Shelley says. "It does indeed call upon us to question what force or power made such a thing." A few steps later he calls Mont Blanc "a vast animal" and the glacier "the frozen blood within its veins."

That night back at the inn, Mary and Shelley write and write. Apparently, the glacier touched something within them. They don't even bother coming down for supper, so Claire is left to eat alone.

Mary

When she was in Scotland, she was so intrigued by the whale boats in the harbor, she began writing a story about a man who embarks upon a journey to the Arctic. But she never completed it; her powers of description failed her when the hero reached the land of perpetual ice. Now, seated at a small table in their room at the inn, she recalls those images and must write as rapidly as she can to keep up with her racing mind.

She glances over at Shelley, who is seated at a similar table against the opposite wall. He's begun a new poem that will show how poetry better than religion can explain nature's grandeur. He pauses and asks her to listen to some lines:

> And what were thou, and earth, and stars, and sea,
> If to the human mind's imaginings
> Silence and solitude were vacancy?

"Read it again," she says.

He does. She holds herself still. The words light upon her consciousness like birds. She says, "Do you intend to answer the question or only pose it?"

"The question is its own answer, is it not?"

She nods, continuing to think. "I shall have more to say when I hear it in its entirety." Then, as an afterthought, "*Vacancy* is a sad word. Among the saddest I know."

And so they resume scratching at their respective sheets with their pens. His words can bring tears to her eyes while at the same time be so unexpected, she can't help but smile.

In her own piece, the broader contours are emerging. Similar to the lines Shelley read, the human mind's imaginings will be at the heart of the design. A man follows his curiosity and passion where they lead but makes a terrible mistake. He fails to consider how a power that's Godlike, that appears at first glance to have beneficial properties, can be misused. As these ideas form, she begins to feel excited; yet she knows it's wise to keep her emotions in check. A week from now she may have abandoned the story. It's happened to her before.

The next day they leave early for Geneva. She's missing Willmouse too much and can't wait to get home. When heavy rains wash out the road, causing a delay, she is nearly frantic with worry and doesn't feel better until she takes her child from Elise's arms. She's forgotten how heavy he is. When his eyes meet hers, he positively beams.

"Has he been a good boy?" she asks.

"Very good. I shall steal him from you."

Mary knows she's joking and that it's Elise's imperfect grasp of English that causes the remark to sound slightly sinister, but she sends her away nonetheless: "Thank you for taking care of him. Do as you wish for the rest of the day."

Now that they've returned, she has more time to think about Claire. The two of them have had their differences, but Mary's feeling increasingly protective of Claire and her unborn child. She presses Shelley: "Speak to LB. Wait no longer. I'm afraid he's becoming bored with this place and then what? There must be some agreement about the child before he leaves." She pauses and shakes her head. "I nearly said *escapes*."

"Tomorrow," Shelley replies. "I give you my word."

That evening they return to their writing. But Willmouse fusses and she doesn't want to interrupt Shelley, so she has to stop. As she paces with him in her arms, she writes new lines in her head. Occasionally, she pauses to jot down a phrase, but it's not the same as sitting at a desk with no distractions. She regrets having given Elise the night off.

When Willmouse is finally in bed, she writes to Fanny about their trip to the glacier. She describes the villages they passed through, the people they met, and the beauty of the mountains and ice. *It was sublime*, she writes. *Someday we'll return and you shall accompany us.* Halfway through the letter, her mind goes back to the time before their father married Mrs. Clairmont, when it was only the three of them. She and Fanny were closer then, as sisters ought to be. On their walks to St. Pancras Church, Fanny would hold her hand.

Upon finishing the letter, she makes a note to herself to go into Geneva and buy something for Fanny—a brooch, a ring, a lady's timepiece. For a while she didn't think they were going back to England, but now, as they near the end of summer, she's all but certain they are. Shelley has even begun musing about where they should live.

"Wherever we end up, I hope we stay for a long time," she tells him. "I don't believe it's healthy to move a child overmuch."

"As you wish," he says.

"I can tell you don't mean it. You're not as travel-besotted as LB, but you have little interest in the making of a home."

"On the contrary. I have written Peacock with instructions to find us a suitable house. I told him to insist on a lease of a hundred years."

"Don't mock my concerns," she says, and gives him a corrective kiss.

Shelley

In the morning he goes looking for Claire so as to keep his promise to Mary. He finds her copying lines of *Childe Harold* yet again.

"Why do you continue to do this?" he asks. "You ought to be charging him by the word."

"I'm the only one who can read his hand. As for being paid, it never occurred to me to ask."

"What will he do without you?"

"What do you think? He shall find some other girl. Or perhaps a boy." She pauses and looks at him meaningfully. "Did you know that about him?"

"It's been hinted at in the papers. Like everything else." He can tell she's in a peculiar mood. Reflective. Cynical. Glum. It's a sad thing when someone so young and fresh begins to feel oppressed by the looming exigencies of life.

"I find it interesting," she says.

"How so?"

"To be carrying the child of a sodomite."

He chooses not to respond. Instead, he says, "I want you to come with me this morning to the villa. It's time to speak to him about who will parent the child." Up until now they've made mention of "arrangements" and "responsibilities" but not the practical facts of the matter. *Parent* seems to him a more appropriate and forthright word.

"Must we?"

"Don't you want to know? Shouldn't you have a plan?"

"My plan, which may be his as well, is to watch him leave for some other country and never see him again."

"Come. Let him express his thoughts on the matter. They may be less cold than you expect."

They make their way to Villa Diodati through a veil of rain. Once inside, they take off their wet cloaks and muddy shoes and follow Byron's man, Fletcher, to a gallery adjoining Byron's bedroom. The drapes are drawn and candles are lit, so it might as well be night.

As they enter, LB is reading; he looks up and closes his book. "Thank you for coming," he says, as though he requested their presence, when in fact it was Shelley who insisted they meet.

He inquires about their trip to Chamonix and they tell him that reaching the glacier was harrowing but that it was thrilling to see. "As a rule I reject the idea of tourism," he replies, "but there are sights one ought to see."

"I believe you know what we've come about," Shelley says. He doesn't want this to be difficult. He hopes Byron will acknowledge the privileges of motherhood, but Claire will need to be gracious and show no predilection toward stubbornness, given his position and wealth.

It starts off badly.

"I suggest we send the child to be raised by my sister," Byron says abruptly. This is the half sister, Augusta Leigh, with whom the tabloid press implied he had an incestuous affair.

Shelley and Claire have taken seats across from him, on a settee. In response to Byron's recommendation, Claire gasps, takes a moment to recover, and then speaks:

"She has her own children to care for, does she not? Why burden her with another?"

"Three daughters," Byron replies. "I can't see how a fourth brat would be much more work."

"Who would benefit from such an arrangement?" she says. Her voice is getting higher and she grasps the sleeve of Shelley's shirt. "I don't understand why—"

Fearing what might come next, he places his hand over hers and interrupts: "Suppose I provide for it," he says.

Byron shrugs. "You want to buy your way into this discussion? Be my guest."

He's still not sure what Byron's intentions are. The man has little interest in children and certainly can't make any claims about how fathers ought to behave. Then again, neither can he.

"You're doing this because you've come to detest me," Claire says. "Must you take revenge on the child?"

Byron shakes his head as if he's getting tired of the discussion already. "I do not detest you. I am indifferent. As for the child, do as you wish. I'll not renounce my rights as a father, but I shall suspend my exercise of them until some future date."

"What do you mean?" Claire wails, and then to Shelley, "What is he saying?"

"He means he doesn't intend to take the baby away from you. He simply wants to reserve his rights."

She tries to say something more, but she's crying and can't speak. Yet this is a better outcome than Shelley expected. He interprets Byron's words to mean he has no intention of interfering for the foreseeable future and might even provide for the child's education when the time comes. "We'll speak of money later," Shelley tells him and ushers Claire away.

Downstairs in the drawing room he stops and makes her sit. As she begins to recover, he expects her to have more thoughts about LB, but instead, she says, "I can't allow my mother to know about this—that I am with child."

"Your mother? Perhaps you should write to her. That might be easier than telling her when we get back."

"It's not the telling I fear. It's the aftermath."

He thinks, *If you'd agreed to allow him to send the baby to his half sister, your mother would never have to know.* But he can see how she's trapped in a sort of triangle with her mother, Lord Byron, and her child, each occupying a side, none of which can be crossed.

"Then we shall choose a place to live far from London, somewhere she'll be unlikely to visit," he says.

Claire looks relieved. "And when the baby is born, I can tell everyone I'm its aunt."

It's an outrageous idea, but he's heard of stranger schemes.

He fetches her cloak and puts it on her as if she were a child. He's not sure what to think about the past hour except that he's glad it's done. He and Mary have never discussed Claire living with them after they return to England, but now he seems to have invited her. As for her child, it appears that instead of being raised by parents, it will have to be content with one eccentric uncle and two adoring aunts.

Dr. Polidori

For the past several days he's been adding to the story Lord Byron began, making use of his leavings like a beggar gobbling up a rich man's scraps. Mary has stopped coming to the villa, so he might as well write. Confessing his love to her was a mistake. People say, "Be forthright. Express your true feelings. What do you have to lose?" But in reality, you have everything to lose. Before his confession he could at least imagine her feelings were the same as his. It was a sweet imagining that is no more. Shelley and Claire came to see Lord Byron a few days ago, and while they were at the villa, he kept looking out the window, expecting Mary to follow. The three of them always arrive together; therefore her absence must have been a statement. He wonders what Shelley and Claire spoke to Byron about. When they left, the expressions on their faces suggested they'd had some kind of row.

As he writes, a certain character in Byron's story (he's still unable to think of it as *his* story), a gentleman named Lord Ruthven, is becoming, line by line, increasingly Byron-like. He is a wealthy aristocrat who makes a habit of seducing young women. He likes to travel on the Continent. He treats his employees poorly. He does as he pleases without regard to the damage done. Were Lord Byron to read it, what would he think?

Currently, the problem Polidori faces is how to braid together the lives of three characters: Augustus Darvell of the ghastly death, the Byron-like Lord Ruthven, and a young traveler named Aubrey, whom Polidori likes to think of as a version of himself. He wishes there was someone he could ask to read his manuscript, to tell him if he's wasting his time. But when he did risk showing his work to them, it was derided. He won't do that again.

The next day he is waking up when some lines from a poem

of Lord Byron's unexpectedly come to him. Not the ones about the peculiar beauty of the fresh corpse but in the same poem, farther up the page. They are the key to Lord Ruthven, to who he really is. He can picture the book and even knows where to find it, on a table in the drawing room on the second floor. He throws on his dressing gown and in minutes is back with the book. Yes, here it is. This will bring everything together: The discussions they've had all summer about the mutability of life and the mysteries of death. Byron's Augustus Darvell, turning hideously to ash. Even his own sorry history, which he would like so much to forget:

> But first, on earth as Vampire sent,
> Thy corpse shall from its tomb be rent:
> Then ghastly haunt thy native place,
> And suck the blood of all thy race . . .

He began with Byron's pages, but the man owes him much more than that. *On earth as Vampire sent.* Why not take this as well?

Claire

The meeting with Byron was the final shattering of her heart. Until then, she'd been hoping that it was all a misunderstanding and that in the end he would take her away with him. Not marry her perhaps, but invite her to be his lover and traveling companion. And copyist— there'd be no avoiding that. Her child would be born and they would raise it together in some exotic locale.

Now, however, she knows how false her hopes truly were, and she just wants to go *home*, although exactly what that word has come to mean, she's unsure. Most days, she is content to have Shelley, Mary, and Willmouse as her family. Yet sometimes, as she walks along the lake, she thinks of her mother (who is a difficult woman but who never failed to provide for her) and her father (who will always love Mary more than her but treats her well enough) and wants nothing more than to be with them again. Then she reminds herself that if they learn she is carrying Lord Byron's bastard, they'll never take her back.

If she were Mary, she would be so very thankful for Shelley—more thankful than Mary presently seems to be. The two of them still dote on one another, but not as much as Mary dotes on her pen. Every day she spends hours writing—in the morning after breakfast, in the middle of the afternoon, and after supper at night. Elise takes Willmouse off for whole days at a time. Claire would be happy to care for him, but no one ever asks.

One rare sunny morning, she walks in the direction of the villa and sees Byron on the balcony, looking across the lake. She decides he resembles a small god of the Greek variety, not the kind who can make worlds, but the kind who can disguise himself as a mortal so as to come into villages and seduce the local girls.

Later in the day she finds Shelley and interrupts his work: "Do you think I ought to change my name back to Jane?" she asks.

Before he can reply, Mary, who is on the opposite side of the room writing, speaks up: "You absolutely may not. Do you want to return to those days?"

She's not sure what she means by *those days*, so she ignores Mary and awaits Shelley's reply. He looks at her with what she takes to be a certain tenderness and says, "Never backward, only forward. You may change it from Claire to something new, but I will not call you Jane again."

"I shall think on it," she says. "But you are correct. I do not wish to turn back."

The next day, Shelley announces that his friend Peacock has secured rooms for them in Bath and they can leave as soon as they'd like. Claire is delighted with his choice. In her more melancholy moments, she has been telling herself she'll be satisfied no matter where they end up. But Bath is lively and stylish. Who knows, she might meet a bachelor or perhaps a widower, one who would consider taking a child-encumbered woman as his mistress if not his wife. She says, "I can be packed by tomorrow—or if you wish, tonight."

However, they don't leave the next day or the day after or the day after that. They have to close up the house and there's no real urgency for any of them—nothing here they're trying to escape and nothing in England they're trying to get back to that cannot wait.

She makes no effort to see LB again. She fears she'd fall on her knees and begin to sob or become hysterical and curse his name—in response to which he'd look down his beautiful nose for a few seconds and then shake his head in disdain. Instead, on their final night there, she writes a letter to leave behind:

> *My dearest friend,*
>
> *When you receive, this I shall be many miles away. I write because I cannot speak to you—were I looking at your face, the words would fail to come. I am sorry we parted on unfriendly terms. My greatest fear is that you will forget me. Pray take care of yourself. I am ashamed to say how much I still love you and hesitate to trouble your heart, and yet I think you might be kinder to me if you could but know how wretched this going away makes me feel. I do wish I could kiss you one last time.*
>
> *Farewell then.*
> *Your own affectionate Claire*

Part Four

September 1816–March 1818

Mary

People say English skies are seldom cloudless, but this one is. The intense blue of late summer, from horizon to horizon. Geneva had its charms, but it's nice to see the sun.

Their new address is 5 Abbey Churchyard, Bath, right beside the Pump Room, where people of quality gather. From the window, Claire watches the ladies on the street below and comments on their bonnets: "Mary, come look. What was she thinking? It's as if a woodcock is nesting on her head!"

At present, only four of them are in residence: Claire, Willmouse, Elise, and herself. As soon as they arrived, Shelley went straight to London. There are new questions about his inheritance—which portions will be available when—and he promised to deliver the final part of *Childe Harold* to John Murray on Byron's behalf. He also said something about paying off some creditors, but when he talks of debt, Mary's attention wanes.

This time they returned by way of Portsmouth to avoid meeting anyone from London who might notice Claire. Notice Claire, that is, in her present condition and carry a report back to Skinner Street, where, in Claire's mind anyway, her mother awaits Gorgon-like, claws unsheathed. Mary tries to convince her that facing her parents now rather than later would have certain advantages. However, Claire seems to think if she never sees them again, all will be well. To which Mary replies: "So instead of giving them the chance to disown you, you intend to disown yourself."

To keep their parents at bay, Shelley sent a letter to Skinner Street explaining that they've come to Bath because Claire is in poor health. One of the details he included was that the diagnosis was made by a Dr. Polidori, which caused Mary to laugh. Her final glimpse of Polidori as they left Geneva seemed to capture her feelings about him—there he stood in the rain, after having helped them load their trunks into the coach in his clumsy, overbearing manner. A perfectly decent man, or at least an unobjectionable man, who was none-theless nearly impossible to like. He tried to give her a manuscript—apparently he'd finally begun a ghost story of his own—but she said she was a poor judge of other people's writing and declined as politely as she could.

The story she herself has been writing in response to Byron's challenge has been going surprisingly well. She expected it to be no more than a few dozen pages in length, a mere diversion, but now she thinks of little else. Having determined (or perhaps *discovered* is the more apt term) that the Arctic explorer in her tale is a con-duit for a story told by a man of science named Victor Frankenstein, she has already written page after page about Frankenstein's happy childhood in Geneva, about his time studying chemistry and natural philosophy at the university in Ingolstadt, and about the emergence of his ardent ambition to discover the source and secret of life.

Now, however, she senses that she's entering a difficult phase—one that will test her abilities to the utmost. If it were a more conventional story, she might turn to other works for guidance, but it's unlike anything she's ever read. Will someone care to publish it? Is this sort of thing even *allowed*? She intends to make use of her ter-rifying dream vision, the one of a hideous pieced-together creature stretched out on a slab. But what then? How will she convince the reader that the impossible is real? She feels a foreboding and expects tragedy. Unless she's mistaken, Victor Frankenstein will pay a price.

When she's not writing or taking walks through the streets of Bath with Claire ("Who *are* those striking young women?" she and Claire pretend the young men say), she's resumed her studies of Greek. She wishes Shelley would return. As confident as she is of his love, she sometimes fears he'll leave her as he did his first wife. He claims Harriet drove him off, but in the end it's always the husband who forsakes the wife and not the opposite. Perhaps that's the best reason to be opposed to marriage. If all bonds between men and women were considered impermanent, then when they are broken, the parties involved might feel less pain. And yet across the room Claire is writing another letter to Byron. If pain is the measure, neither the rites of matrimony nor an individual's unwillingness to embrace those rites seems to matter. Love proceeds according to its own harsh rules.

Jeff Hogg

On a gray autumn afternoon, he receives a letter from Harriet. It's quite unexpected. During the past few months he's written to her a few times, inquiring about the children, but never received a reply. He'd begun to feel he'd never see her again.

The letter begins with an apology: *I'm sorry to have been so silent. I much appreciated your letters and have no excuse for not writing back. I would say I've been occupied with my children, but they now live with my mother and father, so I blame myself alone.*

How unfortunate about the children. No doubt the Westbrooks can provide a good home, but now she's utterly alone.

After the apology, she writes at some length about how she bears Shelley no ill will. And then a new paragraph begins and she turns her attention to him. She would like Hogg to visit again. He wonders what her purpose is. Is there something she'll want him to convey to Shelley? Or is there something she will want from *him*?

He pens a reply and she responds within the week. She asks to meet in St. James's Park. That seems a little odd, but he agrees, and on the day, he arrives early to wait near the canal. He's already planned what he'll say—that whatever she wants of Shelley, he is now devoted to Mary Godwin, and wouldn't it be better to make what she can of her life without him? He doesn't know if Harriet is even aware Shelley is back from Switzerland. If not, he'll tell her, but he won't disclose that Shelley and Mary are living as husband and wife in Bath. She's heartbroken enough as it is.

He sees her coming from a long way off. She looks smaller than he remembers and a bit unsteady on her feet. As she gets closer, he can see that her face is pink from the wind and her clothes appear rather worn; not a single article looks new. Harriet's father has money—surely he could give her more to spend on attire.

They greet one another and go to a bench to sit. He begins by inquiring after Ianthe and Charles. Are they well and when might he see them again?

"You may have more luck if you contact my father yourself. He is angry with me and refuses to answer my letters or invite me into his house."

"Angry with you? But why?"

"I refused to turn over the children until forced to do so, and now he's heard I have taken up with another man."

Hogg hardly knows what to say. This is not the conversation he expected, nor is this the Harriet he knows. "Is that true? Is there another man?" Why didn't she turn to him when he offered? He might have helped her keep her children. He'd certainly have bought her a new frock.

She nods. "He's a captain in the Guards. I'm on my way to see him now."

"And does he intend to marry you?" He can't believe he's asking but he feels the need to know.

"He hasn't brought it up. But I don't know why he would." Her forthrightness is fueled by fury. Not at him or even at Shelley but at what she's become. She needn't put it into words; he can see it in her eyes.

Suddenly, he wants to be done with this, to say goodbye and be on his way. But he still needs to know why she wanted to meet.

"I'm sorry you are in such straits. Is there some way I can help?"

"Thank you for asking. You see, my father has stopped giving me money. Not even the smallest amount. Shelley has always been a good provider but I'm afraid it's not enough."

With that, he understands. Her cuffs are frayed, her hair needs tending, and now that he's looking more carefully, he notices her shoes are falling apart. What arrangement has she with this captain, he wonders? It must not be worth very much.

"I . . . surely . . . you must." He stops in mid-sentence, putting his lips together to keep from saying something he'll regret.

"You owe me nothing," Harriet says quickly. "I promise I would pay it back."

"I haven't much with me so it will have to come at a later date. But of course I shall give you what I can. What address—" he begins, but realizes that the address she would give might disclose more than she'd like. "I'm going to write down the name of my firm. I'll have them hold it for you there."

After Harriet is gone, he remains on the bench for a time

watching people pass. What a turn the girl's life has taken. He fears the money he's promised—which he's certain won't be repaid—will do little to slow her fall.

Shelley

It's good to be back in London. He takes a room in a place he's stayed before, on Marchmont Street, and the next day visits his banker, where he discovers things are not so bad as he feared. Then on to the offices of John Murray to deliver Byron's manuscript into the publisher's hands. The Murray in question is the son of the firm's founder, John Murray of Edinburgh, and although he's met Shelley on only one previous occasion, he greets him like an old friend. Why? Because Byron is his most profitable author, the previous volume of *Childe Harold's Pilgrimage* having sold out in five days. This one is expected to do equally well. Would that Shelley's *Alastor* had such success. As he's about to leave, Murray calls him back.

"I don't suppose you know when I can expect to see Dr. Polidori?"

He stops and turns. What possible business could Polidori have with John Murray? "You know Polidori?" he asks.

"I do. I have a contract with him to produce an account of his travels with Lord Byron. I paid him five hundred in advance."

Shelley shakes his head. So during their time in Geneva that ridiculous man was composing an account about LB. Probably about the rest of them, too.

"All I can tell you is he didn't return with us. I urge you to approach whatever he writes with caution. He's a peculiar fellow and not to be trusted. Lord Byron will be outraged when he finds out what he's done."

As soon as he's on the street again, he begins to laugh. He can picture Polidori in his room at Villa Diodati, feverishly recording everything he's seen and heard. He doubts anyone will want to read it, but he doesn't begrudge the fellow making money however he can.

In the afternoon he goes to Skinner Street—with trepidation. He didn't tell Mary and Claire he was doing this, but he thinks

Godwin and his wife might respond more favorably if he makes the first contact himself.

To his surprise, the Godwins have already heard he's come over from Bath. Apparently, Peacock told someone who told someone else who delivered the news to their shop. London is a big city, but if you count only the poets and philosophers and radicals, you have a rather small circle. Godwin greets him with genial words, while his wife stands two steps behind. Claire was right—the eyes with which Mrs. Godwin glares at him are those of an enraged beast. On the other hand, two of the woman's three daughters have run off, so maybe what appears to be anger is actually unbearable pain.

"We are back and we are well," he tells them. "You must let us bring William 'round. He'll soon be turning one."

"Of course," Godwin says. Mrs. Godwin's expression softens at the mention of her grandson's name.

"And what of Claire?" Mrs. Godwin asks. "Does she plan to remain with you?"

"I'm afraid she's been ill," he replies, using his rehearsed response. "The doctor thinks it's owing to bad food during our travels so he suggested Bath. As you know, the water there is said to have restorative effects."

She seems satisfied, but he can still imagine her showing up in Bath unannounced. With this in mind, he adds, "Don't feel you must come to visit. She's improving rapidly and we'll be returning to London soon." He doesn't see how Claire can keep her pregnancy secret for its full term. Then again, he knows from experience not to underestimate her cleverness and resolve. To change the subject, he inquires after Fanny. They tell him she has begun caring for the children of a nearby family and is presently away.

Tea is served and for half an hour they catch him up on recent events. It has been a bad year in England, with poor harvests in the north leading to food shortages and social unrest. Such talk provokes him, makes him want to run out into the streets and sound the alarm. To recommit himself to bringing about change. But how? About that he vacillates. Can poetry cause change? To do so, it must sell, yet it appears people prefer poems like *Childe Harold*, intended to entertain, over poems like *Alastor* or *Queen Mab*, intended to inform and incite. He's in the early pages of a new one, which he hopes will be more provocative than anything he's written before. In the present climate it may get him thrown in jail, but if he allows his fears to conquer him, then what's his talent for?

Perhaps he should simply return home, reconcile with his father, and prepare to take up his role in society. He would have influence and more money and land and a house. But no, he has renounced that life. Most would say he's mad for having done so. On the contrary, given his principles, he had no choice.

Before he leaves, he hands Godwin a bank draft for two hundred pounds. He can tell it's less than he hoped for, it always is, but still his face goes soft. Tears fill his eyes. How much effort it must have taken Godwin to keep from asking if any money was forthcoming the instant he arrived.

What strange power access to even a few pounds gives one. It almost makes him wish he didn't have it so he couldn't be drawn into encounters such as this. Almost.

On his way back to Bath the following day, he stops to see Peacock in the village of Marlow. Peacock lives with his mother in what seems to Shelley complete and blessed peace. In the daytime he goes to his job as a clerk and at night he writes his gentle satires. Shelley tells him about their summer in Geneva and then about his encounter with Godwin. Peacock finds the latter situation amusing rather than dire. That's what Shelley likes about him—more often than not, he sees the world through a comic lens.

They stroll about the village together and Shelley is unexpectedly charmed by Marlow. It's green and quiet but still near enough to London to make it possible to do business in the city with ease.

"Could you help us find a place here?" he asks.

"Why of course. And after that, where would you like to live? Since it appears I'm becoming your permanent property agent, I should like to stay one step ahead."

"Make it a large place," he continues, ignoring Peacock's remark. "Claire doesn't seem to be going anywhere, and there will be children, two at least and possibly more."

Before he leaves, he gives Peacock an amount of money equal to what he gave Godwin. It's partly as pay for his services, for helping find a house and keeping track of his affairs, but it's also a gift. He likes the man and considers it no great error to reward him not only for what he does but for who he is.

From Marlow he returns to Bath, where he finds Mary even more immersed in her writing than before. He urges her on. It's a pleasure to see her thus. Elise is such a skilled caretaker and so comfortable with Willmouse—and Willmouse with her—that Mary can spend hours and hours at her desk. Presuming she isn't interrupted by Claire. In Marlow, Claire will have her own quarters. He likes a house full of people, while Mary prefers more privacy, with more uninterrupted time to herself.

Claire

In three months her child will be born. She has begun to feel it move within her. She still holds out some hope that LB will rescue her and the baby when the time arrives. Admittedly, her hope is small—though she writes him every week, he has yet to reply. But rescue her from what? This small family of which she is a part, peculiar though it is, keeps her safe and warm.

On the rare occasions when Shelley isn't working, Claire insists he tell her stories or discuss some item in the newspaper, gossip or politics, it doesn't matter, as long as his attention is on her. Mary is generally too prickly to be put to such use. When Claire asks her how her ghost story is progressing, she takes offense:

"It's *not* a ghost story. It never was." Then, more reflectively, "At first I did think it would be something like the ones we read in the villa, but it's gone far beyond that. In truth, I know not what it is. Or what it shall become." If another person made such remarks, she'd consider them pretentious. *What it shall become?* However, Claire is certain it is within Mary's power to imagine something astonishing into being.

As for her own imagination, it is now working upon picturing her child's future. If it is a boy, she'd prefer he grow up to be something other than a poet. She's seen such men up close and their flaws can't be ignored. They are too self-involved. Nor does she think LB would want a poet for a son. If only he'd change his mind and marry her. Then he'd have genuine prospects—her son, that is, assuming it's a boy. If it's a girl, there will be only one question: Can she marry well? Of course, Claire will hardly be able to offer herself as an example. "Do as I say," she will tell her daughter, "not as I have done." She thinks about the years her small family lived in poverty, before Mr. Godwin, when the workhouse loomed. Even as a tiny child she worried about food and lodging, yet somehow her mother refused to give up. She once asked her mother if she knew Mr. Godwin *before* they moved into the house next door to his.

"What are you asking?" her mother replied. "Did I contrive to place myself in his proximity? Did I plot to tangle him in my web?"

She almost didn't pursue the matter but her curiosity was great. "I'm merely saying I can't remember why we moved there. I was very young."

"We moved often, usually because we couldn't afford the rent. Then Mr. Godwin saved us. Whether I found him or he found me is of no importance. What matters is that he is reliable. You will be fortunate to find a man who is so reliable. Notice I do not say wealthy. Notice I do not say clever. I say *reliable* and suggest you take that word to heart."

Of course, that was some years ago, long before she set her sights on Byron. Byron is wealthy and exceedingly clever. She supposes he could be called reliable but only toward his own purposes and not in the way her mother meant. Maybe she should find someone else. Not now—no man would want a woman in her condition—but after the child is born. "Shelley," she could say, "what about your friend Hogg? Do you think he'd like to be married? You should bring him around." Although she doesn't know Hogg well, she's certain he's reliable. In fact, if there were a stronger word meaning the same thing, it would apply to him.

While she's having these thoughts, Shelley wanders through the room, looking distracted. Then Mary wanders through the room, looking distracted. She knows these looks well—they are both writing and any effort to converse will be a waste of time. For Shelley this is nothing new, but Mary has only recently begun to lose herself in her work to such an extent. In response, Claire decides to put on her cloak and go outside.

Lately, she has been visiting Bath Abbey, where she sits outside in the wan October sun. Her favorite place is near the great west entrance, with its enormous window and stone ladders being ascended by stone angels on either side. The story is that some ancient bishop of Bath had a vision of angels climbing a ladder to heaven and the carvers took it to heart. She finds solace in the story and in the angels themselves. They have wings and presumably could fly wherever they please, yet still they cling to the ladder and look down as if they're afraid they'll fall.

She watches people enter the church, heads bowed. Sometimes she wonders what she has missed by not being part of the community of believers. Her father considers religion useless, even destructive, and Shelley does as well. Still, he writes about angels, talks about angels, and is able to describe angels of several different kinds. If there is no God, where then does he think angels come from? How can he write them into being if he doesn't think they exist? She's certain the carvers who placed the angels on the ladders were believers. They look too real to be the product of anything but unquestioning faith.

Mary

She's having difficulty sleeping. Or if she does sleep, she wakes up with a headache and finds it difficult to eat. Shelley tries to take care of her, but she sends him away. "It's kind of you to help, but I believe silence may be the best medicine. Feel free to go back to your work."

Despite her sleeplessness and discomfort, she is writing a great deal. Although there are times when her words seem stale—surely that must happen to all writers—she continues, adding in small increments to the vision she had in Geneva. She was born with a streak of stubbornness and is determined not to give up. She writes a dozen pages and burns them in the fire. A dozen more and they meet the same fate. Shelley looks at her crouched before the hearth, raises an eyebrow, and returns to his work.

Then, on an otherwise unexceptional night, when everyone is asleep, a flood of words and images arrives.

She writes:

> *After days and nights of incredible labor and fatigue, I succeeded in discovering the cause of the generation of life; nay, more, I became myself capable of bestowing animation upon lifeless matter.*

She writes:

> *No one can conceive the variety of feelings which bore me onwards, like a hurricane, in the first enthusiasm of success. Life and death appeared to me ideal bounds, which I should at first break through, and pour a torrent of light into our dark world.*

She writes:

> *It was on a dreary night of November, that I beheld the accomplishment of my toils. With an anxiety that almost amounted to agony, I collected the instruments of life around me, that I might infuse a spark of being into the lifeless thing that lay at my feet.*

Galvani demonstrated how electricity can bring the dead back to life. In this feverish night of writing she feels as if it is not only Frankenstein's creature but herself who has been galvanized. The words come as if from some external source. Her hand moves effortlessly, undirected by her will. So lost is she in her work that when she finally pauses and looks out the window, she sees the morning sun. In the small courtyard below, Elise appears to be teaching Willmouse some kind of dance. How could she have failed to hear them come awake and go out the door? He wobbles about on his short legs. He laughs and hops and Elise holds his hands. He pulls away and she catches him. Then, as Elise lifts him up, he sees Mary at the window and their eyes meet. She feels so much love, she can scarcely breathe.

Later that morning Shelley inquires about her work. She tells him she's made some progress but asks if he'd go out and get some larger paper. She doesn't like working on such small sheets.

"What difference could that possibly make?" he says.

"I don't know that it will make a difference. But it's what I want. My handwriting has gotten unruly. The words run off the page."

"As you wish, my dear," he says and fetches his coat. As regards her writing, he is the best of all possible companions. He praises her when she needs praise and refrains from giving too much advice. If she chooses to burn her pages, he will not ask for an explanation. If large paper is needed, he will provide it. She fears she doesn't do as well by him.

While Shelley is out, she returns to work: *I started from my sleep in horror; a cold dew covered my forehead, my teeth chattered, and every limb became convulsed; when, by the dim and yellow light of the moon, as it forced its way through the window shutters, I beheld the wretch—the miserable monster whom I had created.*

He comes home with a roll of newsprint. When unfurled, the sheets are as long as she is tall. After thanking him, she gives him, with no small amount of apprehension, the sentences she just wrote. Moments later he hands them back with an expression of astonishment on his face.

"Are you Mary Godwin, or have you been replaced by a sorceress? Wherever did you find such words?"

After supper, he reads to them from *Don Quixote*, as he has done for the past several nights. It's a remarkable tale, but her mind wanders. She watches Claire, across the room—she is mere weeks from giving birth. Claire sometimes annoys her, if only because she's ever-present. A week, a day, even a single afternoon when she and Shelley could be entirely alone would be heavenly. Yet she also feels sympathy for her. No doubt Claire would like some privacy as well. Mary forces herself to attend to Sancho Panza again.

That night, exhausted from having worked with scarcely any pause for three days, she sleeps at last, sleeps without dreaming. In the morning, she breakfasts with Elise and Willmouse, bathes as if preparing for some sacred ceremony, and returns to her desk. There, she continues to write, driven by the words themselves, driven by the unnameable forces she seems to have put into play.

In the midst of her passionate spate of work, Shelley announces he has begun a new poem. He says, "It shall be about a youth nourished in dreams of liberty, some of whose actions are in direct opposition to the opinions of the world, but who is animated throughout by an ardent love of virtue."

"I will look forward to it," she says, but to herself she thinks, *While you write of dreams of liberty, I write of death and depravity and good intentions gone wrong.*

In truth, she likes the contrast between them. She is the dark spirit and he the light. She never opens a door without expecting bad news on the other side, while he expects someone has come to bring him money or fame or at least something to eat. And why shouldn't he? His childhood was charmed, he has many friends, and he was born with genius and talent combined.

A few days later, as if to confirm her thoughts, Shelley receives a letter from the editor of *The Examiner*, Mr. Leigh Hunt. Hunt has read his poetry and admires it greatly. He wants to publish some in his radical newspaper and intends to review *Alastor*. Overcome by excitement, Shelley lifts her off her feet, and like Willmouse and Elise, they caper about the room.

Dr. Polidori

After Mary and her companions depart, Lord Byron leaves as well. He'll be back in a few days, but for now Polidori has the villa to himself. Except for the animals. Sometimes he hears the monkey screech—or maybe it's the falcon. He knows a man comes in daily to look after them, but that's all he knows. They're kept somewhere belowstairs.

Now that he's alone, Polidori sleeps during the day, stays awake all night, and at sunrise stands on the balcony and pretends the place belongs to him. As the summer remains unseasonably cold, he builds such huge fires that at times he fears they'll escape the fireplace and burn the house to the ground.

He continues to work on the story he is building upon Lord Byron's leavings. In his tale the vampire Ruthven travels about the Continent exhibiting his abhorrent nature and refusing death. Perhaps Polidori's greatest pleasure is making the heinous Lord Ruthven as Byron-like as possible, inhuman and craven and careless of others' needs.

However, at a certain point he begins to wonder if writing

such tales deserves his time and effort. Since he is a man of medicine and rational thought, aren't creatures of the supernatural beneath him? Then he happens upon a passage in a book by Rousseau (purloined from Byron's collection): *If there is a well-attested history in the world, it is that of the Vampires. Nothing is missing from it: interrogations, certifications by Notables, Surgeons, Parish Priests, Magistrates. The judicial proof is one of the most complete.*

He stops and shakes his head in disbelief. Is this possible? He has always considered Rousseau nothing if not trustworthy; yet here the great philosopher endorses the authenticity of vampires, beings Polidori assumed existed only in myth. After that, he begins writing with increased fervor. This thing he is creating might still be classified as a romance, but if Rousseau is correct, it will be a romance based on truth.

One afternoon there is a knock at his chamber door. Of course he knows who it is. How long was he gone? Five days? A week? Not long enough.

When he opens the door, Byron glares at him. "It's time," he says. Not a single word more.

"You wish me to leave?"

"More than you can imagine."

"What will you do if you become ill?"

"Die, if I have any luck."

He knows he might not see him again, so he tells himself to capture his image and lock it up in his mind. Lord Byron. Lord Ruthven. One and the same. In truth he looks less healthy than at any time since they met, but that's no longer his concern. Not from that moment forward. Let him care for himself, in whatever way he sees fit.

He departs the following morning on foot and travels southward toward Milan. Polidori hopes to visit an uncle there, one he's never met. When he's only a day out of Geneva, the terrain becomes almost impassibly steep and it begins to rain. Yet he continues on. What other choice does he have? Up the mountainsides, across the valleys, taking shelter at night under overhangs of rock and stopping at any cottage or hovel to bargain or beg for a meal. He has the money Byron paid him but refuses to spend it. He'll save it for the future; right now he wants to separate himself from all vestiges of his recent past.

Near Ivrea, he asks a farmer if he can sleep in his barn and discovers in conversation that the farmer's daughter is ill. She has a stomach ailment, and although the farmer seems skeptical of his expertise, he's desperate and allows him to treat the girl. Polidori administers an emetic, and remarkably, she awakes the next morning entirely cured. The farmer falls to his knees to thank him and his wife feeds him like a king. For once he feels useful; for once he feels the title of *Doctor* is something his actions have earned.

That turns out to be one of the few happy events of his journey. For the most part he remains terribly lonely and even at times half mad. Once, in a small village, he's thrown in jail for vagrancy; another time he's beaten by some men who steal the money he was refusing to spend.

Through it all he continues to write, perhaps while seated on a rock in the woods, perhaps at a table in some rude inn. And as the days pass, he begins to live inside his tale, picturing with great vividness and detail the horrors perpetrated by Lord Ruthven: the murders, the dismemberments, the eviscerations, until there comes a period when he can think of nothing but blood.

At last he finds himself on the outskirts of Milan. Without much difficulty he determines the whereabouts of his uncle, who welcomes him with warmth and takes him into his home. After a night of excellent sleep, the first good sleep he's had in weeks and weeks, he awakes and opens his satchel to inspect the smudged and stained and wildly scrawled pages of his manuscript. It takes him only a few seconds to decide to throw it into the canal that runs behind his uncle's house. He is ashamed to have produced such a horrible document, an expression of evil he'd have thought himself incapable of if he hadn't witnessed its creation by his own hand. Just before he manages to dispose of it, a servant calls him to breakfast and he hides it back in his bag.

Jeff Hogg

He hears of the tragedy from a clerk who heard it from a magistrate who heard it from a constable. Apparently, she was unidentified at first and then identified only as Mrs. Smith. Finally, it was determined that she was Harriet Westbrook, found in Hyde Park, drowned in the Serpentine. She was near to giving birth and had been dead for three weeks. He goes to the magistrate and then to the constable in an effort to learn more.

"It seems she'd been living with a Captain Ryan and also a Major Maxwell," the constable tells him, a look partly of pity and partly of disapproval on his face. "At the end it was a stable groom— he's the one called Smith. Young women in her situation generally choose the Waterloo Bridge. It's more certain. But there's no end of ways to get the job done if you've decided it's what you want."

He pictures her as he saw her last—unhappy to be sure, but not in such a state as to make him expect this. All she had to do was agree to let him care for her and she'd have been all right. She wouldn't have had to offer herself to the captain or to the major or to the stable groom. Unable to contain himself, he pounds his fists against the bricks of the nearest wall.

Now he has to tell Shelley. He elects to go to Bath and deliver the message in person. Snow has fallen all across the Midlands, so he waits a few days to depart. He feels no great urgency—given how long poor Harriet's been dead, he will be delivering history rather than news. In the end his report is redundant. A letter from the magistrate has preceded him by a day.

"Why would she do it?" Hogg asks, standing at the door.

"I was hoping *you* could tell *me*." There's a bitterness in Shelley's voice, part of which Hogg thinks may be directed at him.

"I'm so sorry. I don't know what to say."

Then suddenly Shelley embraces him and begins to sob. "I did this to her," he says. Hogg stands mutely, his own tears already expended. He feels a bit like a father holding his son.

When Shelley has recovered, he invites him across the threshold, into an atmosphere of bleakness. The curtains are closed and the fire burns low in the hearth. Mary looks angry and Shelley appears to be unable to face her. Instead, his eyes flash about, like a rabbit expecting to be struck from above by a hawk. Claire is out somewhere with their child and his nurse. Neither Mary nor Claire knew Harriet well. They met her in person only once, when Shelley had just begun visiting Godwin, before he and Mary were in love.

Suddenly, Shelley says, "I intend to get my children back. I will want your help."

Hogg wasn't expecting this, at least not so soon. Of course, guilty grief and confusion can cause one to say almost anything. He may want to take drastic action today, but will he feel the same in a month?

"I can find you someone who does that kind of work," Hogg replies. "It's not my area of expertise."

"I blame her viper of a sister," Shelley continues. "It's she who drove Harriet from her father's house. It's she who made Harriet hate herself. She couldn't stand that Harriet looked to me for guidance instead of her."

Hogg's feelings are a mix of skepticism, sympathy, and dismay. Shelley once loved Harriet, and although that love ended, he never stopped caring about her welfare. After he left her for Mary, he continued to send her money, even if it meant having too little for himself. And yet he seldom visited or wrote. As for the sister, they disliked one another from the start.

Now Mary, who has been silent, speaks: "Shelley never did anything to harm Harriet. If he'd had a large enough house and the means, he'd have taken them all in. As sad as I feel for her, I can't help but think she was being selfish. She's left her babies behind."

She's protecting him, Hogg understands. Once again, he thinks about how different things would be if poor Harriet had opened herself to him when he offered. But now it's too late.

Before Hogg goes back to London, Shelley tells him how Peacock is helping him find a house in Marlow and about the editor Leigh Hunt.

"He intends to review *Alastor*!" he says. "I care not whether he damns it or praises it, at least readers will know it exists. Remain with us overnight and I will read to you from my new poem. And you ought to see what Mary's writing. We'll get her to read as well."

Under ordinary circumstances he would, with pleasure, but for the first time since he's known Shelley, Hogg finds himself wanting to be away from him. From the pair of them. They have become so entwined that Shelley is not quite the Shelley he knew, but a changed being, one who is half of a whole. They seem to encourage one anoth-

239

er's self-regard. Or maybe that's being harsh. In any event, he can't see himself sitting in that room as afternoon becomes evening, with Shelley, Mary, perhaps Claire, and the ghost of Harriet hovering over all. There was a time when he and Shelley were inseparable. But then Shelley's life became so complicated, Hogg could scarcely understand its various parts. If he leaves now, he can get a third of the way back to London tonight.

As he goes for the door, Shelley makes a playful but annoying effort to drag him back. It's pointless—Hogg easily breaks free.

"Well then," Shelley says, "when we have our new place in Marlow, you will come for a long stay."

"Of course," he replies but isn't sure he really means it. It seems possible his friendship with Shelley will never be as it was before.

Mary

Harriet was always something of a mystery to her. Shelley never said much about their life together, although to be honest, she was content to remain ignorant. Now, however, his silence is too much to bear and she makes a request:

"Please tell me what you're thinking? Otherwise I can be of no use."

"What anyone would think, I suppose. Why she chose to destroy her life. Also what she thought of me at the end. If she hated me, I wish she'd said so. Silent suffering does no one any good. But mostly I'm concerned about the children. I dislike her sister and fear Westbrook will allow her to bring them up."

"If you can get them to us, I will care for them. We'd have Willmouse and Claire's baby and the two of them—a lively flock."

She's bending her wants to match his. Although she will never say it, she thinks her preferred way of life would be in a small room somewhere, with her pen and paper and ink, with Willmouse well taken care of by Elise, and Shelley appearing, as if by magic, in her bed each night. But Harriet's death has forced the issue of the children, Ianthe and Charles, upon them and they simply cannot turn their backs.

The next day Shelley tells her he must go to London to see

what it will take to seek custody in Chancery Court. He also intends to visit Leigh Hunt. He's spoken to him a few times, at lectures and the like, but he doesn't know him well.

"I want to thank him for championing my poetry. He's the first one of influence who has."

"Perhaps on your return trip you could see what Peacock has found for us in Marlow." Since the news about Harriet, she has gotten more anxious to leave Bath. An actual house would be paradise. The rooms here are minuscule and she's begun to feel crushed.

Shelley packs and is ready to leave the following morning. Before he departs, he takes her into their bedroom, away from Claire and Elise.

"An idea has come to me," he says.

"An idea?" There's something peculiar about the look on his face.

"No . . . not an idea . . . a *request*. I want us to be married."

"How interesting," she says, "and how unexpected. But why now?"

"Because the court will be more sympathetic to our case if we are husband and wife."

"My goodness. That's hardly a proposal. More like a strategy or a scheme." She'd be taken aback if anything right now was as it should be, but no, she's not taken aback, she's touched. Still, she can't pass up the opportunity to tease him: "I must admit there was a time when I'd have been thrilled but . . ."

"You're not going to tell me no?"

She adopts an expression of deliberation and cool disdain. When he looks sufficiently alarmed, she takes pity on him. "Of course not. However, I have one condition. We must do it in London so my father and stepmother can attend."

As soon as he's gone, she tells Claire and Elise.

Elise says, "You are not married?"

"Surely you must have known," Mary says. "We've spoken about it often enough . . ."

"I did not know," Elise says, straightening her back. "And I am not sure I can remain employed in such a place."

Before Mary can gather her wits to respond, Elise laughs.

As Mary tormented Shelley, so Elise is tormenting her. And doing a better job of it.

With Shelley gone, Mary goes back to work. At first she has difficulty concentrating. She keeps thinking about Harriet Westbrook, imagining how it must feel to drown. Or rather, how it must feel to decide to drown—the true terror would be in the choice even more than the act. Then late that night, something unexpected happens. She finds herself writing in the creature's voice. *Her* creature, the uncanny child of her pen. It's something she never before considered, and as she begins, she's not sure she's capable of such a feat. Yet after only a few sentences it feels natural, inevitable. Clearly, her creation has been waiting for a chance to speak:

> *It is with considerable difficulty that I remember the original era of my being: all the events of that period appear confused and indistinct. A strange multiplicity of sensations seized me, and I saw, felt, heard, and smelt at the same time; and it was, indeed, a long time before I learned to distinguish between the operations of my various senses.*

She finds the process of imagining his consciousness exhilarating. Moment by moment he notices where he is and who he is, what the world around him is made of, and how, by means of his senses, he brings it in to being:

> *I gradually saw plainly the clear stream that supplied me with drink and the trees that shaded me with their foliage. I was delighted when I first discovered that a pleasant sound, which often saluted my ears, proceeded from the throats of the little winged animals who had often intercepted the light from my eyes.*

She thinks about Willmouse and his daily discoveries, but this is different. The creature is not a child. Instead of growing into his perceptions over years, he comes to them in hours. He reflects on his learning and thereby understands what it is to be human—or human-like. As she writes, she sees through his eyes and hears through his ears. Feels through his fingertips and tastes through his tongue. She finds it tremendously exciting and can't wait until Shelley returns so she can tell him about it: "The monster and I have become one."

But he doesn't return. Instead, a letter arrives, calling her to London. The wedding has been arranged.

She tells Claire she should come, too, but Claire is only weeks away from giving birth and holds fast to her belief that her mother would not be able to accept that she is carrying Lord Byron's child.

"She would hate me for it," she says. "Besides, Elise will take good care of me, and once my baby is born, no one will have to know who the mother is. Or the father."

"I would so like you at my wedding ..."

"My spirit will be present. Kiss Shelley for me. Tell Mother and Father I am getting better but still not well enough to travel."

"As you wish," Mary says. In truth, she's not entirely sorry. She hasn't spoken to her father or her stepmother in months and getting married without strife will be difficult enough without the complications Claire would add.

At night, when sleep overtakes her, the creature is in her dreams. How quickly he climbs the glacier and how terrifying is his gaze. She is at once behind his eyes and looking into his eyes. She loves him and despises him. She wants him to possess her and wants to be released.

A week later she arrives in London. Shelley is waiting to meet her. He has just come from visiting her father and tells her all is well.

"He wants to see you as soon as possible. But be prepared, since we saw him last, he has aged somewhat."

His remark causes her a pang of guilt. If their marriage will mend the fabric of her relations with her father, it will be worth it, even if in their minds it remains nothing more than a convenience, a means of tricking society into thinking they are the same as everyone else.

He also tells her that his suit to reclaim his children is underway and that he had a delightful meeting with Leigh Hunt.

"He's quite charismatic," he says. "He was recently released from prison, where he was put for criticizing the extravagant style in which the royals live while so many remain in poverty. I also met his wife, whom I think you would like. He has four children and keeps a contented house."

His face shows how much he admires this new acquaintance: a man who was imprisoned for his principles but whose large family suffers not—what could be better than that? She has yet to tell him that a larger family is in his future as well, as she is pregnant again. She's known for some weeks, but with the terrible tragedy of Harriet followed by the planning for their marriage, she thought the news should wait.

They take supper that evening at Skinner Street and are treated quite differently than they were before. They are congratulated on their upcoming nuptials and given the best seats and the best service, as if they were dignitaries from some far-off land. And when she speaks her mind, no one, not even her stepmother, contradicts her. "Mary, tell us something of your time in Switzerland," her father says, and then adds, "if you are so inclined." He asks repeatedly what he can do to make her comfortable and, at the table, keeps filling her glass. As Shelley warned, he's grayer and more bent. His voice sometimes quavers.

When it's time for them to leave, Shelley pulls her aside. "He said he's proud to have his daughter marry the son of a baronet. Then he asked me if any money would be forthcoming. I said most definitely but I couldn't guarantee an amount."

Shelley

They marry at St. Mildred's Church, Bread Street, with Godwin and his wife as witnesses and his new friend Leigh Hunt and wife, Marianne, as guests. His bride wears flowers in her hair and a simple muslin dress. He'd have liked Hogg and Peacock present, but Hogg is in Manchester on business and Peacock is suffering an attack of gout. Perhaps it's just as well. During the ceremony all he can think is, *I must get out of this place.* The only fitting use for such grim stone edifices is as mausoleums and maybe not even that. The dead, he is certain, prefer to sleep beneath a starry sky. He'd be happy if he never had to enter a church again. Yet both Godwins look entirely satisfied.

Is it because they consider this event evidence that Mary has finally been brought to heel? If so, they are mistaken. She has always done as she pleases and will not stop now.

Later that day Mary prepares to return to Bath. She wants to be present for Claire's parturition and lying-in. Before she leaves, she tells him she, too, will be having a baby before the year is out.

"I am not at all surprised," he says. "After all, it's what married people do."

"Joke if you must, but you had better press Peacock to obtain property in Marlow. We shall need the room."

"Go home and write your book," he tells her. "I'll finish my present business and prepare for any and all eventualities. Do not fret."

He spends the following week in Hampstead with the Hunts. The Hunt household is delightful, full of books and children—four under the age of eleven—and visitors, mostly writers and artists, arriving at all hours of the day and night. It's something like what he knows (based on Mary's reports) Godwin's house to have been when she was a child. However, Hunt's wife, Marianne, is far more charming than Mrs. Godwin could ever be.

At Hunt's house, he meets the critic Hazlitt and a young poet named John Keats. He gets on well with Hazlitt but Keats doesn't seem to like him; when Shelley speaks of how poetry might contribute to the transformation of society, Keats replies that he would agree if only it were capable of that. He says, "Poetry should lift the thoughts of man and diminish his cares—even as society remains as it is."

"But . . . but . . . don't you then become complicit in the evils of society 'as it is'?" Shelley sputters, this matter being of great significance to him. "Is poetry mere entertainment? Is it simply a pretty distraction?"

Keats tries to explain that making poetry into a causal agent diminishes its purity, but Shelley will have none of it: "The great instrument of moral good is the imagination. Poetry enlarges the circumference of the imagination. Therefore . . ."

They fail to reach resolution. Perhaps they are too much alike to be friends.

Later they all take a companionable walk on Hampstead

Heath. Hunt wears a flowered dressing gown and Hazlitt pontificates to such an extent that Shelley finally gets bored and begins making up games with the Hunt children. He twists his hair into horns and chases them as they squeal with delight.

The next day Hunt tells him he intends to publish Shelley's poem "Hymn to Intellectual Beauty," which he wrote in Geneva while under the influence of Rousseau. He wishes Mary were here to share the moment. He reads the poem aloud to the Hunts and their guests and basks in their appreciation. Even Keats has words of praise.

"Such an ear for rhyme you have," he exclaims. "Neither sound nor syllable out of place." He's a slight fellow, no more than five feet tall, yet when he speaks about poetry, his passion seems to add inches to his height.

Shelley is enjoying himself immensely, but the main reason he's not returned to Bath is that he's keeping watch on the Chancery suit aimed at reclaiming Harriet's children. His children. When they were with Harriet, he was able to tell himself it was best if they were with their mother. Now that she's gone, they might be better off with him. He'd at least like that to be an option, not prohibited by the courts.

But the suit isn't going well. The man he's retained to represent his interests sends him daily updates, each one more pessimistic than the last. The problem is Mr. Westbrook. He is as determined to keep the children from Shelley as Shelley is to claim them. He'd assumed that marrying Mary would make it impossible for him to be denied, but Westbrook is using *Queen Mab* and other writings of his to convince the judge he's a heretic, a sensualist, and worse. In a letter to Byron, Shelley writes:

> *A Chancery process has now been instituted against me! The intended effect is to deprive me of my unfortunate children, my inheritance, and to throw me into prison, on the grounds of my being a REVOLUTIONIST and an ATHEIST. It appears I may be dragged before the tribunals of tyranny and superstition, to answer with my children, my property, and my liberty. Yet I will not fail.*

He doesn't really believe he'll be imprisoned, or that his inheritance will be revoked. Still, the affair makes him so furious, he can't help but rant. A few days later, a letter turns up in which Harriet stated that, should anything happen to her, the children are to stay with her sister. He's sure it's a forgery, but he knows it's likely to carry weight. He wants to go into court and make his case, but he's told his chances of winning are now negligible and he's advised to stay away. Therefore, he thanks the Hunts for their exemplary hospitality and heads off to Marlow, where he intends to spend a day with Peacock before returning to Bath.

To his delight, Peacock has been successful once again. The house he has found for them will please Mary to no end. It has two stories, with large rooms and a capacious, sunlit library, which opens onto a back garden of an acre or more. The rooms will be more than adequate, but it's the garden that is the house's true glory. At its center is a beautiful cedar while around the edges fir and cypress trees grow. There is even a strawberry patch. To top it off, it's only a short walk to where Peacock lives with his mother, and the coach road to London is nearby.

"As for the lease," Peacock says, "I'm afraid they wouldn't give you a hundred years. It's only for twenty-one."

Shelley laughs. "If I am alive in twenty-one years, I'll gladly give it up."

He signs the papers and leaves that same day. Peacock promises to have the place in excellent order when he returns.

In Bath, news awaits. Three days ago Claire gave birth to a girl. Mary says she wrote to him but sent the letter care of the Hunts. Claire has decided to name the child Alba, after "LB." Shelley is shown the baby, who, upon seeing him, begins to wail, which provokes much merriment. Then they recount for him the entire story, both harrowing and heroic, of how the midwife never arrived and how Elise and Mary did quite as well as any midwife could.

"Claire was extraordinarily brave," Mary says.

"Mary and Elise were extraordinarily brave," Claire replies. "But Mary, please know that I don't intend to reciprocate when your time comes. Rather, I shall book three midwives so if one fails to arrive there will be two in reserve."

Everyone looks content. Claire reminds them that they are all to pretend the child is not hers, and they feel like coconspirators, proud of their cleverness and exhibiting no shame. Shelley still doesn't believe it's a plan that can be sustained, but there's no harm in trying, at least for now.

"What do you propose to tell her when she's old enough to want to see her mother?" he asks.

Claire looks at him dismissively. "Many things may happen between now and then. The situation will sort itself out."

Over the next few days, he notices that all the joy about Claire's baby combined with all his hard thoughts about Ianthe and Charles has served to deepen his love for Willmouse. He holds him and doesn't want to let him go.

Although he'd like to move them to Marlow as soon as possible, Elise and Mary insist Claire must rest for at least two weeks. In the interim, he turns to Mary's manuscript. Always before, she's prefaced his reading of her work with the admonition that any comments be positive. "Tell me only what pleases you," has been her steady refrain. Yet suddenly she has become confident, handing him the pages without fear.

"Point out every flaw," she says. "I'm certain there are too many to count."

"Should I expect to be terrified?" he asks, realizing as he speaks that his remark might be considered condescending.

"Perhaps. But I hope it does more than that."

He takes the manuscript to a space behind the wardrobe he's taken to calling his library. Seeing it now, with the image of the grand library in the house in Marlow fresh in his mind, he has to smile. On the other side of the wardrobe, Mary and Claire discuss the new baby. Before long the baby cries, but he is so engrossed in Mary's story, he doesn't hear a sound.

Dr. Polidori

In York, Polidori is rereading his own manuscript. Begun in Geneva, completed in the hills above Milan, and carried in his satchel back to England, he has left it untouched for months. In Italy, when he wrote the final pages, he was genuinely frightened by what he'd created. It was too ghastly, too perverse, too filled with evil to expect anyone else to read it. Yet time changes one's perceptions and now he wonders if some publishing firm might take it on. He shall prepare a clean copy with that in mind. Somewhere he has read that "Blood sells."

He's heard nothing from the Shelleys or from Lord Byron. Not even from Fletcher. He thinks of Mary often. She could have changed his life for the better. Could he have done so for her? Probably not. So praise be to her for realizing that and resisting his advances.

He's had more difficulty finding work as a doctor here in York than he'd expected. People seem suspicious of him. As a diversion, he's taken to gambling, mostly whist. He plays several nights a week but has begun to run out of money. This causes him to press forward with this plan to sell his book.

He travels to London and begins calling at publishing houses, manuscript in hand. The first few he visits have difficulty understanding what it's about.

"Can you describe it for me? Give me the flavor so I can determine if it's worth my time." The fellow he's speaking to in this place is ancient, almost dust-covered in aspect, and his voice is a scarcely intelligible croak.

"The flavor? Don't you want to read it and judge for yourself?"

The old fellow waves weakly toward a heap of manuscripts against the wall.

Polidori nods. "I see. All waiting to be read." So he proceeds to explain, to the best of his ability, what it's about. When he uses the word *vampire*, he watches closely for a reaction. There is none. Either the man has never heard of such a thing, has heard of them but considers them ridiculous creatures of fancy, or has been so pummeled by authors, each of whom has an idea he considers remarkable, he's become immune.

Other publishers respond similarly. He'd like to go see John Murray, as he has a preexisting business relationship with that firm, but he never completed the journal of his trip with Byron, so they'll consider him too great a risk. However, from that problem comes an idea. Suppose he were to explain to publishers how the story came about—how he spent last summer with the infamous Lord Byron, how Villa Diodati became a den of depravity, and how, out of that corrupt and sinful slough, came this equally depraved book.

To his surprise, the scheme works. At the firm of Sherwood, Neely, and Jones, on Paternoster Row, he is escorted in to meet the young Mr. Neely—not the old Mr. Neely, who, he is told, has taken to his bed and thank god for that—and upon the mere mention of Lord Byron, Neely's eyebrows go up. He should have known. Why try to sell vampires when you can sell Lord Byron instead?

He is paid 250 pounds as an advance on sales and returns to York feeling as if he's conquered the world. He'll no longer be a doctor; he'll be a writer instead. Eventually. Over the next few months he returns to his game of whist and even meets a young woman who is happy enough to have him spend much of his money on her.

Then, on a brutally cold Wednesday in February, just after a Tuesday evening during which he incurred considerable losses, a courier delivers to him a package wrapped in brown paper. It's his book, he can tell by the size. He opens it with trembling hands and begins to cry tears of joy as he reads the title: *The Vampyre: A Tale*. He runs his fingers over the words in ecstasy. But when he turns to the first page, where he expects to see his name, it says again, *The Vampyre: A Tale*. And below that, *By Lord Byron*. At once his tears turn to tears of fury. How is this possible? Did Lord Byron somehow intervene and take credit? It wouldn't be beyond him. Yet he knows that's not what happened. It's the publishing company taking advantage, twisting the story he told Neely to their own craven purposes.

He writes a letter to Neely, strongly worded, although with a businesslike veneer. Clearly there was a misunderstanding, one that can be corrected in subsequent editions. But their reply is unbending. They appreciate his help in bringing Lord Byron's manuscript to their attention, yet they remain puzzled by his efforts to take credit for it. He was paid a finder's fee—quite a large one—what more does he expect?

After that, he endeavors to contact Lord Byron to ask him to set things right. If nothing else, he'll want to correct the problem out of a sense of pride—he won't want his name on something he'll no doubt consider inferior to what he himself could produce. Unfortunately, this will be a long process. Is he in Italy or Greece or even Russia? Or has he gone to South America as he once threatened to do?

On top of his disappointment about his book, he is out driving when his horse bolts and his gig overturns. He cracks his head on the cobblestones and has to spend several weeks on his back, his head in bandages and his vision blurred. Thereafter, he has difficulty forming words—in his mouth and in his mind. Yet his memory remains flawless. He keeps recalling those gruesome nights in Edinburgh. He keeps recalling the hideous things Lord Ruthven did. It seems irrelevant whether his memories are of events that actually occurred or events that emerged from the tip of his pen. They all play out with equal vividness in his troubled mind. He has debilitating headaches and takes all manner of compounds in an effort to remedy them. Some cause him to hallucinate and others nearly immobilize him, forcing him to spend day after day in bed. He senses that he's fading into a kind of netherworld and fears he'll never be right again.

Claire

She is as anxious to move to Marlow as any of them, perhaps more so. Her infant is a hardy one, already capable of travel. *Alba*. Or so she thought. When she wrote Byron in Italy to tell him of the event and of the name she chose, a letter came flying back, insisting she be called Allegra. It's maddening. He has never laid eyes on the child and cares not for its mother but still wants to give it a name from a thousand miles away. She would resist if she didn't actually prefer Allegra. It sounds more feminine and more dignified, and in Italian, it means "joy." Trust his poet's ear to make a pleasing choice.

Mary and Shelley are working madly on Mary's book. Every day now they ensconce themselves at a table in the corner to edit the manuscript, page by page. They discuss how best to depict clouds or portray remorse or even by what methods a fiend would kill. It's obvious how much her authorship pleases him. Claire wishes she could do something that would please Byron as much. It seems giving birth to a poet's child is but a poor thing when compared to giving birth to a book.

She decides the time has come to write a letter to her parents telling them what she's done. The story she concocts involves a man whose wife has died in childbirth and is himself unable to care for a beautiful baby girl. Only after she posts the letter does she realize her false story echoes the true story of Mary's birth and Mary Wollstonecraft's tragic death. Godwin didn't give her up but the thought must have crossed his mind. Thus Claire fears he will see through her ruse and even consider it mockery. Instead, he writes back with sympathy for the child and praise for Claire. "What a fine and selfless thing you have done," he says. Even if he didn't believe her, she suspects her mother would prevent him from questioning her, so as not to provoke a scandal. On the other hand, perhaps her mother is becoming accustomed to scandal. If remaining unmarried and having children out of wedlock is as wicked as people say, the walls of the house on Skinner Street would have fallen down by now.

Shelley says that in Marlow she can have her own large room. Her own suite of rooms, if she so desires. She hopes Willmouse and Allegra will be playmates. And as Mary is pregnant again, there will be a third. In her mind's eye, she pictures them romping in the garden on a summer day.

So consumed is she with Allegra that time passes quickly. In what seems like a week, a month has elapsed, and the day of their departure is upon them. As they pack, she says to Mary, "We've become very skilled at this sort of travel, haven't we? I remember when it was only the three of us making our blister-footed way across France. But now, even with the children, we collect ourselves and our things in a single afternoon and are ready to depart the following day."

"I suppose that's true," Mary says. "Even so, it's a skill I would prefer someday to stop using. At least this time we are leaving by choice, not because we must."

"It would be much easier," she replies, "if you and Shelley had fewer books."

As has been the case every time they've gone somewhere new, Claire wonders if Mary would prefer it if she and her husband (as he is now called) were going alone. She'd certainly understand if that was true. Any newly married pair must want time to themselves. But about Shelley, Claire has no similar worries. He's always happy to have her along. She can hear it in his voice.

The Marlow house turns out to be as appealing as Shelley promised. With luck, and in accordance with Mary's wishes, they will stay a good long time. The Thames is not far off, and she expects it will be only a matter of days before Shelley obtains a boat. Perhaps that will be enough to keep him from becoming restless.

Before many days pass, her prediction is proven correct: he buys a little skiff. After that other signs of permanence begin to accrue: Mary hires a cook and Shelley a gardener. Shelley buys furniture—he's always bought furniture, but now more than ever before. A table, eight chairs, a bed for each of the five bedrooms, and some small side tables they can't decide where to put.

Next he goes out and meets the neighbors. On his way home he buys a bucket of crawfish from a woman on the street. Yet instead of bringing them home to boil up for supper, he releases them into a pond. A boy sees him doing it and so begins a rumor among the residents of Marlow that he is mad. Not that he minds. "Every village needs a madman," he says. Imagine what they will say when paper lanterns begin to be launched. He sings while he walks and distributes blankets to the poor. Claire's room is as Shelley said it would be, large and filled with light. The garden is as Shelley said it would be, large and filled with light.

Their first visitor is Peacock, which comes as no surprise. In the beginning he's rather formal about it, sending an announcement in advance and standing outside holding his hat until someone notices he's arrived. Before long though, he begins opening the door and entering without even the prelude of a knock. It happens nearly every day, right before lunch. The cook has learned what he likes. Hogg visits as well, although less frequently than Peacock because he has to come out from London. Claire believes she could convince Hogg to marry her, but she hasn't given up on the hope of meeting someone extraordinary and Hogg is not that. Yet she does like him and would be pleased to see him well married, with children at his very large feet.

"Tell me, Jeff, have you a sweetheart?" Claire asks, as they sit in the garden late one afternoon.

He and Shelley have spent the day boating on the Thames. His face is sunburnt and he looks entirely relaxed.

"My goodness, that's an unexpected question," he says, obviously gratified to have her take an interest in him.

"I'm sure you must. Or if not, it's because you are too busy making money, which to my mind is the more important pursuit."

"Can I count a certain lady whose family I have worked for but who does not yet know of my designs?"

"Your designs? You certainly can."

"For the purposes of this discussion, I shall call her Miss X. She lives in London and has a small white dog. I have made no formal declaration, but I contrive numerous reasons to visit and she seems pleased to see my face."

So they continue, chatting like cousins who have known one another since childhood, until the evening stars appears.

A few days later the Hunts arrive, the entire clan. Leigh Hunt, his wife Marianne, and their four young children. Unbeknownst to the rest of them, Shelley has invited them to stay for three weeks. Suddenly, the house is filled to capacity. A boy flies down the banister. Dogs are underfoot.

"I admire your tolerance," Claire says to Mary, at a rare moment when the two of them are alone.

"He can't help himself. And Willmouse is delighted to have so many playmates. Besides, think of where we grew up. Skinner Street had at least as many visitors as this. They may not have slept over, but they often stayed until dawn."

In the midst of the Hunts' visit, a freight wagon arrives carrying a large tarp-covered object. Claire goes outside with Allegra in her arms to see what it might be. Perhaps a new wardrobe, or a cabinet in which to store china. Once you have a china cabinet, you are likely to stay put. But it's neither a wardrobe nor a china cabinet; it's a piano, purchased by Shelley expressly for her. She hardly knows what to say.

"What have I done to deserve this?" Claire asks.

"It's not a matter of deserving. It's a matter of necessity. We have a large house and a need for music. Which you shall now supply."

She'd embrace him, but she's holding the baby, so instead she kisses him on the cheek. Later, she hears Mary ask him how much he paid for it. His reply? "You needn't worry. I bought it on credit and will pay for it in due time."

That same week she buys a collection of pieces by Mozart and begins to learn them by heart.

So the days pass in the Marlow house, through a spring in which the garden bursts with flowers and into a hot summer when they wilt. Peacock and Hogg come and go, the Hunts return, albeit for shorter visits, Mary continues to work on her book, and Shelley goes back and forth between London and Marlow, sometimes to check on his debts, sometimes to look for a publisher for Mary, and sometimes because, for all his satisfaction with life in their house near the Thames, he's simply unable to keep still.

Mary

When she's finally finished her book, when she's read it and reread it and changed ten thousand words, John Murray doesn't want it. He considers it too unconventional for such conservative times. Charles Ollier doesn't want it either. He's already agreed to publish Shelley's next long poem and thinks it might be too complicated to involve himself with his wife. At last, when she and Shelley are about to give up, the house of Lackington's takes it on. They are not considered prestigious, they agree to publish only five hundred copies, and she is paid just twenty-eight pounds. Still, she is satisfied: *Frankenstein-or The Modern Prometheus* is to be printed up and sold for money, which is to say, like a real book. She dedicates it to her father, causing Shelley to become envious until she promises the next one will be for him. And the one after that for their children, "by which time we'll have three or four."

"I see you have quite a career planned for yourself," he says.

Before Shelley began taking her manuscript around to various publishers, she left it with her father to read. She did so with trepidation. For all their difficulties, there is no one, save Shelley, whose opinion she holds in higher esteem. She feared he'd tell her it was ridiculous or incomprehensible or, the worst criticism of all, badly written. Instead, he said, "What you have done is beyond anything I could have imagined for you. It is your own creation, made by your own skilled hand."

"At first it came to me unbidden," she says. "Then I began to take control of it. To mold it and deepen it and . . ." She struggles for a moment to find the words. "To understand what I was attempting."

"The best writing is that which emerges from struggle."

"If that's true, then my book may be better than I think it is. There were times when I felt lost."

"But you found your way to the end. And now I look forward to your next one."

Will there be a next one? She's not sure. Shelley has no such hesitation. Right now he's deep into his new poem. He's calling it "Laon and Cythna," or "The Revolution in the Golden City." Apropos of their recent discussion, he tells her he's dedicating it to her, which causes her to recoil. *Queen Mab* was originally dedicated to Harriet; thus it may be an honor she doesn't want. Yet when he shows her the first lines, they take her breath away:

> *So now my summer task is ended, Mary,*
> *And I return to thee, mine own heart's home;*

"Oh," she says, "how beautiful." And then, "What exactly is the summer task of which you speak?"

"My entire life before I met you. I was in the wilderness."

"But you say the poem is about revolution . . ."

"Revolution is not only what happens to the State. It's also what happens to the individual. For society to truly change, both must occur at once."

Not long after that, she receives a copy of her own completed work, bound up in brown calf. After showing it to Shelley, she takes it to the garden, where she sits alone. There's something ineffable about holding in her hands this thing she made. It's right that she should have dedicated the book to her father. Her love of words and her belief that writing is a worthy endeavor began with him.

As she surveys the garden, she does so with the knowledge that no matter the length of the lease, they will not be here forever, perhaps not even until fall. Already Shelley is becoming restless, looking forward to another place. Before long something will cause him to want to leave, and she will not resist. Her world is Shelley and Willmouse and the child to come—she hopes it's a girl—all of whom accompany her wherever she goes.

After *Frankenstein* has been out for a month, reviews begin to appear. Most are not good. One calls it "a tissue of horrible and disgusting absurdity" and another describes her writing as *uncouth*. She doesn't mind it being called many things, but for some reason "uncouth" causes her pain. However, her father's friend Sir Walter Scott praises it, and one day she happens by accident upon one of Claire's unfinished letters to Byron. She can't help herself and skims the open page. There, she finds an opinion that pleases her more than any other:

> *Mary has just published her first work, a novel called* Frankenstein. *It is a most wonderful performance. The fiction is of so continued and extraordinary a kind as no one would imagine it could have been written by so young a person. I am delighted, and whatever private feelings of envy I may have at not being able to do so well myself yet, I must admire that she is a* woman *and will prove in time an ornament to us and an argument* in our favour.

Mary resolves never again to resent how Claire sometimes interferes with her privacy or her intimacy with Shelley. And she is pleased to see the word *yet*, which she takes to mean that Claire retains ambitions for herself. As for being a woman and doing things women are not expected to do, she considers it perfectly natural, given who her mother was.

Shelley

In the end, three things cause them to leave: First, Lord Byron declares an interest in helping to care for his child. It's unclear what the terms will be, but he is in Italy and going there to discuss the matter with him is the only way to find out. Claire fancies that he might agree to let some nurse in his employ look after Allegra while she finds quarters close by. Second, compared to England, Italy is said to be an inexpensive place to live. And third, up north, in Derbyshire, three workers have been publicly hanged for leading a revolt against the current government's repressive reign. In response, Shelley pours his outrage into a pamphlet. All the rebels really wanted was decent jobs and lower taxes on essential goods. Yet when he's done, Ollier, his publisher, decides it's too dangerous to print. As Shelley sees it, the Italians may not treat their people much better than the English, but they don't hang them for wanting to work.

As they begin to arrange for departure, their new baby is born. Since it's a girl, they decide to name her after her aunt. But does that mean *Jane*, *Clara*, or *Claire*? After some debate, they decide on *Clara*, because none of them like the name *Jane* very much and to use Claire would lead to confusion.

Mary is thrilled to have a girl. She says, "I shall raise my Clara on passages from my mother's books. No knowledge will be kept from her. Instead of resting prettily on a sofa, she'll study philosophy and frolic in the open air." Then her fierceness softens and she looks at the baby so adoringly, Shelley's own heart quickens and his spirits are lifted up. Mary says she now aspires to have as many children as the Hunts.

"Do you mean five as they have now, or six as they shall have in a few months?" he asks. "About such an important matter, I'd like to be precise."

"Have they so many?" she replies, "Then we must begin tonight."

It pleases him to see her in such a playful mood. So immersed was she in her work that he became uncertain about her feelings. Nor has he wished to pry. However intimate a relationship, there are corners that remain out of view. Yet it is also true that important new things continue to happen every day, some large and some small. A child is born; a journey is undertaken; a poem is written. He is confident of Mary's love for him, even as the two of them continue to grow and change.

After vacating their house in Marlow and prior to their departure for Italy, they live in London for a time. As they are now man and wife, he feels free to escort Mary around the city, to take her to concerts and museums and walking in the park. They visit the most fashionable galleries and take in a performance of *Don Giovanni*. For such outings she has had a red dress made, one that displays her white shoulders to advantage. She's always been modest in her attire; now he encourages her to be vain.

Unfortunately, he is again at odds with the Godwins. As usual it's about money, but this time all of them, even Mary, have decided it's his fault. What happened was this: Against his future inheritance, he drew a sizable amount. His intention was to give it all to Godwin, as a sort of parting gift. But after he visited the Hunts and took into consideration the amount of good Leigh Hunt has done him recently and will do him in the future, as well as the large family for which Hunt must care, he changed his mind. A thousand went to the Hunts and five hundred to Godwin. The first amount he considers an investment while the second merely an obligation on which he expects no return. If nothing else, it's one more reason to leave London, one more reason to go somewhere else and start anew.

"You always promise more than you can give," Mary says. "He wouldn't have minded getting five hundred if you hadn't led him to expect fifteen."

"As usual, you're right. I should stop making promises entirely. Indeed, I ought to allow you to serve as my banker and put you in charge of distributing any funds."

Something about this departure seems more permanent than the previous ones. Having the house in Marlow did nothing to diminish his need to wander. In fact, it taught him that no house, however beautiful the garden, can be enough.

One afternoon they visit the British Museum to see the great collection of Egyptian artifacts gathered in recent years. As he studies the broken sculptures, faces without noses, torsos without arms, he tries to imagine the original pharaohs and kings they were meant to memorialize, the subsequent pharaohs and kings who ordered them to be made, and the artisans who carved them out of stone. What would they all think of this crowd of English gawkers four thousand years hence? Upon leaving the museum, he carries these thoughts with him and a few days later he begins a poem. It's to be about a traveler in a far-off land who comes upon two great stone legs standing in the desert. And near them, half sunk in the sand, a shattered visage, as if a once-great statue has fallen to ruin. As he writes, he thinks, *yes, this is what will become of all those who consider themselves immortal, whether kings or saints or emperors, all those who think they can make history bend to their will:*

> *Look on my Works, ye Mighty, and despair!*
> *Nothing beside remains. Round the decay*
> *Of that colossal Wreck, boundless and bare*
> *The lone and level sands stretch far away.*

On March 11, 1818, they leave London. Not three of them as the first time, not four as the second, but eight: himself, Mary, Claire, the three children, Elise, and another girl they've recently hired to help. It's a veritable cavalcade, leaving England with some regrets but in high spirits as they set off for Italy, where they intend to make their mark.

Part Five

Italy 1822

Mary

From the balcony she watches the incoming tide as it crosses a bar of sand and flows beneath the house. The ground floor is open to the sea, the better for boats to be moored, with the living quarters above. Called the Casa Magni, it is theirs for the summer or as long as they desire. It was vacant when they arrived, and owing to the remoteness of this part of the coast, it may be vacant after they depart. But Mary no longer cares where they live. They've been in Italy for four years. It was supposed to bring them opportunity and contentment; yet now she feels empty, hollowed out.

Shelley has gone off to see Byron and the Hunts in Livorno, a few miles up the coast. It is the first extended voyage of the sloop he's had built to his specifications. He calls the boat *Ariel*. With Byron and Leigh Hunt, he plans to begin publishing a new magazine—one that will print the sort of articles and poems that, were they in England, would get the copies of the magazine seized and themselves imprisoned.

Casa Magni is on the Gulf of La Spezia, between Genoa and Pisa. It is not the first place they've lived since leaving England, nor even the fourth, and most certainly not the last. They began with their usual flitting from place to place, yet lately it seems as if the real reason they are traveling is to escape the demons that fly close behind them, snatching at their clothes and hearts.

After they left London, they traveled to Lake Como, where they found a house perfectly suited for their needs. Shelley's plan was to invite Byron to join them and also the Hunts and Jeff Hogg and Peacock, too (although they knew Peacock would never leave Marlow as long as his mother was alive). But Byron declined, so they moved on to Bagni di Lucca and to Pisa after that. Mary had always pictured Italy as a sort of paradise, and in the beginning it was. Lemon trees in the garden with as many lemons as leaves. Cyprus-studded hills. After dark, fireflies in the shrubbery and a moon that seemed to hang uncommonly close to the earth.

Best of all was being with Shelley and the children in such a place. Even with Claire. Perhaps it was because they had so much practice traveling together, but at last they all seemed untroubled and relaxed. They wrote. They read. They cared for one another. Willmouse was coming to love his baby sister Clara and his cousin Allegra. Mary and Claire found great pleasure in their little girls, taking them out together and enjoying how people would stop them on the street to exclaim at how much alike they looked. Willmouse attracted attention as well, especially when he spoke. From the day of their arrival he'd begun acquiring the Italian language at an astonishing rate. Peddlers and carabinieri would stop and stare upon realizing the words they were hearing were being spoken by an English child.

When Byron wouldn't come to them, they visited him in Venice. He and Claire argued about the upbringing of Allegra and, by way of compromise, put the child in a convent school. Ever the optimist, Claire said, "He will lose interest and then I will take her back." To await this eventuality, when Mary and Shelley left Venice, Claire and Elise remained behind.

After their return from Venice, Mary began work on a new novel. It would be about a prince of Florence, the woman he loved, and the battles he won and lost. Shelley, too, embarked upon something new, a lyric drama to be called *Prometheus Unbound*. He told her it would be a sort of reply to Aeschylus and would show how love and morality can repair the damage done by those with unfettered power. As always, it thrilled her to watch him prepare to take on a great subject. Never for a moment did she doubt he'd succeed.

Now, as she looks out across the waters of the gulf, she wishes he'd hurry back from Liverno. She's never liked his fascination with boats—she remembers the times he and Byron were caught in storms—but these days she and Shelley both need to have their spirits lifted, and for him, sailing is the surest method. That and visiting his friends, as he is doing now. If only there was something that worked as well for her.

She thinks back to September. They were just becoming accustomed to Italy but then little Clara became ill. Mary thought she'd gotten rather good at caring for children while traveling and had confidence she could do so now, even without Elise's help. Moving from place to place could induce illness, especially in one so young, but attending to what the child ate and giving it plenty of fresh air were, for most ailments, adequate cures. However, this time none of those things worked. Their baby, their precious little girl, died in only a matter of hours, before they could do anything at all. It happened so quickly that when she realized the tiny body had no life remaining in it, she looked at Shelley in speechless astonishment. That morning, they had a sweet and innocent child. Before the sun had set on the same day, she was no more.

Shelley said, "I had scarcely gotten to know her. I needed more time."

All Mary could do was nod her head in agreement. How much time did you need with those you loved? She was too heart-broken to reply.

She informed her father of the tragedy in a letter. It was the first one she'd written in months. Shelley had been discouraging her from corresponding with him because when he wrote back, there was too much talk about money. Her father continued to think Shelley was wealthier than he truly was and that a portion of that wealth should rightly be directed to him.

After Clara's death, they moved on to Rome. Shelley said it would be a good change, which angered her—what difference did it make? No city, however magnificent, could diminish her pain. And yet Shelley was not wrong. Rome was unlike any place she'd ever been. Even in her mourning, she was excited to be walking through the ancient precincts about which she'd read so much. She fancied she might round a corner and come upon Cicero delivering a speech. Here and there excavations were under way and it was exciting to imagine the grand temples and palaces that might be uncovered next. She was intrigued by the casual manner with which the Romans treated their heritage. Sheep grazed among the ruins and vegetable gardens grew on what she had expected the Italians to consider sacred ground. At first she was alarmed; then she decided that in their eyes, the past was one with the present. It reminded her of Shelley's poem about the broken statues in the museum.

Often, she walked alone, letting herself lose her way, knowing that if she found the Tiber, she could figure out how to get home.

On a cold autumn afternoon she visited the Pantheon and through its open roof the sun streamed down upon her; she felt as if the spirits of the ancients were entering her soul.

One day, as she was walking through the Borghese Gardens, she happened upon Amelia Curran, an artist they had known in London. It was good to see a familiar face, and soon she was making regular visits to Amelia's home at the top of the Spanish Steps. Mary often brought Willmouse with her and Amelia took to the child immediately. She exclaimed about his beauty and insisted she be allowed to paint his portrait. "I can't remember when I have encountered such an ideal subject," she said. "Such a charming, lively boy." Mary watched as Amelia sketched him and then as she began to apply the paint. She found herself wishing she had an image of her dear little Clara. She could picture her face now, but how about in ten years' time?

For several months after the baby's death, Shelley had stopped writing. Then at last he began again, returning to *Prometheus Unbound*. Although Mary was used to seeing him work with great intensity, he now approached the page with what she could only describe as *rage*.

"You will damage your health," she told him.

"Maybe there are some things that are worth damaging one's health for."

She looked at him with concern. Such remarks might be interpreted as selfish or arrogant—*if you ruin yourself, then what's to become of me and Willmouse?*—but she chose not to take them that way. It almost seemed he was asking her to rescue him. Yet she knew he had to find his own path forward, through the writing of his poem.

Mary thought they might settle permanently in Rome, but before they could locate a fitting house, Willmouse came down with a fever. The instant she realized he wasn't well, terror washed over her and she clung to Shelley in utter desperation. A renowned Scottish doctor they knew to be in Rome was summoned. She was determined that what had happened to little Clara would not happen to Willmouse. And yet, after languishing for a few agonizing days, he died. When they'd left Claire's child, Allegra, at the convent in Venice, Mary had thought about what it might be like to be separated from her own children. However, what had actually happened was much worse than anything she'd been able to imagine: two deaths, thrust upon her so soon.

They buried their darling in the Protestant cemetery in Rome, and as they huddled beside the grave, she recalled a line from her mother's novel, *Mary*: *It was the will of Providence that Mary should experience almost every species of sorrow.* Perhaps the book was about her after all.

The day after the burial she opened her journal and wrote, *I am changed. The world will never be as it was before.* She pledged to call her son only William from that point forward. *Willmouse* was a name fit only for a living boy. They left Rome the following week.

After the sun sets, it becomes too dark to see the water, but she remains on the balcony listening to the tide. Although the foundation of Casa Magni is solid rock, the sound of the ocean passing beneath it makes her feel as if she were on a ship, waves striking from all sides.

In the year since Clara's and William's deaths, she and Shelley have had difficulty speaking to one another. Instead of growing apart gradually, they have grown apart in a rush. When William died, she was pregnant again. Their new child, Percy, seems as if he is hers alone—Shelley seldom troubles himself to look at the poor thing. The pain of losing William was too much. He once said William and Clara died to punish him for what he did to Harriet. To which she replied, "*I* did nothing to your former wife. And as for whatever gods exist, I refuse to give them such power."

Perhaps he doesn't care for Percy as he did for Willmouse and Clara because she won't let him. If he offers to help, she pushes him away. This annoys Shelley and he goes out to inspect his boat. She wishes Claire were with them so she'd have someone else to talk to. This despite the fact that in years past, she often wanted Claire to be gone.

Thinking about little Percy draws Mary inside. He is sleeping in the room adjacent to the balcony, only steps away. She checks his head for fever. It's become a compulsion, but a harmless one, she assumes. When he stirs, she takes him in her arms and begins walking back and forth. The sound of the ocean is muffled but still present. A sliver of light enters through the window from a three-quarter moon.

Even during the worst times, she and Shelley have been able to seek refuge in their writing. She has continued to work on her new novel, which she now calls *Valperga*. As it has taken shape, she has begun to find she can address recent events by describing similar ones in medieval times. Human relationships, public as well as private, were much the same then as now. As for Shelley, he is experiencing a period of stunning productivity. After finishing *Prometheus Unbound*, he has gone on to complete several other poems. Among her favorites is his "Ode to the West Wind," which closes with these lines:

> *And, by the incantation of this verse,*
> *Scatter, as from an unextinguish'd hearth*
> *Ashes and sparks, my words among mankind!*
> *Be through my lips to unawaken'd earth*
> *The trumpet of a prophecy! O Wind,*
> *If Winter comes, can Spring be far behind?*

There it is again, his belief that verse can be an incantation, that it can transform the world, even move the winds. If she once agreed, she no longer does. Shelley wants his words to be scattered on the winds; she sometimes thinks she'd like her very self turned to ash and scattered. Blown across the sky.

She finds she can still feel close to him in the evenings when they read to one another from their day's work. Perhaps, after all, their writing *will* be the foundation upon which love can be rebuilt. He has been creating poetry of great ambition, poetry as good as any she's read. And she has confidence about her new novel, in part because *Frankenstein* is becoming popular in England—or so Peacock wrote in a letter that arrived last week.

Mary returns Percy to his cradle and readies herself for bed. It's been hot lately, but this week the wind has been increasing after dark and making for pleasant nights. Somewhere not far off, a nightingale is singing. It is said the ones in this region produce melodies more beautiful than those in other parts of Italy. She listens to it for a time and then falls asleep.

The next morning a letter from Leigh Hunt arrives. In it, he says they had a wonderful time with Shelley and were delighted to see him again. As for the magazine, it's sure to be a success. This is good news. If he comes back refreshed and full of new energy for his poetry, a few days of loneliness will have been no great price.

Then she rereads the letter and notices something worrying. Hunt seems to be implying Shelley's already left for home. If that's true, how is it the letter preceded him? With that realization, she stands and steps outside. Her breathing becomes shallow, almost a series of gasps. He said he'd be back by July 8. Surely he's on his way.

But he doesn't arrive that day or the following day or the day after that. She uses Shelley's telescope to scan the water. She contacts Hunt and Byron, who reply with alarm equal to her own. They inform her they have sent men out to look for signs of the boat. Two more days pass and she begins to prepare for the worst. In the village this is a festival week, so there is singing and dancing on the beach. She probably couldn't get any rest even if it were quiet, but this makes it impossible. When the festival finally ends, Mary is so exhausted, she falls across the bed and is asleep before she has another thought.

Thus, when the messenger comes, it takes her a moment to remember what has happened. "Who are you?" she says. "You've come to the wrong place." But the messenger is not mistaken. A body has been found.

Epilogue

London 1823

Mary

Mary is in a carriage en route to the theatre. Not long ago she could not have imagined herself going alone, but she's managed to grow used to it. Although the journey from Kentish Town to the Lyceum will take almost an hour, it's a pleasant spring evening and there shouldn't be much traffic until they're well into London. For now the horses move along at a brisk and steady pace.

Before she left the house, she explained to the nursemaid where she was going.

"You must be excited," the maid said. "To see your book brought to life."

"More apprehensive than excited. I'm afraid I'll hate it."

The maid gave her a puzzled look, so she attempted to explain.

"They say the actor paints himself from head to foot. That he tumbles about and howls."

"Goodness me."

"Perhaps I'll leave early."

"Don't hurry home on my account. I can manage everything here."

When Mary first returned from Italy after Shelley's death, she'd stayed with her parents. No longer living on Skinner Street, they have a better place at the east end of the Strand. However, their new location doesn't mean her father's financial situation has improved. He still owes hundreds of pounds to the Skinner Street landlord, and without Shelley to help, he's had to turn to Charles Lamb and others to keep him afloat. For her part, Mary has been writing short pieces, essays and stories that can be sold and published quickly, in an effort to give him something, even if only small amounts.

As the carriage enters the city, the gaslights are just beginning to be lit. There are so many more than there used to be. The streets and storefronts remain fully visible even on moonless nights.

Sometimes she actually misses Italy—the stone pines, the sea views from rocky promontories, the sweet-smelling breezes and cloudless skies. One reason she moved to Kentish Town was because she thought its pastoral surroundings might remind her of Italy. Yet now that she's begun to write again, she hardly cares where she lives. While at her desk, she occasionally glances out the window, but for the most part she remains inside her mind, amid the words she writes. She still prefers large sheets of paper like the ones Shelley found for her in Bath.

The gaslights aren't all that's new. Buildings are springing up everywhere, canals are being dug, and the Duke of Wellington is funding an effort to tunnel under the Thames. Mary wonders what Shelley would think of it all. He was not opposed to progress but he had no fondness for the wealthy, and when she looks around London, it appears as though most of the change is happening to improve the lives of the monied class. Larger houses and grander parks where they can live and play. That's only one of the many things she'd like to discuss with Shelley. He was her confidant about matters great and small.

If he were with her tonight, he'd tease her about having become a little famous. It's not because everyone is reading her book, although some are; rather it's due to various efforts to put her story on the stage. Apparently, people want desperately to *see* the monster—the miserable wretch she created. Or rather the wretch whom actors *re*-create, costuming themselves and making hideous sounds and turning a murderous gaze on an audience that responds with cries of terror. Or so the newspapers say. When these dramas—there seems to be a new one every month—are announced and promoted, her name is seldom mentioned, but that hasn't kept the occasional journalist from tracking her down and asking how a woman, with a feminine sensibility, could invent such a godless beast. So yes, a *little* famous. She wishes Shelley could have achieved some small measure of fame. He wasn't greedy for it, but he'd have enjoyed it, probably more than she.

The carriage pauses, perhaps for an obstruction ahead. Mary, taking scarcely any notice, continues to think about Shelley. She now sees herself as the guardian and advocate of Shelley's works. He wrote with such fervor during their years in Italy, imbuing every line with the belief that verse can transform the world. When he finished *Prometheus Unbound* and gave it to her to read, she paused near the end and said, "I see you have described yourself."

"How do you mean?"

"Just here: *ceaseless, and rapid, and fierce, and free.*"

"Perhaps I was like that as a child, but no longer," he replied.

She has since wondered if he somehow knew he didn't have much time left.

Little Percy is now three years old, Willmouse and Clara are four years gone, and Mary feels as though Italy was a very long time ago. She's relieved she doesn't have to occupy the same rooms or walk the same streets she did in that former life. It makes it easier to push the memories away. Although she doesn't always feel the need to do that, she'd rather not be constantly surrounded by objects that bring her departed loved ones to mind.

The carriage jerks and they are in motion again. Now there are vehicles on either side and they are surrounded by the cacophony of the city. Hooves clatter and wheels rumble. They stop again to allow a tram to cross. The driver of her carriage shouts at a reckless horseman and the horseman shouts back. She closes the curtains in an effort to keep out the sounds and smells.

When they arrive at the Lyceum, there's a throng waiting to get in. The play is called *Presumption; or, the Fate of Frankenstein.* She's curious to find out who's presuming what and how fate will be represented. She's also curious to see the painted monster, although part of her doesn't care how the story is dramatized or what the actors do. She almost wishes she'd stayed at home to write. Her work and her son are what give her solace. Indeed, they are all she needs.

As she settles into her seat, she thinks briefly about her father. She sent him a message asking if he'd like to meet her at the theatre but he declined, saying he's getting too old to go out at night. If Shelley hadn't entered her life when he did, she might well have become her father's bookish assistant, reading manuscripts and, as he aged, taking over the shop. Or perhaps not—even at the best of times he makes barely enough to live on, so why would she have sentenced herself to that. The theatre is quite warm, so she removes her shawl.

At last the curtain parts and the play begins. The scene is a gloomy chamber in Victor Frankenstein's apartment. It's not exactly as she envisioned it, but it's convincing enough. Henry Clerval and Frankenstein appear and soon Frankenstein begins to describe his research: *"This evening—this lowering evening, I will, in all probability, complete my task. Years have I labored, and at length discovered that to which so many men of genius have in vain directed their inquiries. I have become master of the secret of bestowing animation upon lifeless matter. But with so astonishing a power in my hands, how should I employ it?"*

They are not her exact words, but she finds herself engaged. She steals a glance at the people sitting near her. All are motionless, all are silent, their eyes fixed on the actors as they speak their lines.

The play continues as she expects it to. Some liberties have been taken, but most of the characters and scenes come directly from her book. The orphan Elizabeth is introduced, and a bit oddly, the playwright has inserted a song.

Then in the third scene there is an explosion, so loud and sudden that the man sitting next to her gasps and the woman behind her shrieks. Smoke billows up, the door of the laboratory bursts open, and out of a wall of flames the monster appears. Advancing forward, he breaks through a balustrade and leaps onto a table. His skin is blue, his ebony mane is long and unkempt, and his face is a mask of rage.

She expected to find any attempt to portray the monster lacking. He has always been so vivid in her mind that an impersonation of him is doomed to fall short. Yet she is as captivated and astonished as the other members of the audience. It's not the blue body, not the brutish way of moving or fearsome growls, it's the actor's eyes. She can't recall his name—is it Cooke? Somehow he is able to make himself appear at once confused, vicious, and desperate. He looks out with a gaze that combines fury and deep distress.

The story continues in the woods near Geneva and then at the Frankenstein home in Belrive. The monster is wounded by a gunshot and Victor begins to descend into madness. Then there's more music, this time a wordless tune, ethereal and haunting, played on a violin. Although in some respects the play is merely lurid entertainment, Mary thinks Shelley would have liked it—for its vitality, for its extravagance, for its resemblance to a dream. But to her, all that truly matters is the monster and his gaze.

As the last act gets under way, Mary wonders if the closing words of her novel will be spoken: *He was soon borne away by the waves and lost in darkness and distance.* But no, this tale ends when Victor Frankenstein and the monster are killed by an avalanche, so there are no waves. It's an impressive spectacle, done with great sheets of white cloth, clouds of shredded paper, and a deafening roar coming from the wings. While the audience is applauding, she slips out of the theatre and into the cool night air.

Acknowledgments

To write *A Storm in the Stars* I drew upon the letters and journals of the principal characters; the scholars who compile and edit such documents are among the unsung heroes of literature. I also made use of a number of biographies. I recommend *Mary Shelley* by Miranda Seymour, *Romantic Outlaws* by Charlotte Gordon, and *Shelley: The Pursuit* by Richard Holmes—which, for me, is where it all started.

One challenge of writing fiction about historical events is deciding what to include and what to leave out. I have chosen to omit the death of Mary and Percy's first child, who was born prematurely and lived for two weeks; the death of Mary and Claire's sister, Fanny; and the death of Claire and Byron's daughter, Allegra, who died of typhus in a convent school. I felt that adding these deaths to the ones I do tell about would have overwhelmed the story and made the final third of the novel difficult to bear.

I'm deeply appreciative of those at Delphinium Books who brought A Storm in the Stars into the world: Jennifer Ankner-Edelstein for her early enthusiasm, Lori Milken for the existence of Delphinium and for her perceptive reading of the manuscript, and Joe Olshan for his excellent editorial guidance and steadfast support.

I also wish to acknowledge my first and best readers: Courtney Angermeier, Mary Buckelew, Andy Goodwyn, Michael Moore, Betsy Noll, Mark Vogel, and, especially, Jean-Louise Zancanella.

Finally, thanks as always to Dorene Kahl. I couldn't do it without her.

About the Author

Don Zancanella's most recent novel, *Concord*, was released in March, 2021 (Serving House Books). Zancanella is well known as a short fiction writer, and his works include his John Simmons/Iowa Short Fiction Award-winning collection, *Western Electric* (University of Iowa Press, 1996) and the 1998 O. Henry Prize winner "The Chimpanzees of Wyoming Territory," which was published in the *Alaska Quarterly Review*. More recently, "Mr. Dog" was cited as a distinguished story of the year in the 2019 *Best American Short Stories*, and "Feed Them" was nominated for a Pushcart Prize (2020). He was born in Laramie, Wyoming, spent more than twenty years teaching at the University of New Mexico, and currently lives and writes in Boise, Idaho with his wife and rescue dogs.